To Annette + George

Please enjoy my
imagination,

Thanks

Dave McDonald

GEORGE & ANNETTE
9 CARAVELLE LANE • BLUFFTON, SC 29909
Lane

Kugi's Story

By

Dave McDonald

Dedicated to
Kugi Chauhan
A strong, wise man with an inner peace
My mentor and great friend

Prologue

October, 1982, Nanakpur, Afghanistan,
A small village northeast of Kabul

Masoud Omar, his black coat and matching turban tanned with dust, squatted in the darkness beside one of a dozen mud brick huts. Lumps of orange embers spewed sparks from the communal ovens across the dirt road. The smell of roasted goat meat hung in the air and teased his hunger. He hadn't eaten since morning. He had been traveling all day, pushing himself, taking chances, coming home. His late-thirties knees begged for relief, but he remained still.

He looked up at the star-filled sky. The gray jagged silhouette of the northern Hindu Kush Mountains rudely interrupted the random pattern of sparkling dots.

He sighed, exhaling a cloud of vapor, a preview of the winter to come. Although a respite from the fighting, the harsh winters killed more Afghans than the Russians.

Adrenaline etched his stomach, a familiar ache just before a kill. Unlike annihilating the communist invaders, his mind wasn't filled with hate. His pride and religious beliefs had pushed him to hide in the dark, to confront, and maybe murder a man he knew. A man he had respected when respect was mutual.

A pebble tumbled behind him. His hand shot to the hilt of the Russian bayonet tucked in his waistband and yanked it free. He swiveled around, tensed to lunge.

The silhouette of a short stocky man wearing a turban stood unmoving a few yards from him. His raised arms held a rifle over his head.

"Hameed, you know better than to sneak up on me." The night breeze wisped away Masoud's steam-shrouded whisper. He stood to uncoil his tensed muscles and to return the long blade to its scabbard. "Did you take care of the dogs?"

1

Hameed Ahmed lowered his old British .303 Lee-Enfield rifle. His head bowed in both shame and servitude.

"They are busy with the bones I brought, Saab," Hameed whispered. He leaned his rifle against the hut. The end of Hameed's turban flapped in the wind. He pressed his hands deep into his coat pockets, shifting from foot to foot. His chin pressed against his chest.

This young soldier, who had saved Masoud's life on too many occasions fighting the Russians, needed a release. "Hameed, you did well. Now watch behind the huts."

Hameed raised his head, nodded, and turned around.

Masoud stared into the night. He recalled the first time he had met Hameed, three years ago, though it seemed more like ten. Hameed was seventeen. And like so many of his Afghan comrades, he was a young, Pakistani-educated and trained Talib, eager to fight. Early on, Hameed had attached himself to Masoud, becoming his shadow, his protector.

Hameed was a gift from Allah except for tonight; this wasn't his fight.

Masoud should have come alone.

Hameed watched Masoud's every move. And when Masoud had tried to leave their camp this night, Hameed had asked him where he was going so late. Masoud had made a mistake by telling him. Now, somehow, Masoud must prevent his friend's involvement in the potentially deadly, personal business at hand.

A distant, throaty, staccato sound disrupted the silence.

Masoud whispered, "Hameed, what is that noise?" He peered around the jagged corner of the squat mud hut. A faint single light bounced toward him on the dirt road.

"Sounds like a scooter," Hameed said his voice inches away.

"Daler Singh has a motor scooter," Masoud said. His hand clinched the hilt of the bayonet.

Hameed, his bearded face masked by the darkness, leaned over Masoud's shoulder. "Shall I go across the road to the ovens?" His breath smelled of curry. "That way you will not be in my line of sight."

"No," Masoud said softly. "Stay here. He may see you if you cross now. You will be closer here." He needed a reason to disengage Hameed. "I doubt you will be able to see to shoot any way. There is only a sliver of moon."

"I can see fine. However, this close to the mountains, a shot would wake the deaf. The whole Sikh village will be on us before we can run."

"Daler and I have met before." Masoud shoved his words through clenched teeth. "This is our last meeting. I have warned him. Either he does what I demand, or he will die." His hand patted the scabbard. "I have my knife. There will be no noise, except for Daler's last gasp for breath."

"I will be here with Daler in my sights should you need me, Saab."

Masoud paused, borrowing time to think of an excuse to occupy Hameed. "If I want you to shoot him, I, ah . . . I will push his scooter over."

"Yes, my leader."

The putt-putting motor scooter slowed and rolled to a stop in front of the hut. A tall, gray-bearded man, wearing a black turban, a heavy black wool coat, and matching pants, cut off the bike's light and engine. He kicked down a stand and pulled the scooter onto it. He bent to open the saddlebags.

Masoud tucked the end of his turban into his coat and strode toward the man. His stride was long and determined, a lion protecting his pride.

The tall man, his arms wrapped around two large packages, swiveled around. "Who goes there?"

"It is I, Masoud Omar." He stopped within arms' reach of the tall Sikh. Masoud looked up into Daler's night-shrouded featureless face. His eye sockets resembled cave entrances. Those blazing copper eyes, which had not long ago conveyed genuine friendship, had to be filled with concern tonight.

3

"Masoud, what brings you to my door in the dark of the night?" Daler asked, easing the bags to the ground.

Masoud's hand slid under his coat flap and gripped the hilt of the Russian bayonet.

This meeting was escalating faster than he had expected. So be it.

Daler's stupid question to mask his hands-freeing move caused Masoud to tighten his grasp on his dagger. All Sikhs carried a Kirpan, a ceremonial knife. Daler's placing the bags on the ground was probably an offensive move versus a defensive one. And, although he respected his one-time-friend's fearlessness, both Daler and his son had underestimated Masoud.

"You know what I want." Masoud emphasized each word with anger. "I have come to take my daughter home. Fatana was born and raised a Muslim, and a Muslim she will remain."

"We have had this discussion before." Daler raised his arms, palms to the sky. "We were friends before this. Let our friendship guide us through this test of life."

"Our friendship died when your son forced my daughter away from Islam."

Daler dropped his hands to his sides. "Your daughter chooses to be with my son. This is not my choice, or your choice, it is our children's decision. I can do nothing but honor it."

Daler's words and outward calmness raised the pressure level of Masoud's heart beat pounding in his head.

"There are no choices. Allah has decreed she is, and will remain, a Muslim." Masoud's voice competed with the breeze for harshness. He gulped some night air, hoping to cool his temper. "You can honor whatever you wish; just tell me where she is."

"Fatana and Raman left yesterday. I do not know where they went."

4

The bayonet slashed the air between them. The razor sharpened edge stopping against the skin of Daler's throat. "Enough lying! Tell me."

Daler grabbed Masoud's knife holding hand with both of his and pushed it away.

Masoud's fist slammed into Daler's solar plexus.

Air whooshed from Daler's mouth, and he doubled over gasping for air.

"Now tell me or I will kill you and everyone in your family."

Bent at the waist, Daler raised one hand. He sucked in air. "I . . . she . . . Fatana is pregnant."

Molten anger boiled and splattered as it raced up Masoud's throat and erupted from his lips, "Nooooo!"

As if the bayonet had a mind of its own, the weapon raised skyward and then ripped through Daler's extended hand.

Daler cried out and staggered backwards, pulling free from the long blade and knocking over the scooter.

The boom echoed off the hills masking the explosion of Daler's head.

Masoud stared at Daler. Half his head was gone. He bent to help his former friend. Hameed grabbed his arm and pulled him down the path between the huts to where they had left their horses.

Chapter 1

June, 2011,

Cincinnati, Ohio

"Hey, Rag Head," a male voice drawled from the adjacent island of pumps.

I glanced over my shoulder at a tall, mid-twenties man dressed in dirty white coveralls with long brown hair surfing the wind. Mud-caked boots spread defiantly; he stood by his dirt-splattered pickup truck. His squinted eyes stared at me.

I frequented this Convenient Mart station because it was local and cheap. The father of an Indian friend of mine owned it and my friend worked there. I had never had a problem at this no-frills store. I attributed that to the owner and its location. The Mart sat along a rolling Route 42 in a rural area just south of Pisgah, a tiny, quiet crossroads burg.

My shoulders sagged prompted by my sigh. There had been so many hecklers especially since nine-eleven. My friends and I called them "turban tormentors," who, like snow in a northern winter, would fall on you often; you just didn't know when.

Although their intentions varied, these harassers all shared the same unworldly, skewed beliefs. Anyone wearing a turban had to be a Muslim, and all Muslims were American haters and potential bomb-strapped zealots.

I glanced up at the sparse clouds flowing by in the noon azure sky. The warm spring-like breeze had carried away the normal heavy humidity, a unique mid-June day for Cincinnati. My eyes returned to the man. I was determined not to let this bully ruin my afternoon.

I sucked in some air and rubbed the steel bracelet, my Kara, on my wrist. My religion had taught me to treat everyone kindly, as equals, no matter who they were or how they conducted themselves. But my disgust had a head start on my frazzled unflappability. And I mentally raced to bring it under control.

The dinging of the gas pump refocused my attention. The almost four-dollar-gallons flowed rapidly and I stopped the pump at twenty dollars, my weekly budget.

I removed the nozzle from my car's tank opening and reseated it on the pump housing. The distraction gave my brain time to shelve my emotional reaction.

"You, with the turban, I'm talkin' to you."

The voice was closer. Here we go again, me and my patience pitted against another's ignorance.

This man's prejudice wasn't his fault. He was a product of his environment, taught to be a self-righteous bigot. Nothing I could say would undo his teachings. He was the victim of deep imprinting. I had no bridge to a common ground with the likes of him. We were from non-reconciliatory worlds. Experience had taught me to let them vent, take no offense, and walk away.

I righted my six foot, stout frame and turned. The tall, in-need-of-a-shave, young man was between his truck and my old rusted Chevrolet. He was a few years older, slightly taller, and outweighed me by a case or two of beer. His lower lip outlined a load of snuff.

"If you are referring to me, I am not a rag head, nor a Muslim, I am a Sikh." My voice was calm, like a summer's night. "I have a name, Kugi Singh. What is your name?"

"My name's none of your business. What I'm makin' your business is my kid brother is over in your camel jockey land gettin' shot at by the likes of you every day. And here you are in my country, walkin' around like you're fuckin' part of it. Now why would I give a shit about what your name is?"

If by camel jockey land, he meant Afghanistan, he was right, or at least close. Wouldn't he like to know my parents were from Afghanistan? That'd convince him I was a member of the Taliban, or, even worse, that I had worked for Osama Bin Laden.

The man spit brown liquid. "As far as I'm concerned your name is Osama Bin Fuckin' Laden."

Great, just great.

My pride tried to sucker-punch my belief that everyone was equal before God. My control side-stepped the blow.

I considered mentioning Osama's death and how my family and I had praised the news, but a mental trial run sounded weak.

I screwed the cap on my gas tank and closed the flap. A thought eased my tension. Maybe, for once, I had found a common ground, brothers in Afghanistan, a means to a peaceful ending with a tormentor.

I stared into his squinted blue eyes. "I am a peaceful man, an American like you, born right here in Cincinnati. I too have a brother in Afghanistan serving in the United States Army. He is a doctor. So we have several things in common. Now have a good day and may God be with you and your family."

I had to walk between his truck and my car to get to the driver's door.

When I reached for the door handle, he grabbed my arm, stopping me.

"So you think you can throw God's name around and then everything will be alright."

He yanked me around to face him. His breath reeked of alcohol.

My unconcerned and yet moist stare fixed on his cold eyes. I pried his oil-stained fingers off my arm. My body chemistry always made my eyes burn and glisten when I was threatened. I hated it, but there was nothing I could do about it. Opponents frequently mistook it for tears of fear, a mistake.

He poked my chest several bruising times with a rigid finger. "I don't give a shit what your name is, or where your spyin' brother is, you're a fuckin' Osama Bin Laden rag head to me."

I blocked his poking finger and shook my head. "You have no idea what a Sikh is, do you?"

"Don't try to con me with your crap." His spit glazed words sprayed my face. "Sikh, shit-head, towel head, rag head, it don't matter. You're all alike. You don't want our democracy, you don't believe in Christ, and you think the only good American is a dead one."

The common brother thing hadn't worked, leaving me with only a direct approach. I held his stare. "Something has upset you. You've tried to fix it by drinking. That didn't do anything but make things worse, so now you've decided to focus your anger on me. I am not your problem."

He leaned his head toward me, his eyes bulging. "Yeah I've been drinkin' and, yeah, you <u>are</u> my problem."

"I'm not your enemy. We're on the same side."

"Home of the free, is that it?" He chuckled facetiously. "Yeah, we all used to drink that bullshit until nine-eleven. You think you can come here and slid in under our radar because you all look alike. No one can tell the good guys, if there are any, from the bad." His sewing machine finger commenced the jabbing again. "So I think we should put all you fuckin' rag heads in one of those deserts over there and nuke all of you and let this God you're talkin' about sort out the good from the bad."

I swept his menacing finger aside. "I'm sorry you feel that way, I respect your beliefs. I wish you would respect mine. I'm leaving now. I pray your brother returns safely and that you have a good day."

"You ain't fuckin' goin' nowhere." His arm shot out and blocked my path. With his other hand, he reached up, hooked a finger in his mouth, scooped out the wad of saliva-soaked paste, and flung it on my shoes.

Anger raced up the center of my back. Years of my father's repeated teachings helped me suppress the heat. Calm invaded me, easing the tension, arresting any fears, and bolstering my confidence. I flexed my fingers, hands, and forearms, an old baseball hitting lesson, tight muscles reduced speed and accuracy.

Further talking would be a waste, unfortunately I'd been to the point of no return on rare, but too many, other occasions. I loosened my tie and unbuttoned my choking top shirt button.

Now everything depended on maintaining mental control, emotional balance, and agility. I widened my stance, turned, and reached for my car door.

He grabbed my shoulder and spun me around again. He cocked his hand to poke me again and I grabbed his finger and bent it back, hard. Something cracked and he dropped to his knees.

I pushed him to the ground and again turned to get in my car.

"You son-of-a-bitch!" he screamed and grabbed both my ankles and pulled my feet out from under me.

My quick hands kept me from doing a face plant. But my chest smacked the blacktop, stunning me.

Then he was on my back, pounding the back of my head with his fists. Each eye-squinting, teeth-clenching blow ricocheted pain from the back of my head to the front as my head bounced off the payment. The second or third blow knocked off my turban. That did it.

I pushed up and rolled him off me. I jumped to my feet and he staggered to his.

I shook my almost waist long hair behind me. "Enough."

"Bullshit." He swung at me.

I dodged his blow, grabbed his arm, and spun him around. With his back to me, I yanked open the top of his coveralls and rolled them down over his shoulders. I pinned him against the side of his truck. I pulled the sleeves down beyond his hands

10

and tied them in a knot behind him. Then I opened the truck's door and shoved him in, face first, so he was lying on his belly.

"Have a nice day." I pushed his kicking feet in and closed the door.

I picked up my turban and brushed it off; I'd have to retie it later. Four steps and I was around my car where I retrieved my receipt, and pulled a paper towel from the windshield washing kit container. I wiped off my shoes and discarded the towel. Then I got into the old Malibu, and, thank God it started, drove away.

What a great way to preempt my first job interview.

Chapter 2

I headed the near antique, V-eight Malibu toward downtown Cincinnati. Normally after a fight, I'd suffer from the after affects of an adrenaline rush; an acidic stomach, the shakes, exhaustion, and regret-induced shame for violating my spiritual principles, but not today. I'd prepared myself and the fight had been one-sided, and the only thing hurt was my attacker's pride and maybe his finger. The intoxicated loud mouth had paid for his mistake. Hopefully a lesson he wouldn't have to relearn, but I doubted he'd learned anything other than more misdirected hate. Sad.

I was guiding the old bucket of bolts down Reading Road when my cell phone rang. Unlike almost everyone else in this world, I refused to talk on a phone while I drove. I found a place and pulled over.

"Hello." My eyes searched for signs about parking.

"Kugi, this is your father." His voice was consistent and calming, like a lake lapping the shore. Although sometimes subtly firmer than others, I couldn't recall him ever raising his tone.

He rarely called me and my curiosity peaked.

"Hey, Pops, what's up?" My fingers traced the knobby surface of the steering wheel.

"Thank God, my father cannot hear how you address me."

How dare he mention the man he refused to talk about? Was he teasing me?

12

"And what would my mysterious grandfather have done, cane me?" My car swayed from the air blast from a passing eighteen wheeler.

"No. He was not a violent man, unless forced to be. He probably would have sent you to an all boys academy to learn proper Sikh manners and respect."

He had opened a door kept closed and locked my entire life. "When are you going to tell me about my grandfathers? I know nothing about either of them."

"When your mother is ready."

His answer flew in the face of everything he preached as right. His hypocrisy ignited my anger. "You always say that. That makes no sense to me."

"And I will continue to—"a car honked at another both vying for the same space.

"What did you say?" I asked.

"There are two reasons I called you. One is do you want this pile of letters, your mother said were resumes, posted today and what are you doing this afternoon? Your mother took the car and I need a ride."

When pinched, change the subject, an always frustrating tactic frequently invoked by my father. I sighed.

"Yes, mail the letters. I feel like I've written enough resumes in the past three weeks since graduating to cause the paper and stamp companies to add a second shift. And didn't mother tell you? I've got a job interview today."

"Wonderful. With whom?"

The flashing vehicles speeding by my car pulled away my emotions and I flat toned my response like I was reading it. "A local small company, Cutler Conveyors, they're looking for a design engineer. They're a family-owned and managed company, an international supplier of conveyer systems of all sizes and applications, customized products. Customization sounds challenging, and I crave challenges. I have an appointment with a Mr. Charles Cutler who's Vice President of Engineering."

13

"Kugi, experience competes only with age for being the best teacher."

I leaned my head back against the headrest, another lecture.

"If they offer you a job, take it, no matter what the pay. Today, finding a job is as probable as finding water on the Dashte-e-Mango; do you remember what that is?"

"The Desert of Death on the western border of Afghanistan."

"You listen well, no wonder you made such high marks in school. If you are awarded a job, continue to send out your resume to companies of interest to you. Family companies are just what the words imply, for families. Getting promoted in a family company is even less probable than finding a stream beyond Herat."

He paused like he was sitting next to me, looking at me. "Now you can come back from your mental nap. I am through lecturing."

I sat up. He knew me too well. Despite the family secrets, he was a great father. He never concealed his love, and his advice had never betrayed me.

"When do you need a ride?" I asked.

"No later than three."

I glanced at my car clock. "You can count on me, Pops."

"Did I just say you listened well?"

Chapter 3

Cutler Conveyors was in an old, rundown section of Madisonville, an enclave of Cincinnati. A place where if you ran into a policeman, he'd search you to see if you were carrying a deadly weapon, and if you weren't, he'd give you one.

I parked my junker on the street. One good thing about having an old, rusted, dented car, no one ever messed with it.

I pulled on my suit jacket, fixed my tie, checked my turban, and crossed the street to the two-story concrete building that consumed the city block.

I opened the steel door with "Entrance" stenciled on it and walked into a lobby fronted by a young receptionist behind a Formica counter. Empty shiny brown leather chairs lined the remaining three walls under framed pictures of all kinds of conveyer systems installed both domestically and abroad. Attached to the wall, above the chairs, ran a soundless conveyer belt from the front door to behind the receptionist, designed to turn the ninety-degree wall corners.

"May I help you?" the striking young blonde with Sarah Palin glasses asked. Her scrunched blue eyes and wrinkled brow inferred she thought I had to be lost.

"Ah, I'm Mr. Singh, and I have an appointment with Mr. Charles Cutler at one o'clock." I glanced at the unique clock above her head. The hands, on small circular conveyer belts, depicted I was five minutes early.

The blonde's dark brown eyebrows arched. "Oh." She sorted through some papers. "Ah, here we are." She held up a piece of paper. "Mr. Singh, you have a, ah," she scraped her top

15

teeth over and over her lower lip while her eyes scanned the paper, "a job interview with us today." Her eyes returned to me and fixed on my turban. "Ah, we, ah, I expected, ah, someone of, ah, with like a Chinese background."

She tucked her chin and raised an eyebrow which seemed synchronized to the same side of her upper lip, raising it also.

I had seen her questioning look so many times before, the way people stared at my father, brother, and I. Unlike the redneck at the gas station, their gaze wasn't hate filled. Our turbans bothered them, as if we were aliens, like a black man at a KKK meeting, we didn't belong.

I forced a smile to try to offset her state of discomfort. "A common mistake. Singh is the Sikh equivalent to Smith or Jones in Punjab, a state of India." I figured India was a better reference than Afghanistan. My appearance already had her off balance.

Her eyebrow and lip returned to normalcy. And she checked her watch. "Have a seat. You're a little early and Mr. Cutler is with another candidate. Would you like something to drink . . . soda, coffee?"

Chia would have been nice, but not probable. "A black coffee, please." I took a seat.

She poured a cup of coffee from a large pot and placed it on a small tray with all the condiments and a napkin and spoon. She turned and sat the tray on the moving conveyer behind her and the coffee laden platter headed in my direction. Then she got up and went through the door behind her. The conveyer conveyed impressive advertising; her hurried exit with an over the shoulder glance conveyed concern.

Five minutes later she returned.

"Ah, Mr. Singh." She motioned at me.

I stood, straightened my suit coat, and took a step toward her until her palm up hand stopped me.

"Mr. Cutler told me to tell you he's sorry for your inconvenience, but the job has been filled."

16

I pressed my lips together, nodded, and left. My emotions bounced from dejection, to disgust, to anger, and then did another lap. If nothing else, I had learned a lesson today. If I wanted to reduce my gasoline consumption, I should enclose a picture with my future resumes.

Chapter 4

Almost an hour later, I pulled into the driveway of our West Chester home, an updated ranch built in the seventies. The summertime reminded me of how we had grown up together, this community and me. My earliest memories were of rolling fields spotted with homes on barren lots. Now the area was saturated with mature trees whose foliage offset the ugliness of too many close proximity thirty to forty-year-old homes.

When I opened the door connecting the mud room to the garage, my father, dressed in a blue suit with a matching turban, stood there. A shiny brown suitcase sat at his feet. It seemed as if each day the man grew older. The tall, slender, slightly-bent man looked tired and his once black beard and hair were now streaked with grey. Lines cut through his copper skin chiseled in place from the countless times his eyes had squinted, his eyebrows had encroached on his forehead, and his mouth had changed shape. The skin hung limp from the point of his chin down to the base of his throat. He was in his early fifties and looked not a day over seventy.

"Pops, what's with the suitcase?" I pointed.

He shook his head, his gray beard jiggled. "Remind me, when I get back, to teach you some manners."

"Get back from where?" I couldn't remember him ever going anywhere overnight without Mom or the family.

He looked at me for a long moment, studying me. He bit on his lower lip, something he did when his mind was burdened. His normally bright brown eyes dull, dimmed from concern or anguish.

He canted his head. "How did your interview go?"

Jai, my older brother, and I had learned his idiosyncrasies a long time ago, lessons necessary for minimizing discomfort. So I knew when he changed subjects, something major was on his mind.

"I didn't get the job." I stepped inside, into the air-conditioning, and closed the door. "Now what's going on and where are you going?"

He folded his arms across his chest and looked down. The man had never lied to me, though I knew he had kept many things from me. This had to be one of those.

"We have a conundrum," Pops said.

When he first came to America and had to learn English, he had gone slightly overboard. He loved to show off his command of the English language, particularly with his family.

"Pops, please. Conundrum? Speak simply," I said, shaking my head.

"It's my mother." His squinted brown eyes met mine.

"Grammy Biji? What's wrong?" I could only think the worst.

My grandmother had come to visit for a few weeks on only two occasions in my life. And my family and I had gone to see her years ago. But on our first introduction, it had only taken her minutes to win my heart. The short, white-haired lady with the big, widespread, brown eyes, hooked nose, and bowed back looked beautiful to me. The wrinkles in her face would triple in number and depth when she smiled. But her smile had always made me want to hug her.

"She, ah, she called ten days ago and told me things were not good in Kabul. She said the Taliban were persecuting Sikhs again, preventing cremations." He unfolded his arms and placed his hands behind his neck, elbows forward. "Like I have done so many times before, I asked her to get out of there and come live with us. But she is a stubborn woman. She still has family and many friends there in Kabul. And the temple she loves, the Gurudwara Karte Parwan with its shrine to Guru

19

Nanak, is there. Plus she says she could never acclimate to the western ways."

His eyes and hands fell.

"So what does that have to do with the bag?" I asked, stepping closer.

"My cousin Maanik called a few days ago. He said the situation had deteriorated overnight. Sikhs in the region around Kabul have become Taliban targets. And . . . and my mother's gone, missing, like many other Sikhs. He wasn't sure if she had escaped or—"he cleared his throat. "Maanik and his family are in hiding, moving every night. They are going to try to get to India."

My eyes dropped to his suitcase. "You're not thinking about—"

"Your mother and I have discussed this. I have her blessing and I have been given a leave from my work." His eyes fixed on mine. A cold sternness seeped into his lifeless gaze. "I am not soliciting either your blessing or advice. I am going to get my mother."

"Then I will go with you." I had been to India years ago but never to Afghanistan. Afghanistan and the Taliban were nothing more than too frequent news clips to me. I had no idea about what he was attempting to do.

"I will tell you what you will do," his voice firmer than I'd ever recalled. "You will take me to the airport." He reached down and picked up his suitcase. "Then you will stay here and look for a job while you watch over your mother."

Driving Pops' Jaguar was almost as exciting to me as the first time I touched a girl's breast . . . well almost.

After I accelerated onto southbound I-75 and punched on the cruise control, I glanced at my father. His stiff thin arms were braced on his knees, his blue turban-covered head tilted forward. His eyes were fixed on the road ahead, unseeing.

20

I had no frame of reference, no way to measure his plight. I didn't have any idea of what he was going to do, how he was going to do it, or how dangerous it was. All I had was my knowledge of him, and he was unlike I had ever seen him. His stiffness, his distance, his abruptness were all foreign to me. The man was deeply bothered. I couldn't discern if it was worry for his mother's well being or the obstacles he had to overcome to find her. All I had was a heap of concern and a whole lot of fear of all the unknowns.

My tingling nerves had no avenue of release. For the first time in my life, I wanted to bite my fingernails.

I had to have some answers.

I cleared my throat. "Father, please tell me about your father."

"So it's 'father' now? I am not sure how to interpret your change of manners."

"What was his name? You've never told us, Jai and me."

"Your mother is such a smart woman. She said you would ask me about him before I left."

"And is she finally ready to tell me?"

He focused his eyes on me. The brightness had returned, lit by memories. "His name was Daler, Daler Singh."

Chapter 5

I grabbed my father's suitcase and locked the car. We walked through the short term parking lot toward the airport terminal.

"Okay, so I resemble my grandfather both in size and looks. He was handsome and strong, both mentally and physically." I swung his suitcase to shoulder height with a stiff arm.

My father pushed my arm down. He shook his head.

"And he was a self-educated journalist who had worked his way up from a printer at a newspaper in Kabul," I said, parroting back what he had told me during the drive. "He met Grammy Biji and life was good until the Russians invaded."

"He was more than that . . . much more," he said with emphasis in his deliverance. "My father had more self-control than any man I have ever met. He could stroll through a riot like he was shopping in the market place. If someone aroused his emotions, he never showed it. He might have talked about it later, relative to what he thought of that person, but that person did not have a clue. Only my mother could affect him outwardly. She could make him smile . . . whenever she wanted to."

Though he continued to walk, I could see him mentally drift away, lost in memories.

I had waited too long for this moment and my stored curiosity made me pull him back from wherever he was. "So what happened to him? Did he fight the Russians? Did those commie slimes kill my grandfather?"

He stopped. "Listen to you. All my years of effort to teach you what my father had taught me, and this is the result? 'Commie slimes?'"

He began walking again.

I hustled to catch up.

He glanced my way. "Your grandfather was a fighter," he said. "He feared no man. And he taught my brother, Amrit, and me to fight just like I have taught you. When the Russians invaded everyone wanted to fight, including Amrit and me, it was our heritage. Our country . . . Afghanistan had been a doormat throughout recorded time. Afghans were always fighting some invader trying to take control of the gateway between the Far East and Europe. From Alexander the Great to Ghangis Khan, up to modern times with the Russians, they all tried and eventually all failed."

My mind whirled. "When did the Russians invade Afghanistan?"

"December 24, 1979."

Pops would have been sixteen or seventeen. "I never thought about you. Did you fight the Russians?"

"The Mujaheddin fought the Russians," he said. "Back then, everything was controlled by the Muslim tribal leaders. Even though there was a central government, the country was divided and controlled by a feudal system."

"Sikhs weren't allowed to fight?" I asked.

"Where we lived everyone, including Sikhs, was forced to fight. Amrit and many of my friends joined the ranks. My father tried to stop him, but he was twenty-one and on his own. So my father tightened his reins on me. He told me over and over again 'One son fighting was enough.'

"It was months before foreign supplies started to flow into the country and up until then it was a slaughter, Afghans on horses with old British rifles charging tanks and helicopters." He slowed and looked away. "Amrit was killed two months into the war. It was the only time I had ever seen my father cry." He took a deep breath and sped up his gait. "And when I got old

23

enough to make my own decisions, your mother came along and . . . well things changed.

"If my father took part in the war, I never knew it. There were times when he would leave for days, sometimes weeks, but my two sisters and I never knew where he went. Our mother would only say that we should pray for his return. When he did come back, he would not speak of where he had been. And, no, the 'commie slimes' did not kill him."

We had reached the terminal building. I waited until we got to the escalator to ask him what he had kept from me all my life.

"So what happened to my grandfather? All this mystery throughout my life, how did he die?"

He turned to face me, his face void of expression with the exception of a hint of fierceness along with a copper hue in his otherwise brown eyes.

"Your mother's father, Masoud Omar, killed him."

24

Chapter 6

I stood at the top of the airport escalator, a statue frozen by an overactive mind. No wonder my parents had kept the secret for all these years. My maternal grandfather, Masoud Omar, had killed my paternal grandfather, Daler Singh. This couldn't be. My father's story sounded like a Kentucky family feud, the Hatfields versus McCoys, not a Sikh family.

Sikhs were taught to respect others and to maintain self-control. Had everything my parents taught me been based on hopes not reality?

How could my mother love her father, a man her husband hated? How could a relationship survive in that environment?

And my grandfathers, two men bonded by their children's love, why would one of them risk losing his daughter's love forever? Why?

There had to be more to the story. There had to be a reason.

My jumbled mind was distracted from its mental chaos by my father. He had stopped several paces in front of me, had turned, and motioned me to join him.

I rushed to his side and grabbed his arm.

"Why? Why did one of my grandfathers kill the other? Why?"

He looked at my hand on his arm.

I released him.

His focus dropped to the floor for a moment. When his copper eyes returned to mine, his features sagged, burdened by some horrendous weight.

25

"Surinder, your mother, changed her name when we married. When we met, her name was Fatana. She was a Muslim."

I gasped and flinched backwards as if struck in the face.

My father looked away, far away, back in time. "I knew the first time I saw her that she was the one. And I could tell she felt the same way. Forget the family arranged marriages; forget the religious dogma forbidding a Muslim marrying a Sikh; I had found my mate. So I summoned all my courage and asked her father, Masoud Omar, for permission to see her. Not only did he say no, he threatened me if I persisted."

He sighed and rubbed his beard-covered chin. "I had this ache inside that would not go away. I had to see her again. So I had a friend of hers deliver a note to her asking her to meet me at a certain place and time. When I arrived early and she was already there, all my questions were answered. We continued to meet, either sneaking off or lying about where we were going. And each time we met, our relationship grew in intensity."

He hesitated. His glazed eyes stared down and away but saw nothing. He had returned to the moment, to his youth.

I side-stepped into his field of view. My arms spread. "So what happened? Did her father catch you with her?"

His focus returned to me. His expression conveyed he didn't want to be here.

I could imagine where he'd gone. I had been there, that warm, exotic, almost fairytale place only young lovers know.

Having been there, I couldn't imagine, didn't want to even think about, my parents being there. Following his lead, I shook the thought away.

"No," he said. "The war with the Russians brought havoc into everyone's personal lives. Her father became a leader in a new group, the Taliban. He was active in the fighting and rarely home. It became easier and easier for us to meet.

"After months of secret meetings, we decided to—"his chin dropped to his chest—"we were young and in love and . . . she was pregnant." He raised his chin, averted his eyes, and blew out a long breath. "Fatana, ah, your mother, ran away from home and came to live with me and my family."

His face reddened, his eyes avoided me, and he chewed on his lower lip.

I had never seen him embarrassed or ashamed until now.

"My father knew there would be trouble," he said with a foreboding tone. "He sent us to live with his brother, Parmajit, in Rawalpindi. When Fatana's father returned from fighting and found his daughter missing, he accosted my father. They met several times, each more emotional than the previous time. Fatana's father's demands for his daughter's return escalated." His eyes returned to mine, but the shame they had conveyed had been replaced with a squinted, piercing hatred. His upper lip quivered. "According to Fatana's mother, the last time they met, Masoud learned of Fatana's pregnancy and killed my father."

His fingers pinched the bridge of his nose. He took a long deep breath. He blinked away the intensity.

His expression migrated back to sadness. How could he be sad? A man had taken his father's life because of religious differences or pride, or . . . who cared. My pulse had quickened and pounded on a kettledrum in my temples.

"When my Uncle Parmajit heard of his brother's death, he sent Fatana and me to the United States." Pops studied my face for a moment. "And yes, Jai knows the story. I told him when he graduated from undergraduate school, after he had joined the army to get his MD."

I could only think of my reaction if someone had killed my father.

"You should have gone back and killed him." The words escaped my mouth before I gave them any thought.

His flush, drooping face hardened, the outline of his bone structure became pronounced. His jaw muscles flexed. His copper eyes bristled with intensity.

27

I had crossed a line, stepped on toes, pushed a button I shouldn't have.

"That was my first reaction. But he was her father. One father dead was enough of a burden. My father would not have acted on revenge nor have wanted me to. It is not what Sikhs do." He paused. Apparently, he wanted to give me time to consume his words. "Plus I had responsibilities, as I do now. I must go. I have a flight to catch."

He started walking.

I caught up to him, matching his long strides with mine. "Is my grandfather, Masoud Omar, still alive?" I asked.

"I think so."

"Will you see him?"

"He is not my priority."

He stopped at the end of a line in front of a Delta ticket counter. He turned and took his bag from me. "It is time for you to go home, take care of your mother, and find a job."

"But what will you do? How will you get into Afghanistan? How will you find Biji? Will you call us, is that even possible?" I snapped my fingers. "Stop in Duty Free and buy an international cell phone."

He gave me one of those 'Don't tell me what to do' looks.

"My Uncle Parmajit still lives in Rawalpindi. He is affluent. He will help me get in country with whatever I need. My mother lives in Nanakpur, just outside Kabul. That's where I'll start searching. And, no, I probably won't be able to call you. But I will call Uncle Parmajit, and he will call you. Now I must go, as should you. You have responsibilities to attend to."

Chapter 7

I felt like I was in a vacuum during my drive home from the airport. No people, no noise, just guilt-ridden thoughts and smells. My father's sweet musky odor hung in his car.

My father, my haggard-looking father, I should have stopped him. He was in no shape to travel half-way around the world and go into a hostile country. What if he had to fight for his life?

I should have gone with him. There had to be another way to get Grammy Biji out of Afghanistan.

We should have called Uncle Parmajit. He had money, lots of it. He could hire people to go after Grammy.

But if the roles were reversed and my mother was in trouble, I would have done the same thing, and no one would have stopped me.

What was I supposed to do now, obey my father's orders?

Look for a job and take care of my mom. My father's and my grandmother's lives were in jeopardy. I'd go crazy.

What else could I do? If Pops and Grammy Biji needed me, I wasn't smart enough to go there on my own. Even though my parents had taught me Pashto, the local language, I knew nothing else. I didn't know anything about the country, the people, the customs, and, most of all, the Taliban. I was ignorant, something hard for me to admit.

I couldn't just sit and wait. I'd start by learning everything I could about Afghanistan.

Where could I get a crash course on—Carl, Carl Thompson, my high school buddy. The tall, handsome weightlifter with muscles on top of muscles hadn't gone to college. He had joined the Marines' ROTC in high school and shortly after graduation, he was shipped to Afghanistan. Recently, a mutual friend had told me Carl had spent two tours there, almost three years.

I hadn't thought about Carl since . . . since the summer after graduation when he left. What a strange buddy. Pops referred to Carl as my 'unique high school chum.' In retrospect, unique was probably the wrong word. Carl and I had violated most of the teenage norms. We had nothing in common. He liked shop. I liked calculus. He played football. I played the other football, soccer. He worked on cars. I worked on getting a scholastic scholarship. About the only thing we had in common was our like for girls and isolated places to take them. We often double-dated, Carl and his girl du jour and Sandy and me.

I pulled the Jaguar off the road, punched on my hazard lights, and fumbled for my pocketed cell phone. All I had was his parent's number, but they could connect me.

On the third ring, to my surprise, Carl answered, "Hello." His voice was deep and groggy, but there was no mistaking his voice.

"Carl, Kugi Singh. What's up?"

"Kugi, the college boy, man it's been awhile."

The way he said 'college boy' made me wonder if he would be willing to help me.

"Ain't nothing up," Carl continued. "Since I left the Corps, I've been sittin' on my ass. How's what's-her-name?"

"Sandy?" Sandy's blue eyes, pug nose, full kissable lips, framed by her blonde hair came to life, high school days. I had to shake reality back into my head.

"Oh . . . life and college got in the way. She married some dude from Clemson. I heard she's currently putting him through med school."

"Whoa. I thought you two would go all the way."

"Back then, we did to. How about you, did you ever get married?"

30

"Only to the Marines . . . I thought I'd be in 'til death do us part.'"

"How long have you been out?" A true friend would have known the answer. Hell, a friend would have written Carl while he was overseas.

"Almost a year. I can't find any worthwhile work. Maybe I should've stayed in, but I didn't want another tour in Afghanistan."

"We have something in common there. I have an engineering degree, and I haven't been able to find a job either." I wasn't sure how to bridge to the subject so I just plopped it out. "Speaking of Afghanistan, do you have some time today?"

"Haven't you been listenin'? That's all I've got." His snarling words made me pull the phone off my ear.

I'd forgotten about his short fuse. An ugly memory quickly surfaced. A memory I had blocked or buried. We were seniors and it was the Spring Dance. A known bully from another school had tried to cut in on Sandy and me while we were dancing. One thing led to another, and I got pushed to the floor. I can still hear the knuckles-mashing-flesh whop of Carl's fist crushing the boy's nose. Blood erupted in a red haze, the beginning of a nightmare. Carl's meat cutting, bone-breaking blurred fists destroyed the boy's face before others could pull Carl away.

I had lain on the floor, not believing the messages my eyes sent to my brain. I wanted to scream protests or jump up and stop him; anything to civilize my raging friend. But Carl's animalistic fury had stunned me, incapacitated me, and most of all sickened me.

Except for rare school hallway encounters, I didn't see Carl after that.

Maybe this wasn't such a good idea. My guts screamed at me to back out, but I had gone too far, plus I needed his knowledge.

31

I cleared my throat. "Can I buy you a beer? I need to pick your brain."

"If you're buyin', I'm drinkin'. But I must warn you, it'll cost you more than one beer, and you're in for some slim pickins'. What do you need?"

"I need to know everything you can tell me about Afghanistan."

"I thought your family came from there?"

"They did, but I didn't. And that was a long time ago. I need current information."

"What's this about, ol' friend?"

"I'll tell you when I see."

"Ah, can you, ah, pick me up? My car got repo'd last week."

My eyes perused the luxurious interior of the Jag. I'd have to stop at home and get my junker.

"Wait 'til you see what I'm driving, my old Chevy's beyond the repo stage. See you in an hour."

Chapter 8

Driving over the speed bumps in the trailer park bounced me right back to driving over them in my high school days, the weekend carefree days.

Carl had been my respite from the books and geek-dom, my source for adventure. He rounded my corners, challenging me with the basics, beer, booze, a little pot, a fight every now and then, and women. And, oh yeah, getting to second base.

I probably should have stayed in touch with Carl. The good times had overwhelmed the bad, or at least that's the way it seemed at the moment.

After three or four horn honks, the door to the doublewide opened and out walked Carl Thompson. He looked different.

I expected him to be older. But I thought his face would be the same. Although his features were similar, a little puffier with a few added lines, he wasn't my pimple-faced adolescent buddy any longer, he was a man.

One thing I didn't expect was for Carl to look stronger, but he did. He wore jeans and a gray tee-shirt with "US Marines" stenciled on the chest. His "V" shaped torso defined fatless muscle and his biceps, lined with greenish-blue distended veins, stretched his shirt sleeves.

Carl made some comment about having seen too many turbans, and then directed me to a small beer joint in Bethany.

The bar was about as wide and maybe twice as deep as my father's two car garage. The interior was dark, sprinkled with neon beer signs, and smelled of stale cigarette smoke and beer. Several men sat hunkered on a half-dozen bar stools.

The size, the dim lighting, all the occupied stools at this hour, I wasn't sure what but something made me uncomfortable.

Carl waved at the bartender, a mid-thirties, pudgy woman with dirty unkempt blonde hair, as we walked by the bar. He yelled, "Two Buds."

We sat at one of four empty tables jammed together, two by two, in the back. The multi-tasking bartender delivered two bottles of beer. She was short and missing a front tooth. Her white shirt was unbuttoned past her red padded bra. And her black jeans failed to hide her cellulite.

After Carl watched her walk away, he raised his bottle and clinked mine. "To ol' friends."

We both took swigs, his consumed half the beer.

He wiped his upper lip with the back of his hand. "Now, what the hell do you want to know and why?"

I sat forward like I was soliciting information from a government spy. "I want to know everything you can tell me about Afghanistan."

His face scrunched up. "Like what?"

"Like who are the Taliban and what are they like? And if you were ever near Kabul; and, if so, what is it like? And—"

"Hey, Carl," a booming deep male voice cut me off. A large hand slapped Carl's shoulder and remained there, fingers pressed into Carl's flesh.

I looked up and saw the largest man I've ever seen. Carl seemed small in comparison. He wore a black leather sleeveless biker's jacket, no shirt, and his head was shaved. He reminded me of 'Mr. Clean,' except for the wide pink scar that crossed his forehead, split his right eye, and thinned as it went down his cheek ending at his chin. His eyes were almost black. His right eye wasn't quite synchronized with his left when he glanced at me.

"Beau and Pinky here," Mr. Clean nodded at two men in the shadows behind him, "they couldn't believe it was you. But I recognized you." He released Carl's shoulder and slapped the back of his head.

Without looking over his shoulder, Carl raised both hands. "Easy there, Moose. I don't like being hit by nobody."

Moose turned. "See. I told you this motherfucker was Carl, the man who fucked me out of all that money."

I leaned back and gave Carl a 'what's going on' look. His eyes met mine. He barely shook his head. What had I gotten myself into? I rubbed my hands together. My palms were wet.

"So did you bring back one of those Taliban guys as a trophy?" Moose asked and nodded his shiny dome at me.

"Moose." Carl looked over his shoulder. "Why don't you and I go to the bar and have a talk."

A faint click was followed by Moose's hand pressing a six-inch blade against Carl's throat. "Now why would I want to hear more of your fuckin' lies, when I can just cut your throat and be done with you?"

The hair on my neck bristled and my beer-coated throat was parched. This guy was serious, too serious. I couldn't just sit there and watch him kill Carl.

I extended my hand, palm out. "Whoa, there. I'm sure this, whatever it is, can all be worked out peacefully."

"Shut the fuck up, rag head." Moose's deep hissed words caused a shudder to ripple down my spine.

There was that name again, 'rag head,' but right now, names seemed trivial.

Carl slowly touched my hand and guided it to the table.

"If you kill me, you ain't gonna get shit from me, Moose," Carl said with his chin raised.

"That ain't true, shit-head. I'll get the satisfaction of removing a lying, back-stabbin' piece of shit from this world."

Carl flinched ever so slightly. A trickle of blood ran down his throat.

"Hey, hey, hey," I yelled.

"Pinky, shut that Arab up," Moose said to one of the dark figures behind him.

35

A shadow stepped forward.

I tensed, despite my training.

Carl, his brown eyes almost squinted closed, raised a hand. "No need for that." He slapped the table with his hand. "Kugi, sit still and shut up."

"Kugi?" Moose asked. "What the fuck kind of name is that? Is that what them fellers over there call a camel fucker?" He laughed, causing his body to shake, including his knife-holding hand.

His partners in the shadows joined in.

Carl's hand lifted off the table an inch and motioned for me to be calm. If that were possible.

"Moose. You're wrong about that money. I didn't take it. Garman's the one who walked with the bread. I didn't get a penny."

Moose grabbed Carl's ear and sliced part of the lobe off with the knife.

"Ahhhh!" Carl yelled. He grabbed his ear and blood ran through his fingers and down his neck.

"You're a liar. You've always been one and you'll die bein' one." Moose wiped the blade off on Carl's shirt and put the edge back against Carl's throat. "While you's was gone. I found Garman. And that's exactly what he said you'd say. Now I know Garman was somewhat of a liar hisownself. But when I had his nuts clamped in a pair of vice-grips, I was sure he spoke the pure truth. Now stand up real slow like. You and me's going out back."

Carl, his face crimson, eased his way upright, the knife never leaving his throat.

"Tell me where Garman is, and I'll get your money," Carl said.

"He's where you're gonna be in about a minute," Moose said.

I had to act, do something.

"How much money?" The words blurted from my mouth.

A deep voice from behind Moose said, "I'll quiet that Arab fucker, boss."

Moose extended his free hand behind him. "Hold on, Pinky. Let the soon-to-be dead terrorist talk." The big man's good eye fell on me. "Fifty grand."

"That's nah—"

"Shut the fuck up, Carl," Moose said, pressing the blade into Carl's skin. "You got that kind of money, boy? You think this lyin' jarhead is worth fifty g's?"

"I can get it," I lied. Anything to stall, to think.

"Didn't I see you and dumb boy get out of a piece of junk out there?"

"Well, ah, yeah . . . but my dad's got bucks, big bucks. He'd give me fifty thousand dollars if I needed it." My words didn't sound convincing to me, so I was sure they didn't believe them.

"Now I guess you expect me and my friends and Carl here to have a little party while we wait for you to go ask your daddy for fifty g's?"

I nodded my head. "Yeah."

My searching mind skidded to a stop. When I was little, my brother and I used to play this game with clothes pins and a bottle. I always won.

I stood.

Two big ugly men came out of the shadows, both wearing biker jackets, and both at least as big as Carl.

Moose pointed the knife at me. "I gonna cut you just for the hell-of-it." Moose's words tinged with disgust. He jabbed the knife back against Carl's neck. "Now move it, Carl."

"I will get you your money," I said, causing Moose to hesitate. I raised my beer bottle as if to drink. When the bottle neared my lips I swiped it through the air and jammed the bottle's mouth over the knife's blade.

In one motion Carl grabbed his bottle and slammed it into Moose's face, spraying me and the table with glass, beer, and Moose's blood.

I picked up my chair, Carl ducked, and I swung it as hard as I could into Moose's hands-covered face. The big man fell back into his two charging buddies.

Somehow Carl's hand came away with the knife and he filleted the arm of the first of Moose's pals who pushed forward.

I'm sure I saw the white of bone through the man's flesh before the gushing blood masked it.

The man howled and stepped back clutching his arm.

The second man backed away dragging the unconscious Moose.

Carl grabbed me and pulled me through the back door.

We ran. I for as long and as fast as my adrenaline would take me.

Chapter 9

Carl and I bent at the waist gulping air. We were in a small stand of trees in a field behind a subdivision.

"Amazing," Carl pushed the word out between pants.

"Amazing?" I squeezed my wobbly knees, and shook my head. My side ached and I couldn't get enough air. "You've, whew . . . you've got . . . to be kidding."

"You . . . you were amazing."

His words, his smile, took my ache away, flooded me with air, and pushed me upright.

I nodded. "Yeah . . . I was."

He threw his heavy arm over my shoulder, and we both laughed between pants.

"No one in their right mind—"he coughed—"would ever match us up as friends . . . no one."

I nodded. "Pops would drink to that."

"How is your ol' man?" Carl asked.

I took a deep breath and blew it out. "At this very moment, he's on his way to Afghanistan."

Carl pushed upright. His jovial expression faded to a concerned look. He nodded. "Now I understand . . . the questions. So why's he going back?"

Pops had always taught us to keep family business in the family. But I couldn't find a reason not to tell Carl. So I told him the whole story, every ugly morsel.

Carl and I were sitting on the ground, fully recuperated, when I finished my story.

39

"Man, that's some bad shit, one of your grandfathers killing the other one. And now your grandmother's gone missing, and your ol' man's going back there." He shook his head. "That isn't a good place to be."

I gave Carl one of those "gee thanks for adding another concrete block to the five already on my back" looks.

"So, Carl, what am I going to have to do to get you to tell me about Afghanistan?"

"Why? What good is that gonna do? You've already got enough on your plate." He extended his arms. "Anything I would say would just add to your worries."

Too late.

I gave him my no-nonsense look. "Carl, I need to know."

Carl skewed his eyes and furrowed his brow like I had just called his mother an obscene name. "Kugi, you aren't thinkin' . . . no way. What are you thinkin'?"

"Are Pops and my Grammy Biji in trouble?" I asked.

Carl looked down and away, and then nodded.

"So what am I supposed to do, just sit here and worry?"

Carl's brown eyes met mine. His expressionless eyes turned to stone. "Yes. Your father and grandmother were born and raised there. They know the people, the country, and . . . their enemies. Your father is a very smart man, slap that with some luck, and he may be able to find your grandmother and get her out of there."

I wanted to climb on his logic train and sit back and ride, but I couldn't.

"You should see him, Carl. He's eaten up with worry and aged way beyond his years. He's frail and out of shape. If that country is anything like he's told me it is, it'll consume what little energy he's got left."

I stood up and paced. "How will I ever live with myself if I do nothing? And," I stopped and pointed, "what if that . . . that place swallows them up, and I never hear from either of them again?"

Carl, his eyes on mine, tapped his mouth with a fisted hand.

40

I knelt down next to him and touched his shoulder. "Tell me, what would you do if this were your father and grandmother?"

He looked away, mind traveling.

"You want it straight?" His eyes questioned mine.

I hesitated and then said, "Yes."

He stood. "The Taliban . . . those young, crazy, brainwashed bastards kill for the fun of it . . . old, young, women, children, it don't matter." He stood. "If I were you, I wouldn't have let my father go because . . . your grandmother was probably killed the first day those bastards went on a rampage. Rarely does anyone survive. Right now, if I were you, I'd call your great uncle, whatever his name is, and make him send your dad home when he gets there."

Oh my God, this man who knew that country so well was so convinced Grammy Biji was dead. I wanted to cry out, but this wasn't the time. My issues were far from resolved.

"You don't know my father," I said.

Carl's head bobbed. "If she were my mom, no one would stop me either."

I sighed and stood. "Shit."

Carl leaned against an oak tree and cupped his chin in his hand. He stared, unseeing, at the ground.

Hands on hips, my mind was banging into a brick wall. We had gone full circle. I had learned nothing except what I had already feared. I was pinched. I had no choice. I had to try to save my father.

"Can I ask you something?" Carl asked.

I scrunched my shoulders. "Sure."

"How will your dying make your father's death any easier for your mother to accept?" His brown eyes fixed on me, a cold, unmoving stare.

I didn't have an answer. I just dropped my arms to my sides and bowed my head.

A long moment later, Carl grabbed my arm.

"Come on," he said and tugged me along with him.

"Where are we going?" I asked.

"You saved my ass back there."

"So? You're my friend. You've saved mine before." The high school dance flashed by. "That's what friends do."

I stopped. "Carl, I need for you to tell me everything you know about . . . that place."

He pulled me into stride with him again. "I will . . . on the way."

"On the way where?" I asked

"I need to get out of this town for a while," he said. He plopped his big heavy arm across my shoulders. "On the way to your uncle-whatever-his-name-is' house."

Chapter 10

"Kugi, you are not going!" My mother, still in her brown business suit, stretched her small slender body to block the doorway to my room. Her brown eyes sparkled with conviction. "Your father and I discussed this. It is his duty to try to save his mother, not yours."

I looked down at my mother. Pops always said she hadn't changed since the day he met her. In my life time, the only changes I had noticed were the age lines in her neck and her recent need for glasses. Though I was a mite prejudice, I thought she was beautiful.

"Then it's my duty to save my father." I tried to sound like a man I had become versus the young son she perceived me to be.

Mom leaned toward me to accentuate her words. Her long dark brown hair somehow, miraculously pinned up in the back, accentuated her small features, nose, lips, and chin. "Your duty is to honor your father's wishes. And those are for you to stay here and find a job."

I didn't want to argue with her, but what choice did I have? If I didn't go, Pops would die. I had to be careful with Mom. She had always taken pride in her motherhood role. I didn't need her permission, but leaving without it could scar our relationship.

I pushed my body erect, raising my height. "Mom, I'm twenty-three years old. I can make my own decisions."

She shook her head. "Not rationally."

43

How could she say that? What in the hell did she think five years of brain-cramming deductive reasoning in engineering college had taught me?

I folded my arms across my chest and tried to compress my irritation. "My reasoning and decision making, though not conforming to your point of view, is totally rational. Just like my respect and love for you. But I'm going. Don't make me pick you up and move you."

"What will you do for money?" she asked.

I patted my pants pocket. "I withdrew my savings, a little less than six thousand dollars."

"The money you earned working every summer? I . . . I thought you were going to use that as a down payment on a new car."

I shrugged my shoulders. "I was. But I don't need a new car, not now."

My mother, who could be the most stubborn woman I'd ever known, dropped her blocking arms and stepped aside. She motioned to my room. "Go ahead."

My eyebrows arched involuntarily. My folded arms fell to my sides. This couldn't be. She wouldn't concede that easily. Had I convinced her I was right? I wasn't going to waste this opportunity by asking. I stepped by her and went to my closet.

"You are wasting your time," she said.

I opened my closet door and pulled out my old battered suitcase. I looked over my shoulder at her. She stood in the doorway, hands on her small hips. The hint of a smirk invaded her otherwise expressionless face. I had seen that look too many times before, she wasn't about to lose this disagreement.

"Why's that?" I asked. I knew this had been too easy. A feeling of insecurity, like being in a chess game with someone you knew was a much better player, bristled the hair follicles on my neck while eroding my competitive pride.

"You are a lot like your father. And I think I know him better than anyone."

44

I put my bag on my bed and opened it. It was time to force her to make her 'check' move. "And?"

"I thought you may try something like this, so I took your passport."

I tried to conceal my mental shock of her invisible fist slamming into my gut. I turned and faced her and mustered all my focus to keep my voice calm and polite. "So, just give it back."

"No."

Miss Stubborn hadn't gone anywhere, she was still here. But I had options.

I flipped my hands out to my sides. "So you'll just cause me to waste some money and time getting another one."

"No." Her tone was so resolute, so assured.

"What's that mean?" She already had me cornered, what now?

"There will be no waste. I took your birth certificate too."

Checkmate.

Chapter 11

"Great Uncle Parmajit, this is Kugi Singh, your great nephew." I bent at the waist and yelled into the speaker phone in Jai's old bedroom. My father had converted the room to an office.

The sun had set hours ago. My mother sat in the dome of light from the desk lamp. Carl and I stood in the shadows bracketing her.

"Who?" a weak male voice asked, cracked with age.

"Kugi, your great nephew . . . Raman's son," I hollered louder. I don't know why I was yelling? I guess it was either because he was so far away in Pakistan, or because he didn't seem to be able to understand me.

Silence drew everyone's focus to the speaker phone.

"Uncle Parmajit, this is Fatana," my mother glanced at me, "I mean, Surinder, Raman's wife . . . Masoud Omar's daughter." Mom spoke softly, slowly.

"Ahhh, Fatana," Parmajit said. "It has been long, long time."

"Thirty years," my mother said. "How are things in Rawalpindi?"

"We had long winter followed by late spring rains, but I think summer has finally arrived. It is cool, seventeen degrees this morning, and the summer winds are here."

"Whoa, that's chilly for June," Carl whispered. "Where is he, in the mountains?"

I leaned behind my mother and whispered to him, "Seventeen degrees Celsius, ah, low sixties. Pops told me Rawalpindi sits on a plateau, near the mountains."

"So why are you calling?" the old man asked. "Raman is not here. He will not be here for two days."

My mother glared at me. This was my call. Since she refused to let me go, I had pressed her to phone my great uncle. I had convinced her there may be another way to rescue my grandmother.

"Uncle Parmajit, my father is too old and frail to make this trip, let alone go into a hostile country," I said in Mom's soft tone. "We were hoping you would do us a favor."

"Favor? What?"

"Is it possible for you to hire someone more able, like a mercenary or some local Afghans to go after my Grammy Biji and thereby keep my father from going? We would pay whatever it costs."

"I am merchant. I own seven clothing stores across Pakistan and—ah, I guess only six now, the store in Kabul has closed. I have no idea about any of these things . . . mercenaries, or Afghans who would do such thing. Personally, I think Raman has lost his mind. I tried to talk him out of coming here. Things are bad for Sikhs in Afghanistan now. Some local Taliban General, near Kabul, has decided to punish all Sikhs. Kabul invaded, airports closed, insane. Sikhs have lived peacefully for centuries in Afghanistan. Then one man with vendetta gains enough power to ruin everything."

"But—"

"My son, Maanik, managed my store in Kabul. He and his family were caught up in this Taliban assault on Sikhs. He called me two weeks ago and asked for help. With the borders closed, there was nothing I could do, nothing for my own son."

"But maybe—"

"Thank God, Maanik and his family arrived here today. You should see them. They have been walking for week. They look like peasants. He and his wife and two small children slept in caves . . . dirty rat-filled caves. I cannot image. They only traveled at night. To avoid borders they crossed those mountains at night . . . with two small children? Many times he

47

and his wife had to muffle their crying children. You should hear his story. Good God, my son, prominent store manager, was reduced to stealing food from poor people." He sighed. "They were lucky to get out of that crazy place alive . . . many others did not."

"Does Maanik know anything about my Grammy Biji?" I squeezed in a question.

"They have heard nothing about Biji. She is old like me. I fear the worst."

"You must stop my father," I pleaded. "Tell him to find another way."

"I stopped him from going back to Afghanistan once before . . . ah, you say it was thirty years ago? Fatana remembers. I doubt I can do that again. Raman inherited his stubbornness. His father, my brother, Daler, and his wife, Biji, were both obstinate. I have tried to talk both of them into leaving that God awful place many times. Now I fear Afghanistan has killed them both."

My mother glared at me. "What will happen if Raman tries to go there?" she asked, her voice trembling.

There was a long pause with muffled voices in the background.

"Maanik just told me this General responsible for this Taliban uprising against Sikhs is . . . is Masoud Omar, your father, Fatana. I fear your running off with Sikh is the reason for his anger. He has old unhealed wound that has festered for thirty years. Now that he is the regional leader of all Taliban, he is using his power to vent his vengeance. He has gone mad, ordering his soldiers to search for and kill every Sikh they find. Hundreds have been murdered. If Raman goes into Afghanistan, and your father, Masoud, finds him, Raman will suffer terrible death."

Chapter 12

When the call to Pakistan was over, my mother pushed back from the desk, got up, and left Pops' office, head down, without saying a word.

I rose to follow her. She shouldn't be alone, not now.

Carl bolted to his feet, grabbed my arm, and stopped me.

His brown eyes stared into mine like he could see into my head and read my mind. "This is not the right time, Kugi. Leave her be."

I had never seen this side of Carl, this caring tenderness. His words made sense. If my mother's stomach ached with fear for my father's well-being as much as mine did, talking with someone wouldn't help. Plus I didn't know what to say to her. My mother and I were beyond words.

I sucked in a deep breath and released it, hoping to unknot my shoulders.

Carl dropped my arm and stretched. "After that call, I need a cigarette. Wanna go outside with me?"

I couldn't believe a man who worked so hard to develop his body would smoke. Was Carl's need for a cigarette a ruse just to get me outside, away from the phone, this room, and the hanging thoughts?

"I didn't know you smoked," I said.

"I'm trying to quit." He led me to the back door. "I picked up the habit in Afghanistan. Between the fightin' we had a lot of idle time and a whole bunch of nerves."

We stepped out of the air-conditioning and were pressed by the heavy humidity. We stood on the back slab and faced the tree-lined yard. Carl lit up a smoke.

Carl blew a gray plume skyward and then turned to me, his brow arched and his arms extended. "So what's this mean?" He hiked his thumb over his shoulder in the direction of the house. "We're not goin'?"

I shook my head and looked away. "No one, not my uncle, not my mom, and especially not the fear of my grandfather, General Masoud Omar, will keep Pops from going after his mother. Unfortunately his intentions are beyond his abilities. He must be stopped or he will die. We're just wasting precious time sitting here."

"So we're goin'?" Carl asked. His expression more confused than his words.

I didn't know what to say. "Well, for Pops' sake, I need to go. I can't think of any alternatives." I touched his shoulder. His eyes met mine. "This is far worse than I originally thought. And this is a family matter. You don't have any skin in this game. All I ever wanted from you is information. All I'll ask of you is to tell me everything I need to know and to wish me well."

"No, no, no. Kugi, we're beyond that decision. That place is as dangerous for you as it is for your father. If you go, I'm goin' with you. Besides, what I can tell you won't help you do it. You'll need me." His arms flipped up from his sides. "So are we goin'?"

"Yes . . . well I think so. There are some issues . . . here . . . complications. They won't be easy to fix."

"'Won't be easy'? That's funny, real funny." He shook his head and dragged on the cigarette. He exhaled several rolling rings of smoke. "We're planning on traveling halfway around the world to Pakistan, not the friendliest place these days. Then we have to either talk your Pops out of going, which you said will be impossible, or tie him up for your uncle to babysit 'til we get back with your grandma . . . fat chance."

"Whoa." I held up my hand. His words, like a dentist's drill, had struck a nerve ending. "'Fat chance' of what, controlling Pops, or . . . getting back?" I asked.

"All the above."

I decided to keep my mouth shut and let him talk. Maybe he would finally answer some of my questions.

Carl sucked on the cig again.

"From Rawalpindi, we have to go about two hundred and thirty klicks to the White Mountains. We have to cross those mountains into Afghanistan, fun." The smoke exhaled with each of his words. "And believe me, these are mountains like you've never seen before. And we can't take the roads with the borders closed so we hike in, more fun. I'm thinkin' backpacks stuffed with food, water, and gear, sixty, seventy pounds, minimum, not countin' any weapons or ammunition. To avoid the border crossin's, we must travel the paths over the passes, like the Khyber Pass for one, that go around and around and up and down forever. We won't have a guide and there aren't any maps worth a shit. We'll need a good compass and a whole lotta luck both to find our way and to avoid the drug traffickers, who like to hold people for ransom. 'Won't be easy' you say?" His eyebrows arched. "Just to get to Afghanistan will be a major feat of accomplishment for the fittest of fit."

His eyes scanned me from head to toe. His hand patted my pouched belly. "And you ain't so fit."

Irritated by his actions though mesmerized by his words, I pushed his hand away.

"Ever hear of altitude sickness?" he asked. "Now there's some real fun for the out-of-shape hiker, dizziness, loss of balance, nausea. Basically done, finished, washed up for days. Got the picture?"

I nodded. My fears for my father turned inward to chew on my core.

"After that we get to the land of rocks, Afghanistan. We have to sneak into a land over-ran with young zealots who love to torture and kill Americans and apparently Sikhs, ah, like you

51

and me." He pointed his index finger at me and his thumb at his chest and ratcheted it back and forth.

Carl took another toke, looked skyward, and released his own little cloud. "If we get that far, we'll be faced with the worst of 'won't be easy.' The 'Ghan' is unbelievable, one craggy mountain after another, endless ambush heaven, with hundreds of uncharted mine fields and too many bad people."

Carl's eyes returned to mine, his eyebrows arched into a furrowed forehead. "If and when we're lucky enough to finally get to where ever we're goin', all we have to do is find an old woman nobody has seen, and get her back through Taliban country and across those friggin' mountains. And she's not likely to be very fit either. And through all that crap, we have to keep ourselves supplied with food and water. There aren't any McDonald's out there."

He pressed his fists into his sides and sighed. "And we're supposed to do that without any weapons, not even a fingernail clipper per the latest dumbass airline rules. And you're talkin' about somethin' here that won't be easy." He took his last drag and flipped the cigarette into the back yard.

I started to protest but Pops wasn't here to find the butt when he cut the grass.

Carl chuckled, exhaling spurts of smoke.

The back door to the house opened and my mom stood there, biting her lower lip. Her squinted eyes went from Carl, to the sputtering smoke coming from his mouth, and then to me.

"Ah, Kugi, I . . ." her shoulders slumped, she jabbed a large envelope at me, "here, your passport and birth certificate. No one will stop your father from going after his mother. I'll talk him into staying at Parmajit's house until you get there. Then you bring him home, whatever it takes. But you must promise me you won't go any further than Parmajit's."

I clutched the envelope, but she held on to it. "Promise me," she said.

I glanced at Carl. I knew there was only one way to stop Pops. And that was for Carl and me to rescue Biji in his place.

As if she were reading my mind, Mom released my documents.

I looked at Carl. "We need to pack. I booked us on a flight leaving for London tonight." How would I ever pay off that credit card bill? I shook away the thought. My focus shifted to my mom. "Don't worry. I, ah, we won't let Pops go after Biji. We should get to Parmajit's about the time Pops is getting up from his journey's rest."

Chapter 13

All my concerns for not knowing what we were going to do were momentarily swept aside by my entrance into the interior of the Boeing 777. I hadn't been on a plane since I had completed my freshman year in high school. Pops had earned a big bonus and decided to take our family to a Singh reunion in New Delhi during the summer. Jai was home on a break from med school. That had been our best family vacation ever. Having my own passport, flying over hours and hours of ocean, seeing London and Big Ben, and finally going to India, that mystery birth place of my ancestors, a place I had only visited via 'Google' and the library.

I looked around the cabin. The interior of planes hadn't changed much since my high school days. For some reason, this wasn't as thrilling as before. Exciting yes, thrilling no. Uncle Parmajit's story of doom coupled with Carl's graphic travel log, had me on edge. Adding the thought of being propelled miles above the earth with my destiny totally out of my control had me jacked up.

I was dependent on a pilot and thousands of mechanical gadgets all doing their jobs for the long hours to come. Maybe I had learned too much 'stuff' in engineering school, the worst being Probability and Statistics. I wondered what the probability was for one of those thousands of parts wearing out or failing during this trip.

My stomach joined my brain in discomfort.

After we stowed our carry-on bags in the overhead, Carl and I sat down a row or two from the "back of the bus" in coach class in the middle section. Having no windows sucked. But last minute reservations had their own baggage.

The ache in my gut got worse by the minute.

Carl punched my arm. "Hey, man, this is cool. We're takin' a trip together and flyin'. Get with the program and enjoy this." He pulled back and squinted at me. "What's wrong with you? You haven't said nothin' since we boarded?"

"I, ah, I don't feel very good." My hand rubbed my stomach. I felt like I had swallowed one of those 'Alien" creatures and it was trying to get out.

"You got the flyin' jitters or is the reality of this trip finally settlin' in?" he asked.

"Both. Let me out, I've got to go to the john before we takeoff."

He got up and I wedged my way out of the row. I passed him, and he grabbed my arm.

"Relax, brother, I've got your back."

I patted his arm and walked away. It wasn't my back I was concerned about.

I had barely got the lavatory door bolted when my mother's dinner surged and gagged my throat. Doubled over, I spewed my stomach contents, every gram, into the toilet between choked breaths.

What a way to start a trip.

Chapter 14

After refusing the offered boxed meal, I whispered my evening prayer. Then I tried to watch one of the flight's movies. I couldn't do it. I needed sleep. Trying to get comfortable in the middle seat of the center section of coach class was like trying to sleep in the back seat of a VW bug between two NFL tackles.

Mentally exhausted from the 'what ifs' of this trip and physically drained by my nervous fear-of-flying stomach, I finally passed out and slept soundly until a thud and bounce jolted me awake. Consciousness brought reality to my dream of having a kinked neck, a sore back, and cramped legs. I checked my watch. I had been asleep less than three hours. No wonder I felt like crap. I turned to my side and closed my eyes.

The cabin lights came on. An invasive, scratchy voice on the intercom announced we had landed in Heathrow, the local time was eight a.m., and the temperature was fifty-seven degrees Fahrenheit.

I desperately needed two things, a soft bed and more sleep, and what did I get, a frigging weather report.

The plane braked and made a hard right turn causing all the head tops in front of me to slid left, including me.

I leaned forward to see a sliver of a window past the six people in between. Water trickled down the outside of the pane. I should have predicted it would be raining in England. Cool and rainy, I was glad to be just passing through.

Carl said something. I didn't have a clue, and didn't care. I just nodded.

When our plane parked at a terminal gate, I said a hushed prayer. I hadn't prayed in a while and I certainly needed to now, I had made a decision without any knowledge of what I doing, an unheard of action for me. I stood on weak, stiff legs and stretched. My lips and tongue were almost as dry as the stale cabin air. My wrinkled clothes clung to me. My breath and body had to smell musty like the people close to me.

Having fallen asleep just after the 'Preview of Coming Attractions', my mind did not want to wake up. And my body didn't want to lug my carry-on let alone walk.

I wedged into the grumbling jam of stinky passengers and let the human tide move me up the aisle and off the plane. A jet way later, and I was in a narrow hallway packed with people squeezing onto an escalator rising into the ceiling.

I glanced over my shoulder and couldn't see Carl. But it didn't matter. Nothing matter to me in my half-awake state except finding a big soft chair in the transit lounge and getting some more sleep.

I stumbled onto the escalator and almost fell on an old woman in front of me. Damn, I needed to wake up. What I really needed was a soft bed and eight hours of sleep followed by a hot shower. Unfortunately, all I had to look forward to was more airplane rides, three to four hours to Athens with a couple hours lay–over followed by another five to six hours to Lahore, another lay-over, and then an hour flight to Rawalpindi. Three more body-punishing flights in the same clothes for God's sake.

But first things first, I wasn't sure of what I had to do to catch my next flight. I had to find my flight's gate somewhere and check-in or something. Hopefully this throng of bleary-eyed passengers would lead me to where I needed to go. But I doubted if any of them were going to Pakistan. And I had no clue where Carl was, so I'd have to depend on my own wits to find my connecting flight. And, in my current condition, my mind required hot stimulants just to tie a shoe.

What I immediately had to have was hot tea or coffee, plenty of it, and now.

57

Two longer than long hallways later, I found the transit lounge, a huge yellow-painted, crowned-ceiling room, and Carl. Carl somehow looked fresh and wide awake. Maybe he didn't require much sleep. Military training I supposed.

People and their baggage were everywhere, either flopped in chairs or rushing past. A wall on the end of the football-field size area was covered by a large screen depicting all departing flights and their status. I checked my ticket, found my next flight's number, and scanned the board. I found the flight number and my eyes slid over to the flashing word "Delayed" under the status column. Shit. Carl said this wasn't going to be easy, but I figured the problems would surface in Pakistan, not in London.

Anguish became my caffeine fix.

This had to be a mistake. I needed to get to Pakistan on time to stop my father. An hour or two delay could result in Pops leaving Rawalpindi before I got there, and I'd probably never see him again, ever.

I motioned to Carl to follow me. I spotted the Pakistan International Airlines desk, shouldered my bag, and pushed my wobbly legs in that direction.

A young Pakistani man dressed in a gray PIA uniform stood behind the desk reading the London Herald.

I clumped to a stop, drop my bag, and asked in a morning voice, "Excuse me, but why is Flight 483 delayed?"

The man lowered his paper and looked up at me like I wasn't allowed to ask questions.

"PIA Flight 483, it's listed on the monitor as delayed." I pointed at the gigantic screen. "Do you know the reason why?" I asked, like I was a detective in an interrogation room and the clerk was a suspect.

His eyes shifted from me to a computer. He tossed his paper aside. He sighed like I was forcing him to dig a ditch. His fingers tapped the keys.

"That flight is routed from here to Athens and then on to Lahore." The man spoke with a clipped British accent.

"Tell us something we don't know," Carl blurted.

Maybe he did need sleep.

The clerk eyed Carl with a raised brow and then fixed his gaze on the monitor. "There are weather conditions in Athens, heavy rain and fog. That is why the flight is delayed."

"For how long?" I asked.

"Until tomorrow." His response sounded apathetic.

My already sensitive stomach gurgled. "What? I need to be in Lahore early tomorrow morning, as originally scheduled. I," I glanced at Carl and nodded at him, "ah, we have a connecting flight from Lahore to Rawalpindi, tomorrow morning."

"That is no problem, sir," the clerk said in well-rehearsed politeness, though his body language conveyed irritation for being put to work. "If you will give me your tickets, I will reschedule everything for tomorrow and you will be in Rawalpindi the day after."

This man either didn't understand me or wasn't listening. I took a deep breath hoping to inhale my frustration. "How can I, ah, we get to Rawalpindi tomorrow?"

He glanced at me and sighed again. His attention returned to the computer and his fingers jabbed at keys like he was trying to hurt them. He steadied the screen. "There is one other flight from here to Karachi," his head tilted, "but it is full."

My rest-starved mind failed to control my emotions, despite a lifetime of training. My cheeks warmed, my eyes burned, and my hands formed knuckle-white fists. I blurted through clinched teeth, "My father's life depends on us getting there tomorrow, not the next day."

I knew anger rarely achieved desired results. I looked up and shook my head. Why should this man care about my father?

The clerk gazed at his computer and rubbed his smooth chin. "Are you and your friend frequent flyers?" he asked.

I glanced at Carl. "Ah, no," I said.

His eyes roamed over the screen, and then, as if he were speaking to cyberspace, he said, "Ah-ha." His eyes returned to me, brows arched, and his hands spread out to his sides. "I think I may have found a way."

"Great." My tension-knotted muscles relaxed allowing my shoulders to sag.

"I think I can get you both on that flight to Karachi, but . . . it will require a bond."

"A bond?" I asked. I looked at Carl for some guidance, but his eyes were fixed on the agent. "What is a bond?"

"Basically if you are bonded, you can displace any stand-by passengers and this flight has several," the clerk said keeping his eyes on the screen.

"And how do we get bonded?" Carl asked and stepped closer.

"You must purchase a bond from me. For this flight they are, one moment," his fingers tapped away, "ah, here we are, two hundred US dollars each."

"And I'll bet you only take cash for bonds," Carl said.

"So you have flown before," the agent said, his eyes finally fixing on Carl. "There is a money machine just to the right of the last Duty Free shop, over there." He pointed.

Carl stepped between me and the PIA clerk. "And I guess the only way we can get to Rawalpindi close to our original reservations is to pay you four hundred dollars?"

The agent averted his eyes to the large wall monitor. "That is correct, sir."

An older man dressed in a PIA uniform came out of a door behind the counter.

"Excuse me, sir," Carl yelled.

The elderly man stopped, "Yes, may I help you?" His eyes rolled to the young clerk. "Aktbar, is there a problem?"

The young agent chewed on his lower lip and then held up a palm out hand toward his senior associate. "No, sir. I just need to perform some of my computer magic." Then his hands dropped to the computer and his fingers were a blur on the keyboard.

A moment later, the young Paki looked up and a smile spread his lips. "I worked the system backwards and found a way." His words were saturated with self greatness. "There is a Lufthansa flight from here to Munich with seats available. From there you can take a Turkish flight to Ankara and connect with an Emirates flight to Rawalpindi. You will arrive tomorrow about an hour later than your current plans, but you'll be there tomorrow."

"Fantastic," I exclaimed.

The older agent nodded at us and walked away.

"There is only one problem," he said.

"What's that?" Carl asked, his words smeared with skepticism.

"You will have to run. That flight is scheduled to board in—"he checked his watch—"eighteen minutes and you will need new tickets from Lufthansa. You must run, fast."

My hand, still clutching the boarding pass for the morning flight to Munich, shook causing me to fumble with the seat belt. Carl, panting from our long run, plopped down across the only aisle from me. This plane was smaller, much smaller, but I didn't care, the only thing that mattered was we were on board the only flight that could get us to Pops before he left.

I pulled my travel packet out of my pocket and thumbed through my newly acquired flight plan. I shook my head. My anguish had only just surpassed the weanling stage. I still had three flights, ranging from three to six hours in length, interspersed with six hours of layovers, to suffer through to get to Rawalpindi, barring no more delays. I did a mental calculation of the total travel time in the same clothes, sitting in seats made for midgets who could sleep sitting upright. Unbelievable.

I pulled out a corner of the plastic wrapped blanket that someone had tossed in my lap and used it to wipe sweat from my brow. Then I leaned across the aisle. "Hey, Carl, per my figures, it's going to take us over thirty hours to get from Cincinnati to Rawalpindi. I'm so sorry you have to suffer through this crap for me. But I'm glad you're here. I'm so naiveté. You saved me four hundred dollars back there."

He patted his wet forehead with an ironed white handkerchief.

Did I really know this man, an ironed handkerchief?

Then he carefully folded the cloth and wedged it in one of his back jeans pockets. He pressed his lips together and slowly turned his head to face me. He tilted his head down so he looked at me out of the tops of his cold brown eyes, his eyebrows peaked, his jaw muscles flexed.

"Kugi, all I can say is <u>this</u> is the easy part." He sat back and closed his eyes.

Chapter 15

The endless trip, one rigid airplane seat after another followed by yet another flop in a transit lounge, and I had become a Pavlov dog responding to intercom voice commands. "Flight blah-blah-blah is now boarding through gate blah-blah, present your boarding pass at the gate." A slow shuffle on board followed by, "Please pay attention to the following video which will inform you of the safety regulations on this blah-blah-blah aircraft." And normally right after I'd dozed off, "Your flight attendants will be coming through the cabin to serve you refreshments," that is if you call stale pretzels and a six-ounce drink with more ice than liquid refreshing. "We are on final approach to blah-blah, please raise your seat backs and stow your tray tables." If I would have barked, nobody would have listened, and I was too worn out to wiggle my tail.

And then there was the fun part. Each flight bracketed by knotted, stiff-legged herding. People, like cattle, herded onto planes, and then herded off and then back on, again and again; announcement, moo, announcement, moo.

Planes with seat backs that wouldn't recline, window shades that wouldn't elevate, and audio systems with no sound. And to think I had paid a bunch of money, for me, for all this misery.

Being an infrequent traveler, I wanted to remember as much as possible, but my tired mind and body, between cat naps, tumbled and blurred most of the events. I recalled Munich, a modern airport with service people Carl called 'resolute, strutting Bavarains.' Ankara was old, cold concrete.

But Rawalpindi at four a.m., I remembered in vivid detail. The last of the series of bounced landings for my dulled nerves and tired back. The last of the long stinky lines of pushing, grumbling passengers bumping through health, immigration, baggage claim, security, and money exchange.

Of that process, immigration was the most memorable, the little Pakistani man dressed in a gray uniform with questioning beady dark eyes. He must have glanced from my passport to my face six times. His blank, cold expression had me convinced I was guilty of something. If he would have accused me, I was too exhausted to protest. I would've just extended my hands for cuffing and reacted to whatever voice commands he dictated, bow-wow, moo-moo, or whatever.

After clearing security, Carl and I were jostled outside under wattage-starved street lights to be greeted by a menagerie. A throng of beseeching beggars swarmed by big green flies either lay, sat, or stood pressed against the door. The crowd consisted of all ages, from old to newborn babies. Men, woman, and children all skinny, each one with more distracting conditions than the next, missing limbs, eyes, and teeth, enlarged extremities, and what looked to be open, running leprosy sores. We wedged our way through the congested mass, and several men and boys tried to forcefully take our luggage. Somewhere in the background, taxi cab drivers screamed at us and each other. The chaos was shrouded by late night thick hot air tainted with the smell of sewage.

We had arrived.

Chapter 16

Carl and I hired a cab, a shouting process I let Carl handle, to take us to Uncle Parmajit's home. I placed waking up the uncle I didn't know in the early morning second to saving my father. We were wearily surprised by the cabby's clipped British accent as he gave us what Carl called a practiced 'tip pleading' spiel on costs while he drove through empty streets.

The drive through the city pummeled my already airline battered spirits. Sparsely staggered dim street lights cast an eerie gloom over the ghost-like structures gliding by the old Mercedes taxi. My first awareness of being in a foreign place since my high school trip, but this was different. We were more like unwanted invaders than foreigners.

The first light of day diluted the dark horizon when the cab stopped. We were in front of one of many adjacent homes surrounded by high walls, the tops of which sparkled in the faint street lights.

Carl paid the driver while I rang a bell at an iron-gated entrance. The house windows remained black. I rang again.

The taxi putted away and Carl walked up strapped with luggage.

"What's happenin'?" he asked followed by a yawn.

I glanced at my watch in the weak light of a nearby street light. "It's half-past five, I guess everyone's asleep." I wiped my forehead with my sleeve. "Damn it's hot."

"I could climb the wall," Carl said.

I looked up at the ten-foot high wall. "There's broken glass embedded in the top."

Carl picked up a hefty rock and shrugged his shoulders. "So?"

The trip had been too long. I lacked the energy to reply. I rang the bell again. A light appeared in one of the front rooms.

The front door creaked open. A male voice asked in Punjabi, "Who is there?"

My parents had taught me both Pashto and Punjabi. My parents conversed in Pashto at home, their Afghan native language. And my religious teachings were both written and spoken in Punjabi.

I responded, "Kugi Singh."

The door clicked closed.

Carl and I looked at each other. He dropped the rock, sat the bags on the ground, and lit up a cigarette.

I swatted at ear-buzzing mosquitoes.

A half-a-cigarette and too many insect bites later, the front door burst open.

"Kugi is that you?" my father's voice asked.

His voice washed away my weariness. I had made it here in time. Carl and I would save my father.

My smile tugged my sagging shoulders upright.

"Yes, Pops. I . . . it is so good to hear your voice."

My father rushed to the gate and opened it.

I stepped through the opening, hug-searching arms extended to be greeted by a stiff arm.

"What the hell are you doing here, Kugi? And . . . is that Carl with you? And are you smoking, Carl?"

Stabbed by a stiff arm and then shelled by a barrage of questions. Yeah, my father was alive and well.

"Pops, slow down. Can we come in and sit down, and have some tea?" I glanced at Carl as he squashed the cigarette under his boot. "And maybe some coffee? We've been traveling forever and we're beat. But we need to talk."

My father stepped aside and motioned us inside the gate.

Carl shouldered the bags and eased past my father. I had never seen Carl so wary of another human.

66

My father led us on a flagstone path to the front door. "You have awoken the entire household. We will all need chia." He glanced over his shoulder at Carl. "And I would hope Uncle has some coffee also." His shadowed eyes returned to me. "You better have a damned good reason for being here, son. I can't believe your mother let you come here." He shook his head. "I thought she could control you."

We walked into an air-conditioned, thank God, living room. The lit, white-painted, stucco walled room had a large multi-colored patterned rug covering most of the concrete floor. Flowered cushion-covered wooden framed furniture lined the walls and a wide, oval coffee table inlaid with carvings of animals sat in the middle of the room.

Pops was dressed in a robe and sandals. His sleep-deprived eyes sagged into the puffy skin topping his flushed cheek bones. His waist-length gray hair hung down his thin back.

He walked into a hallway and stopped. "Parmajit, you have early morning guests. My son Kugi, ah, and his friend, Carl, are here. Please get dressed and join us. I would not want you to miss this wonderful story my son is about to tell." His eyes glided to me. "Or should I call it a fairytale?"

Chapter 17

The four of us, Pops, Carl, Uncle Parmajit, and I, sat in the living room of Uncle's Rawalpindi home. The first rays of light beamed through the eastern windows.

The naukar, the house servant, Saddique, had served us several rounds of chai. An empty tea pot sat on a woven pad on the table along with plates of half-consumed betel nuts and betel leaves accompanied by a partially used bowl of powdered lime.

When Saddique brought the tray earlier, Carl and I had exchanged glances thinking the powdered lime was cocaine. But then Uncle Parmajit explained the ingredients and the process of chewing betel nut. He took a partially cracked-open nut and filled the crevice with powdered lime. Then he wrapped the filled nut in a betel leak and put in his mouth and chewed it.

Carl and I both had refused an offering but Pops had chewed a wrap.

The drinking, chewing, and small talk had ended. The time to explain my purpose for making this long, horrid trip was upon me, and I had no clue what I was going to say.

Uncle Parmajit sat next to me. He patted my hand as if he knew my quandary. He reminded me of one of the Sesame Street muppets, an aged 'Oscar the Grouch' with a turban. His gray hair was pushed down, out of his hastily wound turban, lapping his bushy black eyebrows. His gray-splashed beard grew high on his cheek bones, leaving only his glasses perched on the end of his large hooked nose, an island of skin in an ocean of hair. His teeth were partially stained red, which he later explained was from chewing betel nut, an apparently addictive habit. He had the body of a short Santa, his shoes hidden from his vision by his distended belly. I had never met him before and based on our purpose, I doubted I'd get a chance to know him very well during this visit, and maybe never. He was old and I had other obstacles, like I may never return from Carl's 'land of death.'

My father slid forward in his cane chair and placed his tea cup on the table. "Okay, Kugi, you have met your uncle, have had your chai, and now have both Uncle's and my undivided attention. So tell us why you and Carl have pursued me halfway around the world within hours after my departure."

I glanced at my uncle. Our eyes locked for an instant and he waggled his head. He hadn't told my father anything about our phone conversation. No wonder Pops was shocked by our presence.

I swallowed the last of my tea and then fidgeted with the cup. To challenge one's father was acceptable if done respectfully, but to disobey your father's orders was heresy.

"We are waiting," Pops said.

I looked at Pops and felt more tired than he looked, if that were possible.

"I, ah, I—"

Carl grabbed my shoulder.

I turned to him.

A little empathy glinted in his cold brown eyes. "Let me give this a shot."

Carl's aggression had me off balance. This was not the Carl I remember. But I was stumbling under the pressure. I nodded.

"Mr. Singh and ah . . ." Carl's eyes locked on Uncle Parmajit.

"Just call me Uncle Parmajit, everyone else does." The old man's voice cracked with age.

"Okay, Uncle Parm-a-jet. If you don't mind, I think it would be easier for me rather than Kugi to tell you why we are here. I recently spent almost three years in the US Marine Corps in

69

Afghanistan fightin' the Taliban. I know how brutal the people are. I learned a lot about the God-awful terrain. And I will never forget the life threatenin' winters."

Carl released my shoulder and sat down his cup of untouched tea. "So with that said, my long time friend, Kugi, came to me askin' for information. He wanted to know everythin' I could remember about Afghanistan. He told me about the Taliban uprisin' against Sikhs and your trip, Mr. Singh, to rescue your mother." His brown eyes looked at me. "Kugi was determined to join you in your attempt."

Carl looked away and coughed into his hand.

"After I shared some of my knowledge, Kugi was even more determined to come here and stop you, to go in your place. With all due respect, a man of your age and conditionin' will never survive the trip, trust me I know. If the terrain doesn't kill you, the Taliban will. If I learned anythin' from my experiences in Afghanistan, if the Taliban have decided to kill Sikhs, they'll kill every Sikh they find, and they will be relentless in their search."

I wanted to stand up and cheer. Carl, the knowledgeable Afghan veteran, had said everything I needed to say and had saved me from possibly disrespecting my father in front of others.

"I was born and raised in Afghanistan," my father said with a hint of indignation. "I was about your age when I left. I still know many people there, people who would protect me. And," his copper hued eyes fixed on Carl, "I'm not as frail as you deem me. I will be fine."

Just when I thought Carl had won the game, Pops put us in overtime.

Uncle Parmajit cleared his throat and his hand squeezed my arm. "Raman, I think your thinking is . . . how do you say . . . not clear. The people you knew have either died, left the country, or are in hiding. There will be no one to protect you. And you are not a young man. The trip alone almost killed my son and he is half your age."

70

I wanted to hug my Uncle Santa-look-a-like. He had given me an early Christmas.

Carl nodded at Parmajit, and then turned his gaze on Pops. "And why take the risk? We're younger, stronger, and I've been trained to perform missions like this, plus I know the Taliban far better than I hope you'll ever know them." Carl took a deep breath and blew it out through pursed lips.

The man had scars I couldn't see.

"If your mother is alive, and I pray she is, you've got to agree that we," he pointed at me and himself, "have a far better chance of findin' her and gettin' her out than you do."

Carl had just swished a three-pointer with only seconds left.

"Why did you come all this way, Carl?" Pops asked. "Why would you risk your life for my mother?"

"'Cause your son is my only true friend, plus I owe him." He patted my back. "He saved my life."

My father looked at me with raised eyebrows. Then he looked away and drained his cup.

Carl received a goose-bumped raise above all my other friends.

Pops' eyes returned to Carl. "I admire you both for your courage and I appreciate your concern for me. But you have wasted both your time and a lot of money. Biji, is _my_ mother. She is my responsibility. No one will take my place. I will not let them. No one will risk their life to do what I am honored to do . . . must do. If I didn't go and something happened to my mother or either of you, I would be a broken man. I am going and that is final. Your trip was not necessary. We could have had this same discussion on a phone call." He chuckled.

Carl and I looked at each other, and we both shook our heads.

Carl, my high scorer, had just fouled out, and I was the only one left on the bench.

My stomach was upset though I didn't have what people frequently refer to as 'a stomach full of butterflies,' my stomach contained bricks being tumbled over and over.

I had no choice. This trip was my idea. The fate of this negotiation game rested on my shoulders, where it belonged. I sucked in a chest full of air and stood up, bracing to my maximum height.

"Father, there comes a time when a boy grows into a man, not just physically but mentally as well. All boys go through it, your grandfather, your father, you, and now me, have had to face the realities of manhood. Each of us has to assume the responsibilities of his father. That day has arrived for me. Today is my day, my coming of age, my turn. I'm going and you are staying here. I will not let this man, this Masoud Omar, kill my grandfather, maybe my grandmother, and also my father."

My foundation built on conviction, resolve, and courage was slashed to rubble by Pops' laser stare.

I had been fouled at the game-ending buzzer. We were a point down. I missed both free throws.

A giggle followed by a mop of brown hair and two little dark brown eyes peered around the hallway entrance close to the floor.

"Raja," Uncle Parmajit said and extended his arms, "come here to your grandfather."

A toddler, wearing a child's nightshirt, pitter-pattered across the floor into his grandfather's arms.

A mid-thirties Sikh with his long brown hair tied in a bun on top of his head also wearing pajamas, followed the youngster into the room.

Parmajit motioned to the medium height and build man. "Gentlemen, this is my son, Maanik."

After Carl and I exchanged names and handshakes with Maanik, he walked over to my father. "Raman, I have been standing in the hall for minutes trying to keep my son from interrupting your discussion. I overheard all I needed to hear. This man Carl and your son Kugi are right. The trip alone is nightmare. And this madman, this General Omar, has excited the Taliban into Sikh-killing horde. For Sikh to travel in Omar's territory is too risky for untrained young man let alone

72

untrained elder. Believe me I know. There were so many times we—"his eyes locked on his son—"we were . . . what is the word, oh yes, we were lucky."

My father shook his head. "But she's my mother . . . they don't know who to talk to . . . how will they get through the mountains, they—"

"I will take them," Maanik said. He patted my father's shoulder. "I know the way and I know the people who know Aunt Biji. If we're going to find her, we will need to talk to them. And, if necessary, they will also hide us if they are still there."

"But—"

"This is the best way to find Biji," Maanik said. "We just need to brown Carl's face and leave soon." He turned to his father. "We will need some equipment, can you ask your friend Jaya to help."

Uncle Parmajit nodded.

I looked at Carl and smiled. "I can't wait to see you with dark skin, another brother." I laughed more to break the tension than at the thought of Carl looking like me.

Chapter 18

Two days didn't dampen my father's demands to go with us, nor did it hamper our joint desire to keep him in Rawalpindi.

Carl, his face skin a copper color, wearing a camouflaged jump suit, clomped into the lit living room at three a.m. in his new combat boots. We looked like dressed-alike twins. "Maanik told me to tell you, 'The car is packed and my face is black.' Real cute. But if we're gonna get to the drop point before sunup, we must leave now."

Pops, fully dressed, paced the room.

I looked at Carl. "I'll be right there." I head motioned him to leave.

Carl closed the door and Pops stopped and spread his arms.

"This is all wrong, Kugi. I am the father here. It is my mother who needs help. The son obeys his father. That is the way it is, the way it must be. Why are you disobeying your father? Are you trying to alienate me?" He covered his face with his hands. "Why?"

My deep love for this man and my great respect, both of which he had earned versus dictated, pushed against my resolve. He was a good man, here, halfway around the world, to save his mother. And he had raised me to respect my parents and all elders. The last thing I ever wanted to do was hurt him or alienate him, but I couldn't let him get killed either.

"Father, we have plowed and re-plowed the same ground. You know why. Now I must go."

He dropped his hands and spread his arms. "Kugi, look at me. I am dressed, my clothes are packed, at least let me go with you."

74

"I came here because of my love and respect for you, father." I walked over and wrapped him in my arms. He was skin stretched over bones. But he smelled like the man who used to hold me when the bad things came into my room at night. Those moments seemed so recent. I missed them.

I stepped back to arm's length, my hands on his sagged shoulders. "Let me show you how much I love you. Let me do this for you. If something should . . . Carl and Maanik will take care of me. And we'll find Biji. I'll call when I can."

I turned and walked out.

The warm night air embraced me. I took a deep breath. If only my resolve equaled my assuring words.

Chapter 19

Carl and I sat in the back seat of Uncle Parmajit's new Mercedes. The strong, new leather smell made me realize how much I wanted a new car. What a silly unconnected thought at this point in my life, a mental dodge from reality.

Maanik sat in the front, next to Uncle's driver who guided the car through the empty streets of Rawalpindi in the middle of the night.

Maanik turned to face me. The car rolled past a street light. The dull illumination slid over his round bearded face. His expression was warm, but his eyes were serious. "Kugi, would you join me in my morning prayer? I can't think of a better thing to do at the beginning of our journey."

I looked at this man, maybe ten years my senior, and wondered what had inspired him to accompany and guide us. He had a wife and kids. Biji was his aunt, not his mother or grandmother like she was to Pops and me. Biji was my responsibility, not his. Per his words, he and his family had barely escaped the horror he had volunteered to go back into, why?

"I would love to, Maanik. But before we start, I must tell you how much I appreciate what you did to dissuade my father by volunteering to guide us. I will never be able to repay you."

"Thank you. Don't ask me why I am doing this. I do not have answer. But it will give us chance to get to know each other."

Carl said, "You can count on that."

Whispering the scriptures with another Sikh in the mixed language of Gurnukhi focused my mind on goodness versus the possible horrors that awaited me, just hours away. What a relief.

After the hushed prayer, the interior of the car overflowed with quiet. I wasn't sure if it was the relief from the constant tension at Parmajit's, the praying, or the swaying of the car in the early morning, but I fell asleep before we left the city.

I was surrounded by men with turbans with their Kalashnikovs pointed at me and a commanding voice yelled, "Fire!" and then my body bounced.

"Kugi, wake up," Carl said. "Kugi. We're at the drop point. Get up and shake the cobwebs loose. We've got to load up and get out of here."

I opened my eyes. The car was stopped on the edge of a road cut into the side of a mountain. We were just below the timberline in the shadows of tall pines. The gray light of dawn outlined the peaks.

I climbed out of the back seat. The air was cool, much cooler than Rawalpindi, and smelled of pine. A stream roared somewhere down below. My back and legs stiff from riding, I stretched upward and then bent to touch my toes, nestled in my new hiking boots. I loved my new boots. I eased upright.

"Where are we?" I asked through a yawn.

"Ten or twenty miles north of Peshawar," Maanik said from behind the opened trunk lid. "Welcome to the Suleiman Range."

"The White Mountains," Carl interjected, standing next to Maanik, both blocked from my view by the trunk lid. "Come here, I have something for you."

I walked behind the car to find Carl and Maanik wearing light camouflaged jackets over their jump suits, wide floppy-brimmed green hats on their heads, and large gray-green backpacks strapped to their shoulders and waist.

Maanik dropped a hat on top of my turban and pointed into the trunk. "That gear is yours. Get it on, quickly. We do not want to be found here. We are near one of many Taliban madrassas in this area."

77

"I haven't heard that word in a long time. Interesting, do you know what a madrassa is Kugi?" Carl asked. He inserted a clip into an automatic rifle and chambered a round.

"It's sort of a school . . . probably more like a training camp," I said. "What's that?" I asked pointing at the weapon.

"This," Carl held up the rifle, "is the Army's new M14 rifle with a Bushnell Tactical scope. The military modified the old M14 to accommodate fightin' conditions in Afghanistan. Mountain fightin' requires added range. It's a honey. We each have one plus a US Army issue M-9, 9 mm automatic pistol." He patted the holster strapped to his thigh. "I feel like I'm dressed again."

"I know nothing about guns," I said. "The only gun I ever shot was my cousin's Daisy BB gun. And I couldn't hit anything with that. I'm an engineer, not a mercenary."

"I have been in retail clothing sales all my life," Maanik said, his eyebrows arched. "I don't even know what a BB gun is."

Carl shook his head. "I feel sorry for the Taliban if they find us. We'll overwhelm them with calculus and inseams."

My stomach bricks tumbled into action again. "Seriously, what will we do?" I asked.

Carl smiled. "Don't worry. I made sure we have enough ammunition for some target practice. When I'm finished with you, you too won't feel dressed without your guns."

His smile and confidence smoothed the surface wrinkles of my fears but didn't penetrate my layered concerns.

I slipped the jacket over my camouflage jump suit and heaved the backpack onto my shoulders. "My God, this thing must weigh a hundred pounds. I can't lug this up and down mountains all day."

"It weighs sixty-five pounds and contains your food, water, sleeping bag, and ammo," Carl said. "And, if you want to survive up there, you will lug it." He patted me on the shoulder. "The fun starts now, my friend."

Chapter 20

"How much farther?" I asked for the umpteenth time, trudging up another steep hill. "I've got blisters. I need to get out of these boots for a while." Though my hips bore most of the backpack burden, my thumbs pulled on the shoulder straps of the backpack to reposition the still bruising load.

"You sound like my nephew whenever I take him somewhere," Carl said, followed by a chuckle. "Maanik, let's take a break. Our young team member needs—shhhh." His arm raised, Carl tilted his head. His eyes squinted. He stood motionless for a long moment. "Get off the trail," he whispered. "Someone's coming."

The three of us scattered into the surrounding forest. I dropped into a clump of bushes ten or fifteen yards from the trail and eased the rifle Carl had loaded off my shoulder. I wasn't sure how to shoot it, but I could always use it as a club.

I lay there, unmoving, my heart thumping faster than the slow moving seconds. Minutes had to have passed when I realized I was holding my breath. I eased the air out of my aching lungs and took a shallow breath and listened, nothing. I looked around and couldn't see Carl or Maanik. Had they separated in the all encompassing shadow-blotched woods? Had they kept on going, farther off the trail? Were they lost? Had they abandoned me? I bit my lip, trying to stem the rising panic, but the panic persisted.

A twig snapped in the direction of the trail. I didn't think it was possible for me to become more rigid, but I did. My heart beat boomed like rolling thunder inside my ears. My neck hair bristled. My hands squeezed the rifle.

Someone was near. I could sense it, like when I played hide-and-seek as a kid. You knew when someone was close to your hiding spot. I couldn't breathe if I wanted to, nothing moved but my eyes. The only thing visible was the thick bushes, a good thing, if I couldn't see them, they—

"People are here," a voice whispered in Pashto. "I heard them talking."

The voice was close, off the trail, a rifle lunge away. I closed my eyes and tried to envision what I'd do if discovered. I'd jerk my knees under me and swing the rifle like a club as fast as I could. Maybe I'd get lucky and hit something.

"Ali, none of the others heard anything, including me," a second voice whispered. And then in a normal tone, "It was the wind or an animal. Who would be on this trail other than us? No one uses these trails anymore, except students, and we are the only ones in this area. Come, we must get to the road on time to meet the trucks."

"Those are the same words Choudry spoke two days ago. You were there when we returned to camp. I also heard something then. And what did we find?"

"Ali, you are right, you are always—"

Boom! Boom! Boom!

The shots were deafening close. Although all my muscles bunched, I don't think I moved. I opened my eyes and the unmoving bushes were still there. I had no pain. I hadn't been shot, but had Carl or Maanik?

The ringing in my ears eroded into many footsteps from the direction of the trail pounding close, coupled with sliding noises of rifle breeches being loaded with bullets. There were many, too many.

Carl's words to my father echoed in my head, "If the Taliban have decided to kill Sikhs, they'll kill every Sikh they find, and they will be relentless in their search."

These men, these killers of Sikhs, were only a step or two away. They were bound to find me. Should I jump up and fight, or run, or just lie here and pray they'd leave?

To find Biji, I had to survive. My only chance was to stay still, perfectly still, which was so hard to do with my insides shaking apart.

A breathless moment, maybe two, and then, "You see? The American was alone just like he said. After what you did to him that first night in camp, he had to speak the truth. There is nothing here. Not even a bird flushed; nothing. Now let us go. It is a long walk if we miss the trucks."

Bodies moved away, coupled with soft, mumbled comments, intermixed with laughter. Then silence.

I risked a gulp of air. The tension burned my fatigued muscles, but I remained still. These young men with guns, these killers Carl had warned me about, had found an American. And they'd almost found another. What was an American doing in these mountains? The man's words blared in my head, 'After what you did to him that first night in camp, he had to speak the truth.' What had they done to him? I wanted to shake, to tremble away my fear, but I couldn't. My God, what had I gotten myself into?

The silence, interspersed by my pounding heart, grew heavy, pressing on my lungs. I needed to move, to stand, to breathe normally again, and stretch. But my mind wouldn't let me. Was someone still there, just being quiet, baiting me to move? How much longer could I contain the trembling?

Where were Carl and Maanik? Had they ran away? Were they still running? They could be miles from me by now. How would I find them? I had no clue where I was. We had been walking for hours since leaving the car, up and down through the thick forest, rarely seeing anything but trees and undergrowth. I couldn't even see the sun through the canopy of trees to get an idea of time or direction. I was alone and lost.

No, Carl wouldn't leave me, not Carl. He was near, he had to be. But why wasn't he moving? Had he been shot? Or did he see or know something I didn't? Were there still people with guns nearby?

Somehow, I remained motionless, a comatose body with a brain screaming for help.

Something bumped my leg. I twisted around jerking the rifle over my head.

Carl squatted next to my legs, his finger across his lips.

Thank God for Carl, but were the Taliban still here? They had to be if Carl wanted me to stay quiet. Damn. Had they heard me flip over?

I eased the rifle down to my chest and released my lung captured air.

His rifle at ready, Carl eased to his feet, like a mushroom pushing up through the earth, silently. His eyes scanned the area.

"Don't move," he whispered. "I'll be right back." Then he was gone, a ghost through the brush.

I wondered if he knew what he was asking, 'Don't move.' I was on the verge of exploding.

I lay still on my back, propped up on my backpack, my neck muscles straining to support my unsupported head.

Like an apparition, Carl was back, his hand extended down to me. He pulled me to my feet.

"That was too fuckin' close," he said.

Maanik appeared out of the brush.

"Did you hear them?" I asked. "They said they found an American, a man, two days ago." My words spewed out of me like too many happy-hour beers at my first bathroom visit.

"Are you sure?" Carl asked.

"My Pashto isn't that rusty." I gave Carl my 'don't question me' look that accompanied my tone.

"Many Sikhs tried to escape," Maanik said. "But why would an American be out here?"

"I have no clue," Carl said. "But if we don't get moving, he won't be the only American they find."

82

I couldn't think about this other man any longer or what had happened to him. I wasn't sure my shaking legs could hold me or my lungs could get enough air. The only thing I was sure of was I had nothing else to say. Words were useless to me, almost as useless as the damned rifle clutched in my white-knuckled hands.

Chapter 21

    I sat in a dense fir and white birch woods on a moss-covered log with my boots off along with that thousand-pound backpack. It was hard telling which felt better; my shoulders, my waist, or my feet.

    I wasn't sure what time it was, but I knew it had to be close to sundown. We'd been walking since sunup and that was forever ago.

    The heels of my socks were wet and red. I was hesitant to remove my socks for fear of what I would find.

    Carl and Maanik had left me to rest while they scouted the area. And I needed it.

    I peeled one sock down exposing a torn blister about the size of a quarter on the back of my heel. The raw exposed flesh burned and oozed blood. I carefully slid the sock off my foot. I repeated the process with my other foot, only to find a bigger, ripped-open blister that burned worse.

    I unzipped my backpack and rummaged through the contents looking for something to put on my wounds. I found dehydrated food, bottled water, a sleeping bag, a slicker, a flashlight, ammunition for both the rifle and pistol, and three sets of underwear and an extra shirt and pants. I was fucked, no socks. I'd never get those bloody socks back on, not that I wanted to try.

    And then a memory jolted me. I reached into my pants pocket and removed the two pairs of socks Carl had given me when he gave me the boots. He had instructed me to wear the socks with the new boots. But I hadn't put them on with the

84

new boots because they were so thick and coarse. They both looked and felt rough to the touch. So I had put on a pair of my soft Argyle socks; obviously, a big mistake.

If Carl saw my bloody feet and the socks I wore, he'd be madder than Pops was when we left this morning.

Hopefully, Maanik would have a first aid kit and I could treat my feet without Carl knowing.

"What the hell?" Carl's voice was right over my shoulder.

The man made less noise in the woods than a tree.

I looked over my shoulder and there he was, Mr. Stealth, with his arms out to his sides.

"Kugi, I told you to wear the socks I gave you. Look at your feet. How do you expect to walk thirty miles a day on those?"

I lowered my eyes and shook my head. I tried to look as stupid as I felt.

He shrugged off his backpack and fished inside. He removed a white plastic box. He opened the box and took out some Moleskin and an antiseptic ointment.

"Wash those blisters out, dry them, put this ointment on them, and leave then exposed to the air tonight. Tomorrow, cover the blisters with the Moleskin. Then, put the socks on I gave you. Then change your socks daily. Wash the old ones and hang them on your backpack to dry while we hike. We've got a lot of mountain miles to hump tomorrow. And if you complain about those feet tomorrow . . ." he tossed the ointment and Moleskin at my feet.

I needed to heal the soon-to-burst blister I had rubbed into being on our relationship.

"Carl, I-"

"Take care of those feet, get some food and water in you, and unroll your sleeping bag." He glanced at his wrist watch. "It's almost nine o'clock and it'll be dark soon. You won't be able to see your feet in a few minutes. We'll have no fire, no flashlights, and no talk. We need to grab a few hours of sleep before hoofing some more. We'll try to get started before dawn. It'll be safer."

85

He was gone, poof.

Chapter 22

I was snuggled in my mother's arms. I was so warm, so comfortable, and so secure. I curled into a tighter ball and languished in her warmth.

Something about nuzzling into my mother's lap was different. It was her smell; my mother smelled different. Her normal lilac and soap smell had been replaced with a mixture of cloves, pine, and musky decay.

Mom tugged at my shoulder. I opened one eye and saw nothing but blackness. It wasn't morning yet, so why was she waking me up? I pushed her hand away. I mumbled an inaudible complaint. The hand came back, this time harder.

"Go away." I turned over placing my back to her hand. "It's still dark."

"Shut up and get up. Now."

Oh shit, it was Carl not my mom and I was somewhere in Afghanistan.

I opened both eyes and pushed up out of my cocoon of warmth. The cool mountain air, heavy with dew, greeted me like a cold shower. I so desperately wanted to slide back into my sleeping bag.

The freshness of the mountain air made me realize for the first time in my life how awful the air was at home.

"I can't see anything," I whispered.

"Did you not hear what I said?" Carl's voice bordered on anger.

I unzipped my bag and fumbled for my jump suit. My hands trembled in time with my teeth while I slid the suit over my bare legs and wiggled my trunk and arms into the one piece garment and zipped it closed. The suit was cold and damp like the night air. My entire being shook, and no one part was in time with another. I was like a band with each instrument playing a different song. My hands fumbled inside the envied warmth of the sleeping bag to find the Moleskin, and coarse socks. This should be a real trick, putting Moleskin on blisters I couldn't see with trembling hands and frozen fingers.

Somehow I got the protective coverings on the blisters, but not in the timely manner my new self-appointed drill instructor thought acceptable. Once a Marine, always a Marine.

"Kugi, are you packed and ready to move out?" Carl asked, his whispered words had to raise the air temperature.

"I haven't even got my boots on yet." My response sounded more like a hiss than words.

"You've got two minutes," Carl replied.

"Bullshit. Who made you General?"

"The United States Marine Corps. Now move it or we'll leave without you."

"Carl, you're—"

"Shut the fuck up. Dig a hole with your hands, pee and take a shit if you can and cover it. And don't use any toilet paper. You could misplace a piece in the darkness. Tap me when you've packed, pooped, and are ready," he whispered close to my ear.

"You've got to be kidding, no toilet paper? What am I supposed to use, my hand?"

"You're a quick learner." His hand patted my back.

Dig a hole and shit in the dark and wipe my ass with my hand? How crude, I had never even taken a dump outside. And besides, it was too damned cold to take off my nearly warm clothes.

"I can't hear you digging." Carl stood nearby.

Mumbling under my breath, I jammed the boots on, and slid the suit back down my legs. The night air attacked my skin with its cold flames. I dug a hole using the knife sheathed in my

88

jump suit sleeve and squatted over it. I needed a magazine or a Sudoku puzzle to have a bowel movement; that was routine, not a pitch black icy breeze freezing my testicles.

I pissed what little water I had been rationed yesterday that I hadn't sweated, and covered the hole. Then I redressed and packed my sleeping bag along with the medical supplies and the extra pair of coarse socks. I had my coat and hat on, ready in less than two minutes. I wadded my turban and old bloody socks into my jacket pocket. I'd head-wrap my turban later. It wasn't until I stood up that I realized I hadn't even thought about my blisters.

I reached out in the darkness and tapped a nearby hard body. I assumed the muscles had to belong to Carl. A man I was getting to know less and less each day.

Who was Carl? This trip kept exposing bits and pieces of the man I had never seen. Last night he was Carl the healer, but this morning he was a mean order-snapping dictator. Or was he a psychologist hiding behind harsh commands?

Hands touched my waist and then something, a rope, was tied around me.

"If you feel me jerk the rope twice, like this," he jerked me forcing my hips to sway forward and back twice, "then you stop. Three tugs, we continue, one tug we go fast. Whatever happens don't talk, not a word. Maanik, will take the lead. He has a pen light, but you won't be able to see it. If you hear, see, or sense something out of the normal behind us, jerk the rope twice. If you need to stop for anything before daybreak, too bad."

Chapter 23

Trying to walk in dense mountain woods at night hopefully was the closest I'll ever be to being blind. The world was void of light but everything else was there, trees, branches, bushes, the cool air, the undulating ground, noises, smells, and that damned pulling rope. My senses went into a hyper-mode. I could hear noises, chirps, hoots, cries, howls, screeches, things I didn't even know existed in the woods. I could smell scents, most of which I couldn't identify, making the odors both puzzling and bothersome. And I could feel every temperature change on my skin. And I became aware of obscure obstacles and their proximity based upon the strength of the chilly night breeze.

My mind was bombarded by all the input from my acute senses along with all the hazards my imagination could conjure, mile-high cliffs, jagged rocks, trees, Taliban waiting in ambush, mines, snakes, the rope coming loose, and on and on.

At first I stumbled in the dark, tripping over rocks, logs, and uneven earth. I learned by touching the rope whether Carl was stepping up or down. But my technique soon got overwhelmed when my inner ear became confused. Five minutes into the walk, I had no clue whether I was going up or down, it was like the time I was in a 'white-out' on a skiing trip to the Rockies one spring break. Standing blind on skis, my senses had gotten so confused I couldn't tell if I was moving, so I plopped down. I had the same powerful urge now, just to plop down, but the rope had other ideas.

I stumbled along forever, stubbing toes into rocks, getting smacked in the face by branches, and banging shoulders against

90

boulders. I learned to keep my head down to use the hat brim for a deflector. Plus I kept one hand on the rope and one waving back and forth in front of my face.

At some point in the trek, things changed. The myriad of smells dissipated to nothing but fresh air and the cool wet breeze became cooler and more consistent, more encompassing. There were no more branches or bushes to push away. My leg muscles burned, my breathing had become labored, and the pack grew heavier. The fatigue was a good thing; it focused my exhausted mind on walking and nothing else except we had to be climbing, above the tree line.

I prayed Maanik knew where he was going and that there would be no life-threatening surprises along the way. But I couldn't be that lucky.

Chapter 24

Up, up, and up, I had no doubt now. We were climbing at a steady pace. My laboring legs, back, and lungs were certain.

A dull light transformed my world from a blind black to a blind gray. We must have walked above the woods into cloud cover when the sun rose.

The rope demanded each step, one after another, all my attention centered on moving one of my legs one more step.

The gray air grew lighter until I could see my feet and the rock strewn ground.

Initially, being able to see the ground alleviated my fatigue. However, when my vision of the surroundings improved, I realized how steep the terrain was, and my fatigue came roaring back.

But the rope continued up, one cold air breath-demanding step after another, each more difficult than the last. I couldn't get enough air. The rope was stretched taunt. I couldn't maintain the pace, and I didn't care.

When I was assured I was a couple of steps away from collapsing, the rope tugged twice. I stopped. My body was too busy recuperating to let my mind worry about why we had stopped. I bent and braced stiff arms against my knees.

I stood upright and put my cold hands into my jacket pockets. One of my hands found my bloodied socks. I would have laughed out loud, but I didn't have the lung capacity. My mind had been so busy I hadn't even thought about my feet. Either the coarse socks were working or my feet were numb. I slid the socks over my hands and returned to the bent, braced position.

The rope slackened and I heard muffled words. A hand appeared out of the fog and touched me.

"Kugi, we're getting off the trail," Carl whispered. "Maanik thinks there are caves nearby. We'll find a place to rest while its light." The hand lingered on my bowed back. "You did good, my friend."

Carl, my friend, was back.

Chapter 25

When the sun evaporated the cloud cover, I found we were in a rock and shale strewn pass between mountain peaks. Carl and I sought concealment in the shadow of a boulder while Maanik searched for a cave. The world below us was cloud-covered with snow-capped mountain peaks rising out of the whiteness all around us. The air was cool but the sun was warm. Carl and I removed our packs, rifles, and our jackets and sat. I leaned my rifle on my pack, Carl held his.

"How are your feet?" Carl asked, his head swiveling, his eyes constantly searching.

"From now on, I will do everything you tell me," I said with a head bow. "How much farther to Afghanistan?" I removed my hat and wrapped my turban around my knotted hair.

"I'd say we're in country now."

"Let me rephrase, how much farther until we're out of these friggin' mountains?"

"In these mountains? A day, maybe two." His eyes continued to roam.

I put my hat on over my turban and rubbed my shoulders. "There are more mountains like these?"

"Well not quite like these, but eastern Afghanistan is anything but flat."

I looked up at the gap in the mountains. "Is this the Khyber pass?"

"No. That's west of here and much too busy for us. This is a lesser used pass. Maanik used this pass a few weeks ago to get his family out of Afghanistan."

94

"Do you know this area?"

"We went on search ops in these mountains a few times. But all we ever found were empty caves. I always thought that either our interpreters or the Pakis informed the Al Qaeda about our missions. We never found them, but they found us wherever the terrain was on their side." His eyes came to rest on the ground at his feet. "A lot of good young men lost their lives in these fuckin' mountains."

"What was your rank? What did you do?"

He stood and peeked around the boulder. "I was a—"his extended arm flew up behind him in my direction, palm out, then blurred back to the rifle stock.

I froze.

Seconds ticked, and then Carl's shoulders sagged ever so slightly. "It's Maanik."

Maanik hustled around the boulder and squatted, breathless.

Carl peered out to check Maanik's trail.

"There . . . there are many . . . caves," Maanik said between pants. "The only one . . . I could reach . . . without climbing . . . the largest."

"The trap cave," Carl said over his shoulder.

"I . . . I do not . . . think so." Maanik removed his hat and wiped his sweat beaded brow beneath his turban.

"Why is that?" Carl asked. He turned and locked his focus on Maanik.

"At the entrance I . . . I heard someone crying . . . a woman."

"Sounds like a trap cave to me," Carl turned back to scan the area.

"What's a trap cave?" I asked, spreading my arms, exposing my ignorance.

Without turning, Carl said, "They hide a motion sensor near the entrance that sets off a recording of either a baby crying or some other plea for help. And the cave is either laced with mines or trip wires."

95

Neither my father nor I could have survived this trip without Carl.

"So what're we going to do?" I asked, the student beseeching his teacher.

"Well, we can't stay here," Carl said.

Maanik stood. "We go help woman."

"No. We climb and find another cave," Carl said.

Maanik and I exchanged glances. I couldn't leave the subject open-ended. "But what if there really is a woman in there and she—"

"Do you remember the first thing you said to me when we sat down?"

I looked down, sighed, and nodded.

Chapter 26

The sun slowly eroded the cloud cover below us. Every minute we spent in the barren gap between the mountains increased our risk of being seen. We climbed into the heart of the pass where Maanik pointed out the caves. The steep mountainside was riddled with caves, most of which were several stories above the pass floor. The largest cave entrance was at the base of the mountain. The dark hole was at least ten feet in diameter, a perfect resting spot.

Carl stood and eyed the mountainside. He pointed to an aperture about ten feet up the mountain to the right of the large cave. "Maanik, check out that cave," he said in a hushed tone. "See if there's room for all of us to lie down and maybe have a fire." His pointed finger swung to another opening further up the mountain and roughly fifty yards to the left of the base cave. "Kugi, check out that hole. And be careful, both of you."

"What's that mean, be careful?" I whispered back to him. "What if there's someone in there? What should I do?"

"Good questions," Maanik said, standing next to me.

Carl looked from Maanik to me.

"When you get up there, use your flashlight. If you see any movement get the hell out of there. If you see a person with a gun, ah . . . surrender. But make some noise when you do." He sat his rifle down and unbuckled his pack harness.

Great. If I saw a person with a gun, I'd be too scared to say a word. I'd probably faint. How was I supposed to make some noise? Maybe Carl would hear my body smack the ground.

"Surrender?" Maanik asked with a look of bewilderment on his bearded face. He removed his shoulder-slung rifle.

"You don't know how to use your weapons, what choice do you have?" Carl asked.

Maanik looked at the rifle in his hands, shook his head, and leaned it against a large rock.

Carl slid his backpack off his shoulders and sat it on the ground and laid his rifle on it.

"What're you going to do?" I asked.

"I'm gonna check on this large cave, the one where Maanik heard somethin'." He looked at me like a placating father looks at his concerned child. "We must be sure there's no one in there. If there happened to be a woman in there, she could attract the bad guys."

I couldn't stop my smile. Despite his efforts, Carl couldn't contain his goodness.

Nodding my head, I slid my rifle off my shoulder. I sat the gun down and then shrugged out of my backpack.

Following my lead, Maanik also unbuckled his pack and we both slid the packs to the ground.

My back and hips sighed internally.

"Hold up a minute," Carl said. He chewed on his lip and looked away. After a long pause, his eyes returned to us. "Surrenderin' is probably not a good idea. Even a blind man could tell you're Sikhs." He rubbed his chin. "Watch what I do and copy it."

I watched Carl pull out his pistol. He pointed the weapon at the ground, and chambered a round.

I had never held a real pistol before. I removed the holster strap. My fingers pinched the plastic grips on the 9mm automatic. I slid it out of the holster like it was a vile of nitroglycerin. Grabbing the barrel with my free hand, I wrapped the fingers of my left hand around the handle copying Carl's grip. A strange, unexpected feeling, a good feeling, swept over me, like the first time I tasted ice cream, or touched a girl's breast, I wanted more. There was something about having a pistol in my hand, something almost natural. The weight, the fit, the power, all seemed right. I had never liked guns, didn't have a need for one, and never wanted one. And yet here I stood, my hand wrapped around a weapon like it had been designed for my palm and my fingers. And the weight and balance made the pistol seem like a natural extension of my hand. It fit.

I clutched the slid with my right hand and slid it back like Carl had done. It was smooth. A bullet appeared in the top of the clip. I eased the slid forward and the shell disappeared into the barrel. I had unlocked the gun's power and the power was mine. I sensed a slight upward tweak in my heart rate, like the first time Pops had handed me the car keys. I had power at my fingertips.

I watched Maanik. His pistol hand shook. He copied Carl's actions in a jerky manner. His body language spelled immense discomfort, lack of trust, and fear. Was there something wrong with me?

"The gun is ready to fire," Carl said. "All you have to do is aim and squeeze the trigger. The pistol will buck a little when it fires. Don't anticipate the kick, just let it happen. Pull the barrel sight down to the target and your ready to squeeze off another round. If you see a man with a gun, aim at his chest and pull the trigger, lower the barrel back to his chest and fire again, and repeat this process until the gun is empty." He holstered his gun and scratched his head. "Be careful. Holster the weapon while you climb so you don't drop it or accidently pull the trigger. When you get to the cave have your pistol in your shootin' hand with your finger off the trigger, and the flashlight in the other before you enter. Okay?"

We both nodded our heads and holstered our pistols.

The weight of the gun against my thigh no longer seemed foreign.

I shook Maanik's hand. His skin was clammy.

"Good luck," I said, the novice cowboy condescendingly addressing the dude.

"May God be with you," Maanik replied. His eyes looked through me at something life threatening.

Maanik and I split and walked toward our assigned caves. When we got to the place where we needed to climb, I watched him start his ascent and whispered a prayer for him.

I looked up at the small dark mouth of the opening roughly twenty feet above me and wondered what awaited me. My untested new power waned, pushed aside by the unknown, by whatever could be lurking inside the small black opening.

I shut down my imagination before it could feast on all the possible bad things inside that hole. If I was going to complete my assignment, which I must, I needed a positive attitude.

I looked over and Maanik, the scared one, was slithering his lean body into his cave. If he could do it, so could I.

I found a hand hold and started to climb. The pock marked mountain face made the climb easy. I found a place to kneel next to the opening. The entrance was small, too small to crawl through on my hands and knees. I'd have to snake my way into the opening, not an easy thing to do with both hands full. Maybe I wouldn't have to go in at all; maybe it wasn't deep enough to enter.

I took the flashlight out of my pocket and switched it on. Then I removed the gun from its holster, the gun was cool and heavy in my hand. My finger lightly touched the trigger. Could I actually shoot someone, maybe even kill them? I couldn't dwell on the thought, not now.

I eased my finger off the trigger and gripped the handle. I leaned close to the opening and listened. Nothing.

I leaned my head close to the opening and stuck the flashlight into hole. I peered inside and was glad to see no cob webs blocking the entrance. The thought of crawling through a system of sticky, clingy spider webs full of spiders caused me to grit my teeth. A second thought wisped that image away but stiffened my jaw. The lack of webs across the entrance may mean that someone or some large animal, like a bear, has recently entered the hole. I shook away my thoughts and relaxed my clamped mouth. I had to go into this cave webs or no webs.

I scanned the interior. The cave opened into a larger space just beyond the aperture. I would be able to crawl once inside. The floor looked smooth and free of any signs of animal or human habitat. About six feet in, the tunnel curved to the left. The only way to know if the cave got bigger, big enough for all of us, was to go inside and explore. Damn.

I sat on a rock next to the opening and took a deep breath. I never liked close quarters. Small dark places had embedded me with a lasting fear when I was a kid. Playing outside in the dark was one thing; hiding in a dark closet was another. I didn't like confinement especially when I couldn't see anything. There were hairy legged things that crawled around in the dark. Who knew what other creepy things may live in a dark cave? A shivered ripped through me.

I looked down, Carl was gone. I looked to my right and Maanik was gone. They were doing their jobs and here I sat.

I had to do this, I had to. This whole thing was my idea.

I positioned myself at the mouth of the cave and inserted my arms and head. With my finger caressing the pistol's trigger, I swept the light over the interior. All I could see was a rock wall. There wasn't a sound. The cave smelled musky, like wet mildew, but the walls were dry. I found a foothold and shoved inward. Once inside I rose to my knees, brought the pistol up, and listened for a long moment. I should have been happy with the silence, but dark quiet places have always been creepy to me.

The cave spanned about a four-foot diameter, so I could sit or crawl or turn around, if need be. I crawled to where the tunnel turned. I eased my flashlight hand around the bend and swirled it around, thinking if the Taliban were in there they would shoot at the light. All I received for my efforts were

101

silence and confinement. I had to go further in if I were going to do what had been asked of me.

The cool dampness of the cave didn't stop sweat from beading on my forehead. I breathed like I had earlier, during the climb. I looked down at the gun in my shaking hand. Something gnawed on my insides. I wanted out of this hole, now.

I sat down and stared at the opening just inches away. After several deep breaths, my composure returned at least to the point where I didn't think I'd throw up.

I had to do this.

I rolled onto my knees and crawled to the bend. I hesitated, listening, praying for a noise, any excuse for exiting, but there was nothing.

My head followed my arms around the bend. The empty tunnel continued growing slightly larger in size. Ten or twenty feet in, the cave looked almost large enough for me to stand up. I pushed myself forward, my breath rate accelerated and raced with my hammering heart.

Fifteen or twenty bruising knee slides inward, I could stand in a head bowed position. I swept the light around and found I was in a jagged square area about ten-feet by ten-feet, plenty of room for three men to recline. In the middle of the area on the cave floor lay a black heap of—something struck my hat brim causing me to jerk upright striking my head on the ceiling. Thank God I had my turban on under my hat. I squatted, gun at ready, and looked up, just in time to get smacked in the cheek with a drop of water. I rubbed the bump on my head with my gun-holding hand. I swung the light back to the black heap, a pile of ashes. Somebody had been here. Goosebumps sprouted on my arms.

Across from where I had entered this space, the black tunnel continued, large enough for me to walk into. Did I really need to go any further? But what if I had startled someone and they were hiding further back in the cave?

I scampered on my knees to the ash pile and touched them with a fingertip. They were cold.

Between my palpitating heart and my starving lungs, I was exhausted and more than tired of being confined in gloom.

I made a snap decision. If Carl decided to stay in this cave he and Maanik could explore the rest of it.

I exited the cave in a minute at best.

I swear the sun had never been as soothing to my flesh or the air as fresh to breathe. I looked down and saw Maanik, but not Carl. I holstered my pistol, pocketed the flashlight, and climbed down.

Words escaped my lips like steam from a pressure cooker. "Where's Carl? Did you find anything? Should we go in after him?"

"Kugi, slow down," Maanik said and clutched my shoulder. "Breathe. Small dark places make me the same way. Try to relax."

I nodded and gulped some air and slowly exhaled it.

"My opening was a deep crevice, not a cave," he said. "I barely fit and had horrible time getting back out. It was so small I had to go outside to change my mind." He chuckled, more a nervous release than a laugh.

I smirked and shook my head. Maanik was one of those people who couldn't tell a joke. And, even if he were a stand-up comedian, I wasn't in a mood for humor.

Maanik's eyes searched my face for a hint of humor and when he found none, he pointed at the large cave whose entrance sat on the floor of the pass. "Carl is still inside the big cave. Large caves are normally very deep. It may take awhile for him to explore, especially since he is being cautious. What about your cave?"

I sighed, burdened by the memory. "It has a very small entrance, but about twenty or thirty feet in, it opens into a room large enough for all three of us. Somebody has used it before. There were remnants of a fire."

103

"Is there a bend in the entrance to the left?" His hand made a swooping turn to his left.

My eyebrows involuntarily arched. "Why yes, there is."

"My family and I stayed there. I thought we stayed around here somewhere. It was dark and we were scared. Everything jumbles in your mind when you are—"

"Eeeech!" A woman's scream erupted out of the large cave.

My hand found the pistol grip and I fumbled the gun out of its holster.

I motioned Maanik to one side of Carl's cave entrance and I took the other.

I eased close to the opening. Bodies tussled somewhere inside interspersed with incoherent words. The noises paused followed by muffled grunts and moans accompanied by multiple footsteps getting closer. Carl wasn't alone. Maybe he needed help.

I pulled the flashlight out of my pocket and flicked it on.

Carl needed me.

I leaped into the entrance, gun hand extended, tracking the shaking, searching beam of light.

Carl, his one arm around a woman, his hand over her mouth, his other gun-filled hand pointed at me, froze in the beam.

"Kugi, is that you?"

Chapter 27

The four of us stood in the entrance to the large cave at the base of the mountain pass. Our guns and backpacks were stacked on one side. Based on the position of the sun, it had to be close to eight o'clock in the morning. Carl, Maanik, a muffled woman whose face was concealed by Carl's hand and a droopy hooded sweatshirt, and I stood, faced outward, as if posed for a group picture.

Carl held the woman's back tight against him.

"If you promised not to yell or scream, I'll take my hand away," he whispered in her ear. His harsh tone competed with his expression. "We ain't the Taliban. We ain't gonna hurt you. Do you understand me?"

She nodded causing a strand of blonde hair to fall to the side of her face.

My mind went into warp mode. I looked closer. She also had blue eyes, beautiful blue eyes. What the hell was a blue-eyed blonde woman doing in these mountains by herself? What was she doing in Afghanistan? Was she a German tourist who got sidetracked, a whole bunch sidetracked?

"Do I have your promise?" Carl asked.

She nodded again.

"And you won't kick or scratch or bite me anymore?" he asked.

She rolled her blue eyes and nodded again.

Carl took away his hand.

The woman's face around her mouth was smeared with blood.

"What the hell?" I exclaimed. "What did you do to her, Carl? Did you hit her? Did you hit a woman?"

Carl released the woman and shook his hand. Blood splattered the front of the woman's coat.

I grabbed his hand and turned his palm toward me. There were two parallel rows of teeth marks, several through the skin.

"She bit you," I said. My eyes went from Carl to the woman.

"You've got a firm grasp on the obvious," Carl said.

He tried to pull his hand away, but I held it tight.

"These wounds need to be cleaned and disinfected, now," I said. "The human mouth can have all kinds of those little squiggly fellows in it. Maanik, grab the medicine kit from Carl's backpack and some water."

"It serves him right," the woman said, her voice coarse from screaming. "He shouldn't have snuck up on me in the dark and put his hand over my mouth. What'd he expect me to do, kiss his hand?"

Maanik handed me a water bottle.

"Who are you and what are you doing way up here? Are you alone?" I asked and poured water over Carl's wounds.

She shook her head, causing more long hair to show. "Too many questions. Alone? No, I wasn't alone, at least not until, let's see," white, perfect hand-biting teeth clamped her lower bloody lip and her blue eyes looked skyward, "two-three days ago. Are you Americans?"

"Carl and I are," I said. "Maanik is from Punjab, ur, Rawalpindi, Pakistan."

"Do you mind if I sit down?" she asked.

"Of course not," I said,

The woman took a step toward a nearby rock and collapsed onto the cave floor.

"What the hell did you do to her, Carl?" I dropped his hand and rushed to her.

"Nothin'," Carl said. His hands raised.

106

The woman curled into a fetal position. Her face creased in pain.

"What's wrong?" I knelt and touched her shoulder.

"My ankle." She moaned and pointed at her right foot.

I bent and pulled her pants above her ankle. The surrounding skin was black and ballooned outward from her low cut leather shoe.

"Good God, is it broken?" I asked.

"No. It's just a ba—bad sprain. Unfortunately, it's not—damn that hurts—my first. I inherited weak ankles from my dad. He . . . he always said they kept him out of pro ball."

Her face looked up at Carl with squinted eyes. "Now you know why I was screaming when you dragged me out of the cave. I should have bit you harder. Damn that hurt almost as much as when I did it."

"I'm sorry," Carl said. He spread his hands. "I, ah, I didn't know."

"Maanik, put some of that ointment on Carl's hand and wrap it in gauze and then tape it. I'll see what I can do for the lady. Ah, what's your name?"

"Montana, Montana Simpson. Could I have some of that water? I ran out, ah yesterday I think."

"Sure." I handed her the bottle. "Let me wipe the blood off your face first." I pushed the hood off her head, freeing her long, straight blonde hair.

She shook her hair into place, it folded onto her shoulders.

I took some gauze from Maanik, wetted it, and dabbed her chin, nose, cheeks, and mouth. Her skin was tanned and soft. I wiped Carl's blood off her face, revealing her features. She had full high cheek bones, a long, slender turned up nose, and full lips with a vertical scar that sliced through her upper lip almost to her nose. Her round chin concluded the tour of a pretty but not beautiful face.

"Thanks." She took a gulp of water. "I'm a reporter with a network affiliate out of Chicago. My partner, John Sparks, and our cameraman, Bill Monroe, and I were in Kabul to report on

107

the recent uprising between the Taliban and the Sikhs. We—"she looked away. She took a deep breath. "We were in the outskirts of Kabul, some village, interviewing some Sikh refugees, six, no seven days ago when . . . they came out of nowhere, hundreds of them in their Toyota trucks, guns firing. Everyone panicked, men, women, children, running in all directions. The situation got ugly so fast . . . in an instant. Those bastards were shooting everybody they could. John grabbed my arm and we sprinted for a hut. I stepped in a hole and sprained my ankle and went down just as one of those damned trucks came roaring up. Bill Monroe was running behind us, lugging all that damned equipment he valued so highly. About a half dozen of them in the bed of the truck opened up on us with AK-47's. Bill dove on top of me and he . . . he was dead when he landed on me." She sniffed back her tears. "I . . . I could tell. He never moved, never breathed, nothing." She wiped away an escaped tear. "All he did was bleed. And he did plenty of that, but not enough for those sons-of-bitches." She burst into tears. "Another truck full of those fuckers—sorry I just can't control . . . they came by and shot him again and again. I felt each slug jerk his body and that . . . that damned equipment. Between him and all that stuff, I was . . . was sheltered. Bill gave his . . . his life . . . for me." She sobbed.

I took her in my arms and held her. Her body jerked against me as if she were being shot over and over.

I looked up at Carl and Maanik. Maanik had stopped in the midst of bandaging Carl's hand. The two men stood unmoving, their heads bowed, their faces blank. They knew. They both knew exactly what she was describing. They'd seen it. Both had witnessed the works of the Taliban.

What had I gotten myself into?

108

Chapter 28

Maanik added the last piece of tape to Carl's bandaged hand while I sat and cradled the sniffling, blonde woman. The four of us were just inside the cave entrance, out of sight from anyone below the pass. The high sun had burned off the cloud cover revealing the green, undulating forests far below us. The surrounding mountains sprouted up and out of the greenery.

I looked at the woman snuggled against my chest. Her undisclosed figure, bundled in men's clothing. I had encountered a lot of new, courage-testing obstacles in trying to get to my grandmother, blistered feet, the Taliban, humping up a mountain in the dark, wielding a loaded gun like a drunken cowboy, exploring an eerie cave, but this crippled woman may yet be the toughest obstacle to overcome.

When her crying spasms stopped, Montana wiped her tear-wetted face on her coat sleeve. "I'm sorry. I rarely cry. You have to be tough in my business. It's just that I've never had someone close, a friend"—she shook her head. She inhaled deeply. Her facial expression became stern, chiseled in stone, as if she were prepping for a monologue. "Cub reporters get the shit jobs. Field assignments are a test of a reporter's guts and ability to stay cool in life-threatening circumstances. I've had my share." Her finger touched her scared lip. Her eyes looked down. She was somewhere else.

"What happened to the other guy, John was it?" I asked and glanced at Carl.

One of Carl's eyebrows arched ever so slightly. He knew why I asked the question. He gave me a barely perceptible nod.

"John, John Sparks, a damned good man. John hid until the Taliban left . . . after they thought they had killed everyone." She clamped on her lower lip again, flexed her shoulders, and stared at the cave floor. "He found me. I couldn't walk so he made a travois for me."

"A what?" Carl asked.

"It's a North American Indian term for a carrier or stretcher made from two poles and leather straps dragged by a horse . . . except John was my horse."

Carl and I exchanged glances. We both knew she was going to need a new 'horse.' And that presented a big problem. We couldn't leave her here. Who would drag her and where would they take her?

"We were cut off from Kabul so we only had one choice, get out of the country through these damned, endless mountains," Montana said, refocusing on me. "John stole some food and water and we left. He dragged me up and down these trails for days, three, four, I don't know, my ankle throbbed and . . . he was amazing.

"We were running out of food and water and John was exhausted. We weren't going to make it if he had to drag me any further, he couldn't do it. So he found this cave and we spent the night. The next morning, two or three days ago, I, ah I'm not sure, John left. He said we had to be close to Pakistan. He'd cross the border and get some help; it was our only chance.

"Despite my insistence, he took nothing, leaving me the remaining food and water. He said he could find water."

She hesitated. Her blue eyes played tag with each of us as she chewed on her lower lip. Then her focus rolled down and away.

Her mention of short supplies set off an alarm in my head. Carl had packed enough food and water to get us into Afghanistan. Though that damned backpack weighted a ton, he

110

had given each of us just enough for a one-way trip. Then he had monitored our consumption daily. There wasn't enough for a fourth person. I was about to ask her how much food and water she had left, when she tilted her head up, locked her blue eyes on mine, and disrupted my thoughts.

"What are you doing here?" Her eyes questioned me. "Where'd you come from?" Her eyes squinted.

I glanced at my traveling companions. "We're going into Afghanistan to find my grandmother." I lifted my hat and exposed my turban. "My cousin, Maanik, and I are Sikhs. Maanik lived in Kabul until this uprising happened. And Carl, well he's just an extraordinary friend who spent some time in country. Hopefully, Biji, ah, my grandmother, is one of the refugees you mentioned earlier."

Montana looked up at Carl. "So, Carl, you aren't a Sikh. What are you, an American Indian?"

"Oh that." Carl touched his face. "That's several applications of suntan spray. I didn't want to stand out when we traveled through towns and villages."

She nodded. "You've been here before. Army reserves?"

"Marines," Carl said. "Two tours."

"Bless you for serving," she said, giving Carl a look I envied.

"Kugi, is that right?" she asked, her blue eyes scanned my face, almost like they were softly touching me.

My chest tightened and I had to force my response. "Yes, Kugi Singh."

"Were you in the service, too?" she asked.

"No." My head dropped down ever so slightly from embarrassment. I wasn't a hero like Carl. What was wrong with me, I wasn't a loser. Although I didn't have a battle plan, I did have a career plan. I eased my head back up and fixed on her face. "I just graduated from college, UC, ah, the University of Cincinnati."

She nodded. "Well, I can understand why you're here, Kugi, but these other two should know better. And they should have talked you out of coming."

111

"You don't know Kugi," Carl said and shook his head, and then as if giving birth to a thought, he added, "I'd say you two are cut from the same bolt."

She looked at Maanik. "How did you come, what Paki border town did you go through?"

"Peshawar," Maanik said.

She pushed off my chest and sat upright. "That's where John was heading. You had to have passed him." Her eyes played tag with us again.

This wasn't the right time for guesses. But I couldn't look at her, so I looked at the others, hands out and palms up. "We didn't see him," I said.

Chapter 29

The three of us carried Montana to her camp site, forty or fifty yards deeper into the cave. Carl had unpacked his sleeping bag for her. And Maanik and I eased her onto the opened bag. Then Carl, General hardnosed Carl I must add, gave her food and water, supplies he knew we couldn't spare.

I needed to talk to Carl and Maanik, alone. Sprained, maybe broken ankle Montana was a problem, and we didn't have a solution. We needed a plan.

I rubbed my arms. "Man, it's chilly back here."

"Try spending three or four days in here alone," Montana said and pulled the bag's flap over her. "The chill is quickly overwhelmed by what you can't see and your other overloaded senses and mind make up."

"I'll bet," I said and pushed the images aside. "We'll be right back." I motioned to Carl and Maanik. "We'll see if we can find something to burn."

Carl gave me one of his 'no fires' looks.

Before he could say anything, I head motioned him toward the opening.

She reached up and grabbed my hand. Fear filled her face. "Ya-you aren't going to leave me are you?"

Were my excuses for leaving her that transparent? Had she experienced people who would leave a person who was a burden? Her friend John had left her. I didn't want her to think we were like that, ever.

"No." I patted her hand. "We will not leave you. We'll be right back." I removed her clamped hand. "I promise."

At the cave entrance, out of Montana's sight and hearing, I stopped my companions.

"So what are we going to do? Either the Taliban has her friend, John, or he's dead; regardless, he's not coming back. She can't walk. And we can't leave her here. And we can't take her with us and look for Biji."

Carl placed his hands on his hips. "Sounds like you answered your own question."

"He did," Maanik added.

"We have to take her to Pakistan," Carl said.

I canted my head. "Well . . . _we_ don't have to take her back, but _one_ of us does."

Carl and I both looked at Maanik.

His index finger touched his chest. "Not me. You will need me when we get to your grandmother's village. I know those people. Without me, you will not find her." Each word became progressively higher and louder.

"Biji lived in a Sikh village." I raised my hands with two fingers on each hand curling like quotation marks. "'Those people' as you call them are probably either gone or dead." I squeezed his shoulder. "You got us through these God-awful mountains, and I'll always be in debt to you for that. But I've got to go on. This whole thing was my idea. Biji is my grandmother. And if we delay our search for Biji, our chances of finding her alive decrease. Carl and I must go on. Carl knows the country and can find the village. And neither you nor I would last very long in country without Carl. Soooooo," I spread my hands.

Maanik stepped back, shaking his head. "I did not come all this way to be babysitter."

I clutched his arm, stopping his retreat. "No, you didn't. You came here to save a life and you will. Without you, this woman will die."

114

He shook his head and wrung his hands. "And without the two of you, she and I both may die."

"Travel at night and hide during the day, like we did coming here," Carl said. "You'll be safe."

Maanik spread his arms. "It will take days dragging her. I am not sure I can do it. She will need food and water. We do not—"Carl's palm-out hand almost touched Maanik's face.

"You can have most of our supplies," Carl said, his words firm, his tone soft. "We'll get more in country. And I would guess it will take you close to four days. You'll have to travel by night until you get into the tree line. Then you'll have to be extra careful on the trails. That contraption you'll be dragging has to make a lot of noise and leave a trail that Ray Charles could follow."

"All the more reason, we should all go back," Maanik said. "Two of us could carry her. That way the trip would only take two days; less time exposed in the Taliban woods and more eyes to look for them."

Carl looked at me. "He's got some good points."

If we all went back, that would mean Biji, if she were alive, would have to survive at least another week, maybe two. We'd have to get more provisions.

I scratched my head.

Chapter 30

I sat on a large rock in the shadows of the cave entrance, my forehead resting on my hand. The sun was only an hour and change from the horizon. Carl smoked while Maanik, squatted amongst the stacked backpacks, fidgeted with our pooled supplies.

If my grandmother were alive, which was not very likely, and we made it to her village, if the Taliban hadn't found her by now, how could we? And if we did find her alive, how would we ever get a damned near seventy-year-old woman through these mountains?

Maybe the only reason God got us this far was to save this American woman. And saving Montana would take all of us and too much time, greatly reducing the probability of ever finding Biji alive.

Returning a second time would be insane. I couldn't ask Carl and Maanik to make four trips through these mountains, the risks were too high.

I was pinched, either save a living but hurt young woman or risk the lives of her and my cousin to try to find an old woman who was most probably already dead. And if Biji weren't dead, and Carl and I were lucky enough to find her, the trip over these mountains would probably kill her.

There was only one logical choice. We had to take Montana back to Peshawar.

I had failed, failed my grandmother and my father.

116

Maybe I should go on by myself. It'd be certain death. But at least I would have tired. Pops could have done as much and had wanted to. Going on alone was better than going back and facing Pops without even having tried to find Biji.

I'd do it.

Maanik sprang to his feet and snapped his fingers. "I have it!"

"Have what?" Carl asked.

"I have the solution to our problem," Maanik said. His round face beaming like he'd just discovered a cure for cancer.

I raised my head. "Let's hear it," I said, lilting my words to feign enthusiasm.

"We are near Gerdi," Maanik said.

"Gerdi?" I asked.

"It is a small town in Afghanistan on Route A01 near the border. I have friends there, Afghan friends, Muslims not Sikhs. We could take the woman there. They would hide her. Plus they have an old car. We could probably borrow it, or rent it, or even buy it. We need a car to get to Nanakpur . . . where your grandmother was living. Miss Montana could rest her leg until we get back. Then the five of us could crash the border in a car and not have to worry about these mountains again."

"How far to Gerdi?" Carl asked.

"My family and I stayed with them for a couple of days when we escaped. We left there early one morning and arrived at these caves at sunset. I'd say carrying Miss Montana would cause us to go at about the same pace as my wife and I and two small children . . . twelve to fourteen hours with rest stops."

I rose to my feet. Maanik's words were words of salvation for me. "I like your plan."

I liked it a bunch, but it couldn't be that easy, nothing about this trip had been easy. "Are you sure they would take care of Miss Simpson?"

"Yes. They are good people. And they hate the Taliban."

I looked at Carl. "Wouldn't the Taliban have control of the road?"

117

He stubbed out his cigarette. "Not during the day, they're afraid of our drones." He nodded his head. "This might work."

"And they have a car?" I asked.

"Well, they did when I was there, an old one."

I didn't care, I could make it run. I would make it run. I had a history with old cars, a good history.

I patted Maanik on the back. His smile offset the gloom in both the cave and my mind.

"We need to get some rest," Carl said, his voice alive with purpose. "We'll leave just after dark."

I raised my hands. "We're going to carry that woman down in the dark?"

Carl chuckled. "Yeah. "What's the difference between being tethered by a rope versus a stretcher?"

Chapter 31

This trip was 'my idea' which Carl and Maanik both asserted when it came time for someone to talk to Montana.

They were right.

I walked back into the cave and found her lying on Carl's sleeping bag. Her facial features blended into a silhouette in the diluted light from the cave entrance a half football field away. At least I had darkness on my side, she couldn't see my anxiety. Anxiety about telling her we were taking her north, farther into Afghanistan.

"Kugi, is that you?" she asked.

"Yes. I didn't wake you did I?" I sat on a nearby baby boulder.

"No. I've had plenty of sleep. That's all I've had to do for . . . I don't know. I can't walk so I sleep. I'm nothing but a burden." Her trailing words dropped an octave closer to depression.

"We, ah, we need to talk."

"I know," she said, sitting up. "I've become an unexpected obstacle to your plans. You need to find your grandmother. You're a good man, Kugi. And all I pose to you is a . . . a conundrum as my father would say."

I couldn't believe her father's word choice could be 'conundrum.' He had to be like Pops. Was there more than one? No way. A tickle started in my throat and migrated down to my side gaining strength and volume on its way.

My laughter caused her to sit up. I could sense more than see a slight smirk on her face. "What on earth . . . what did I say? What's so funny?"

I couldn't stop laughing. Laughter was my relief from all the pain, tension, and worry this trip had bestowed on me. And it was going to take a lot of laughter to offset my issues. I needed to laugh and I did, loud and hard.

I gasped for a breath and squeezed out, "Conundrum." I thought I heard her softly giggle. A breath later and she was laughing with me.

We laughed until we couldn't laugh any more. With tears streaming down my face I watched her dab her face.

"Conundrum is a funny word, but I never thought it would make me laugh like that," she said.

"Believe it or not, my father uses that word. And then you say 'as my father would say, conundrum.' I can't believe there are two men in this world who use such a goofy word. You have to know my Pops to appreciate how funny it is that your father uses that word too." I couldn't help but chuckle again.

"That is funny," she said. "Conundrum . . . who would have guessed?"

"I needed that," I said.

She reached out in the darkness and found my hand and held it. "Me too."

Her hand was warm and her fingers toyed with mine. Her warmth migrated up my arm into my chest causing my heart to go from a walk beat to a trot tom-tom.

I didn't want to talk. I didn't want to do anything but play with her fingers, forever.

She broke the wonderful silence. "You said we needed to talk." She released my hand.

My fingers had never been lonely until that instant. Not knowing what to do, I put my hand in my jacket pocket.

"Ah, yeah, we do. Carl, Maanik, and I have discussed our . . . conundrum and—"

120

"All I need is a little water and enough food to last John and I until we can get to Peshawar. He should be back no later than tomorrow. You and your friends need to go. Leave me, I'll be fine. I know John. He'll be back."

I eased out a long breath. "John's not coming back."

"What? John will be back." Her tone bordered on indignation. "John would die before—no. Kugi, is there something you haven't told me? Kugi . . . don't . . . what? Tell me."

I wanted to make her laugh and play with my hand some more, not cry. But I had no choice. I couldn't lie to her. And I couldn't give her false hope or let her think John was coming back. She couldn't stay here and wait for a man who was probably dead.

"We had to hide from a Taliban training group yesterday." My voice was an octave lower than normal and my pace slower, more selective. "I overheard them talking. My parents were from Afghanistan, they taught me Pashto. The Taliban said they had captured an American . . . a man, a few days earlier."

Her long pause added to the cave's gloom. "So? That doesn't mean he was John. It could've—"

"He was on the same trail, about where John would've been after leaving you here." I thought about her already depressed state. "Maybe the American wasn't John. Maybe . . . regardless, we can't take the risk of leaving you here."

"But your grandmother—"

"We thought about that. We have a plan that will keep you safe while we search for Biji, ah, my grandmother. But we need to take you somewhere safer."

"Just leave me. I need to be here when John gets back," her voice waned.

I stood. "Listen to me!" The cave absorbed my exclamation. I gulped a breath and released a sigh. I reached out in the semi-darkness and touched her shoulder. "We are not going to leave you. There is a small town, Gerdi I think, just

121

north of here. Maanik has friends there who will take care of you until we get back. We'll carry you there tonight."

Her fingers found my hand in the dark. She pulled me down next to her. Her arms wrapped around my neck and she hugged me, a warm, dependent hug, like a lost child hugging a found parent. A weak strawberry scent cut her stale musk. A shudder rippled through her frail frame.

"I've never felt so alone, so helpless, so afraid." Her words weak, cracked with fear. Head on my shoulder, she sniffed back her tears. "I thought I was tough. I've had to be, but . . . but I've always been able to fend for myself. But that was when I could walk. I . . . I need you."

"We will take care of you. And," the dark thought of us not coming back from where ever we were going wasn't timely, "we will make sure you get to Pakistan."

Chapter 32

Carl and I rigged a stretcher from the travois and Carl's sleeping bag while Maanik slept. Carl took the first four-hour watch and I crawled into my sleeping bag. I guess the combination of altitude, physical exhaustion, and mental anxiety overwhelmed my mind caught in 'what if' loops. I slept.

Carl woke me just after sunset. The cave was spookier in the dark, a black hole enshrouded in blackness, thank God for flashlights.

I suggested we flip coins or draw straws to see who carried the woman, but I lost. Recently self-promoted General Carl Thompson dictated the decision. He and I would carry Montana since Maanik knew the trails and should lead.

Great. I was about as enthusiastic as Jackie Kennedy being invited back to Dallas.

I stood at thousands of feet above sea level some forty or fifty yards into a black void, already breathing hard from putting on a pair of clean coarse socks, my broken-in boots, and that damned heavy backpack, when Carl said, "Okay, Kugi, take the back of the stretcher. Lift with your legs not your back, on three."

Ugh.

For the hundredth time, Montana said, "I'm sorry."

I heaved my end of the stretcher. My back and legs agreed with her.

I had thought the trip up the mountain tethered to Carl had been the second worse experience of my life, the first being my encounter with the murderous Taliban. I was wrong.

123

Walking down the mountain in the dark carrying Montana, who looked slim and trim but had to weigh four hundred pounds, was a bitch. My feet were blind and yet responsible for Montana's well-being. I couldn't drop her or fall no matter what my toes smashed into or how deep the next step down was, or how often my lead foot slipped when I stepped on scree. Like a dumb animal, I learned from pain what to expect based on the angle of the stretcher and Carl's pace. If the poles suddenly tilted downward or upward, there was a serious change in the ground. If he slowed, there was some kind of obstacle, a large rock, a step up or down, something that gave my feet a clue and a brief second to search in the dark, my toes taking the lead.

After what seemed like the first millennium of the trip, Carl whispered over his shoulder, "Kugi, we're stopping for a break. Ease her down, on three. Use your legs."

'Use your legs' like my aching back was my biggest concern? I was convinced I had at least two broken toes on each foot.

After lowering the stretcher with Montana to the ground, my body decided to sit versus trying to stand up again.

"Are we going to do this all night?" I asked with whispered words. I removed my boots and flexed my bruised but unbroken toes.

"We should be off the mountain before daylight." Maanik's soft reply came from somewhere close in front of me.

"How long?" I asked. My hushed voice conveyed my need for an accurate response.

"At this pace, six maybe seven hours," Maanik said.

Great.

Chapter 33

The sun came up and I went down, flat on my belly. We had stopped in a shallow ravine not far from Route A01. The mountains were about an hour behind us. Just before it had gotten light, we had seen the lights from a few vehicles and could faintly hear their tires singing.

Montana was asleep. She was asleep when we sat her down. How she had slept with all the jostling of the stretcher down the mountain was beyond me.

Maanik and Carl slept on top of the remaining two unzipped sleeping bags.

I stood watch or rather laid and watched. It was just as well, my back, legs, and toes hurt too much to sleep. The early morning sun cooked the night's chill from my exposed skin. I slid my coat off and rolled it into my pack. I had Carl's binoculars. I held the glasses with one hand and swatted at menacing flies with the other. I lay near the rim of the ravine and scanned the surrounding area. The view was monotonous, one jutting rock formation after another. Trees were nonexistent. Now I knew what a flea must think trying to traverse the back of an alligator. The only break in the terrain was to the west, a small section of A01 could be seen through a gap in the interlaced rock projections.

Per General Carl's instructions, I scanned the surrounding area, all three hundred and sixty degrees of boulder strewn landscape. I viewed the surroundings in ninety degree segments. When I got to where I had started, I started over again. I saw nothing alive, not a person, an animal, a bird, an airplane, nor a vehicle, nothing, but the damned flies. I got bored to the point of struggling with my concentration in the first hour.

I remembered a game we played as kids when we were bored. We'd lie on our backs and see who could come up with the best description of clouds. So I decided to give the rock formations names. I started my rotation again with Dolly Parton's boobs, a ten gallon Stetson cowboy hat, Rod Stewart's lips, Owen Mason's nose, Don's King's hair, the Incredible Hulk's bicep, Reggie Miller's ears, Jennifer Lopez's butt, a buffalo's head, a—something moved, just to the base of the buffalo's head, not far from the gap to A01. I braced and focused the glasses.

Maybe three or four hundred yards away a child, a boy, ran in our direction. I edged forward. Why would a small child be out here alone? He wouldn't. He had to be running away from something, but what? The boy tripped and fell, looked back, got up, and ran.

Then I saw what he was looking at behind him, a woman. She darted into view and stopped, picked up a rock and hurled it at something behind her. Then she started running again. Seconds later, two men with turbans appeared chasing her. I tweaked the focus on the binoculars. They were carrying rifles. The two men dodged out of view when the woman hurled another stone. She was slowing them down, increasing the distance between them and the boy at the price of the men closing the distance behind her.

I glanced at Carl. His mouth was gaped open, his limbs limp. He was deep into a much needed rest. He had taken more watch shifts than Maanik and I combined.

I needed to do something. I wiped my flooding eyes and refocused on the chase. The boy was within three hundred yards of us, but the men were only steps away from the trailing, sprinting woman.

I slid down the ravine, hopped to my feet and dashed to Maanik's side. I nudged him.

126

His eyes squinted open. He shook his head. "It can not be time for my watch." His voice and demeanor were like sandpaper. "No way." His eyes fixed on mine. "Are you crying?"

"Get up," I whispered and sawed my forearm across my eyes. "Take the watch. I, there's, ah . . . I must do something." I had no clue what.

"No." He laid down and closed his eyes.

I grabbed him by his coat collar and snatched him into a seated position.

His eyes snapped opened resembling fried eggs. "Are you insane?"

"Shut up and get up." I tried to make my hushed orders sound as demanding as Carl's.

He grimaced and grunted to his feet.

I clamored up to the rim and lifted the binoculars to my eyes.

The boy, obviously getting tired, was closer but now moving at a trot versus a gallop.

The woman was down. One of the men straddled her and pulled at her clothes, while the other man kneeled at her head holding her arms.

I couldn't sit here and watch a woman get raped.

I pulled the glasses off my neck and sat them down. I stood and darted toward the closest boulder, maybe one hundred yards.

As I ran, I heard Maanik's hushed voice behind me. "Where are you going?"

I didn't look back. When I got to the cover of the rock, I peered around the side. The two men were too busy wrestling with the woman and her clothing to notice me.

I leaned back against the cool stone, out of sight of the men and took a long breath. I was numb all over, like I wasn't really doing this, like an out of body experience, whatever that was.

The woman shrieked something I couldn't understand.

There was no time. I had to move.

127

I peeked around again and picked my next spot for cover. The smooth stone disruption in the earth's surface was a good fifty yards away. I'd be in the open unprotected for five or six seconds. My hand dropped to the holster. I unsnapped the strap, and pulled out the pistol. Just like Carl had demonstrated, I chambered a round.

With gun in hand, I sprinted for the next rock. The boy was close and I think he saw me. His head jerked. He hesitated. He saw me. I didn't break stride.

I slid to a stop behind the age smoothed boulder, waiting for my breath to catch up to me.

The woman screamed followed by the men yelling at each other in Pashto, something about holding her still.

I stood there gathering myself and a frightening thought slammed me. What was I doing? I was running from rock to rock like an Apache on the hunt. And I was getting closer and closer to two armed men, who were acting more like beasts than men. What was I going to do, if and when I got to the woman? Would these men surrender to a gun-wielding fool? Would they think I was a killer? What if they were Taliban? Didn't killers only respect killers?

I hadn't fired the gun. I wasn't sure I could shoot the gun let alone hit anything. And could I kill a man? Hell, the woman was in more jeopardy if I started shooting than she was from these rapists.

I looked down and my gun-holding hand was shaking so badly it would have made a coiled rattlesnake jealous.

What the hell was I doing?

Chapter 34

Although the sun had just risen, the morning air was warm but not hot, and yet I was sweating. Either fear or sprinting or both had taken my wind and beaded my forehead with perspiration. I wiped my head with the sleeve of my jump suit.

Leaning against a boulder, the 9mm automatic in my trembling hand, the little boy trotted into my view and stopped. His wide open eyes went from my face to the gun in my hand. I reached out and pulled him behind the rock. He was small, maybe six or seven years old. I had to hold him when his mother released a horrific scream.

"Run toward that ravine over there," I whispered in Pashto and pointed. "There are good people there who will help you. Go." I gave him a little shove.

I peered around the stone. There was about a hundred yards of barren ground separating me from the now wailing woman and her attackers. The man holding her arms had his back to me. The other man faced me but was busy unbuttoning his pants. The woman's naked legs thrashed at him. He laughed at her.

I watched the man fumble with his fly buttons, and I remembered an old adage bantered by women. A man with his pants down around his ankles wasn't very mobile. This was my chance, my only chance.

I watched and sucked in air. When the man's pants fell, I took off, sprinting as hard as I could directly at them.

Twenty yards into my gallop, the man with his pants around his ankles had knelt between the woman's forcefully spread legs. Just as he positioned his body to enter her, he saw me. He pointed and yelled. He turned, stood, and tried to run for the guns leaning against a nearby rock. He fell. That move gave me another ten yards. His comrade looked over his shoulder, his eyes enlarged, and he yelled something. He released the woman, dove over her, and scrambled on his hands and knees toward the rifles.

The bare legged man tried to kick off his pants bunched at his ankles. He stood; his back to me. I slid to a stop and aimed, fifty maybe sixty yards away. Using both hands to steady the weapon, when the gun-sights filled with his broad back, I squeezed the trigger. The pistol roared and bucked. The man arched forward and went down. I pulled the gun down, targeting the other crawling man who had grabbed his rifle. The woman sat up. She was in my line of sight. The man shouldered his weapon and spun around.

In that split second, I knew I was going to be shot and wondered how it would feel to have hot bullets puncture my skin, shatter bones, and destroy organs. I knew I should fall and make a smaller target, but my knees were locked. I was a frozen shooter with only the woman in my sights. I braced to take a bullet.

A rifle boomed. You weren't supposed to hear the shot that killed you.

My eyes couldn't believe what I saw as my rigid body sagged into relief. Blood splattered the rock behind the second man. He fell backwards and dropped his rifle.

I turned to see Carl, prone on top of the ravine, lower his M14 and stand. He must have been over three hundred yards away.

Chapter 35

The rustle of clothing interspersed with a woman's weeping brought me back to gore splattered horror.

It was as if I had fallen asleep and been awoken to find my nightmare was real. My senses slowly returned from an involuntary time-out. I could hear and see, but the rest of my body was still numb. Unfortunately, my mind both absorbed and reacted to all inputs.

I stood over the half-dressed man whom I had shot. He lay on his chest, head turned to the side; arms spread. Twisted pants around his ankles held his hairy thin legs together. A small red circle spread over the middle of the back of his brown shirt. The dust covered black turban had come off when he fell. Long oily, matted black hair seemed pasted on the man's copper cheeks and forehead. Brown blank eyes stared. His mouth gaped open forming an "O," like he'd been surprised. Uneven teeth, blackened at the gums from chewing betelnut, pressed against cracked lips.

I guessed him to be in his late twenties.

Who was he?

What was his name?

Where was he from?

Was he an Afghan? Was he a Taliban? Did he know my grandfather?

Was he married?

Did he have a wife and kids?

I shook my head. What was I doing? I forced my eyes away. All these questions were now meaningless, erased forever by a bullet, my bullet.

My eyes returned to the dead man, driven by inquisitiveness with death.

If he had a family, because of me, he'd never see them again. He'd never see another sun rise. He'd never see anything. His life was over. Because of me.

I wondered if he were a bad person or just mislead. Maybe he was just a naïve, young man who had been programmed to believe in a different set of rights and wrongs.

Could he have been right and I have been wrong? How could raping a woman ever be right?

A shudder rippled through my fading numbness.

What if she wasn't being raped? What if this dead man had been her husband and they were just having a fight? What if she were running away from her husband? But if that were the case, who was the second man and why did he hold her down while the other man stripped her clothing?

I really didn't know what was going on?

So what gave me the right to kill him? I wasn't a soldier in a war. My home wasn't being invaded by men with guns. My wife and kid weren't being chased and my wife raped.

I didn't really know who these people were or what they were doing.

If I had seen two men chasing a screaming woman through a field back home, in Cincinnati, would I have shot one of them?

No.

So who had made me judge and executioner of this man?

Just me.

Only me.

My God, what had I done?

What had I become?

Tears welled and then overflowed.

My tear-blurred eyes stayed fixed on the man's face.

None of this mattered, not for him. Nothing mattered. Not now.

What _did_ matter was he was dead, and I had killed him.

In my haste, I had hurdled a barrier into another dimension and I could never go back. The old innocent, good hearted Kugi was left on the other side. He was also dead. A new, different Kugi had emerged on the other side, a tainted man, a man whose conscious now had a hole in it, a big gaping hole leaking guilt.

Someone touched my left hand. I should have been concerned about being touched, but I wasn't. A hand eased the gun from my left hand. I didn't even know I still had the pistol in my hand.

"Well, I guess I don't have to teach _you_ to shoot," Carl said.

I felt him put my gun in my holster.

Carl's heavy hand rested on my shoulder. "I know where you are, and there's nothin' I can do or say that will help you. Only time will help you, time to digest what you did and why it had to be done. But only you can do that." His fingers dug into my shoulder. "You are a good man, Kugi Singh, and I am proud to be your friend. You saved two lives today, this woman and her boy. That's what you need to focus on if you can. Come on, let's leave this place. It's not a good place to be."

133

Chapter 36

The sun had transitioned from an orange ball kissing the earth's rim during the start of my watch to a blinding yellow ball about midway to overhead.

Things had happened around me as if I had been asleep or rendered unconscious, and I hadn't been either. Things I hadn't seen or remembered doing.

First of all, I was sitting on the ground. I don't remember sitting down. I remember running, stopping, and . . . and shooting. And I remember standing over the man I killed and staring at him. And I recalled how different I felt inside, how foreign.

Our little group, now larger with the exception of a missing Maanik, were clustered in the shadow of the 'buffalo's head,' not far from the blood splattered boulder. How and when had Montana and the little boy gotten there?

The woman I assumed to be the boy's mother sat on the ground. Her copper cheeks and chin spotted with red, swollen welts. Her nose was swollen and the swelling had spread to the bridge of her nose and into her eye sockets. One of our band aids striped a cheek bone. Now fully dressed, she cuddled her son.

Montana sat upright on the stretcher near the woman. She broke pieces off a chocolate bar and maneuvered the temptation in the air in front of the giggling child, teasing him with the old airplane-in-the-hanger game.

Carl scanned the area with his binoculars.

And Maanik, his long thin legs moving briskly, walked towards us from the direction of Route A01.

The two dead men were gone. Two parallel shallow troughs in the sand formed a trail leading behind the blood stained boulder. I assumed someone, either Carl, Mannik, or both, had dragged them out of sight.

What had happened? Where had I been and what had I done between Carl's shot and when I stood over the man I had killed and since then? I had lost at least two segments of time out of my life.

I rubbed my hands together and my feelings were intact. I could touch, see, hear, and smell. I hadn't been shot. Nothing was physically wrong, but my short term memory had some major problems. I had never encountered anything like this. I had friends who told me about drunken blackouts in which they did things they couldn't remember, but I had never experienced one. And I had gotten drunk before, absolutely stumbling, mumbling drunk on rare occasions. Carl knew. My college buddies knew. But I had always been aware of my surroundings, my actions, and time.

Maanik's yell redirected my attention.

"Hey, Carl and Kugi. Guess what I found? It is just as I thought. These two rapists had a truck, a Toyota truck. They left it on the side of the highway. They must have pulled over and left it when they saw the woman and boy. The keys were in it and the gas tank is almost full. Plus there are two five-gallon cans of gas in the bed, plus another five gallons of water. I would guess they were Taliban. And they were on their way to pick up some of their Taliban buddies from one of the madrasses just across the border in Pakistan."

"A truck and gas and water, fantastic," Carl said, and then held his arms out to his sides and scrunched his shoulders. "But why didn't you drive the truck back here?"

"The damned thing is a standard shift," Maanik responded, extending his palm-up hands. "And I do not know how to drive

135

anything with all those peddles. But I have got these." He held the keys in the air.

Carl gave me a once over look and then said, "I'll go get the truck. Maanik, get the women, the child, and, ah, Kugi ready to travel." He snatched the keys out of Maanik's hand and jogged away.

No one was talking to me. Did I have "Killer" written across my forehead? Were they all afraid of me? I raised my hands in front of my eyes and turned them over to see if they were blood splattered.

I wondered if I looked different, mean, or cold, or something? Maybe if I slept, this would all have gone away when I woke up. Maybe it was all part of a dream, a nightmare. I pinched my hand. I wasn't asleep.

"Maanik, what do you see when you look at me?" I asked.

He was bent over Montana. He helped her up so she could lean on one leg against a large stone. Then he turned and looked at me. His eyes washed over me.

"What do I see? I see a hero. That's what I see. Now help me with the packs and sleeping bags."

'A hero.' Why didn't that make me feel good?

Chapter 37

The paved road to Gerdi was empty in the mid-day sun. Thank God for the truck, the flowing air offset what had to be close to one-hundred-degrees Fahrenheit temperature.

Between Maanik and Rashi Sundri, the almost-raped Afghan Sikh woman, they guessed the trip to be ten kilometers.

Carl drove the Toyota pick-up truck and Montana sat with the boy, Jodh, in the cab. There was no need to risk a wisp of Montana's blonde hair flying in the wind and being seen.

Rashi rode in the bed of the truck with Maanik and me. She was in her mid-twenties and, although facially bruised and swollen, very attractive. Her face was oval shaped with high cheek bones, a straight, once thin nose, and a small mouth with thin, but perky, lips. I had only seen her smile once, when I helped her into the bed of the truck. But when she smiled, her dimples drilled deep into her cheeks and her eyes sparkled like showcased diamonds.

When she wasn't smiling, her eyes spoke of things a woman her age shouldn't have known. She had a war-bloodied young soldier's eyes.

I wondered if mine looked like that.

On the way to Gerdi, Maanik explained who we were to Rashi, why we were here, and where we were taking her.

Rashi frequently interjected questions or comments during Maanik's story. Her Pashto was clear and crisp, her word choices succinct, she obviously was a well-educated woman. Her mannerisms and conduct implied she was anything but a commoner.

When Maanik finished, she focused on me and said, "Your grandmother is from Nanakpur. I have been there. My husband has a cousin, or did have a cousin there. It is such a small village." Her brown eyes sparkled with a thought. "I probably met your grandmother."

I couldn't help but smile. "If you met her you'd remember her. She is the sweetest woman . . . ah besides my mother, I've ever known."

She reached out a hand and touched my hand. "She would have to be, to have a grandson as brave and caring as you."

My face flushed. I needed to change the subject. "Where are you from?" I asked her.

"Originally, Herat," she said. She withdrew her hand. "After our arranged marriage, we moved to Batawul. My husband—"her hands covered her mouth, failed to block a moan, and then dropped. "My husband worked in Jalalabad, he was a geologist."

"I know Batawul," Maanik said. "Why did you stay in such a small town like Batawul when you could have the conveniences of a large city like Jalalabad?"

"I was a school teacher," she said with a hint of pride.

"God bless you," I said. But my need to know who the man I had killed pushed me to ask. "What happened?"

"A week ago, the Taliban raided Batawul at night looking for Sikhs. My husband hid me and Jodh and diverted those killing bastards by gaining their attention and running in another direction. I watched him in their headlights as they chased him pointing and laughing." Her focus dropped to the truck bed. "He ran . . . they made him run . . . he never had a chance . . . they killed him . . . slowly." She bowed her shaking head.

"I am so sorry, I cannot imagine losing a loved one," I said.

She slowly raised her head, her eyes brimming with tears. And she nodded. "We did not have what your American movies portray as a romantic marriage. My parents selected him. He worked long hours. Jodh and I only saw him on weekends. But

138

he was a good man and a good father. He did not deserve to die like that, like an animal." She shook away an image.

"I . . . I cremated my husband the next day. There were many to bury." She wiped away a tear. "We stayed in Batawul for a few days, but we were afraid they would come back. So Jodh and I packed some food and water and started walking for the border. We traveled during the night and hid in the rocks off the highway during the day. This morning, Jodh got up to pee and those two Taliban monsters passing by in this truck saw him. And we ran. It seemed like we ran forever before they . . . before you came." Her soft brown eyes touched me.

"You and your son will be safe now," Maanik said. "When we get back, we will take you to Pakistan and see you get to wherever you want to go."

I gazed at this beautiful, sweet lady who deserved none of this lunacy. What could drive men to kill innocent people, like it meant nothing, like it was a game? Could the stored up hate of one man infect so many others? Adolph Hitler had succeeded in bending millions of minds. Was Masoud Omar another Adolph Hitler?

My grandfather had put this woman and her son through hell. And how many hundreds, maybe thousands, of other Sikhs had Omar hurt or killed? It embarrassed me to be related to this murderer. Worse yet, I was in the same gene pool.

Rashi's stories coupled with Montana's horrific experience diminished what little hope I had for finding Biji alive. But I had to try. If she were dead, I had to at least find out what happened to her for Pop's sake. I had to go on. Plus, I had killed a man. My actions had to be made accountable.

The thought of me being a killer was so incomprehensible, an indelible mark on my soul. I couldn't go back and undo what I had done. But could I kill again? Our search for Biji would probably force me to take another life, maybe more. Could I?

For Biji's sake, for my father's sake, I had to go on. So I had to face the prospect of killing again. Just the thought caused me to shudder.

139

Killing didn't seem to affect my grandfather or Carl. I wondered if their first kill was as difficult for them as mine had been. Carl had inferred his was.

Could taking another person's life become easier? Or did people just become calloused and uncaring? If so, I didn't want to become one of those animals. But my choice had been made, I was continuing the search.

Maybe I did have Masoud Omar's genes. Maybe I was destined to become a ruthless killer like him.

No way. If I were forced to take more lives, I'd only do it in self-defense or to save Carl or Maanik.

A thought jerked me upright. Maybe I had one other reason to kill again.

If we couldn't find Biji or we found her dead, there was another purpose for this God-less trip, kill Masoud Omar. So what if he were my grandfather. He'd killed Pops' father, was responsible for Biji's disappearance and most probably her death, and had ordered the deaths of hundreds maybe thousands of other Sikhs.

I glanced at Maanik and the back of Carl's head. If we didn't find Biji alive, I could send them home and make up an excuse for staying. Then I could search for Omar.

The sight of a nearby river caught my attention. The brown-gray torrent, swelled from the summer's snow melt, raged over and around protruding rocks.

Hell, my grandfather would be like one of those rocks, impossible to reach without great risk. He was a Taliban general, for God's sake. He had to be a wanted man, most probably on the American military's top ten list. He'd be protected. How could I, the son of the man he hated, get close enough to kill him?

And if by some stroke of luck I got close, could I kill my mother's father?

Chapter 38

Gerdi was small enough to forget but large enough to hide in. Gigantic gray boulders randomly interrupted and towered over the three or four dozens one-to-two story buildings lining the main street. The dwellings were separated from the crowned road by a high curb used to channel waste. Unlike home, there was no greeting sign introducing the town. All summer traffic was greeted by the smell of human feces mixed with urine coupled with small clouds of roaming, buzzing insects.

The homes and businesses were combinations of wooden single-gabled roofs with brick or stone walls. There was no color, just the drab brown and gray of the local bricks, stone, and wood.

Our entrance suspended a children's game of soccer in the street. I hoped the primary purpose of the game was to keep the ball out of the gutter. The children stared at us.

The few adults, veiled women and fez-topped men, out in the peaked sun, also stared at us.

The expressions on their faces were too familiar. It was the same glare I got at home, a mixture of fear and encroachment.

The truck, our age, our clothes, they had to think we were Taliban.

We passed a couple of inns in the middle of town. From external appearances, I would've rated these lodgings at a negative three on a grid of five. I wondered if they had running water, if so, it probably wasn't drinkable or available in hot or cold. I couldn't guess what they charged for a room, but I was sure the bugs were free and plentiful.

Route A01 made almost a ninety degree turn at Gerdi, going from a northwestern direction to almost due west. The large river I had seen earlier flowed just east of the town. The river and the bend in the road were the only points of interest in the area.

We rolled through Gerdi and Rashi looked at me with her tender brown eyes and she touched my hand. "You saved my son's life and my life. Those horrible men would have raped me and then killed me. And then they would have chased down Jodh and killed his as well. They are known for such things. Just when I was sure of the worst, you appeared. It was like God had sent you. I will be forever indebted to you. I will pray for God to be with you on your quest."

Rashi's words, like an anti-inflammatory drug, found my infection of guilt and destroyed it. "Your words are too kind," I said.

Maanik rolled onto his knees and pounded his hand on the roof of the cab. Carl responded by turning onto a dirt road which turned off A01 near the north end of town. The road took us to a small cluster of brick homes. Maanik slapped the roof of the cab again and Carl stopped in front of one of the larger huts.

Maanik jumped out and knocked on the door. A woman opened the door and embraced him. Words were exchanged and he turned and motioned us inside.

Nasiba and Abdul Hanifi, a childless mid-thirties couple, were surprisingly glad to see us as we crowded into their small home. There was only one room separated into two by a curtain with a loft. And to Montana's good fortune, the couple's parents were from Punjab so they both spoke English. They agreed to house Montana, Rashi, and Jodh, until we returned.

"We've got to go if we're going to try to make Kabul before nightfall," Carl said.

I turned to Abdul, a short, balding man dressed in a white cotton gown. "We should be back within a week." I clasped his hand with both of mine, with four thousand Pakistani rupees cupped in my palm. "This is to help you with food and . . . whatever."

"*Shukriah*," he said, Urdo for 'thank you.'

I turned for the door and Montana, seated in a rough-hewed wooden chair, grabbed my hand. "Kugi, you're probably getting tired of hearing this, but you will come back, won't you?"

I nodded and masked my concerns behind a smile.

"Be safe," she said. "And thanks, so much, for all you have done for me."

She pulled me down and kissed my cheek.

Her lips were wet, warm, and soft. I wanted to turn my head and plant my lips on hers. But kissing her seemed inappropriate now, maybe when we got back.

I was feeling good about her kiss until she motioned Maanik over and kissed his cheek too. Damn.

Then my hopes for a future kiss were pulverized when she kissed Carl on the lips, a long lingering kiss.

I couldn't take my eyes off them.

I had worked hard to get through engineering college. Many who tried failed, but not me. I made it. And I had plans. I was going to make something of myself. I would get a job and work my way up the management chain and live very comfortably.

So I was a college graduate, who gave a shit?

You would've thought that being the instigator for this trip, not withstanding everything else I'd done, would've gotten me the kiss on the lips. I wasn't muscle-bound like Carl, but I was toned, tall, and, per a lot of girls I knew, an attractive dude. But who gets Montana's luscious lips and probably her tongue? Carl, the big fuckin' deal Marine.

Maybe I should have joined the Marines instead of going to college.

143

Hell, knowing my luck, I'd probably have gotten my ass killed or maimed if I'd served one term let alone two terms as a jarhead in this God forsaken place.

Rashi motioned to me. She stood, wrapped her arms around my shoulders, and pressed her soft body against me.

She had probably watched my reaction to Montana kissing Carl and felt sorry for me.

If her intentions were to divert my thoughts, she almost succeeded. Beneath her loose fitting clothes, when she pulled me tight against her, her mounds and valleys became defined.

She whispered in my ear, "You are my God sent angel. May God watch over you and bring you back."

I was the only one she hugged. That helped repair a few of the many cracks in my ego.

Maanik and I climbed into the cab of the truck.

Carl checked the equipment in the truck's bed.

Abdul, wearing what looked to be several neck scarves, brought food to us.

"Thank you, Abdul," I said. I took the food and shook his hand. "If, ah, we um-hmm . . . we aren't back here in a week, would you please drive the two women and the boy to Peshawar?"

The stocky man put his palms together at his chest and gave me a little bow. "I would be honored." His English was clipped, spoken like a Brit. He slid the scarves off his neck and handed them to me. "I would suggest you replace those floppy hats with these turbans before you get to Jalalabad. And tie them like a Moslem would. Jalalabad is forty-one kilometers from here, and Kabul one-hundred-forty-four." He patted my arm. "May Allah guide you to your grandmother and bring the four of you back here unharmed. _Inshallah._"

"May God's will be with you as well," I rephrased and returned his Arabic send-off.

Carl keyed the engine and we left. He steered us back to Route A01 where we headed northwest toward Jalalabad.

144

I tried to formulate a plan about what we would do when we got to Biji's village. But my mind kept returning to the dead Afghan man lying in the dirt. His eyes, those blank staring eyes, seeing nothing. I had to think of something else or go crazy.

Five or ten miles into the trip, I nudged Maanik who sat between Carl and I. "Did you ever see Biji when you lived in Kabul?"

"Yes. I would see her often at Gurdwara Karte Parwan. She came there to worship almost every week except in the winter."

"How was she? Was she healthy? Could she take care of herself?"

"She seemed hearty. She looked and acted much younger than her years."

"What do you think Biji would have done when the Taliban came to her village? What options did she have?"

"Well, village people take care of each other. I think someone would have—"

"Did you hide the rifles under the backpacks, Kugi?" Carl asked.

Obviously Maanik's and my conversation wasn't important to the kissing General. Whatever popped into his mind out ranked us.

"Yes, I covered them with the packs." I glanced over my shoulder and the pot-hole infected road had jarred the packs off the guns. "But I can see them now. Why?"

He braked the truck and pulled to the side of the road in the shadow of a towering boulder just before a bend in the road.

Carl's eyes searched the sky. "Kugi, go get the guns. See if they'll go behind the seat. All we need is to have an UMA spot us, three men in a pick-up with guns in the back. We'd be vaporized."

"UMA?" I opened the door.

"That's what we called them when I was here, unmanned aircraft. Would you believe there are pilots sittin' at a control panel somewhere in California flyin' drones armed with missiles over this country? Amazin'."

I retrieved the rifles and slid them behind the seat.

When I climbed into the cab, a paneled truck came around the bend. The truck slowed as it approached us.

Carl jerked his pistol out, and Maanik and I copied him. "Keep the guns out of sight, but be ready," Carl said.

Two men wearing turbans came into view in the front seat.

Carl put the truck in gear and rolled onto the road. He shifted into second gear and accelerated by them.

They craned their heads, staring at us in our floppy hats.

"It's turban time," I said.

Chapter 39

Carl, pistol in his lap, challenged the truck's and his abilities to keep the Toyota on the curvy, pot-hole strewn road. His eyes darted back and forth from the road to the mirrors.

Maanik and I holstered our weapons and removed our floppy hats. We glanced at each other knowing we were violating Sikh rules by removing our turbans, but it wasn't like we were cutting our hair. We were just substituting one turban for another. We untied our turbans and replaced them with turbans tied in the Muslim fashion, with a tale of the cloth hanging down.

Maanik pulled off Carl's hat and tied a turban around his head while he drove.

Maanik had just finished Carl's head gear when we sped around a curve to see another oncoming vehicle.

"It's a Humvee," Carl said, his free hand griping his pistol. He leaned forward. "Better yet it's a MAC. Semper Fi, boys." Carl saluted. "Go get'em. It's the United States fuckin' Marines, boys. That block of iron comin' at us is a Marine Armor Kit on a High Mobility Multipurpose Wheeled Vehicle."

Maanik, his eyebrows peaked, tapped my shoulder. His eyes made a full circuit from my eyes to my turban and back again. A message screamed in silence.

"And I'd bet they're followin' that truck we just passed." Carl holstered his gun and extended an arm out the window and waved. "This is fan—"he jerked his hand inside and touched his turban and then his copper colored, whisker-stubble cheek—"oh shit."

The Humvee slowed and swerved into the middle of the road. A head appeared in the turret mounted on top of the vehicle.

Carl slammed on the brakes, and Maanik and I slammed into the dashboard.

The road-blocking Humvee screeched to a stop about fifty-feet in front of us.

"Get out of the truck, now, with your hands up," Carl yelled. He flung open his door and hopped out of the truck, arms up.

I'd never thought about encountering American troops. Our intent was to blend in with the locals. The thought of being killed by my own people overwhelmed my nervous system and I couldn't find the door handle.

Maanik pushing on me didn't help matters. After several hard shoves, he slid out Carl's side, shot his hands skyward, and joined Carl in front of the truck.

My shaking hands finally found the lever and I shoved the door open half-falling out in my haste. I stumbled a step or two, and a metal-on-metal sliding noise grabbed my attention. The turret rotated and a machine gun stopped with me in its sights. A helmet over sun-glasses was all I could see behind the gun. Had this person witnessed the madness of the Taliban? Had he or she lost a friend, maybe a relative to these young zealot killers? Had this gunman killed before?

I got my legs under me and rapidly raised my arms. I couldn't breathe, and I was sure if one of these Americans didn't kill me, I'd die from a heart attack.

A deep voice, speaking in Pashto, blasted from a speaker. "On your knees."

Maybe these Marines had murdered other men suspected of being Taliban. We were in the middle of nowhere. They could kill us and no one would ever know. Each of them, in their own way, probably had reasons to terminate us.

Maanik and I dropped to our knees, hands still extended. Carl stood there.

"Carl, on your knees," I yelled.

148

Chapter 40

I was going to die. I knew June was almost over, but I had no idea what the date, day, or time was. Had I lost track, or had my ability to think been compromised by the black mouth of the machine gun pointed at me? Who cared? What difference would it make? Dead was dead.

I had never been so vulnerable, so controlled. My knees in the hot sand next to the road in front of all things a Toyota Taliban truck. My trembling arms raised with a damned Muslim turban on my head.

A short stocky black man with a sergeant's chevron on his camouflaged uniform sleeve got out of the truck. Sun glasses and the chin strap of a camouflaged helmet hid most of his features. The helmet had what I guessed to be a camera mounted on the front. He wore a flak vest and his shirt sleeves were rolled up exposing well defined biceps. He had all kinds of gadgets and small containers hanging on him. And his uniform had enough flapped pockets to make any magician jealous. He held a rifle, just like ours, at ready.

Unbelievably, I found myself thinking he had to be burning up in all that clothing and gear. At any moment, I could be riddled by American bullets and I was thinking about the sergeant's discomfort. My mind had to be trying to block my fears. But when my eyes slid back to the machine gun, all my fears returned.

"Johnson," he shouted over his shoulder. "Get out here and talk to these people. You know I don't speak that crap."

"That won't be necessary," Carl said. "Semper Fi, Sergeant."

The black sergeant's head rocked back like he'd been smacked in the forehead.

"We're Americans, well at least two of us are," Carl continued. "I was here a year ago, with the Third, in the Kunar Valley."

"What?" The black man's squinted eyes fixed on Carl. He eased his rifle down. "A Muslim Marine? In Kunar? Ain't no way."

"I'm not a Muslim or an Afghan," Carl blurted. "This is, ah . . . I'm in disguise. It's a long story."

"Are you a spook? CIA?"

"No. Nothin' like that." Carl hunched his shoulders. "Probably more complicated than that."

Another Marine, a young thin white man with red hair, clambered out of the Humvee. "Yeah, Sarg. What do you want me to ask them?"

"Stand down, Johnson. This man," he waved his gun at Carl, "says he's a Marine."

"I still wear my tags," Carl said. "Let me drop my arms and—"

"You keep your arms up," the sergeant ordered. "Tags don't mean nothin'. Some of the Taliban wear'em like the Indians wore scalps." His eyes roamed over Carl. "Pretty stout for an Afghan. Where'd you take basic?"

"Parris Island."

"What's the name of the little town where the Naval Airstation is?" the sergeant asked.

"Beaufort," Carl said, pronouncing it bew-furt.

The big sergeant bit his lower lip and nodded.

"Who was your DI?"

"Gunny Sergeant George W. Hannerhan . . . but everyone called him Gunny Hammer."

The sergeant slung his weapon and reached out a hand to Carl. "I know the Hammer well, Semper Fi. Staff Sergeant Charles Mason, First Marines."

Carl stepped forward and grabbed the big man's hand. "Former Sergeant Carl Thompson."

"Now why don't you start telling me this 'long story' of yours," Mason said.

Carl glanced at his watch. "I will, but I'd bet that the truck you were followin' should be comin' around that bend any second now."

Sergeant Mason gave Carl a 'how did you know' look and then turned. "Parker, Egghead, out of the vehicle now. Simpson, cover the bend in the road. And you," he pointed at Carl, "ah Sergeant Thompson, move that truck off the road now. And you two," he motioned at Maanik and me, "get behind the Humvee."

Two additional men climbed out of the Humvee. The Sergeant brought his hands together at his chest and then spread them apart. The men jogged to both sides of the road and dropped into a prone firing position.

Carl pulled the pickup off the road, behind the military truck.

Maanik and I got up and jogged behind the Toyota.

Not more than five seconds later, the paneled truck we'd passed earlier came around the bend.

Chapter 41

The sun was two to three hours from ending this day from hell, the worst day of my life. And just when I thought it might be over, I'd become part of a military patrol blocking a highway to confront what was probably Taliban men in a truck racing at us.

I used the sleeve of my jumpsuit to wipe the excess moisture from my eyes.

Carl was out of the Toyota truck, and handed Maanik and me rifles. Maanik and I both copied Carl as he cocked his weapon. The three of us crouched behind the bed of the pickup and aimed at the panel truck as it screeched sideways to a stop. The sliding van came to rest about fifty yards away, the passenger side facing us.

The sun was at our backs. Advantage us.

The men in the cab had disappeared into the back of the truck, and the vehicle sat there idling for what seemed like forever.

Staff Sergeant Charles Mason leaned against the opened door of the Humvee, M-14 pointed at the truck through the door window.

"Johnson," he yelled. "Tell them to come out of the truck one by one with their hands up and empty. Tell them they have a minute before we destroy the truck."

The red headed marine standing at the other Humvee door shouted the Sergeant's words in Pashto.

There was no response.

The truck idled and my rifle grew heavier with each passing second.

"On my command, Simpson, fire a burst through the cab doors of the truck." The sergeant raised his hand.

The passenger door of the truck opened. The seat back had been pushed forward. A hand grabbed the seat and then a small girl appeared in the doorway and climbed out of the truck. I guessed her to be eight or nine years old. She raised her trembling arms and exposed a band of plastic explosive strapped around her waist. A red light flashed in the band. She stopped, turned her head, and looked back at the truck. A small boy, a little younger, with his hair wrapped in a small white bun on top of his head, a Sikh, followed her out. His eyes opened wide with fear, he also raised his arms revealing his belt of explosives.

This boy, and most probably the girl as well, was a Sikh. I could understand how soldiers could be programmed to hate another sect; history books were full of such atrocities. But how can hate be focused on children? I couldn't comprehend hurting kids. These men, Taliban, bastards, whatever they were, had captured two small, scared children and turned them into human bombs.

I didn't want to be here, not in this insanity.

"Hold your fire," the Sergeant bellowed.

A muffled male voice inside the truck said something I couldn't make out. The two unmoving children, faces wet with tears, looked back at the van. They glanced at each other. And then they walked toward us, slow unsure strides, as if they had been summoned for punishment.

"Fuck," the Sergeant said. "Simpson, tell those kids to stop, now."

The red head yelled at the children in Pashto.

Maanik laid his rifle down and ran forward next to the Sergeant. He repeated the command in Urdo and then in Punjabi.

The shaking kids, side by side, kept walking.

153

"Son-of-a-bitch," the Sergeant said and shook his head. "Those bastards—again Johnson, again."

The red head repeated the command yelling in Pashto. Maanik stepped away from the door of the truck and went forward a step or two. He waved and screamed for the children to stop in Pashto, Urdu, and Punjabi.

"Hey you," the Sergeant said, "get back here, now."

I dropped my rifle and ran to the side of the Humvee, next to Staff Sergeant Mason.

The bawling children continued; one small, hesitant step after another.

Maanik, his raised arms waving, took several steps toward the kids.

"Maanik, come back here," I said.

"Johnson," the Sergeant yelled. "Tell whoever's in that truck to call the kids back or we'll destroy the truck."

The redhead hollered the order in Pashto.

An arm appeared in the opened door of the truck and pulled the door closed. The engine roared and the truck jerked forward, turned hard, and sped away.

"Fire at the truck, now!" Sergeant Mason ordered.

The machine gun rat-tat-tatted and rifles cracked pockmarking the back of the truck before it sped around the bend.

The firing stopped.

The children stood crouched with their heads ducked.

Maanik sprinted toward the kids.

I jumped out from behind the door of the Humvee and ran after him. "Maanik, no!"

An invisible force slammed into my whole body, like a giant fist, and lifted me. My world went silent, and I was flying in slow motion backwards, in the air, above and past the Humvee. The air around me was spotted with fragments of stuff, some pelting me while others whizzed by me. The only thing I recognized was a turban, a wet turban, Maanik's turban, as it hit me in the face.

154

Chapter 42

"Kugi, Kugi." Carl's distant voice sounded soft and caring like my mom's when she would wake me on a school day.

The smell of gun powder hung in the air, a singed smell, the smell of survival.

A cool damp cloth swabbed my face, a relief from the surrounding heat. I kept my eyes closed. My forehead and cheek burned. Something wet trickled down my cheek only to be absorbed by the damp cloth.

I could feel my face, I could breathe, smell, and hear, but my body, my arms, hands, and feet, where were they? Obviously my brain, nose, ears, heart, and lungs were working. But with the exception of my face, everything else was there and yet detached, dream-like, like I was floating in a pool with only my face out of the water. I was at rest and after all I had been through on this trip, particularly this day, I wanted to stay there.

"Kugi, open your eyes." Unlike the other Carl, the self-appointed General Carl Thompson, this Carl's words were more of a plea than an order.

But I didn't want to open my eyes. I wanted to revel in my relaxed state. Of late, reality had been a bitch, so why go back there.

Cloth tore and—oh shit, something pierced my arm, again and again and hurt like hell. As if someone had flipped a switch, my entire body came to life with certain areas overwhelming all the others. My violated arm and both legs burned. My head throbbed.

Why would someone stab me in my arm? Why would Carl let them?

My eyes opened defensively. I blinked repeatedly adjusting to the glare.

I was on my back, but I wasn't floating anymore. I was in the dirt next to the Toyota Truck. Carl knelt over me. A man with red hair was doing something to my right arm.

Carl's eyes darted to mine.

"Kugi, say something, anything."

Rashi stepped into my view, above and behind Carl. The skin around her eyes wrinkled with concern. "How is he?" she asked in Pashto.

Funny, Carl didn't acknowledge her. He didn't move, turn, or even speak to her.

Rashi raised her hands in frustration.

"I'm fine, Rashi." The Pashto words scratched my dry throat. "Why don't you go to the truck and see to your son," I said.

She disappeared.

"What did you say?" Carl asked. "Speak English, it's me, Carl."

"I, ah, I was talking to Rashi."

"Rashi?" He shook his head. "We left Rashi in Gerdi. Don't you remember?" He touched my forehead.

"What? What are you doing? What happ—" 'Remember.' Maanik. Oh my God. A shudder quaked through my soreness. Chasing Maanik as he charged toward the bomb-strapped children, the horrific body-bruising force, flying in the air, the . . . the wet turban. Reality was a bitch for sure, a cold, sobering bitch.

Fear overwhelmed my pain, fear that what I thought had happened really had.

Like Pops always said, 'the truth will always find you.' I couldn't run from it, I couldn't hide from it. I had to face it. I didn't want to hear the words I knew would come, but I had to

156

know. I took a deep breath; my chest expansion tortured bruised muscles.

I forced my thoughts into words. "Where's Maanik? The little children?" My voice sounded like a weak, pathetic man, a broken man, searching for a loved one he knew was gone.

Carl looked at my arm. "You've got some shrapnel in your tricep and some in both legs. We're gonna have to dig it out. This Marine patrol, thank God, has both a medic and a medical kit. We'll have you patched up before you know it."

I reached up and grabbed Carl's jumpsuit sleeve. "Those kids . . . Maanik . . . is Maanik . . . what happened?"

Carl's eyes returned to mine. He peeled my hand off his sleeve. His jovial expression remained, but his eyes became the eyes of a child caught stealing. He chewed on his lower lip.

A passing sneer erased all expression. He looked away.

"Those bastards detonated the bombs strapped to those kids. Maanik was only a step or two away. He's . . . he's gone."

I tried to sit up, but Carl restrained me. I needed evidence. 'He's gone' were just words, immaterial utterances, larynx formed noises, lacking structure or a visual memory.

Maanik was dead. I knew he couldn't have survived. I knew it, but I couldn't accept it.

I visualized his round face, outlined by the thick black beard, the brown alive eyes, the broad nose, and his contagious smile.

Dead, no way, I couldn't ingest the word, the image, the pain. He and I had been together, close, for these past several days. We'd shared food, and water, and prayers. People next to you, touching close, they didn't die. It just didn't happen, not in my life. We were related. He was married and a father, his big-eyed little boy that first morning at Uncle Parmajit's, they were so close, so family.

The thought of Maanik being dead sat on my chest like a weight too heavy for me to lift. The heavy thought wouldn't go away, I couldn't budge it. This burden made it difficult to breathe, difficult to think about anything else. Thoughts of his death eluded logic and birthed emotions. Grief, anger,

157

resentment, vengeance, guilt, and hatred toured my brain, one after another tumbling over each other in no repeated order.

I knew there was danger, Carl had warned me. But I never thought anything terminal would happen to any of us, particularly Maanik. He had volunteered to guide us. This was his home. He knew these people. This was freaking wrong. Insane. What kind of world was this where good, God-abiding family men and little children die and their savage killers survive?

Maanik dead, why? He shouldn't have been here. He wasn't a soldier or a fighter. He had never touched a weapon until this trip. He was a dad. That's why he was trying to save those children. He was a dad.

Biji wasn't Maanik's responsibility. She was mine. He had come back to this damned country because of me, me and my father. Maanik was dead because of me.

My deductive mind reasoned Maanik was here because he chose to be, but my guts gurgled with guilt. Acid churned and sought an escape. A man I had wanted as a friend, a man I had wanted to get to know so much better, a dad who risked everything for me, was dead. Carl's words, 'he's gone,' echoed in my head.

Suddenly I was hot, so hot. A tinge of nausea ballooned into an unbearable threat to consciousness. I rolled to my side and gagged. Vile tasting vomit burst from my mouth and spurted out my nostrils. I coughed and spit and fought to breathe, but air was blocked by another eruption of bile. I gasped between spitting and hacking. My stomach convulsed again but nothing was left to eject. I sucked much needed air between spits.

Carl wiped my face again with a cool cloth. "Easy there, take it easy."

I rolled onto my back and focused on the wonderful, cool, wet rag gliding over my face and neck.

"Sergeant Mason and three of the Marines are chasing those sons-of-bitches," Carl said. "I hope they blow them to hell. He left his medic, Johnson, here to patch you up."

A red head leaned over me. "Lance Corporal George Johnson, Opelika, Alabama, at your service." He poured fluid from a brown bottle over something shiny in his hand. He sat the bottle down. "I'm going to remove the shrapnel from your arm now. I've given you a shot of morphine and I injected the tissue around the wound with Lidocaine, a local pain killer mixed with a coagulant. But this may still hurt. I don't know how deep I'll have to go." He nodded at Carl.

Carl moved around and knelt at my head. One of his strong hands clamped down on my right shoulder and the other pressed my right forearm to the ground.

"If you want to scream, scream," Lance Corporal George Johnson from Opelika, Alabama said.

I clamped my teeth together and nodded at him.

The pain that followed made me scream through my clinched teeth and went on and on and . . .

Chapter 43

Consciousness returned. I kept my eyes closed, hoping to go back to sleep, away from what I feared lurked beyond my eyelids. I was lying on my back, stretched out. Cool air, like an ocean's spring breeze flowed over my bare chest and legs. A gentle rocking motion helped nestle my body into the softness under me. I always slept in my underwear, so I must be home, in my bed, in my air-conditioned room. I had to be there, all the elements were right, except for the swaying, but there had to be a logical answer for that.

The idea of being home in my bed eased every fiber in my being. Afghanistan, Maanik's death, men killing children, me killing a man, all had to be just a bad dream. I'd wake up and Mom and Dad and I would have breakfast together like we had done thousands of times before.

I had never felt this tired and yet so relaxed and comfortable. Maybe I'd just sleep through breakfast. Maybe I'd spend the day in bed, what a novel idea. I'd never done that unless I was sick. But I wasn't sick now. I was just clean-sheets-comfortable and in need of more rest. I'd sleep in.

I normally slept on my side. I rolled onto my side and excruciating pain flared, exploded, knifed, and needled through my arm and legs.

Fuck.

Although I wasn't quite sure where I was, the agonizing wounds in my arm and legs gave me 20/20 clarity. Now the swaying made sense, I was being transported.

I kept my eyes closed, my last defense against reality. But the thin tissue of my eyelids didn't block the Technicolor, three-D visions in my head. The wet turban. What had to be body parts. Blood. Bone. Flayed skin. Tension laced fear consumed comfort. All my horrors were real.

I opened my eyes. I was in the Humvee. The front passenger's seatback and the rear seatback directly behind it had been folded down to make a cot. The redheaded Marine, something Johnson from Opelika, drove and Sergeant Mason and the machine gunner sat in the back.

Sergeant Mason patted my bare leg. "Welcome back. You're safe now. We're just coming into Jalalabad. We've got a camp on the western side of the city. There's a doctor there. He'll have you as good as new in a day or two."

His deep voice was surprisingly soft and reassuring. Though I couldn't spare 'a day or two,' I was 'safe.'

The memory of a television newscast showing the burning hulk of a military vehicle after the detonation of a roadside bomb in Afghanistan flashed vivid in my mind. There wasn't a safe place in this God-less country, nowhere.

Safe? The word should be expunged from all languages in this place where humans have become beasts. People, friends, and small children were dying all around me. Hell, even I had become a killer. Who could be safe?

What was I doing? I didn't belong here. I needed to go home, not to Jalalabad, not deeper into Afghanistan. I was getting people killed. If I went on, I had no doubt more people would die. Who would be next, Carl?

I'd rest up at this camp and—Biji. Pops and I had made a commitment. I had come all this way. If I returned now, Maanik's death would be for nothing. What would I say to Uncle Parmajit or to Pops? "Maanik was killed, and I got scared and came home." Right. No one in my family along with Carl would speak to me again. How would I live with myself? And what if Biji is alive, out there hiding, and praying for help?

161

I had no choice. I would go on and not in "a day or two.' And I'd kill any son-of-bitch who tried to stop me.

I pushed up on my elbows. "Where's, where's Carl?" My voice sounded like it hadn't been used in a week.

The Sergeant jerked his thumb pointing hand over his shoulder. "He and Egghead are following us in the Toyota."

My eyes surveyed the interior of the Humvee. There were three Marines in this vehicle and one in the Toyota; that made four.

"Weren't there five of you?" I asked without thinking.

The Sergeant's blank brown eyes looked through me. His expression changed as if he saw something he didn't want to see. He nodded.

Safe, yeah, we were all safe.

Chapter 44

The sun had slid out of sight and the day's last light dimmed with each ticking minute. Reclined in the Humvee, I watched portions of stone and block buildings of downtown Jalalabad flash past my limited window view. It took us fifteen to twenty minutes to traverse the city at this late hour. A mile or two later, in the outskirts of the town, we pulled into another city, a city of tents, now glowing with lights.

I was helped from the Humvee onto a stretcher by two Marines and carried into an air-formed, large plastic dome used as a hospital. The cool interior air was such a contrast to my brief encounter with the day's lingering humid heat.

Lying on a gurney, I was startled when a woman's head, lipstick and all, appeared over me.

"Hello, I'm Nurse Samuels," she said brushing brown hair away from her chubby face. "Do you speak English?"

"Yes," I said.

She held up a clip board. "I need some information from you before we treat your wounds."

Although I never thought I'd smile again, I did. "It's good to be back in the bureaucratic world of the good ol' USA," I said.

Her dark eyebrows arched. "Are you an American?"

"Born and raised in Cincinnati, Ohio," I said.

"I've been to Cincinnati several times to see Reds' games. My daddy was a big fan. I'm from Fort Wayne, Indiana." She flipped my hair off my shoulder. "Your hair . . . you're not military. Who are you?"

I reached up and touched my loose hair and realized all I had on were my Jockey shorts and nothing else.

"I'm a Sikh. My parents were born here. I came here to try to find my grandmother before the Taliban does."

Her face flinched back. "Wow. Sounds like movie material to me. How cool. Here," she laid the clip board on my chest, "fill out this form. I'll be right back."

Another face appeared; Carl's, dirt smudged and copper stained.

"At last, Rip Van winkle has awoken," he said and smiled, his teeth pearl white in contrast to his dark face. "How're you doin'?"

Why tell him about my pain? He knew pain on a much larger scale, a scale that I was unfortunately climbing. "I'm okay. But what am I doing here?"

"You need some stitches. All the medic could do was butterfly bandage your wounds."

I handed him the clipboard. "Fill that out for me would ya?"

"Sure." He printed on the form. "Think your medical insurance will cover this?" He chuckled and glanced at me.

My stern look cut his laugh short.

"There were five Marines in that patrol, one is missing. What happened?"

He eased the clipboard to his side. "They found the panel truck a few miles away, blocking the road. It was in an open area and there was no one in sight. They couldn't see anyone in the van, but they heard a woman inside crying. Apparently the kids' mother. Sergeant Mason sent Parker to check it out. He peered in the windows and signaled he could only see one person, the woman. Then he made a mistake. He opened the door. The van exploded."

His words slapped my mind with a wet turban. My empty stomach gurgled a too familiar message.

My thoughts involuntarily formed into words. "How do people become such brutal animals? They're certainly not born that way."

164

His empty hand slid down his jaw line. "Now, there's an old question, really old." His jaw muscles tightened. "I'm not sure I can answer it. But Kugi, I'd bet if you stay here much longer, you'll find out."

I didn't want to explore this subject. I didn't need to extend my stay to 'find out.' I was waging an internal war to keep hate from gaining total control of me.

I had other questions in need of answers.

"Carl. What did you do with Maanik's . . . his body?"

His brown eyes bore into mine. "Kugi, this place taught me to not dwell on the past. It'll find its way into your dreams too often as it is."

I grabbed his arm. "Did you bury him? He's a Sikh. He should be cremated."

Carl slowly shook his head. "He and those poor kids were blown to bits, vaporized. There weren't any parts big enough to identify. We left them."

I released his arm and my eyes drifted to the ceiling. "What will I tell his father, his wife, and . . . and his kids?"

"Tell them the truth, without the painful details. Tell them he died tryin' to save two children. That's all that needs sayin'."

"They'll want to know what happened to his body."

"Just say it was taken care of." He averted his eyes as if reflecting on the past, as if he'd had to stretch the truth before. "It's sort of the truth. That's all they need to hear."

I looked at him and his hardened face couldn't mask the compassion in his eyes. He was one hell of a good man. He had found a way to live with his demons. I hoped he'd teach me how to live with mine.

The nurse returned. "We're ready for you. Did you fill out the form?"

"I will," Carl said, wagging the pen at her.

She went to the foot of the gurney and pushed me down a hall.

I raised my head and looked around the nurse at Carl standing in the hall in his dirty jump suit, clipboard in hand. "Carl, I want you to go home."

Chapter 45

I was taken to a bed isolated from rows of beds by a surrounding curtain. A doctor joined the nurse.

Nurse Samuels removed the tape from my wounds, resurrecting each area's original pain. Next, she cleaned the wounds, another lip biting experience.

The doctor injected a local anesthetic in multiple places around each wound and left, adding stinging to the now inflamed, gaping, seeping wounds.

The nurse opened the curtain and half-turned toward me. "We'll be back in ten or so minutes. We need to give the drugs time to numb you."

"I hope that happens faster than ten minutes. What's your name?" I asked.

"I told you my name, Nurse Samuels. And yes, you should be pain free in seconds."

"Your whole name."

She put her free hand on her hip. "You young boys are all the same. You always want to know our names." She pursed her lips and then sighed. "Sara, Sara Samuels."

"I'm Kugi, Kugi Singh. I just wanted to thank you, Sara Samuels. That's all."

"That's sweet. But, I'm sure you must realize," she waved an arm in an encompassing circle, "this is not a good place to get to know people."

"No. I can't, although my brother has told me similar stories."

"Your brother?"

"He's an Army doctor. The last time I spoke with him he was somewhere near Kabul. But he moves a lot."

She sighed. "I can relate to that." She looked up at the ceiling. "Dr. Singh, hmmm, I don't recall him."

Without thinking, the words just spilled from my lips. "He'd be wearing a turban."

She shook her head. "No. I would've remembered that."

I dodged the inference. "I can understand why you don't want to get close to these soldiers, but I'm sure they will never forget you."

She waved at my words. "You're one of the few lucky ones."

"How's that?"

"This doctor is good. You may not even have scars to remind you of this, this God-awful place." She left, closing the curtain behind her.

I was confident I wouldn't need physical scars to remind me of this 'God-awful place.'

Chapter 46

An hour later, I guessed around ten or eleven p.m., stitched, bandaged, and wearing one of those stupid hospital gowns, Nurse Samuels wheeled me in a wheelchair back to the hospital's entrance. Carl sat in a folding chair by the door.

"He's all yours," Nurse Samuels said to Carl. "He's got pain pills, and he needs at least a week of inactivity to preclude opening one of these wounds. The dressings should not get wet. Bring him back in a week."

Carl plopped my floppy hat on my head and rolled me out into the darkness to a Humvee. He helped me into it and then returned the chair.

Whoever was in charge of the Marines' logistics and planning knew what they were doing. The hospital seemed centered in a mass of intersecting rows of faint-glowing lit tents nearing 'lights out.' A large sandbag walled and roofed structure across from the hospital was marked with a sign 'Bomb Shelter.' The lay-out emphasized discipline to detail and structure.

The truck's driver door jerked open and Carl slid in and keyed the ignition. "Sergeant Mason gave me directions to a tent where we can spend the night. And we could probably spend the week the nurse said you'll need."

"I don't have a week. Where's the Toyota?"

Carl wove the parking-lights-on Humvee through the maze of tents. "It's parked on the periphery. The Sergeant didn't think it would be a wise idea to drive it around in the camp."

"Yeah."

169

"Kugi, I've seen a lot of superficial wounds here that weren't taken care of turn nasty, even life threatenin'. I've had men lose limbs to infected wounds. You need to take a break. There's a reason the military removes wounded soldiers from battle. And we both need some rest."

"I'm leaving in the morning. I can rest while I drive."

"If that's what you want. We'll eat breakfast in the mess and get some rations from the Sergeant. I can probably even get the Toyota gassed up. We can be in Kabul in less than two hours, barrin' no more disruptions. Gettin' from there to your grandma's village may take the rest of the day. We'll need to sneak in there."

"There isn't going to be a 'we' anymore, Carl." I reached out in the blackness and clutched his shoulder. "I owe you more than I can ever repay for just getting me this far. But Maanik's death was . . . I can't risk losing anyone else close to me. Biji, if she's alive, which I doubt, wouldn't want that. I only knew her briefly, but I'm sure she would rather die than cause someone else to lose their life trying to save her. She is old. She has had a long life. If she could talk to us I know she'd tell us both to go home. As for me, I have no choice. Minimally, I must go on for my father's sake to try to find out what happened to her."

"I've got the same problem," Carl said. He parked the Humvee next to a numbered tent, turned off the running lights, and shut off the engine.

Sitting in the darkness, I could sense his eyes looking at me.

"If I were to leave you now, I'd be responsible for your death and you know it. You've seen enough to get a small taste of what you're up against if you continue. The deeper you go into this country, the longer you stay, the higher the risk. You lack the trainin', knowledge, and fuckin' mother-of-all-nightmares experiences to survive here on your own. For God's sake, you haven't even fired your rifle."

Something snapped followed by metal sliding on metal, and then clicked closed.

170

"If you insist on me leavin', here's my gun, loaded and cocked. Just blow your fuckin' brains out here and now and save me the gut eatin' shame of lettin' you go on by yourself. I don't need any more shit that keeps me from sleepin'." He nudged my arm with cold metal.

I eased his gun-holding hand away with my right hand. The movement stretched the sewn skin, reminding me of my limitations.

"Please, Carl, go home. This is my decision to go on alone, not yours. If I don't make it back, it's not your problem. Just do me a favor, call Uncle Parmajit and tell him about Maanik. I know I'm ducking my responsibilities, but I think you can do that much better than me. And tell Pops . . . tell Mom and my father how much I loved them and that it was my decision to go on alone. Pops will understand."

"I'll tell you what I _will_ do." The General Thompson tone had returned. "I'll call your Uncle in the mornin' for you. And then _we'll_ go find your grandma together. And if you say one more word about goin' on alone, so help me, I'll break both your fuckin' legs."

Chapter 47

Someone very close to me yelled, "Hey, Shithead!" and I woke up on a cot, the only occupant in a four-man tent. People, men, women, many people were going by the tent, some dragging their feet others running. They talked, coughed, sneezed, belched, laughed, squealed, and made whatever other noise people make before the sun has risen. I had no choice but to get up also.

My body was stiff and sore. I slowly grunted my way into a sitting position. The pain killers I had taken last night had helped me sleep, but were no longer effective. Although I wouldn't admit it, Carl was right, we both needed a rest.

Carl's morning baritone greeted me from the entrance at my back. "Feel like you've been run over by a tank, don't ya? Want me to go get that wheelchair?"

I knew he was pushing my buttons, but it was too early and I was too sore to sustain control. My words began flowing even before I swiveled my head. "I don't need no fucking—"he wasn't alone.

Montana, her long blonde hair draped over the collar of her too large, camouflage Marine blouse, stood next to him. Although her smile bent the scar through her lip, she looked so kissable. Unlike yesterday, she looked clean and . . . and she was standing. Was I dreaming?

"I think your hair is longer than mine, Kugi," the dream-woman spoke. "I'm jealous."

I pulled the blanket around my shorts and grimaced as I stood. I turned like an old, bent over man and faced her. I needed more of those damned pills.

Montana's blue eyes scanned my body. "My God, you're a walking bruise covered in bandages. What happened to you? I ran into Carl in the communications tent," she glanced up at him, "and he said you had some trouble, but . . . are you okay?"

My hand touched the bandage on my forehead and slid to the one on my cheek. All my other wounds had made these seem superficial.

I glared at Carl. He grinned.

I didn't want to talk about yesterday, not now, not ever.

"I'm fine, just a little sore. How'd you get here? And you're standing."

She glanced down. "I'm standing thanks to a boot cast. And I'm here because of my transponder. The company injects all of the field people with a transmitter. I'd forgotten about it, and I guess it didn't work very well in the cave. But shortly after you left Gerdi yesterday, a Marine helicopter arrived." She flung her arms outward. "And here I am. Where's Maanik?"

Yesterday came swinging back like a wrecking ball, aimed at destroying whatever was left of me. I was there, the kids, Maanik, and that freaking wet turban. I looked at Carl, his smile was gone. I looked away, seeing nothing but Maanik charging to his fate. My eyes welled.

"Oh no," Montana whispered. "No."

Chapter 48

The early morning sun sliced through the tent's flap. Montana sat between Carl and me at one of fifteen long tables, in three rows of five, per Carl, one of the many large mess tents.

Before we had entered the tent, I had decided to shield Montana as best I could from the young horny Marines.

Montana's reception was rather benign with only a few men averting their eyes from their food or companions to scan her. To my surprise, there were many women in uniform at the mess tent.

Every chair was filled and the din was such that you had to yell at the person next to you to be heard. This was a blessing. I suspected Montana would want to know all the details about Maanik's death, and I wasn't ready to talk or to listen about it.

The breakfast was some kind of scrambled eggs, probably powdered, sliced ham, toast, and coffee or juice. Either it was great or I was hungry, probably some combination thereof.

Each of us consumed every morsel of food.

I sipped my second cup of coffee. The crowd had thinned and the noise level had diminished to tolerable.

Carl excused himself to get fuel for the Toyota.

Montana leaned close, her red lips almost touching my ear. She smelled shower fresh.

"I cannot tell you how glad I am to see you and Carl. I'm so sorry about Maanik."

I turned and looked at her, our lips almost touching. I wanted to kiss her. It had been forever since I had kissed a girl. All I had to do was lean forward, just a smidge and our lips would meet. Hell, she'd probably scream. She didn't want to kiss me. She wanted Carl. What the hell did it matter? I could be dead tomorrow. So why not just plant a big kiss on her? No, I couldn't. I hadn't been raised to take what wasn't offered.

I held up my opened hand and shook my head.

She nodded and again leaned close to my ear.

"I know." Her breath bathed my ear. "It hurts too much to talk about. I know how you feel. I also know talking about it will help you heal. When you're ready, I'm here for you."

"I . . . we won't be here that long," I said, my lips touched her soft hair.

"You don't look fit to travel. You need time to heal."

I pushed her hair off her tiny ear. She smelled like Ivory soap, like my mom. I spoke into her ear. "We're leaving this morning. Every minute could be the difference between life and death for Biji, ah, my grandmother."

"After I found out you were here, on my call to the office this morning, I told my management about you and your quest. They loved the story. They, ah . . . they want me to go with you."

I pulled back and she eyed the puzzled look on my face.

Before I could speak she was at my ear again. "I've got another cameraman arriving here this morning. We have an armored Humvee, military issue, and maybe I could talk the Marine commander into giving us an escort. My boss is confident he could get your filmed story aired on one of the networks. He's even willing to pay for all your—"

I grabbed her shoulders and pushed her to arms' length.

This furrowed brow, gaped-mouth woman wants to go with me to film the death that awaits us, maybe hers, or mine, or Carl's, or death's remnants of what was a kind, loving old woman who never hurt anyone. She and her boss want to pay me to record my suffering and the gore I would surely cause, death as entertainment. What a fucked up world?

Control, I had to find it and squeeze it hard to keep from telling her what I thought of her and her boss.

175

"You're not going!"

Her eyes squinted and her lips pouted, like a child refused candy.

I closed my eyes, took a breath, maintaining control, and relaxed my vice-like grip on her shoulders. I stared into her azure blue eyes.

I spoke loud but in a soft tone. "I'm sorry, but I will not be responsible for losing another person's life. If I had it my way, Carl wouldn't be going either."

"Kugi—"I crossed her lips with my index finger.

"It's not negotiable."

Chapter 49

It must have been after eight a.m. by the time Carl guided the Toyota onto Route A01 climbing out of the Jalalabad valley toward Kabul. The morning air was dry and short-sleeve tolerant. A mile or so west of the Marine encampment, bouncing through the rolling hills, I turned to Carl. "Pull over."

"Kugi," he waved two fingers at me, "two cups of coffee, I told you to pee before we left."

"I did. It's turban time."

"Oh." He wheeled the truck to the side of the road. He reached out the window and patted the roof of the truck. "I meant to tell you, we've got an emblem on the roof. Sergeant Mason had it painted on so the UMA's won't attack us."

"UMA's . . ." I shook my head, "oh, those unmanned aircraft. Good. I was convinced those Marines were going to kill us. I don't want to be threatened again by our military. That was smart of Sergeant Mason."

Carl punched me in the arm. "It was my idea. And so were the IOTV's in the back."

"The what?"

"Improved Outer Tactical Vest, flak vests, they're in the back with our packs."

"Great ideas." I rubbed my arm wondering if I really knew him. The old Carl wasn't that sharp, or at the time I hadn't thought he was.

I quickly tied Carl's turban on his head and was almost finished with mine, when he jerked out his pistol.

"We got company." He motioned behind us.

I drew my 9mm pistol and swiveled in the seat to look back. A military Humvee slowed to a stop a quarter mile behind us.

I grabbed Carl's binoculars and focused on the occupants.

"Shit," I said. "It's Montana and I assume her new cameraman behind the wheel. Her boss wants her to go with us and film our little adventure. She asked me if they could join us after you left to fill the truck. I told her no. Obviously she doesn't understand 'no.'"

Carl slipped the truck in gear and barked the tires as he accelerated onto the highway. "Ain't no big deal. If you don't want them followin' us, I can lose them in Kabul. It's one big fuckin' town."

"Bigger than Rawalpindi?"

"Oh yeah." He glanced at his mirrors. "I spent some time there. There's over three million people in Kabul."

"Damn." I had no idea Kabul was that big. Greater Cincinnati was only one-and-a-half million. It had to be like Atlanta, a city I'd scratched off my interview list because it was too big, too many people.

"My old CO said if it wasn't for everyone invadin' this country, Kabul would be a pretty cool place. And it is that, a cool place. It's over a mile high and is located at the base of the Hindu Kush Mountains. In the summer, the days are warm and the nights are sweater weather. The winters are a bitch. My old CO was a nut about geography, which I hated in school. But he was interestin'. He said the city was over three thousand years old. Unfortunately, the Taliban in their many attempts to capture the city have destroyed most of the ancient stuff."

I stared at Carl. He had remembered useless numbers and facts about something. I was almost as shocked about his retention, the roof emblem, and the vests as I had been when he had graduated from high school with me. I never thought he'd graduate. He'd hated school and never did homework. I really didn't know this man.

"Carl, you're scaring me," I said. My eyebrow arched when he glanced at me.

178

He chuckled. "I was here, so that stuff seemed more interestin'." He sawed on the end of his nose with his index finger. "Anyway, the city is in our control now, but suicide bombers, and roadside bombs go off too often." His eyes darted from the road to the mirror and back to the road, while one of his hands searched a pocket. "They're keepin' their distance."

"We do need to lose them," I said. "We'll need to slip into Biji's village versus come in like the Ohio State Marching band."

"Ya got that right." Carl guided the truck on the winding road paralleling a river. He checked the rear view mirror again. "If they stay back that far, they'll be easy to lose."

"Speaking about Biji reminds me." I looked at Carl's week-old beard and envied how thick it was. "How'd the phone call go with Uncle Parmamjit this morning? I wanted to ask you earlier but Montana was there and . . . well I just didn't want to answer any of her questions about Maanik."

Carl sucked in a deep breath and blew it out through whistled lips. "Not good."

I slammed my left fist into my other hand, jarring my stitched upper arm. Damn it, I had made a big mistake. I should have made the call. Poor Uncle Parmajit had to hear about his son's death from a stranger.

"Did, ah, did he break down? I'm sorry. I should have made the call. I—"

"Yeah, he cried." Carl shook his head. "But that wasn't the worst part."

A tingling sensation rose up my spine and spread from my neck across my shoulders. "Why? Wha—what happened?"

Carl glanced at me, his lips pinched together and his eyes squinted. A sigh blanked his expression. "I should've told you earlier, but . . . I didn't know how to tell you. I, ah, I—"

"Damn it, Carl, tell me!"

"Your father flew out of Rawalpindi yesterday."

"So? Did you ask Uncle Parmajit to call him when he got home?"

"He, ah, he wasn't going home. The US Army and Afghan police have regained control of Kabul and opened the airport. He flew into Kabul."

Chapter 50

Since Carl dropped his little secret on me, the only noise inside the Toyota cab was the howling, warm morning air blowing through the opened windows and buffeting the interior. The road wove through the boulder-ruptured landscape, ascending westward to the mountains on the horizon.

We both frequently checked behind us to assure that Montana and her cameraman were still following in the Humvee.

Open-ended thoughts ping-ponged back and forth in my mind. My father was in Afghanistan. Just what I needed. Now we would have to find two people in this vast land of rocks and try to get them out safely.

Pops was stubborn. I should've known he wouldn't go home without looking for his mother. The only way to find him was to find Biji and hope he found her too.

We approached a small village nestled among a scattered growth of trees bordered by cultivated fields.

Carl fumbled in his pocket and pulled out one of the international cell phones I had bought us in Cincinnati. "Kugi, keep an eye out for anything unusual when we pass through this village, a lingering stare, a hard look, anything. I've got to make a call."

"Who you calling now? You know the reception is crap in these rocks just like it was in the mountains. So far, those phones were a bad investment."

As if I hadn't spoken, Carl held the phone against the steering wheel and punched in numbers and then placed it against his ear.

"Hey," he said. He glanced at me. "Yeah, I know. He doesn't want you here. You need to go back." He rubbed his jaw while he listened. "I know what I said. But that was then and this is now." He paused and looked at me, his eyes off the road.

I pointed at the road ahead.

Carl returned his eyes but not his focus to the highway.

"Yeah I know it's a good story. But—"he nodded and rocked his head from side to side again and again—"I know. It's more complicated now . . . and probably more dangerous. Go back." He chewed on his lip and shook his head. "These small villages are known to have Taliban spotters. They'll see a military truck followin' a Toyota pick-up with two Taliban look-a-likes, and they'll call their friends down the road and take you out. Go back." His hand slammed against the steering wheel. "Well, I was wrong. We were both wrong." His head nodded and his jaw flexed in time to words I couldn't hear. "Okay", another pause, "okay! A klick or two on the other side of this village. Fine."

He disconnected the call.

"More surprises, Carl?" I stared at him.

We had entered the village, a few dozen stone or mud-brick huts lining A01. Veiled women pulled children off the road. Old men and young boys stared at us. Their faces blank, but their unmoving bodies seemed tense, like a diver looking at an approaching shark.

Carl kept his eyes on the road and the people. "I, ah, I like her, Montana . . . a lot. I . . . damn it I slept with her last night."

"What?" I liked her and wanted her too, 'damn it.'

Something rotten had invaded my stomach. I was such a fool. I had almost kissed her this morning. Wouldn't that have been a mess? I was totally out of control. I clamped my teeth to hide my disappointment and my bruised ego.

182

"And I'd sleep with her again tonight if I could," he said. "She begged me to come along. I, I couldn't say no."

I looked at the people passing by in the village but all I saw were two naked, sweating bodies pounding against each other.

"You knew?" My rhetorical question slipped out.

I couldn't let a woman I hardly knew come between Carl and me. I'd write Montana off and not let it continue to be the two men and a woman on a deserted island scenario. Carl and I had to be able to depend on each other. And Montana needed to leave.

And what about Carl? I definitely didn't know this man. A woman had gotten under his skin. A woman was in control of his mind. Where was Carl, the kid I grew up with, the teenager who only kept a girl long enough to get what he wanted?

I pushed my ego and issues aside. "So what are we doing a few klicks from here?"

He flipped a hand skyward. "We're goin' to pull over and talk."

"About what?" I wasn't sure if my frustration was caused by jealousy or that no one was listening to me. "There is nothing to talk about."

The last of the huts slid behind us.

"I'm sendin' her back. But she does have some good points." He glanced at me. "You do have a good story."

Erections kick logic's ass every time. I wondered if he noticed my head slightly nod.

"You think all these people dying because we're trying to find a woman who's probably dead is a good story?"

"Well, it isolates you and your family from the rest of the herd, that's for sure."

"Yeah? All her readers would think is one turban against another." But a thought lingered. Carl's use of 'isolation' and my reference to 'turban' made me wonder if my family's story would separate the Sikh turbans from the Muslims' in the reader's mind. Could such a story sway the biased minds of

183

some of her American readers? I'd have to nest on this thought and see what hatched.

"Okay. I'll send her back."

"Thank you." My ears heard him, but my heart didn't believe him.

Chapter 51

A few kilometers on the other side of the cluster of huts, Carl pulled the Toyota truck off the road. The morning sun glistened on small plants in an irrigated field on the north side of the road. An eight-to-ten-foot high mesh fence topped with barbwire barricaded the rows of grayish-green leaves topped with red flowers. Other small, fenced fields with more red, orange, and white bloomed plants interrupted patches of trees and rock plateaus in the surrounding northern area. Several larger stone homes spread among the cultivated ground commanded views over the fields.

While we waited for Montana and her cameraman to catch up to us, Carl reached into the glove box and removed a map, obviously another Sergeant Mason gift. He unfolded the map and his finger traced a path.

"For what it's worth, that little village we just went through borders the town of Khayrow Khel. It's just to the northeast of the highway, can you imagine, just a couple hundred rows of poppies from here. Looks to be a decent size town."

"So?"

"Just somethin' to pass on to your grandkids. You were ten or twenty million dollars worth of poppies from Khayrow Khel, Afghanistan."

His efforts at a pun pushed one of my buttons, a raw button. "Do you really think we'll live to be grandpas?" I couldn't keep the sarcasm out of my voice.

He looked into my eyes. His expression hardened. "Kugi, I _will_ become a grandfather. But with your attitude, I'm not so sure you will. Trust me, if you don't believe you'll get through this, you won't. I've seen that 'I'm not going to survive this place' attitude before, too many times. And none of them did, not a one."

The Humvee pulled off the road in front of us and Carl got out of the truck before I could reply. His exiting really didn't matter for I didn't have a reply. Carl's message gave me goose bumps. I did want to survive. But I wasn't sure I had the skills to do it. I was scared. I didn't want to be here. I was trapped.

I watched Carl and Montana hesitate a step apart. They looked at each other like they were each reliving their naked intimacies from last night. I longed for a woman to look at me like she looked at him. Then, they embraced. I could imagine how her body must feel pressed against him. I envied Carl. I needed what he had; someone shapely, soft and warm who smelled like scented shampoo. An attractive woman snuggled against him who both cared for him and lusted for him. I hadn't been there a long time ago, and I wanted to go back.

But I wasn't going to satisfy my needs here. I had to find Biji and Pops first and take them home before I could even think about my needs.

Carl was right. I needed to regroup and get back in control of my life. Pops had raised me to greet adversity with a controlled calmness. And I wasn't even close. I took a deep breath and rubbed my Kara, the steel bracelet, on my wrist. My mind cleared. Damn it, I would survive. I would.

Chapter 52

The sun was climbing toward noon, and we weren't making any progress. I had sat in the Toyota truck parked on the side of A01 for what must have been fifteen minutes watching Carl and Montana holding hands and chatting. They talked like they hadn't seen each other in years versus an hour or two. Yack, yack, yack.

I assumed these two lovers were talking about how to convince me to let Montana and her cameraman go with us. She was a reporter. She needed a story to embellish, one probably already promised to her boss. I wondered if Carl's earlier words were his or hers, 'it isolates you and your family from the rest of the herd.' Regardless, his words echoed over and over in my head.

I needed to clear my mind so I tried to visualize how Biji looked. Thoughts of her, made me anxious to get on the road; a lost minute here or there could cost her life.

I could now relate to the impatient man's prayer, "Lord, please give me patience, and please hurry!"

Minutes after exceeding my tolerance for wasting time, I got out of the truck. Carl and Montana stopped talking and looked at me as if they were naughty children, and I was their scolding parent. I stepped next to them.

"Kugi, I think we've reached an acceptable compromise," Carl said, a smile creased his copper skin.

"Compromise?" I asked. I glared at Montana. "I already told you there would be no negotiations. Didn't I make myself clear?"

"Kugi, hold on a minute," Carl said. He patted my shoulder like it was on fire. "Montana and George, her cameraman, have agreed to wait in Kabul until I call them. If you and I find your grandmother, and the area is safe, I'll call them and they'll come and film your story." He squeezed my arm. "You've got to agree, as I said before, it's a great story."

I looked at Carl and shook my head. Where was the independent and fearless, war-bloodied hero? Obviously he was parroting her words, not his. This woman owned him.

I knew my father wouldn't want his efforts to save his mother turned into a syndicated TV program for everyone in the world to see. He kept his personal life private. I doubted if his closest friends knew any of our family issues. Just as I prepared to blurt my negative response, my hibernating thought from my earlier conversation with Carl hatched.

But what if we found Biji alive? That would be a great story. But how could it be great when the effort cost Maanik his life? But overall it was a good story about Sikhs, a family willing to risk their lives for a loved relative. If she didn't find out about my Muslim, Taliban grandfather, our family could be portrayed as a typical loving American family. I made a mental note to get Carl to promise not to tell her. Maybe a story like this would change how many people, particularly Americans, thought when they saw a turban. What if 'our story' at least mellowed some of the 'turban tormentors'? If a few bigots were eliminated, it would be a start.

My hesitation caused Montana to drop Carl's hand and place both her hands on her hips. "So you agree, it's a great story," she said. Her follow-on smile bent her lip scar.

I wondered if my lips would feel that scar during a kiss. I'd bet—damn it, my self-control needed work.

I adjusted my focus from her lips to her magnetic, azure eyes.

"Tha-that would all depend on how it turns out." I glanced at Carl. I needed to remain positive in my thinking. "My intent is to make it a great story."

"So you agree, George and I can wait in Kabul?" She spread her hands stretching the fabric of her blouse across her pronounced chest.

My focus dropped. Those babies had been hiding under clothes since—shit, I was out of control again.

I looked away clearing wayward mental images.

"I guess so." I looked at Carl. "But what about what you said on the phone call, the spotters? I don't want to endanger anyone other than you and me."

Carl thought for a moment. "We'll follow them, closely. Hopefully, anyone observin' the road will think the Taliban is chasin' some Americans."

"I hope you're right," I said.

"Me too," Montana said. "This is an older Humvee without all the flak protection."

She saw me roll my eyes.

She shrugged her shoulders. "Maybe I shouldn't have said that?"

I flipped my hands out and back. "I'm okay. For the sake of your story, did Carl tell you that my father is also in country?"

Montana's eyes went from me to Carl and back to me. "No, he didn't. Well I would think that was a good thing. Two different approaches and efforts for finding your grandmother; that should help."

"Or two additional Sikh targets for the Taliban." My eyes slid from Montana to Carl. "Okay, I'm working on it. I'll get better; two different efforts, how's that?" I refocused on Montana. "You will need my father's approval along with my uncle's and mine, before you release anything. Okay?"

"Okay." She smiled.

Her smile was worth all this hassle.

Carl smiled. "Let's go get some lunch in Kabul. I'll buy."

Was this Carl, the high school guy who stole another boy's boutonniere and corsage for prom because Carl was too cheap to buy them? No. This was a new, mature, Carl, no longer a

189

punk kid without a purpose. Carl had a purpose, although it had been slightly redirected by his penis.

"Montana, we've got several more villages and small towns to go through before Kabul," Carl said, his tone emphasized seriousness. "If you see anything suspicious, call me," Carl said.

"Like what?" she asked.

"Well . . . like a man smiling at you," Carl said.

"Carl, men smile at me all the time," she said. "You aren't the jealous type are you?"

He reached out and cupped her chin, fixing her eyes on his cold brown eyes. "Even if these people aren't terrorists, they don't want you in their country. You're just another invader. The peaceful ones look at you wishing you weren't here. Then there are the ones who hate you. If they smile at you, it's because they've seen a soon-to-be corpse."

Chapter 53

Montana's blonde hair fluttered out the window of the Humvee in front of Carl and me, not a good thing. Her cameraman, George whatever-his-last-name-was, I never was introduced, drove past the colorful poppy fields. He drove fast like he'd been raised here and knew the road. All the cultivated ground was north, next to the bottomland near the river. The land south was barren, wind-smoothed mounds of stone.

The warm, mid-morning air whipped through the open Toyota cab as Carl tailgated him. Thank God the road was generally flat and straight where it bordered the farm land.

But being an engineer, I couldn't help but calculate the time Carl would have to brake if George decided to lock up his wheels. It would be really close, tenths of seconds. Carl might make it. His words about attitude jabbed me. I convinced myself he would be able to stop if George did.

Just when I was almost comfortable with Carl's driving, he reached down and picked up the map wedged between the console and his seat.

"Accordin' to this map, the next city we come to is—"Carl took his eyes off the Humvee's bumper to scan the map.

I wanted to scream, but I had to be positive. So I did the only thing left to do, I reached over and grabbed the steering wheel.

Carl glanced at me and took both his hands off the wheel, giving me control. "Thanks," Carl said.

My right foot pressed an imaginary brake pedal into the passenger's floor.

191

"Ah, you mind backing off a little. If something were to happen to cause the Humvee to stop, a flat tire, a runaway camel on the road, whatever, I don't want to have come all this way to be killed in a car wreck."

His brown eyes fell on me. He smiled. "It's good to hear you're worried about livin' again." He eased up on the accelerator. His eyes returned to the map.

"Ah, Carl, would you do me another favor?"

His eyes followed his finger tracing over the map.

"Would you mind not telling Montana about my grandfather, Masoud Omar, the Taliban General?"

My words 'Taliban General' got his attention. Our eyes briefly met and then mine returned to the road.

"Why?"

"If I'm going to allow her to write my story I want it to portray a loving American Sikh family. Maybe it will reduce the bigotry in America against people wearing turbans. But if she prints that my grandfather is a Muslim and a Taliban General, it'll just make things worse."

"You've got a good point. Makes sense. I won't tell her. You have my word."

'Thanks." My old friend, Carl, could always be depended on when needed, a true friend.

His eyes returned to the map.

"Let's see, oh yeah, here it is, Sar Kand Ow Baba Ziarat, what a mouth full. The map calls this place a city. I don't remember any city out here, but it's been a while since I was here. This stop in the road is about eighty kilometers from Kabul. After Ziarat, we should start climbin' back into the hills."

"Good. All these poppy farms make me nervous. Because of their value, they've got to be guarded."

Carl jammed the map into the gap next to his seat and took the wheel.

I wondered if he heard my sigh.

"I'm sure there's somethin' more than fences protectin' these fields. But the farmers ain't so bad," Carl said. "It's the

192

traffickers you've got to worry about. The Taliban gets most of their support money from these crops."

I looked at the fields, each a different color. The adjoining bloomed-plant plots created a patchwork quilt of green, orange, red, and white rectangles. The view reminded me of my grandmother. She loved to quilt.

I needed to stay focused. We were both fixated on women. I needed a clear mind. One of us with his mind controlled by a woman was enough, probably too much.

I wondered if the different colors of blooms meant anything, different ages of plants or different genders?

The multi-colored fields were tainted by a blue-brown river that wound through the farms with a wall of jagged, gray rock hills as a backdrop.

"Why don't we destroy the fields?" I asked.

"It's the biggest export business this country has. These farmers are dependent on what little the Taliban pay them for their crops. So, without it, even more Afghans would starve. The world is tryin' to feed them, but fallin' short. It'd take some major changes to convert these poppy farms to produce farms, major."

I leaned forward to catch his eye and gave him my best puzzled look. "How do you know all this stuff, Carl?"

He smiled. "You've always thought I was a dummy, haven't you? I told you, my ol' CO loved geography." He shrugged. "For some reason, all his preachin' stuck with me."

"The longer I'm around you, the more I realize how smart you are and how dumb I am."

Carl shook his head. "I never thought I'd hear you say somethin' like that."

"Talking about smart, what's going on with you and Montana? You two act like newlyweds and you barely know each other."

He rubbed his chin. "She's special. No one has ever made me feel so alive . . . so good about myself." He scratched his head. "She probably ain't herself. This place has most likely gotten to her, the constant threats, the tension, the need for somethin' to take your mind off death. When she gets back home, I'll probably be just a hazy memory."

"For your sake, I hope not." I studied his face. His mind was with her. "When we get to Kabul, why don't you take her back home with you and find out how real the feelings are."

The old Carl, my old high school buddy, looked at me. "Maybe I will . . . after we find your grandmother." His attention returned to the road.

His words gave me a glimmer of assurance Biji was alive. Carl was such a wise man, the advantages of positive thinking. His words along with his protective physical presence made it almost possible to live with the fear.

Then I saw his finger pointing forward at the skyline. A plume of black smoke billowed skyward.

Chapter 54

George, the cameraman was driving fast, too fast, right toward the rising smoke ahead of us.

"What the hell's he doin'?" Carl yelled, accelerating to keep up with the Humvee in front of us.

"She's a damned reporter and she smells blood," I said, grabbing the dash as Carl yanked the screeching truck through a curve in the road.

Carl eased the Toyota closer to George's Humvee, retrieved his phone, and punched in numbers.

"Hey . . . tell that son-of-a-bitch to pull over. That smoke is comin' from a town up ahead. We don't want to go chargin' in there without knowin' what's happenin'." His eyes opened wider. "What?" His jaw muscles flexed. Veins distended in his forehead. "Tell him to pull over now, or I'll force him off the road!"

The Humvee slowed and pulled to the side of the road.

Carl stopped behind the military SUV, and we both got out. Carl went to the bed of the Toyota, pulled off his turban, and replaced it with his floppy camouflaged hat. He tossed me a flak vest and my hat.

"Here put these on," he said and pulled on a vest. "Somethin's goin' on in this town. We need to get close and find out what caused the smoke. I'll guarantee you someone ain't burnin' leaves."

My heart rate had to double. If I needed a vest, we were heading for trouble. I took a deep breath but my fears dominated any composure. My trembling fingers struggled with fastening the thick torso protector.

The vest shape, with its crotch flap, produced a weird thought. Why would I even want or need a penis if I had no legs? Who would want me? I shook away the thought. The male ego was too influenced by perfection.

Montana, scarred perfection, jogged to Carl's side. "What're you doing?"

He glared at her, handed me a rifle, and slung another over his shoulder. He jammed some extra clips into his pants pockets and stuck his bayonet into the breast sheath sewn into his jump suit. "Kugi and I are goin' to check out the town. You and your damned racecar driver, stay here. If we're not back in an hour, go back to Jalalabad and bring the Marines."

She spread her arms. "Why are you acting like this?"

"Kugi was right, you shouldn't be here." He handed me some rifle clips, a knife, and gave me a 'you were right' look.

"What?" she asked.

Carl picked up the third rifle, slid a clip into its breech, and shoved it at her. "Give this to George. I hope he knows how to use it, 'cause he may have to."

He nodded at me and walked away from the Toyota to a fenced field. He took out his knife and hacked at the fence wire.

Rifle slung on my shoulder, I followed him but couldn't help looking back to see Montana's reaction.

The rifle dangled in her hand. She cradled her bowed forehead in her other hand and shook her head. Her long blonde hair swayed on her shoulders glinting in the afternoon sun.

I wanted to hug her . . . *control, lad, control*.

If I had things my way, I'd prefer to stay with her. But none of this trip had gone my way.

My whole body was numb. I wasn't sure I could walk let alone run. But somehow, I followed the running Carl through the field toward the river.

196

Ahead of us and to the right was a house. A door opened on the side of the house.

A chill danced up my jogging spine. I remembered Carl and my discussion about farmer's protecting their poppy fields.

Two large, furry, black dogs bolted out of the house. Throaty, hair-raising bellows announced their intentions as they raced toward us.

Carl slid to a stop. He unsheathed his knife, took his rifle off his shoulder, and fixed the knife to the end of his rifle barrel. He turned to face the oncoming teeth-bared dogs with his gun clasped in both hands in front of him. He looked like he was prepped for an inspection.

Without knowing why, I did the same thing.

Without looking at me, Carl said, "Kugi, these ain't dogs. They're man-killin' beasts. When the first one goes down, stab him."

The dogs were on us before I had time to respond or worry.

The first bounding dog, jaws gaped, leapt at Carl's throat. Carl jammed the rifle butt into the side of the dog's head. The dog flipped in a cartwheel to the ground.

The second dog's feet were just leaving the ground when Carl rotated his rifle to point at the dog. He thrust his rifle toward the air-born, teeth-bared animal. The bayonet buried in the dog's chest.

I sidestepped Carl.

The first dog pulled his legs under him.

I thrust my bayonet into his side.

I loved dogs. Both my brother and I had had pet dogs throughout our adolescence. My last dog died when I was in high school. I had filled his grave with more tears than dirt.

I had never hurt an animal, never, until now.

With trembling hands, I yanked the bayonet out of the dog and turned away. I had become a different person, a stranger, a killer. I didn't like me.

Chapter 55

I stood in the middle of a poppy field with blood dripping off my bayonet. This day had barely started and I had already killed something.

It was like I was in a trance, like I wasn't really standing over a dead dog, a dog I had stabbed.

"Kugi, let's go." Carl's harsh, whispered words cut through my physical fog, but my mind didn't respond.

Carl took several running side steps, his eyes fixed on the farm house. Then he turned and sprinted for the river, a few hundred yards ahead.

Like an obedient, preoccupied child, I tagged along, stumbling and struggling to keep up with him.

After Carl descended to the riverbank, he stopped, scooped up some mud, and smeared it on his face.

When I caught up to him, he wasn't even breathing hard. I braced my arms on my knees and gulped air.

He stepped in front of me and slathered mud on my face. And before I could protest or even catch my breath, he took off again. He sprinted west along the flat river bottom toward Sar Kand Ow Baba Ziarat and the billowing smoke.

Step after wobbling step, I shadowed him.

After what seemed like an all out run of at least five miles up a mountain, Carl stopped. He knelt, barely breathing hard, on the river bank at a spot where a stand of field-separating trees led to the town of Sar Kand Ow Baba Ziarat.

I could remember the town's name, but I would never be able to say it, not now. I was having trouble breathing and not just because of the long run. I could hear gunshots.

He pulled his M14 rifle off his shoulder and chambered a round.

I copied him with shaking hands.

Carl studied the trees. "Kugi, we're gonna go tree to tree until we're close to the town and can see what's goin' on. Follow my lead . . . and, Kugi, if shootin' starts—"

"I'll be fine," I blurted. I hoped he couldn't see or hear my quivering spine.

He turned and settled his intent eyes on me, scanning me up and down.

He made me wonder if I had forgotten something.

"Stay low and move fast . . . tree to tree," he said. "And remember, these men don't take prisoners, not for long anyway. You're better off dead than captured."

I reached out and squeezed his arm. My mouth was too dry to talk. I worked up some saliva. "So what are you saying? Are you telling me to shoot myself if I'm wounded?"

He glanced away. "Actually, I was thinkin' about me. If I get hit and can't move or I'm unconscious, you can't carry me. And I don't want to be left . . . alive." His soliciting eyes returned to mine. "I'd want you to kill me. Deal?"

I looked skyward. "Maybe we shouldn't do this?"

He shrugged off my hand. "We have no choice. There's only one road and we can't wait here forever."

This conversation was the last thing my raw nerves and rumbling stomach needed.

"Then if you go down, I'll carry you somehow, end of subject."

He laid one of his big arms around my neck and squeezed me. "You are my brother." He released me. "Just remember our reason for bein' here is Biji, she comes first. So don't get yourself killed tryin' to save me. She's your first priority."

"You talk too much."

He smiled. "Oh . . . one more thing, don't run with your finger in the trigger guard. I'd hate for you to stumble and shoot me."

I looked down and my finger was on the trigger. Then I realized why Carl was worried. He was going into action with an untrained idiot, me. He was afraid I'd get him wounded or killed. I wrapped my fingers around the stock like his.

"Gotcha," I said with all the confidence I could muster.

"Okay, here we go. I'll go first. You stay here and wait for my signal."

He climbed out of the riverbed and ran in a bent position to the first tree. He stopped there and peered around at the town. A deep breath later he ran low to the next tree. He peered around the tree, turned, and motioned for me to move.

I could do this. This was just another game of 'Cowboys and Indians,' there was no other way to think about it, another game. I glanced down and made sure my finger was wrapped around the stock. The rifle seemed so much heavier off my shoulder. I bent low and sprinted for the first tree.

Chapter 56

The distance from the riverbed to the first tree couldn't have been more than thirty yards. But running in a bent-over position, on numb legs, carrying a lead rifle, made it seem like a mile to me.

I just got to the tree when Carl darted from his tree toward the next one. I followed sprinting to the tree he had left.

Four or six or ten trees into our reconnoiter, I wasn't sure, I heard gun shots coming from the town, followed by screams.

Carl never looked back. His focus was on the town. He kept going, getting closer and closer, until he had ran out of trees.

Panting, I slid down next to him.

He covered his mouth with a vertical finger, and then motioned for me to stay down.

I lay motionless trying to suck air quietly. Someone was near. I could sense it in Carl's fixed, intent stare.

There were more gun shots. Men yelled, women screamed, and children cried. This had to be a Taliban raid. The bastards were brazen, raiding a town at mid-day this close to the Jalalabad Marine base.

I looked up at the sky through tear-filled eyes, praying to see a drone. But the sky was empty. Were these men brazen or did they have counter intelligence? Did they know where our troops were and where the drones were flying?

"Gohar, the General wants you," a man yelled in Pashto very close by. "We have unwelcomed visitors. He's at the school. They are torching it. I'll take over."

Carl's questioning eyes met mine. Then he bent his head next to mine. I whispered the translated words into Carl's ear.

Repeating the guards words to Carl spawned questions. General? Company?

Why would a General lead a small raiding party, unless this wasn't a small force? The thought added to my growing mountain of worries.

Maanik, gone forever Maanik . . . had said my grandfather, Masoud Omar, the Taliban General leading the Sikh uprising, was a regional leader. Maanik had lived in Kabul and Biji lived in a village close by. That region had to be around Kabul. We were within one hundred kilometers of Kabul. How many Generals could the Taliban have, ten, twenty, hundreds? Could this General be my grandfather?

And who were the 'unwelcomed visitors?' Did these killers of women and children know about Montana and George? Or had they watched Carl and me? Were we entering a trap?

Carl laid his rifle next to me. He took out his knife. "Stay here," he mouthed the words. "I'll be right back." He got on his stomach and crawled away toward the voice.

I didn't want to be here alone. I had to suppress my memories of my near encounter with the Taliban in the mountains.

I rolled over on my stomach and eased my head around the tree until I saw a young man, too young for facial hair, wearing a turban and hugging an AK-47. He walked slowly, patrolling the edge of the town. He was twenty yards of knee-high grass away.

Flankers, smart, these Taliban.

More shots boomed from the town. I shouldered my rifle.

Carl used the edge of the poppy field and the grass as cover, as he crawled toward the guard, a bush at a time.

The guard, framed in my scope, moved parallel to the line of buildings. His eyes scanned the area between the town and the river. Each time his eyes slid in my direction, I would duck into the high grass behind the tree.

202

The next time I dared raise my rifle-rested-head to see what the guard was doing, he had stopped, his gun raised, and his wide eyes fixed. My heart stopped, my breath caught in my throat. His eyes weren't fixed on me. He stared at Carl.

Chapter 57

I lay behind a tree in two-foot high grass near a small town I couldn't pronounce. It was hot. I had been running. I was on the verge of succumbing to fear. My lungs couldn't get enough air. Sweat rolled down my cheeks onto the stock of the M14 rifle. My finger lightly touched the trigger.

A young Taliban guard bounced in my gun scope as he took aim at Carl. The guard couldn't miss Carl. He was laying in the grass on the edge of the poppy field within twenty feet of the young Taliban.

There was no time to think.

I held my breath, brought the gun's scope to the biggest part of the target, his chest, and squeezed the trigger.

Boom!

The young Taliban disappeared from my scope, replaced by a standing Carl looking over his shoulder at me. His face scrunched into a look of disbelief. He took off running toward the downed guard.

Knife raised, he bent over what had to be the guard's body, the high grass blocking the horror of my actions. Carl stabbed once, and rose to stab again when a rifle shot slammed him backwards.

Oh my god, he's been shot! Carl's been shot. Shit. Is he dead? Maybe he's just wounded?

My first instinct was to run to his side. But there was a shooter out there.

I needed to get to Carl, fast. Maybe he was alive, and I could stop the bleeding and save him.

But I dare not move, not until I located and killed the fucker who had shot Carl. I had to kill him. And the son-of-a-bitch needed killing.

The flash had come from above. I looked up and saw a head with a turban leering over a rifle on the rooftop of a building to my right.

I slide my feet to my left, aligning my body in the shooter's direction. I used the side of the tree to steady the rifle until the head was centered in my scope. Then I pressed the gun against the tree, sight locked on the target.

I eased my finger onto the trigger and let my rage squeeze the explosion. The head disappeared. The turban flew up in the air. The sniper's rifle dropped off the roof.

I was on my feet and running before the rifle hit the ground.

Carl was on his back, eyes closed. I dropped to my knees and felt his carotid artery. His heart was pounding at a steady rate. I looked at his chest. There was no blood on his . . . vest, of course, the vest ate the bullet.

I patted Carl's face once, twice, and then I slapped him. His eyes batted open. He shook his head and half sat up.

"What the fuck you hittin' me for, Kugi?"

I started laughing out loud, probably too loud, but I didn't care. Carl was alive and well. My friend Carl was okay.

"Who kicked me in the chest?" He rubbed the vest over his chest. His hand stopped. His finger probed a small hole.

"My gun, where's my gun?" Carl bolted up, onto his knees. "Get down! There's a shooter out there. The bastard shot me."

I touched his shoulder. "He's dead. I shot him." And my own words hit me. I hadn't given a second thought about killing the man who had meant to kill Carl. I had no remorse. I had avenged Carl. I was actually very pleased with myself.

Then I realized what I had done. I had killed two men in a matter of seconds. I wasn't happy about the guard, he was so young, but he would've shot Carl. But shooting the man on the roof had quenched my anger to the point of satisfaction.

205

Pops would have called this a defining moment. In one of our many lesson sessions on life and how to live it, he had told me I would experience things, either done by others or myself, that would change either me, my life's course, or both. I knew this was one of those moments. I had done something I thought I could never do. I had killed not just one man; I had slain two men without remorse.

I had changed.

Had I become a cold-blooded killer?

Chapter 58

Carl and I lay in the tall grass a few feet from the young man I had shot. I didn't want to see him.

Carl clutched my arm. "Kugi, for the second time, you saved my life. What can I say?"

"If we were actually keeping score on how many times you saved me versus me saving you, I'm sure I'd be losing."

"That kid told the other one, 'we have unwelcomed visitors.' I've got to find out what he meant by that. Unfortunately, I don't think he was talkin' about you and me."

"What are you, ah, we going to do about it?" I had already had enough action to last me a lifetime. I wanted to go some place safe and sleep, for a long time. But Carl was right, we did need to know. And I couldn't let him investigate by himself.

"I'm goin' up to that rooftop," he pointed at the roof where the sniper had been and rubbed his chest, "and find out what's goin' on in town."

"Don't you think they'll send someone to check out the gunshots?" I asked.

"This is a pretty large town and there are gun shots goin' off all over. I doubt they send anyone."

"That building you want to climb . . . that's where your sniper was." I handed him his rifle. "Let's go."

"Why don't you wait here in the trees? Rooftops have advantages, but they can also be traps. There's no reason for both of us to go up there. If I get caught up there, I'll need you down here to help me."

207

I wasn't sure if he was trying to protect me from seeing the man I had shot, probably killed, or if he was just thinking of both our safety. I wasn't sure which Carl I was dealing with, there seemed to be so many different Carl versions since this trip started.

"There is only one flaw in your logic. I speak the language, so I should go up on the roof and you stay here."

He scratched his head. "And you think you don't know me. I have no clue who you are." He looked at the buildings. "We'll both go."

I followed Carl. We crawled through the grass toward the building. The tall grass made me wonder if there were poisonous snakes in Afghanistan. I had most probably just killed two men, and I was going to climb on top a building in a town full of Taliban who knew they had 'visitors.' And I was worried about snakes. I had no business being here.

Chapter 59

Like most buildings in small cities and villages in
Afghanistan, this concrete structure had a flat roof. The sides of
the roof were at least three-feet high, designed to catch rain
water. There were drain holes around the periphery of the roof
wall opening to a deep channel in a bordering ledge. The ledge
had several drains in the rear of the building that led to a
cistern.

The building was comparatively large, probably some kind
of store or storage facility. It was centrally located on the main
street.

Carl and I got to the roof probably the same way the sniper
had. We climbed on top of an adjoining shed in the rear, then
up to the wall ledge, and then onto the roof.

When I peered over the roof's wall, I saw another man on
the roof of the building across the street. He was looking south
at the rolling rock hills. I motioned to Carl who was below me.
This guard and probably another had been assigned the same
duties as the two men I had killed. They were assigned to watch
the flanks and were obviously immune to all the gunshots being
fired, particularly mine.

I knelt on the roof, watching the lookout's back.

Carl climbed over the wall.

The sniper who shot Carl was there on the roof, laying on
his back staring at the sky. He had a small trail of blood across
his brow from a hole in the middle of his forehead. His still
wrapped turban lay next to him.

I crawled a few feet, squatted next to the young Talib, and closed his eyes.

Carl pulled me away and whispered in my ear, "Remember that man shot me, and he would have shot you too, maybe killed you, if you hadn't killed him. You had no choice."

Pops had told me on more than one occasion, "The only thing accomplished by replowing the same ground is to wear out the horse." And I was tired.

Carl's logic had worked on the ground. But when you see a dead man up close whose life you took, reasoning fails to justify the finality of death. You needed a whole bunch of hate to be able to kill without remorse. I wasn't there yet, but I sensed I was getting close.

Men shouting and automobile engines racing refocused my attention on the street below the front of the building.

The mid-morning sun was warmer on the concrete roof. Carl and I knelt and removed our hats and vests. We duck-walked around several water puddles to the front of the roof. At the front wall we separated and crawled to different drain holes to spy on the street below.

I lay on my belly and peered through a hole. A crowd of ranting, armed, turban wearing men had gathered in a semi-circle on the street.

I crawled to another hole. In front of the horde was a stack of lifeless human bodies, children, women, and old men, all Sikhs.

My grip tightened on the stock of the rifle. My pulse throbbed in my temples and my eyes burned and flooded. I was on the verge of either throwing up or standing up and shooting as many of them as I could. Remorse for taking a life was no longer an issue.

Pops' words resounded over and over in my head, "Control, a man without control is a loser." I looked away and rubbed my bracelet.

What if one of those dead Sikhs was Biji? I forced myself to look again. I couldn't see her, but she could be under the pile. I couldn't even count how many there were.

How could they do this? How could they murder innocent defenseless people? Why?

I rubbed my bracelet harder. I couldn't let my emotions take over. Unjustified atrocities were committed everyday all over the world. This was not the time or place to try to figure out why.

These murdering bastards were aroused about something. I had to find out what it was.

The small aperture limited my view, so I slid to several holes. There had to be over a hundred men gathered on the street. They faced east and were cheering and shouting. I moved to a side wall drain hole so I could see what they were looking at. A string of pick-up trucks, two abreast, slowly approached, engines revving and men waving from the cabs. In the middle of the line of trucks, rolled Montana's Humvee with a human body tied across the hood, like a hunter's deer kill.

My pulse quickened and my mouth became a drought zone. I couldn't spit if I had to. I looked around and found a loose stone. I tossed it and hit Carl. He turned and looked at me. I motioned him to me.

Carl crawled over and I pointed him to the side hole. He took one look and pulled his knees under him.

I had anticipated his reaction and grabbed his arm, hard.

His wide eyes met mine and I shook my head and motioned him back down.

He blew out a sigh and lay back down. I leaned close to his ear. "There are over a hundred men down there. If she's still alive, the only way we'll save her is to outsmart them."

He closed his eyes for several seconds and then opened them and nodded.

I released him, patted his back, and crawled to another side hole.

211

The line of trucks got closer. The man strapped to the hood of the Humvee was George. His shirt was saturated with blood. Although I didn't know him and didn't respect his reason for being in this country, he was still an American and these people were beasts. I hoped he took a few of them with him before he died.

The trucks stopped and dozens of turban-wearing, screaming zealots disembarked. Two of them pulled a person from the Humvee. Another roar erupted from the crowd, accompanied by shots fired into the air. I could tell by her size, her clothes, and her limp, it was Montana. Her shirt had been removed, her hands tied behind her back, and then her shirt had been buttoned and pulled over her head and shoulders, hiding all of her head but her eyes, those blue, blue eyes. Her blouse had been transformed into a short abaya or Arabic women's cloak covering her head. Her trim midsection and the bottom of her white bra were exposed.

I glanced at Carl. He covered his face with his hands for a moment and then returned his eyes to the melee below us.

The two men pulled the stumbling woman with the walking cast to the front of the line of trucks.

A whistle sounded and the din quieted. A hunched over man with a white beard contrasting with his black turban stepped out of the crowd and approached Montana. He stood in front of her and cupped her shirt-covered chin with a hand, forcing her bowed head up to his eye level. He studied her eyes for a long moment. Releasing her chin, he searched her blouse pockets until he found her press badge. He clipped it on one of her blouse pockets. Then, grabbing Montana by the arm, he turned and stood next to her. With his free hand, he raised what looked to be an AK-47 into the air and froze. The crowd roared.

The son-of-a-bitch was posing for a picture or a film.

Was that the General? Was that man my grandfather, Masoud Omar?

Chapter 60

Was this a dream? It was mid-day, it was hot, and I could use a drink of something. If it weren't for the cacophony, the heat, and my thirst, I would've bet these images before me, like the rest of this trip to hell, were unreal. How could I be in a place like this? I didn't want to be.

Carl and I were laying on the roof of a mid-town building in Sar Kand Ow Baba Zariat, Afghanistan, surrounded by Sikh-killing Taliban. I'm watching a Taliban General, who might be my grandfather, pose before a camera with Montana, Carl's new lover. If we didn't rescue her, they would eventually kill her, if she didn't die from the repeated raping first.

Carl motioned to me. We had to get off this roof. He crawled to the dead man and grabbed his arm and dragged him to the rear edge of the building. He checked the guard on the building across the street, and then heaved the dead man over the side. Carl slid back and retrieved his turban and a spent shell casing.

When we were on the ground, Carl clutched my arm.

"Kugi. We have to hide these bodies. Hopefully all the excitement will cause them not to look for them. But we can't take the chance. Pick up everythin' belongin' to the other one, rifle, turban, shell casin's, everythin'. Then pick him up and we'll take them to the river."

"Pick him up? You've got to be kidding? I can't—"

"Do it! If we drag them, we'll leave a trail through this high grass a blind man could follow."

213

Carl and I were back at the riverbed on the outskirts of the town of Sar Kand Ow Baba Zariat. We squatted, side-by-side, just below the eroded riverbank, out of sight of the town and out of breath. It had to be close to noon.

Picking up the young man I had killed and placing him on my shoulder was not an easy task. He wasn't that heavy, but he smelled like a Monday morning locker room and he was covered with fresh blood and flies. Dozens of the pesty flies had followed me to the river.

Having killed him was no longer an issue to me. I wanted to kill all of them. But carrying the lifeless, limp, lump of meat was just too personal, too close, too awful. But I did it; just like I had done so many other things I never would have guessed I would do in my lifetime, ever.

Squatting on the riverbed, the shoulder of my jumpsuit stained with blood, I regained control of my breathing and my bewilderment. "I think, ah, I think that may have been my grandfather back there." I swatted at the flies. "The one with the white beard, posing."

Carl bolted to his feet. "Fuck your grandfather!" He spit on the ground. "I don't give a fuck who he is. He's got Montana."

His eyes were enlarged and he kept rubbing his hands together like he didn't know what to do with them.

I tilted my head at him. He was fine a few minutes ago. Lugging the dead Talib back to the river must have given him too much time to think about Montana. I didn't know him. He was either losing control or already had. I had witnessed this muscle-bulging man before when he was enraged. He was dangerous. Easing my butt onto the ground, I grabbed a handful of pebbles, picked one, and threw it into the river. Plop. Plop. Plop.

Carl walked in a tight circle around the dead men. "They . . . they'll be leavin' soon. That's what they do. They hit and run." He swallowed hard and wiped sweat off his forehead. "They've

214

got our truck and the Humvee. How we gonna rescue Montana?"

I wanted to scream at him that he was the military expert here, not me. But he was in no mental condition for rebukes. I scratched my head.

"Where will they take her?" I asked not knowing what else to say. Plop. Plop.

He stopped. His chin dropped to his chest. He clasped his hands close to his chest as if he were praying. He rocked back and forth on his feet. "They'll go off road into the mountains. They probably have a large cave complex somewhere nearby."

"What will they do to her?" I hesitated from tossing another pebble. I shouldn't have asked the question. And now it hung there, like the tension, requiring a response, a release, and trailing ugly images.

He retraced his steps in a circle, around and around. "What are we gonna do? If they leave, we'll never find her . . . alive. Fuck." He pounded his fist into his hand. "Fuck!" He smacked his hand again. "Fuck!"

"Settle down. We need to think." Plop. Plop.

He stopped next to me and spread his arms. "I . . . I can't! I'm blank." He reached down and pulled me to my feet and slapped the pebbles out of my hand.

I stepped back, expecting him to take a swing at me.

Instead, his shoulders sagged. He clasped the sides of his bowed head with his hands.

"Kugi, I, I don't know what to do? Those bastards right now are probably—she doesn't deserve this. We got to get her out of there. Soon. Tell me what to do."

My tough, fearless friend had finally gotten too close to someone, too close to be rational when his mate needed him in the worst way. I had more than my share of being led around by an erection or the anticipation of one, but I never recalled acting like him. He hadn't fallen 'in like'; he had dove in, head first, and was now suffering from a love concussion.

215

This war-bloodied veteran was asking me for help, me, a neophyte. I didn't have a clue. I didn't belong here. I wanted to run away, away from all the killing and insanity. And he wanted me to tell him what to do. God save him.

He reached out and his powerful fingers dug into both of my arms. "Kugi?" His pleading eyes fixed on mine.

I pulled free from his bruising grasp and raised both hands palms out. I needed to think.

I had been educated to think deductively. Logic had gotten me through five years of engineering school. Why wouldn't it work now?

Review everything you know, the facts.

"There must be a hundred of them," I said.

"I counted one hundred and sixty four, not counting the two you killed," he said.

Good, the soldier in him was coming to life.

"We can't sneak in there in the middle of the day, not dressed like this anyway." I touched my camouflaged jumpsuit. "We'd get caught for sure."

Carl nodded. His expression begged me to continue.

"Do they always travel in those pick-up trucks?"

"Generally. Sometimes they use horses or walk. Depends what they're doin'."

"Trucks. That's all I saw today. Do they travel two to three in the cab and some in the bed?"

He nodded. His expression more focused.

"They had spotters all over town, on the flanks and I assume on the road leading into and out of the city. That's how they had to have found George and Montana. So won't they do the same thing when they leave? Won't they have a trailer to watch their back?"

He nodded again. A glint of control had returned to his sad eyes.

I had averted his focus. I had his attention. Now all I had to do was come up with a plan that didn't get us both killed.

I shoved all my personal concerns into a mental recess. Carl was right. He and I were the only hope Montana had.

I took a deep breath and blew it out.

"Tell me about them. How they fight, how they travel, their defenses, anything?"

He sighed. "They, ah, fight like our American Indians use to fight the pioneers and cavalry. They ambush you and run, and lure you into a fight on ground of their choice. Then they outflank you and attack. They're a cunnin' adversary. They always cover their flanks both when they stop and when they're on the move. Yeah, they'll have a trailer. You can count on it."

"How many?"

He rocked his head from side to side. "Maybe two or three in a truck. Possibly two in the cab and one or two in the back probably with a machine gun."

"How long would it take to get an armed drone here?"

Carl's eyebrows arched. He pointed at me. "Fifteen, twenty minutes."

"Did you get a number for Sergeant Mason?"

"I did." He pulled out his cell phone.

"Call him now. Tell him where we are. Tell him we've stumbled onto a couple hundred Taliban, and we need as many armed drones here as possible. Oh . . . and tell him we'll put an 'X' on the roof of our truck and . . . don't attack the Humvee. They will put Montana back in the Humvee won't they?"

"Probably." He started dialing. "What's the plan?"

"We'll put these turbans on and sneak back into town. When they leave, we'll have to take out the men in the last truck and replace them. We'll follow the main body and guide the drones to them. When the drones attack, the Taliban will have to scatter. That will be our only chance to get Montana."

He clasped my shoulder with his free hand and sighed. "I owe you so much, my friend."

I touched his hand. "Hell, you wouldn't be in this mess if it wasn't for me. I'm the one in debt." I squeezed his hand.

217

"Now, don't you go get yourself killed trying to save Montana. I needed the calm, cool Carl by my side, and so does she."

Chapter 61

I sat on a rock on the damp riverbed and leaned my back against the bank, a few yards from the receded water. Cool tree shade and the gurgling flow of the river enticed me to lie down and pass out. The day was young, barely past noon, and I was already spent.

Carl, bent at the waist, stripped the clothes off the dead roof sniper, the only one of the two men I had killed without blood stained clothing. He struggled with the man's shirt and gave me a guilt-glance that would have made my mother jealous.

I pushed off the rock and helped him.

Carl held the shirt up to his chest. He looked like a man checking out shirts in the boys' department.

I shook my head and snatched the shirt from him. I held it up to my shoulders. The shirt would fit me, but not if I wore the vest. Fuck.

If Carl and I were going to capture the rear guard of this Taliban force, at least one of us had to get close enough to surprise them before they drove away.

Silent logic dictated that since I could speak Pashto and could wear the clothes, I would be the one to go into town before the last truck left. The thought of going in there amongst those killers without a vest made me shudder.

Carl was the damned soldier. He was the one whose lover was being held captive by these bastards. He had the purpose and the anger-driven energy needed to eliminate the Taliban rear guard.

219

My purpose was to save my grandmother, an innocent victim of the Taliban. I hadn't suffered through all this hell to try to save a story-chasing reporter, a crazy woman who had voluntarily come here for the sake of being promoted. If I got killed going after Montana, what would happen to Biji and Pops?

Plus, I was already physically and mentally whipped by today's dose of fear. I didn't want any more.

I looked at Carl. Despite his copper skin, the turban looked out of place on his head. His eyes were fixed on the town.

Time was Montana's enemy and he knew it. We both did.

For the umpteenth time he disengaged the clip from the AK-47 and checked to make sure it was full.

He was here for me.

Now I had to be here for him.

With the exception of the dead man's pants being a little short, his clothes fit. The shirt smelled like goat's cheese and the turban was damp with the man's sweat and hair oil. My fear of head lice and the nauseating smell of the clothes were the least of my problems, and yet I had to fight the urge to strip naked and dive into the river.

I stuffed my jumpsuit and hat into my backpack and gave it to Carl. He adjusted the straps and was slinging it on top of his when truck engines revved.

We ran toward the town.

Chapter 62

My tucked run through the four or five hundred yards of trees to the town of Sar Kand Ow Baba Ziarat was like running naked through a police station. I was exposed and vulnerable. What if the Taliban sent someone to summon their flankers? I'd be caught in the open.

Five years of digesting high order math and science hadn't made me a marshmellow. I had played intramural sports all through college, basketball in the winter and softball in the spring and summer. I could run but never as fast as today.

Or at least I thought I was fast.

Carl passed me in the first fifty yards.

He quietly weaved through the trees like a spooked snake, one hand holding the rifle, the other securing the turban on his head.

Carl had skills I wanted to emulate, but my eyes were too busy scanning the rooftops to ingest his mechanics.

When Carl got to the building we had previously climbed, he stopped with his back against the wall.

I stopped next to him. My eyes glistened with tears. I so wished my tear ducts would dry up, forever.

Trucks were rolling past the front of the building.

My biggest struggle wasn't for breath. I focused all my energy on trying to keep my trembling internal. *Control, damn it, control.*

On the verge of panic, I grabbed Carl's arm. I needed a mental shove to go around the corner of the building and into a street full of Sikh killers.

"Carl, wha-what sha—should I—I do?" My pitchy voice cracked through chattering teeth, like my first speech to an audience.

"Did you bring your pistol?" His head swiveled from side to side looking for people. The old Carl was back.

I patted my waist under the shirt.

"Back into the street like you're checkin' the flanks. When the main group rolls out of town, walk to the last truck like you own it. My ol' CO always said most of these Taliban fear authority, that's how they became brain-washed as kids." He checked his AK-47's clip again. "Don't hesitate for anythin' or anyone. Get in on the passenger's side. When the driver gets in, shoot him. I'll take care of any others."

I'm supposed to walk into the street like I'm in charge and shoot a man sitting next to me? I wasn't even sure I could walk.

Shooting someone trying to kill me or my friends from forty or fifty yards was one thing, but killing a man inches away who isn't posing a threat was far different. It was premeditated murder.

"I, ah, I don't think I can do this. I, ah, I'm—"

His vice-like hand grabbed my shirt front and yanked me, my face inches from his.

"These fuckers spent all mornin' rapin' and killin' Sikh women and murderin' their ol' men and children. For all you know, your grandmother may have been one of them. And these bastards probably spent the last half-hour rapin' the woman I think I love. Each and every one of them needs killin'."

So tell me something I didn't know. I grabbed his wrist and saw my Kara, my steel bracelet. Not only was I sick with fear, I hadn't been raised to hate. Anger was a vice. I had been raised to do good deeds and to forgive those who didn't. My religion taught me that everyone was equal and capable of change.

But Sikh history also taught me self-defense mandated religiously approved action. Sikhs could and would fight when provoked, and fight well.

222

These Taliban Sikh-killers nurtured hate and anger, challenging my teachings. My grandfather, Masoud Omar, had attacked Sikhs, vowing to kill all of us. This was war. He had become the enemy, and life-threatening enemies, if at all possible, must be terminated.

Although Carl was right, these people needed killing, he wasn't going to brow beat me into hating the Taliban. He didn't need to, God forgive me, I already hated them.

I had proven I could fight and even kill, but committing a cold, merciless murder wasn't an incentive to go into that street.

I pried his hand off my shirt. Calmness flowed through me. I don't know why, maybe the thoughts of my faith and Sikh history. My fears remained unscathed, but not in control of my nerves. Like the time Pops rescued me when I was a small child, when the neighbor's ferocious police dog had attacked me. I was afraid and yet calm.

Trucks were driving by and had been for minutes.

If I were going, I had to go now.

Chapter 63

I peered around the rear corner of the mid-town building through a small alley to the main street. I could see pick-up trucks jammed with Taliban rolling through a dust cloud past the gap.

I slid the AK-47's bolt, chambering a round, and checked to make sure the safety was off.

I glanced at Carl and he nodded assurance.

The dust gave me an idea. I pulled the tail of the turban across my face and tucked it into my shirt collar. Then I willed my legs to walk down the alley toward the exiting trucks.

When I got to the street entrance, the last of the string of trucks rolled past. Just as I had thought, a single truck sat idling a few buildings to my left on the opposite side of the street. Four men, features blanked by the tumbling, polluted air, stood off the road near the driver's door. Two of them smoked cigarettes. Their hands free of weapons. The other two, both cradling AK-47's, had their backs to the dust and, thank God, had their mouths and noses covered with their turban tails.

I turned around and acted like I was checking the flank.

Carl peered around the corner.

I held my hand against my chest so only he could see it. I pointed four fingers vertical and then in the direction of the truck.

He gave me a 'thumbs up.'

Now if I could just clear my emotions and perform the mechanics? A robot, I needed to become a friggin' robot, an R2D2.

Carl's instructions echoed again and again in my mind, 'like you own it.' I inhaled a big slug of air, turned, and walked diagonally across the street toward the truck. I took long, unhurried strides, like a man in charge, a trembling man.

The thick billowing dust was my friend. If I couldn't see their faces, they couldn't see mine.

I reached the truck, opened the passenger's door, slid inside, and close the door.

All four men looked at me through the dust covered glass.

One of the smokers spoke in Pashto. "Are you alone?" Each word spurted smoke.

I nodded.

I wanted to leap out of the truck and run for my life.

Instead, I sat the rifle on the floor with the barrel leaned against the dash. I reached inside my shirt with my left hand and removed the pistol. Then I realized I would have to hold the gun in my right hand both to conceal it and to be able to shoot in the cramped cabin space. Until this trip, I had never shot a pistol, now I was going to have to shoot one with my unskilled hand. The urge to run grew stronger.

I took a deep breath. It was too late for running.

I cocked the pistol in my lap and then held it in my right hand between the seat and the door. I pressed my hand against the seat to minimize my shaking.

One of the non-smokers, pointed his finger at me and then at the bed of the truck. "That is my seat. Get in the back."

If I got out and climbed onto the bed of truck, shooting the driver would be difficult. But that wasn't my worst fear. When the shooting started, in this poor visibility, Carl would shoot me. And the man in the passenger's seat would most probably kill Carl.

The man jabbed the air with his finger again, pointing at the bed of the truck. This wasn't the time for an argument. I didn't need any close-up scrutiny.

The pointing man glared at me.

I didn't know what to do.

225

Toeing a sure death drop into panic, I looked away. My eyes came to rest on the mound of dust covered Sikh bodies.

Carl's words resounded in my mind. "For all you know, your grandmother may have been one of them. And these bastards probably spent the last half-hour rapin' the woman I think I love. Each and every one of them needs killin'."

Throughout my adolescence, I had been programmed not to be controlled by anger. But I had never experienced anything like this slaughter of defenseless people. Today, my programming failed.

The one concerned about his seat stared at me. He cocked his head. "Where did you get those bandages?" he asked.

A shudder of fear forced me to look away. I had forgotten about the bandages. I was trapped. There was only one thing to do and no time to think about it.

I switched the pistol to my left hand, opened the truck door, and walked to the front of the truck.

All four men stopped smoking, stopped talking, and watched me.

I moved until the truck was no longer between me and the group of men. Three steps from the men, I raised the gun, pointed at the nearest one with a rifle, and shot him in the middle of his back. Boom!

The three others froze, watching the man fall forward. A wail squeezed out of his pinched lips as he squirmed onto his back on the street. His hands covered the blood pulsing hole in his chest.

The other man with a rifle jammed the gun to his shoulder and swiveled toward me.

I swung the smoking pistol in an arc until his head filled my sights and squeezed off a round. Boom!

The man dropped like his entire body was trying to get into his shoes.

One of the remaining two dropped his cigarette and lunged for an assault rifle leaned against the truck.

I took a step forward and shot him in his side. Boom! He tumbled into the waste filled gutter.

When I turned my pistol toward the fourth man, he raised his hands.

A rifle boomed from behind me, and the man fell backwards, clutching his chest.

"What the hell did you do that for?" I asked, without taking my eyes or my gun off the four sprawled men. "He had his hands up."

Footsteps pounded the dirt behind me.

Carl raced past me. "Fuck'em. Fuck'em all."

He slid to a stop over the men. He yanked out his knife, bent at the waist, and slashed one man's throat.

I gasped and turned away. The slashing continued.

"We're supposed to mark the top of our truck with an 'X', right?" he asked, talking to himself.

His words made me look at him.

Carl took one of the men's turbans and dipped it in blood. Then he stood on the seat of the Toyota and painted a red 'X' on top of the cab.

I really didn't know Carl.

I glanced down at the smoking gun in my shaking hand.

Worst of all, I didn't know me.

Chapter 64

The Taliban convoy left the road, like Carl had predicted, a few miles to the west of Sar Kand Ow Baba Ziarat. They headed south leaving a dust cloud and us behind them.

Carl and I rode in silence, weaving through and climbing over age-smoothed mounds of rock. He drove and I tried to reload my pistol in the jolting, bouncing truck.

I fumbled in my pants pocket and retrieved a box of shells Carl had given me at the riverbed. I removed three bullets. I pressed the first bullet into the clip. The image of a man in my gun sights returned, the gun boomed, burnt gun powder smelled, and the man's body jerked, I was there. The first killing had been effortless, mechanical, cold and uncaring. The memory chipped at my core, my foundation of beliefs. However, when I fumbled with the second bullet another image appeared; an image of the pile of dead Sikh bodies. Hate countered my reaction to the first kill. My opposing emotions tumbled, blended, and produced justification. My only regret was I hadn't had the time to sort through those Sikh bodies to make sure Biji wasn't one of them. Carl was too wired. If we were going to save Montana, we had to stay within visual range of this gang of murderers. So here we were, per the plan, dust eaters.

I finished loading my pistol and pulled out my phone. "Are you ready to do this?" I asked.

"Hell yeah." He patted the six Ak-47's and two M14's we had stacked between us.

228

I punched up my GPS and found our coordinates. "Call Sergeant Mason. I've got our position."

Carl punched a number into his phone. "Sergeant Mason, Sergeant Thompson. I've got some coordinates for you."

I held my phone up in front of Carl's face with the coordinates displayed.

Carl glanced at my phone, voiced the numbers, nodded, and listened.

"Yeah, a red X, that's us, trailin' the pack. How'd you—"

He listened for a long moment, squinted, checked the sky, and pushed my hand away.

"Yeah, I see the clouds." Carl swiveled his head and scanned the area. "They're entering a pass, can you wait 'til they come out the other side?" Cal rubbed his beard. "I understand . . . low clouds, poor visibility, and mountains. So what's the plan?" He grimaced and flipped a hand palm up. "How's that gonna work?" He chewed on his lower lip and drove. "Okay, we'll make it work." He glanced at me. "Yes, we're ready. Remember, don't target the Humvee." He nodded. "Yeah we'll need it. And thank you, I owe you one." He disconnected and pocketed the phone.

"What's going on?" I asked.

"Sergeant Mason assigned a drone to follow us when we left. That drone picked up the Taliban force and followed them. More drones have joined the effort. He says a thunder storm is rollin' in, so we don't have much time. Low clouds, rainy poor visibility and high mountains will cause our fly boys to pull the drones. Unfortunately we won't be able to pick a good spot to attack. It's now or never. And Montana won't last 'til never. So, lock and load, the fun's about to start."

Chapter 65

A mountain range ran east and west across the path of the Taliban force. The convoy headed toward a gap. The break in the range was wide at the top and narrowed to a truck's width at the bottom. Falling rocks had formed a vee with steep sides at the base of the notch. The convoy of Taliban trucks slowed, the flankers arrived and assembled into a single file.

Dark mountain-touching clouds blocked the afternoon sun and a strong wind swirled the convoy's dust skyward. The visibility had decreased to dusk conditions in a matter of minutes.

Carl and I, trailing the band of butchers, closed the distance.

Blinking away the damned fear-produced moisture in my eyes, I searched the skies for the drones. Only black thunderheads flowed over us from the north.

I had to do something. I didn't know what we were doing. I just knew hell was about to erupt. I picked up a rifle and checked the clip.

"What's the plan?" I asked, inserting the full clip into the stock.

"Not now," Carl said. "Keep your eyes on the trucks. Let me know when the Humvee enters the pass."

The dark sky rumbled along with my stomach.

Carl slowed the truck and stopped about a quarter mile from the back of the convoy.

"There," I pointed, "the Humvee just entered the pass."

"Count how many trucks are behind it." General Thompson ordered.

I glanced at him and we both counted as the trucks filed into the mountain gap.

The last truck entered and Carl accelerated the truck toward the pass. "How many?"

"Nine."

"That's what I counted," he said. "About sixty men. That's good, most of the force is in front of her."

I slapped my opened hand on the dash. "Tell me what we're doing, damn it. My life's hanging out here too."

"The drones will attack the head of the column, hopefully blockin' the pass with debris and stoppin' the column. Then they'll knock out as many trucks as they can. We're goin' to block the rear exit and take out anyone who tries to come this way. If all goes to plan, which never happens, when the smoke clears, all that will remain untouched in that pass is the Humvee and Montana."

Carl drove the Toyota into the mouth of the pass. He maneuvered the truck across the narrow path, the ends of the truck inches from the stacked rocks.

"Get out and take half of those rifles with ya," Carl said.

He grabbed half of the rifles and exited the truck before I could get control of my share of the weapons.

I got out of the truck clutching four stacked rifles in my cradled arms and kicked the door closed. When I turned to follow Carl to the side of the truck opposing the gap, a ground-shaking explosive roar caused me to duck and drop several of the rifles.

Black smoke billowed nearby in the gap and men screamed.

"Kugi, get your ass behind the truck, now."

I set the rifles into the truck's bed and picked up the ones I had dropped.

Two back-to-back explosions close enough to pelt me with pebbles and sand made me clamor over the rocks for the cover of the truck.

"Get those guns out of the bed and stack them against the fender. You're gonna be needin' em in a minute or two."

231

I did as ordered. I picked up one of the M-14's and checked the clip with shaking hands. I was more familiar with this weapon. I had killed men with it, too many, and if a drone didn't blow us up, there would be more. Today was a long way from being over.

Three more explosions boomed one after the other, each closer and piercing my head with needles of noise and buffeting my body with shock waves. I fought the urge to crawl under the truck. Instead, I dropped and hunkered behind the truck's cab, next to Carl.

"Kugi, you're left-handed. Take the hood and I'll take the bed."

We switched positions, keeping low as two more drone released missiles exploded.

I shouldered the M-14 and rested my stock-gripped hand on the hood.

Large rain drops fell slanting in the swirling wind. I wrapped the tail of my turban over my eyebrows to shield my eyes from the blowing water. And then men, many men, came running at us through the downpour.

"Here they come. We've lost the drones," Carl said. "Deep even breaths. Sight and squeeze. Don't panic, but be quick about it."

I filled my scope with a chest just as Carl opened up with his AK-47. I fired, found another target and fired again, over and over.

The remaining rain-soaked Taliban took cover in the rock-piled sides of the gap. The pass lit up with muzzle flashes. I jerked my body down behind the truck. What seemed like hundreds of bullets thudded into the truck's body, shattered the truck's windows, and creased the hood. The truck sagged as the tires were punctured.

I crouched behind a fender, eyes closed, jerking as if the staccato of bullets smacking into the truck were striking me. I had never been shot at before. I wanted to hide. A warm liquid ran down my legs. Concerned about being wounded and bleeding, I opened my eyes to sadly realize I had peed my pants.

Carl's rifle never stopped firing. How could he stand there partially exposed in all those bullets? Was he insane? No one could become used to this, no mattered how seasoned. He had to be crazy. I wondered if I would ever love someone that much.

"Kugi! There movin' on your side. Stand up and fire."

I couldn't move. My legs weren't connected anymore. Even if they were, they were shaking too much to hold me.

"Damn you, Kugi, start shootin'. Now!"

I pushed up, sliding my back against the fender. I rotated my head and peaked over the hood. Six turban-wearing men moved in the rocks towards the hood of the truck and a dozen others were climbing up the rocks to get above us. If their progress wasn't stopped, in a matter of minutes, Carl and I would be exposed with no cover.

I spun on shaking legs, shouldered the rifle and fired a burst in the direction of the running men. Two fell and the others kept coming, close. One of the men pointed a tube at the truck. I had seen these weapons on news highlights.

"Carl. RPG! Get away from the truck."

I scampered low into the rocks in front of the truck. My world became a hot, fire and debris felled roar. An invisible force slammed and twisted my body. I landed on my back against a rock. The air born truck rolled and landed on its side. Another explosion followed as the gas tank exploded.

In the black cloud of smoke, dust, and debris, I couldn't see Carl.

I shook my head hoping to clear my fear-filled mind. Carl's existence couldn't be an issue, not now, not at this God-less moment. Those Sikh killers would be charging. I was my only source for survival.

Somehow I had held onto the M-14. I ejected the clip, retrieved another from my pants pocket and inserted it. I crawled to the edge of the road, dirt flew all around me.

233

Something stung my right calf and then branded it with a red hot poker. The bastards up high in the rocks were about to flank me. Ten or twenty men were running at me on the road.

"Sight and squeeze," I whispered Carl's words. "Sight and squeeze." And I did over and over and over again. Another piercing fire bolt stung my thigh, but I continued to fire until there were no moving targets left on the road. Whether they were dead or taking cover in the rocks didn't matter. They were gone. Then I dragged myself behind a boulder, reloaded, and found new targets in the rocks above me.

Bullets careened and chipped rocks all around me, but I kept firing.

When I inserted my last clip, I took a second and scanned for Carl. Either the rolled truck blocked my view of him or he was under it. Suddenly I could feel the rain pelting me and my leg wounds burned. Being wounded and drenched paled in comparison to the thought of being alone. Like the incessant rain, loneliness drenched my nerves.

Halfway through my last clip, the rain stopped. I checked the area near the truck. I spotted two of the AK-47's we had brought with us. A fire ignited in my leg when I pulled it under me. Grimacing, I had to try to get to those weapons. I had no choice, die here with an empty gun or maybe die hopping into the open going for another weapon. Dead was dead. If I could grab the weapon and get behind the truck I had a chance.

I refocused on the rocks above me. A turban came into my scope. I squeezed and sent the bastard to Meeca or wherever these dead killers went.

I decided to stay still for a while. Let them think I was finished. Then I would fire my last burst and either hop or crawl for the nearest rifle.

Ten chipped rocks later, I tested my leg with weight. The throbbing, teeth-grinding pain escalated into a bout with consciousness. I eased my weight off the leg. I'd fire the burst and go from there.

A high pitched buzz sounded in the skies over me. A drone burst through a low cloud and circled over me. Guns erupted in the pass. The airplane wing-tipped in a tight turn behind me and aligned with the gap as it angled toward the earth. Just before it got to our truck with the red 'X' on the roof, a wing rocket fired and ripped past me, exploding in the rocks above me. I hugged a rock as stone fragments pummeled the area around me.

A second later, I stood with a muffled scream and one-legged hopped to the nearest AK-47. Four leg-torched hops and I dove for the gun and rolled with it behind the overturned truck.

Chapter 66

I lay behind the overturned truck blocking the mountain gap. My thigh and calf burned like wounds of my youth when my mother had poured a whole bottle of Mercurochrome on them. I wished I was with her now.

Another thunderhead rolled over and the rain poured down again. I peered around the end of the truck. Big water droplets splashed the mud near my face. There was a huge smoking hole in the rock pile on the side of the pass. The road was dotted with rain and blood-soaked bodies.

The only movement was three Taliban, two dragging a limp third. They hurried away in the direction of the convoy. These three men had to think I was dead. Why else would they expose themselves?

Thoughts bombarded me as I watched the three men hobble away. Carl possibly being dead, the dead Sikhs piled high, Montana raped and probably dead along with her slain driver, Maanik and those bomb-strapped kids blown to bits, all these images made me realize there were no innocent Taliban in this force or probably anywhere.

And they thought I was dead.

Wrong.

I shoulder the assault rifle, slid the bolt, and raked the three men with crossing bursts. The three men dropped into a heap, a pile of dead Taliban, one pile for another.

There were no innocent Taliban.

I scanned the pass several times. There was no other movement.

No noise except for the pattering rain.

Could it be over?

I wanted to stand up and scream that I was alive, that I had survived, that I had won, but I was too tired and my leg hurt.

All I could think about doing was to lay here in the mud and close my eyes and sleep. Sleep, a respite from the pain, an elixir for exhaustion, a place to—Carl. I had to find Carl.

I pushed up on my good knee and crawled to the tailgate-end of the destroyed truck.

I saw something move in the rocks. I leaned the AK-47 against the truck's roof, pulled out my pistol, and cocked it. I crawled toward the spot.

A man moaned.

Pistol pointed, I pushed up on my knees. A jolt of joy raced through me. Carl lay in the rocks on his back, hatless. His face smeared with rain washed blood.

I checked over my shoulder, a long scan of the gap entrance, nothing. Then I worked my way through the rocks, stopping frequently to eat pain.

When I reached him, I could see chest movement. His arms spread-eagled over the rocks. His left arm sleeve dripped blood and his hand dangled at a strange angle.

"Carl. Carl, speak to me."

One blood-caked eye opened, then the other. He half smiled. Then a look of fear mixed with hate caused him to jerk up only to collapse back onto the rock with a teeth-clinched cry.

"Kugi. God, it's good to see you." Startled again, he grabbed my sleeve. "Where's my gun? I need my gun. They're . . . comin' . . . my gun."

I patted his hand clinched on my arm. "The bad guys are gone, Carl, all gone."

"What? How?"

"Sight and squeeze, Carl, sight and squeeze." I couldn't control the smile that redistributed the rivulets of rainwater

237

running down my face. We had survived; me and my friend, my brother.

"Montana. Kugi, did you look for Montana?" His expression begged for good news.

"No. I looked for you first."

He slumped. Then he raised up at the waist. "Help me up. We need to look for her."

"Carl, your head's gashed open and your arm—"

"We're goin'." He fumbled inside a pants pocket and pulled out his turban. "I knew this would come in handy again. Tie a knot in it and loop it over my head."

I did as I was instructed and then gently tucked his bad arm into the sling.

"Get me a gun."

"Carl, I don't think I can walk."

He looked at my bloody pants leg. He reached in a flapped pocket and pulled out a small encased needle. He flicked off the plastic tip. "Come closer."

I hesitated. "What's that?"

"Morphine. It'll relieve your pain."

I stepped forward and he stuck my leg through a tear in my pants. Then he fumbled in his pocket for another vile and stabbed himself in his bad arm.

"You'll be fine in a minute."

"What about your head?"

"It's just a nick. It can wait. Ain't nothin' wrong with my legs. I'll help you. Now help me get up."

General Thompson wanted to look for Montana.

Carl was right. We had spilled all this blood to find her.

My wounds seemed superficial compared to what she must have been through. I doubted if she were alive. But I needed to be positive for his sake.

I stood, resting my weight on my good leg, and helped him up.

We found his pistol and, thank God, my vest and headed into the pass, two broken men leaning on each other.

238

Chapter 67

Carl, his distorted arm cradled in his turban sling, leaned against what was left of our overturned truck. The rain poured down, diluting the blood seeping from his head wound.

He looked at the pistol in his hand. "Kugi, does this gun have a full clip and is it cocked?"

I stiff-armed the butt of an emptied assault rifle, my makeshift crutch. Looking at him, I cocked my head and arched my brow. "Do Sikhs have long hair?"

"Then, let's do this. I'll take the lead. I'll cover our front and right." He waved his pistol-holding right hand in the air. "You cover the left and our back. Okay?" He pushed off the truck. "Ready?"

I hesitated and released a long sigh. My leg had sent fire-bolts up my thigh with each step getting to the truck. I wasn't sure I had enough courage or energy to take another painful step. The fear-filled gun battle coupled with the adrenaline production and consumption had left me looking for a dry place to collapse. I bordered on being too tired to care. And that was dangerous for both of us.

But Carl was going to look for Montana with or without me. I had to go with him. And for the first time I could remember, my eyes didn't tear-up at the threat of a physical confrontation.

I weighted my good leg, leaned the rifle against the truck, and cocked my pistol. Retrieving my AK-47 crutch, I spotted something on the ground a few yards behind the truck. "Hold on a second." I tucked my gun in my pants and hopped over and picked up Carl's floppy hat. The morphine and crutch made

239

walking tolerable, reducing the pain from red-hot knife cuts to needle stabs. I limped back and plopped the hat on his rain soaked head. "Let's do it."

"One more thing, check each and every body," Carl said. "Make sure they're dead. We don't want any back-shooters left behind us."

"What if I can't tell if they're faking or dead?"

"Quietly get my attention." His gun-holding hand patted his knife. "I'll take care of them."

I shook off the images of Carl and his knife.

Carl pulled the hat brim down and eased his way around the truck into the open. His head swiveled back and forth from the front to the hard right with each step.

I limped behind him, my wounded leg growing number and more untrustworthy with each step. Leaning more heavily on my crutch, I continuously checked the left and our rear. My stomach gurgled over the slapping rain drops.

A haze of gray-black smoke hung over the narrow gap in the mountains.

This was crazy, two men, two pistols, no match for a Taliban force of over one-hundred men with automatic weapons.

We weaved through the unmoving twisted bodies, stopping to poke and prod each of them. I didn't like jabbing or kicking them, but I did. I checked each one for a killing wound. If I couldn't find a mortal wound, I'd hiss at Carl. With his good legs, he could kneel. He'd tuck his gun under his bad arm and retrieve his knife. That's when I'd turn away.

We worked our way past the smoking hole in the rocks from the last drone's missile. The twenty minutes our progress had taken seemed like an hour. There were at least twenty to thirty dead men on or near the road. More than I had imagined. More than I wanted to poke.

Carl, his good hand streaked with rain–washed blood, stopped at a curve in the road.

We peered around a rock at the burning remnants of the rear truck in the convoy. The acrid smell of burnt plastic and gun powder mingled with the gut-exposed smell of death.

My eyes never stopped roaming, left and rear, while my stomach ate itself, an acid-releasing bite at a time.

Carl raised his index finger on his gun hand, pointed at me and then pointed down. He wanted me to stay put. He bent at the waist and darted around the corner, stopping at the back of burning truck.

Gun raised, he stepped around to the side of the truck and pointed the gun into the cab.

He looked at me and motioned me forward.

I hobbled to his side. The truck was empty.

A line of five more trucks, half of which were destroyed, led to the next bend in the mountain-splitting road.

Again Carl motioned for me to stay, and he hunkered and darted to the next truck, visually undamaged.

I turned to scan our rear and every fiber of my body jerked with the crack of a pistol shot. My head cranked forward.

Carl, his smoking gun aimed into the cab, scanned the ground in front of the truck. He swiveled his head, motioning me forward.

Hopping on my good leg, my wounded leg totally senseless, I bounced my way to him. I moved like I was barefoot going through a colony of fire ants.

He leaned in close. "One less zealot." He motioned at the truck. "Stay alert. That gunshot will bring'em out."

Did he really think his words were necessary? Hadn't he heard my stomach?

Four trucks of Carl's game of tag later, we crouched behind some rocks at another road bend.

Leaning against a rock, I wanted to sit down. Maybe I shouldn't have taken the morphine. At least before, I could tell when my leg would support me. And the pain had kept me from thinking about how tired I was.

Carl peeked around the bend. "I can see the Humvee. Thank God, it looks okay. Those fly boys are good. It's three trucks up, just like we counted. Same as before, we'll tag-team our way to it. Remember, you've got left and rear." Bent low, he disappeared around a rock.

I stepped to the rock. Carl was halfway to the next burning truck when he slid to a stop, raised his gun and shot to his right. His parting words, 'left and rear' overwhelmed my instincts to look at what he was shooting at and forced me to scan left.

A man wearing a rain-soaked turban rose up from the rocks above the road and sighted a rifle at Carl's back. I aimed and shot in one motion, and squeezed off a second round as the man fell backwards. His body jerked as the second bullet slammed him as he fell.

I scanned the terrain to my left and rear, twice, three times, nothing. I risked a glance at Carl. He stood by the cab of the burning truck. His eyes roamed front and right.

I hopped-ran to the truck. Watching rear and left, I said, "I got mine, did you get yours?"

"Yeah, except I only needed one bullet."

Probably an hour ago this conversation would have disgusted me, but at this moment, Carl's barb tickled me. Maybe I just enjoyed being alive.

"What are these men still doing here?" I asked over my shoulder. "The drones should've forced anyone with good sense out of this pass. Are they stragglers?"

"Maybe, they might have gotten trapped. Maybe they were a rear guard."

"So do you think there are more?"

"I'm gonna act like there are. See ya at the next truck." He tucked and ran.

A moment later, I joined him.

He darted to the last truck between us and the Humvee. This truck, like the Humvee, was undamaged. Carl stared at the Humvee for a long moment. He squatted by the side of the truck, head down.

Even though he hadn't motioned me forward, I went. There was something wrong. I hopped next to him. "What're you doing?" I asked. "Something wrong?"

"Prayin'," he said, his head remained bowed. A moment later he looked up at me. "Don't say nothin'. I've seen it work for others."

I spoke without thinking. "It didn't work for Maanik."

"Sounds like you and the Big Man need to talk. But do it later. We've got a mission to complete. Stay here until I motion for you." He pinched the pistol between his knees to free his only useful hand. Then he slid the breech open and verified he had a round chambered. He snatched the gun, stood, and darted for the Humvee, low, quiet, and quick.

The man could be a ghost when he chose to be.

Bent below the windows he eased to the driver's door. He shot to a standing position with his pistol aimed in the driver's window. Leading with his gun, he stuck his head inside. He removed his head and walked to the rear door. His features sagged along with his shoulders. He slid the gun under his useless arm and opened the door. He leaned inside and came out holding a piece of paper. Holding the paper inside the vehicle, he head motioned me to his side.

I limped toward Carl. "No one, nothing?"

"Just this." He bent inside the cab, out of the rain, and held the paper close to his face. "Somethin' written in Sanskrit or whatever you call it. But I think it must mean somethin'."

"Why?" I asked as I stopped near him.

His questioning eyes met mine. "It's got your name on it."

Chapter 68

The late afternoon sun was blocked by angry clouds and dense, heavy rainfall. Carl and I stood in the mountain pass next to the empty Humvee, Montana's Humvee.

Water streamed off a crease in Carl's floppy hat. The heavy rain seemed to pound Carl down, drooping not only his head and shoulders, but his features. He had prayed to find Montana alive in the Humvee. And all he had found was a note addressed to me.

I took the folded paper from his extended hand and sat down in the back seat. My overworked good leg thanked me. "Kugi Singh" was scrolled on the outside of the single sheet of paper.

This could only mean one thing. The old man, the General, was Masoud Omar, my grandfather. Montana must have told him everything she knew.

I unfolded the paper and read the scribbled Pashto. "This woman reporter tells me of a young Sikh named Kugi Singh, born in America, searching for his grandmother named Biji. How strange, I too have a grandson who is an American born Sikh and has a grandmother with the same name. Could you be that grandson?

"If you want this woman to live, and you want to know where Biji is, go two kilometers south, an escort will be waiting for you. Come alone and unarmed."

Montana had survived the attack, but so had my grandfather. But that wasn't the part of the note that tickled the hairs on the back of my neck. I couldn't stop my surge of hope, the thought that all of this hell had been worth it, Biji was alive. I reread the note. Had the words been carefully selected or just hastily written? Knowing where Biji was, didn't necessarily mean she was alive. Maybe all it meant was that the bastard knew where he had buried her. Regardless, the hook had been set.

"What's it say?" Carl asked, a glint of hope in his tone. "Is Montana alive?"

"Yes, she is."

As if inflated with life, Carl's head and shoulders rose and his eyes sparkled. "She's alive. Oh thank you, Lord, she's alive. Where is she? Do they want somethin' for her? What's it say? Read it . . . ah, in English."

I read the letter to him.

"We've got to get going. We'll need weapons." His eyes searched the area. "It'll be dark in an hour or two.

I tucked the letter into a pants pocket. Then I grabbed Carl's good arm. "Carl, you're not going. I'm going alone without weapons, as specified. Guns wouldn't do me any good anyway."

"Don't be stupid. This is the man who's responsible for murderin' all the Sikhs. The only reason he would know where your grandmother is located is because he killed her. And he'll kill you too, but slowly. Trust me, I know."

"It's the only way to free Montana and for me to find out about Biji."

"That letter doesn't say he'll free Montana, it just says if you want her to live, how long she lives is another question."

I spread my arms. "So what do you want me to do?" My words skewed with exasperation.

He sat the pistol down next to me on the car seat and used his good arm to cradle his injured limb. "I'll shadow you."

I couldn't contain the laughter that burst from my lips.

Carl cocked his head and looked at me like I was the crazy one.

245

Bracketed by chuckles, I said, "Between the two of us, I'm not sure we have enough undamaged parts to make one person let alone a soldier. I can barely walk and all you can handle is a pistol. And you have a devil of a time reloading it. If we were fighting cannibals, they'd have the fire blazing, the water boiled, and the table set by the time you reloaded."

He gave me a sideways look of no-nonsense conviction. "We have no choice. You can't trust those bastards. I'm going."

Chapter 69

The incessant rain reminded me of a wonderful little book I'd read in high school by Ben Franklin, Poor Richard's Almanac. I loved the simplistic wisdom Ben shared such as excess is not good. A little precipitation was tolerable, but this heavy, pounding, continuous deluge made me crave shelter. Good ol' Ben and his words to live by; strange memories at stranger times.

I limped back to our truck along with Carl and we retrieved our backpacks. I couldn't stand the Taliban's clothing any more. The wetter the clothes got, the stronger the prior owner's musky odor became. Plus the big brimmed hat would keep the water out of my eyes.

Sitting in an undamaged truck, Carl helped me remove my vest and the wet smelly clothes. He checked out my leg wounds. He was surprisingly gentle.

"You're lucky. Both are superficial grazes that took out a little meat and no bone."

I didn't feel lucky. The wounds had burned like fresh brands. There had to be some permanent damage. But I just nodded and ground my teeth. Complaining wouldn't do either of us any good.

He retrieved the medicine kit from his backpack. He tore open packets and covered the wounds with pre-treated large adhesive bandages. Then he bound them with strips of cloth from the shirt I had worn.

No matter what, I wasn't going to completely rid myself of the dead man's B.O. I didn't need the smell or the memory jogger.

"That should stop the bleedin' and hopefully prevent any infection. And it may even help you walk better. The bindin' will hold the muscle to the bone. 'Though I was startin' to get used to the limp."

"Thanks. You'd make a pretty good one-armed nurse."

He grinned and helped me put on my jumpsuit and vest. It was good to see him grin.

"Now let me dress your head."

"I'm fine."

"Bullshit." I pulled off his hat, found some gauze, and dabbed antiseptic on the slice through his scalp. "It's stopped bleeding, but I'll need to shave your hair to get a bandage to stick."

He grabbed his hat. "That's good enough." He reached in the packs and removed ponchos. "Help me get this on."

Dry clothes and a poncho, I had to be close to Heaven.

He sat my floppy hat on my bun-tied hair and helped me out of the truck, back into the downpour.

With my calf and thigh wrapped, I could walk stiff-legged without a crutch. I tried several steps and then a few quick darts. I discarded my mud-caked AK-47 crutch.

Then Carl and I, armed with assault rifles, extra clips of ammunition, and our food and water containing backpacks, snaked through the debris filled pass. We chewed on dried mystery meat from our packs.

"I think we could plow one of those trucks free, Chester," he said, looking back at the twisted metal blocking the gap in the mountain range.

"Chester?"

"Yeah, you remind me of Matt Dillion's sidekick in Gunsmoke."

"Cute," I said between chews with a head shake. "We don't have time to mess with the trucks. I need to get there before

248

dark. I won't be able to find my escort after the sun goes down. Hell, the light's so dim now it's going to take some luck to connect with them."

"All the better for me," Carl said chomping on the jerky. "They won't see me flankin' you."

"They'll have a truck." I spit out a piece of gristle. "How are you going to keep up with a truck on foot?"

"I hope to have the Marines here before then. They got video feedback from the drones. They have a pretty good idea how big that Taliban force is and that alone should entice them to bring some numbers. This damned rain must be holdin' 'em up. They're probably on their way. If they aren't here soon, I'll call Sergeant Mason and see if I can get a ride. Turn your cell phone on in case we need a means to track you."

"They can track me via my phone?"

Carl shook his head at my ignorance and then scissored another piece of jerky into his mouth.

"They'll search me and destroy that phone."

Carl extended his hand. "Then turn it on and give it to me."

"Why?"

"Just do it."

I held the remnants of my jerky in my mouth and retrieved my phone from my pack. I switched on the phone. "There's no signal," I said around the chunk of meat pinched between my teeth.

"Don't matter." He snatched the phone from my hand. "Now drop your jumpsuit down to your ankles."

I gave him a scrunched look. "It's raining."

"Do it," General Thompson ordered.

The cold rain on my bare skin made me fold my arms and shiver.

He knelt and wedged the phone into the wrapping around my inner thigh.

"They may find it, but they'll have to do a lot of searchin'." Carl chuckled.

I pulled my previously dry clothes back on and looked at the fading light. "The Marines had better get here soon, because I can't wait. The letter said the escort would be two kilometers south, that's a little over a mile. If the Marines don't get here in the next quarter mile, you'll have to call them off. The Taliban may hear the choppers, even this rain won't dampen the low frequencies those big blades produce. We can't take that risk. They'll kill Montana. And in this poor visibility, they'll vanish into the mountains. And I doubt I ever see my Taliban grandfather or my Sikh grandmother again. You and I will both lose."

Carl nodded and pulled out his phone.

Chapter 70

Carl, phone to his ear, and I plodded through the mud away from the mountain pass full of death. I could hear a faint whop-whop noise growing louder in the rain-dumping clouds above us.

Carl put his phone in his pocket.

Four huge, heavily armed helicopters dropped down through the black clouds and landed within fifty yards of us.

We both clutched out hats to our heads and turned our faces away from the blast of pelting mud-water. When the engines wound down, we turned back to face sixty, gun-raised Marines scattered around the choppers.

Short, burly Sergeant Mason trotted toward us.

"Where are the bad guys? I've got four more choppers up there awaiting orders."

"What's left of them went south," Carl said. "I'd guess close to forty of them are dead in that pass." He head motioned at the gap in the mountain range.

"Our drones would've gotten more of them if it hadn't started raining," the Sergeant said.

"Well I can't give your drones all the credit. Kugi, here, took out at least half of them."

"Good job, uh, Kugi is it?" the Sergeant asked.

"We don't have time to chat," I said. "They have Montana."

The Sergeant gave me a questioning look.

"The blonde reporter. They killed her cameraman and kidnapped her. They left me a note. I'm supposed to meet them about a mile from here. Unarmed and alone. I've got to go now before it gets dark."

The Sergeant's dark brown eyes met mine. He had the look of a surgeon baring bad news. "They'll kill you."

His tone was so matter-of-fact, a shudder rippled through me.

The Sergeant looked away, rubbed his chin, and then fixed his gaze on me.

"They left you a note?" he asked. "Why do they want you?"

"It's a long story," Carl said. "He's turned on his cell phone, can you track him?"

"I've got a drone up there that can sense infrared. That's how we found you two. We'll track him to the rest of the force and go from there."

"Whatever that means," I said. "I'm leaving." I handed Carl my weapons, turned, and stiff legged my way south.

Chapter 71

Slopping through the mud and rain puddles in the near darkness, alone and unarmed, had not been a good idea. Not only was I vulnerable, I had no one to talk to, no one to divert my thoughts. Sergeant Mason's blunt warning echoed in my mind, "They'll kill you."

Did my grandfather hate Sikhs enough to kill his own grandson? If he had the chance, he'd definitely kill my father, the man who stole his daughter away from both him and Islam. But would Masoud Omar kill a blood relative, his daughter's son?

The image of the pile of dead Sikhs in Sar Kand Ow Baba Ziarat amplified the Sergeant's words.

Masoud's note didn't promise me safety. Nor did it promise to release Montana. So why was I going? Did I believe my grandfather would tell me where my grandmother was and then release Montana and me?

Did he just want to meet his grandson? Or did he have another purpose?

Montana had to have told him my father was in Afghanistan.

Masoud Omar hated my father. That hatred had to have fermented in him for all these years of missing his daughter and thinking of her with a Sikh. Finally, he had been awarded a means of releasing his hatred, power, the command of a region of Taliban militia. He had to have started this Sikh genocide because of my father.

A deductive thought stopped me in the downpour. Masoud Omar didn't want me, he wanted my father. I pounded my fist against my palm. Why hadn't I realized his intentions before leaving Carl?

My grandfather was going to use me as bait to capture and kill my father.

My knees became untrustworthy, I needed to sit down. I had been so stupid. Why hadn't I seen through my grandfather's ruse when I read his note? Maybe Carl and I could have planned something.

Wobbling on unsteady legs, I shook my head. I hadn't accrued enough hate in my life to think like these people. I had no business being here. My grandfather's intentions were on the other end of life's spectrum from mine. His purpose was life-ending vengeance, while mine was life-enhancing love.

If I went to this rendezvous I could be responsible for my father's death. I shook my head, I couldn't imagine being responsible for Pops' demise.

I stood in the rain, stuck in mental quicksand.

I should turn around and get Carl and try to find my father and grandmother and take whoever was still alive in my father's family out of this horrible country.

But what about Montana? I didn't want to think about what she was going through. And if I turned around and didn't meet with the escort, she'd most likely be killed.

If my grandfather killed Montana, Carl would never forgive me and probably wouldn't leave until he terminated Masoud or was killed, and most likely the latter.

I owed my friend, Carl, and I more than liked Montana. I didn't want either of them to die.

What if I could talk to Masoud Omar and reason with him? Maybe I could get him to stop killing Sikhs. After all, he was my grandfather. Maybe I could arrange for him and Mom to meet, somewhere safe, like England or France?

What was I thinking? How could I reason with a man I didn't know anything about, except he was a killer. He'd joined the Taliban and fought against the Russian when my mom was a teenager. Apparently he had been a soldier most of his life, how else could he be a General? He had been subjected to the horrors of war for decades. Taking of lives and the loss or maiming of friends and family. All the death, with its finality and horrible imprint of smell and visual gore, had to have brutalized him. He had to have lived a life tormented by his emotions; the never-ending fear, sadness, and hate, deprived of normalcy, without his family. He had to be a man plagued with the long list of war-related ugliness, the list I now knew too well. In my brief exposure, I had changed. What would twenty or more years of fighting do to a man?

Why would a hardened man like Masoud ever listen to a naïve American college kid like me?

Because of my father, Masoud hated Sikhs. And now he had the opportunity to capture and kill the man who had ruined his life, my father.

Masoud Omar would probably laugh at my selfish pleadings.

This had to be a trap, a death trap for Pops.

I was cornered, boxed in, stuck. If I went on, Pops could die. If I went back, and were lucky enough to get my family out of here alive; Montana would die, and Masoud would continue to murder Sikhs, probably with a stronger fervor than before. He'd kill hundreds more and probably Carl as well.

I glanced up, the light was fading. I had to do something.

The risks of going on had cemented my legs in place.

Then I thought of my mom, the kindest, most compassionate human being I had ever known. How could a man create and raise such a person without having some of those traits himself?

I stood there and shook my head splaying water off the brim. My mother's father wouldn't kill me, no way. No matter how hardened he had become, he wouldn't hurt me. I just knew it. But would he care if I hated him? That was the leg stopping question.

Then I thought about my dad. If Pops were in my fixed shoes, what would he do? Would he risk my life to save hundreds of others? Knowing my dad, he would figure out a way to save all of us, me, Montana, Carl, Biji, and the remaining Afghan Sikhs.

All these mental perturbations left me with only two choices. Either I had to convince my grandfather to stop murdering Sikhs or I had to kill him. In either case, I had to confront him.

I'd let my stomach acid gnaw on the risks.

Digging a compass out of my pack, I verified I was faced south. I summoned my energy reserves and moved toward the rendezvous at an increased pace through the dense rain.

I had to try.

Chapter 72

The rain continued as did I, heading south by myself. I glanced up at the black clouds and prayed there was a drone up there somewhere tracking me.

I had been humping for about twenty-five minutes. Based upon the rough terrain and my stiff-leg gait, I calculated that I should reach the rendezvous location in the next ten minutes.

My race with the sun would be close. I checked my watch. I guessed I had about twenty minutes of light left.

What would Carl do if he were here? I picked up my pace. I needed time to scout the area before exposing myself.

I had never seen rain this dense. The visibility was less than one-hundred feet. The terrain changed, I was going up a gentle grade.

Dozens of elephant-sized rock outcroppings appeared, causing me to alter my course as I weaved through them. Every rock made me wary. It would be so easy for a man, or several men, to hide in ambush among all these boulders.

It had taken me a long time, too long, to learn that my nerves, like my appetite, would take control unless my focus was diverted. I was going to a rendezvous. Somewhere, someone was waiting for me. So what if it was behind one of these rocks? I had more important things to think about, like what I would say to my grandfather.

My quickened pace was slowed by the increase steepness of the terrain. Plus the rain made the rocks slippery. I checked my watch, I had to be close.

A few paces later, a mass of stone spread before me and rose into the blackness above. This had to be the place. There was nowhere else to go. My eyes swept the area in front of me. I couldn't see anyone. I moved closer and then I saw it, to my left, a black jagged void, a cave. This was just what I needed, another dark, probably bat-infested hole in the earth.

Montana had to be in there. There wasn't anywhere else she could be. What was it about Montana and I and caves? Well at least we'd be out of the rain.

I limped-ran to the base of the mountain, twenty or thirty yards from the entrance. I removed my backpack and found a flashlight. I flicked the switch and, thank God, it worked. I turned it off.

Checking all around me, I edged my way to the mouth of the cave. I stubbed my toe on a hefty stone. Instead of cussing, I picked it up. Carl was right; I should've brought a damned gun.

Stopping next to the entrance, I peered around the corner. Light flickered off the cave wall about thirty feet inward, the light source around a bend. I stepped inside and could smell wood burning. Warmth, dryness, and maybe death awaited me around that bend.

With my back to the mountain, I looked into the rain-filled grayness, into the direction I had come. I so wanted to run, as fast as my gimpy leg would take me, back to Carl, back to all those Marines.

A thought pressed me against the rock face. My grandfather wouldn't allow himself to be trapped in a cave. He had to have a perimeter set up, a means of escape. I couldn't go back now, I'd be stopped. Hell, I couldn't go back anyway. This whole trip, my purpose for being here, hinged on the two choices awaiting me in that cave.

I put the flashlight back in my pack and sat the stone on the cave floor. Neither of them would help me now.

I took a deep breath and eased it out through pursed lips. My grandfather, my blood relative, my parents' best kept secret, had arranged this meeting. It was time we met, long overdue. I needed to be in control, calm, cool, confident.

I limped to where the smooth cave walls turned. There was no going back now.

I touched my vest, my only defense, and stepped into the light.

Chapter 73

The bend in the cave led to a domed enclosure, the end of the cave. I scanned the domed area. Other than one person and a pile of dry fire wood, the stone room was empty.

Montana lay unmoving on her side on the cave floor next to a blazing fire. Her back faced me and her chest faced the fire. Her hands were tied behind her back and the rope linked her tied hands to her feet. Her water darkened blonde hair smeared across the shoulders of her jumpsuit.

I prayed she was alive.

Relieved and yet disappointed I hadn't met my grandfather, I half whispered, "Montana."

"Kugi?" Her head moved, and she strained to look over her shoulder. Those stretched-open beautiful blue eyes came to rest on me.

I hopped-skipped my stiff leg to her side. My leg hadn't bothered me since Carl had wrapped it. But when I bent to kneel next to her, the wounds pulled open and burned as if some of the nearby blazing logs had been laid on them.

Gritting back my desire to moan, I pulled out my knife and cut her bindings.

She slowly pushed up into a sitting position, turned, and faced me. A wisp of relief tinted the hurt etched on her face.

She reminded me of a homeless street person, oblivious to her personal condition, desolate and hopeless. Her face smudged with dirt. Her dirty, wet hair matted to her head. Her soggy, grit-crusted jumpsuit unzipped to her abdomen. Void of underwear, red blotches dotted her exposed skin.

Someone, probably many, had removed her dignity shortly after they removed her underwear.

Her tongue wiped over her cracked lips. "Thank God, you—you're here." Her eyes swept the entrance to the room behind me. "Where's . . . where's Carl?" She grabbed my arm and her questioning eyes explored mine. "Is he, ah, is he okay?"

"He's had better days, but he's okay. He's with the Marines. They're following me." I motioned with my hand. "Where are your guards? There was supposed to be an escort here to meet me."

"An escort? I don't know. Three of them . . . they dumped me here, built the fire, and—"she looked away and her expression changed as if she saw something awful and then she tried to sniff her reaction away—"and, ah"—her voice broke into sobs.

I wrapped my arms around her and hugged her. Her limp body shuddered against me with each sob. I wanted to hold her until she had no more pain, no more memories. I wanted to assure her nothing bad would ever happen to her again as long as she hugged me.

An emotion I had been pigeon-holing for the past several hours forced its way into reality; I wanted to kill the men who had hurt her, each and every one of them, slowly. I envisioned killing them as a source of joy and accomplishment.

What had I become and would I ever be the man I used to be? And if not, how would I ever be able to function back home, if I ever got there?

Montana pressed into me, erasing my thoughts. My concentration converged onto every square inch of where our bodies touched.

She quieted. Her body became rigid and she pushed back to arms' length. "The sons-of-bitches left," she wiped her face on her sleeve, "about ten minutes ago, after . . . after each of them had his fun." She closed her eyes and shook her head. "God, there have been so many, so many." Her eyes opened and squinted, creasing her temples and brow. I—"

"Shhhh." I touched her cracked lips with my finger and pulled her back into my arms. I eased her head onto my shoulder and stroked her wet hair.

She nestled her face into the crook of my neck. Her warm breath bathed my skin. Her hands caressed my back. The heat from her body overwhelmed the cold dampness of our clothing.

Nothing else mattered, my leg, the pain, this fucked up country, my inhuman Taliban grandfather, nothing. This frail, abused woman was the focus of every fiber of my being. She had become the center of my world, my reason for being here. I wanted her to be dependent on me. She feed my craving for her to need me. No one had ever needed me, not like this. She was so soft and warm, so everything wonderful. I had never experienced such bliss. My desire to have her in my life peaked. My desire to kiss her and tell her things I had never told anyone before was all I could think about. I was totally out of control and didn't care.

Courage and boldness took a backseat to need, mutual need.

I eased her head away from my neck. Our faces, our lips just inches apart.

"Montana!" Carl stood at the entrance, dressed in a clean, dry jumpsuit with his arm in a white medical sling.

Chapter 74

It was like being awakened just shy of having the most wonderful dream ever. I had been mere inches away, less than a second from kissing Montana, touching and tasting her scared lip, when Carl arrived.

Shit!

Carl rushed across the cave floor to where Montana and I sat, cuddled by the blazing fire.

Montana pulled away from my arms. She pinched the sides of her unzipped jumpsuit closed and stood on wobbly legs. She took a weak step, faltered, and collapsed into Carl; his good arm grasped her waist and supported her.

The cool cave air bathed my chest, stealing her warmth along with my peaked emotions and physical wants. In a nanosecond, I had transitioned from a state of ecstasy to being cold and alone in a foreign place. No wonder babies cried at birth.

I got my good leg under me and stood. Invisible knives stabbed my thigh and calf. Who cared?

I hopped away from the embraced couple, my back to their swooning eyes, out of ear shot from their endearing whispers.

Who needed a dry warm cave anyway? I needed the cold saturating rain. I needed to have my foolishness and stupidity washed away.

I limped out of the domed room. The tunnel was filled with light forcing me to shield my eyes with my floppy hat. I hesitated for a step thinking there really was a train at the end of the tunnel.

I moved forward into the light streaked with thousands of raindrops.

The heavy, cold rain greeted me, splattering on my wide brimmed hat and shoulders. Several of the trucks from the pass faced the cave, idling, headlights on high. A dozen or more Marines stood in the shadows, braced with weapons, behind the trucks.

I bowed my head, shook it, and released a steam cloud of exasperation. How could I ever think this was about me? None of this insanity was about me. Clinched teeth and fisted hands didn't divert my disgust, my failure. In one selfish moment, I had uncaringly abandoned everything important to me, my scruples; my self–control; my purpose for being here; and most of all my friendship with a man who was risking his life for me.

A thought added to my burden of self-loathing, forcing my bowed head to chin-bottom on my chest. How long had Carl been standing there?

Chapter 75

The darkness and the cold rain didn't help my mood. I was back to where I had started; no, I was worse. I had no clue where my grandmother or my father was and I had probably pissed off my best friend. And who knew what my Taliban grandfather's intentions were?

A deep voice called to me, pulling me out of my self-loathing funk. It sounded like Sergeant Mason. "What's going on in the cave? Who's in there? Any bad guys?"

I held a hand up to shield my eyes from all the lights. I shook my head. "Just the woman, she's alone."

"Johnson, form a perimeter guard and turn out those damned lights. And you, ah, Kugi, come here and get out of the rain. You and I need to talk."

The time factor for morphine coupled with all the bending I had done along with all the walking had awoken my wounds. I grimaced as I hobbled toward the voice. Then the lights went out, stopping me until my eyes adjusted.

The frozen moment returned my focus to my purpose. I needed to get out of here and head to Biji's village. Knowing Pops, he'd be there or close by.

Carl and his arm needed rest. He and Montana could use some time to heal together, him physically, her mentally. I prayed he hadn't been standing there watching Montana and I too long. I both wanted and needed his friendship post-Afghanistan, if I ever got there.

Through the pouring rain in the darkness, I could now distinguish faint images, grays versus blacks. One of those black images held the Sergeant who wanted something from me. Maybe I could manipulate a favor or two from him in return.

"Over here," Sergeant Mason hollered. Obviously patience wasn't one of his stronger traits.

Locking my knee, I limped to a nearby silhouette of a truck. As I got closer, I could see it was the Humvee the Sergeant had loaned Montana and her cameraman, what seemed like a year ago.

I climbed into the passenger's seat of the idling vehicle. It was good to get out of the cold hard rain and off my leg.

"Is, ah, is the woman alright?" he asked, the outline of his face fixed forward not looking at me.

"Although she's alive and has no visual wounds, she's not good."

"Fuckers." He spit more than spoke the word as if it was refluxed stomach bile. "Days like this make me want to extend my tour." He leaned back, jammed his right hand in a pants pocket, and rummaged. "Most of these Taliban are young kids, too stupid to have a mind of their own. They're given a gun, some half-assed training, some ultra-conservative religious cause, and then allowed, or most probably commanded, to do all the most horrific things humans can do to one and other." He pulled his hand out of his pocket. "The leaders are the ones we need to eliminate. Without them, none of this would be happening."

I looked out into the blackness, not replying. His focus on the Taliban leaders had me concerned.

He stuck something stubby into his mouth. "Mind if I smoke?"

"No, not if you open a window."

He cracked a window and thumbed a lighter to flame. The light danced over his flat features as he held the flame to the end of a half-smoked cigar, puffing and puffing until the tip remained a mixture of orange and red. He extinguished the lighter's flame leaving the cab interior shadowed in a dim pink glow. The wafting smell reminded me of a college professor I had whose clothes reeked of cigar smoke.

He blew a cloud of smoke toward the window. "What's your last name, Kugi?"

"Singh, it's the Joneses for Sikhs." I opened my window an inch to create a cross flow to help the smoke out his window.

Sergeant Mason removed the cigar from his mouth, turned the lit end toward him, and checked the burn. "So you're a Sikh?" The cigar returned to the corner of his mouth. "And you and your buddy Carl came here to save someone?"

In a puffed glow of the cigar, his eyes fixed on mine.

"My grandmother." I didn't like where he was going but at least it took my mind off my leg.

"So why does a Taliban General want to see you, Kugi?"

I released a long sigh. "He's my grandfather."

"What? That . . . that makes no sense. The Taliban are Muslims, they're not—"

"He is a Muslim. Years ago, my father, a Sikh, impregnated the General's Muslim daughter, my mother, and ran away with her to the US. That's why he hates Sikhs and, now that he's a General, why he is killing all he can find."

"Damn." He took a puff, the glow lighting the blue-gray smoke filled interior. "Makes sense now. And you and your family really didn't have a way to save your grandmother except to come here."

I rubbed my bandaged forehead. "That's what the General hoped would happen."

"You're lucky he wasn't here. He probably would've killed you."

"I don't think he really wants to harm me, it's my father he wants."

"Where's your father?"

"Unfortunately, somewhere in country looking for his mother."

"Oh shit."

I pushed back into the seat and angled my body toward him. I needed to study his reactions to what I was about to say.

"Carl needs medical attention, and he and Montana need some healing time. I could use some help."

He puffed. "Like what?"

"Have you ever heard of Nanakpur?"

"No."

"It's a small village northwest of Kabul, probably sixty or seventy klicks from here. Think you could use one of those choppers to drop me off there? That's where my grandmother lived and my father is probably there."

The Sergeant rubbed his square chin and looked down. "I could get in a whole heap of trouble if I did that. What's in it for me?"

"If I can find my father and hopefully my grandmother, maybe we could set a trap for that Taliban General, my grandfather, Masoud Omar."

Sergeant Mason's head snapped toward me, eyes enlarged. "Masoud Omar is your grandfather?"

My palms out and up, I said, "Yeah."

"Don't you know who he is?"

"Yeah, haven't you been listening, he's a damned Taliban General."

"Have you ever heard of Amir Mullah Mohammed Omar?"

His tone insinuated I should know this man. I hated being ignorant so I searched my memory carefully. Finally I shrugged my shoulders. "No, don't have a clue."

"Mullah Omar is the head of the Taliban, the top dog, and your grandfather's brother. Now that Bin Laden is dead, Mullah probably tops the CIA's 'most wanted list.' And he's your great uncle."

Chapter 76

I stared out of the Humvee's windshield into the darkness. Why hadn't Pops told me my great uncle was the world leader of the Taliban? What else had he and Mom kept from me?

A light bounced on the cave floor twenty or thirty yards in front of us. The light stopped at the mouth of the cave and then searched the darkness until it found the cab of the Humvee and my face.

I blocked the light with a hand. "Will you help me?" I asked Sergeant Mason.

"Yes, but this is going to have to go up the chain. It's above my pay grade, plus it'll take some major planning."

"No. I can't risk a big operation where one little miscue by someone could cause my grandmother or father getting hurt. I just need transportation to Nanakpur, some weapons, and your help convincing Carl we're all going back to the base. He's done more than enough for me. He's too emotional right now and he's hurt. I don't want to be responsible for getting him killed."

"So you want me to lie to my commanders and to Carl?"

"No. Just tell Carl we're all taking choppers out of here. And you won't be able to tell your commanders what you don't know. I'll have to set up something and then call you."

He pulled on the high-beamed headlights.

Carl, with Montana clutched in his good arm, stood in the cave's entrance. Montana held a flashlight.

Sergeant Mason pushed a button on a shoulder-mounted microphone. "Johnson, go help those two into your truck and let's head back to the choppers. Tell them you're taking them

269

back to the base. And Johnson, take the lead, and as soon as you get to the choppers, load them with the Lieutenant and some troops, and get them out of here before I get there." He released the button and puffed a plume of smoke. His eyes studied me. "You've got to realize that if I drop you by yourself into some Sikh village, you'll probably get your grandmother, father, and yourself killed."

"Or maybe get you credit for capturing Mullah Omar's brother."

He levered the truck into gear. "Okay, kid, it's your family and probably your funeral."

Chapter 77

Two helicopters had lifted and disappeared into the darkness by the time Sergeant Mason and I, along with four other soldiers, climbed on board one of the smaller gunships.

I strapped myself into a seat and Sergeant Mason conferred with the pilot. Thanks to Carl and Sergeant Mason, I had my trusted M14 rifle in hand as well as my pistol. Carl had stowed our equipment in the Humvee before he and the Sergeant had tracked me.

On our way to the landing zone, I had sorted through my backpack. I kept about two hundred US dollars worth of Afghanis, local money I had obtained at the base. The rest, a little over a thousand US dollars, I gave to the Sergeant to give to Carl. For some reason, I trusted the Sergeant, though I wasn't sure it mattered what happened to my money. Who could count on tomorrow?

The Sergeant leaned over the pilot's shoulder and they talked. Their words were masked by the idling engine over our heads.

Sergeant Mason, bent at the waist, turned to return to his seat.

The pilot yelled over his shoulder, "Okay, Staff Sergeant, but you need to get this cleared before we lift off."

The Sergeant keyed his shoulder mounted mic twice. "Lieutenant Kastings, Sergeant Mason," he yelled over the motor. "I was told by the kid—"

"Who?" A voice blasted from his speaker.

"The Sikh kid we followed here. He said the band of Taliban might be hiding out in a small village about fifty klicks from here. With your permission, I thought I'd go scout the place on the way home."

"Okay, Sergeant, but if you see activity, do not engage. I'll keep the choppers loaded at the base and await your findings. Where are you going?"

The Sergeant hollered into his mic, "A small village near Kabul called Nanakpur."

"Good hunting."

Sergeant Wilson disconnected, nodded at the pilot, and took a seat next to me. He strapped in, put on a headset, handed me one, and motioned for me to put it on.

I donned the earphones and had instant silence until Sergeant Mason spoke.

"You heard the man, Lieutenant Zak. We're a go. Take this bucket of bolts to Nanakpur, a hop, skip, and pole vault northwest of Kabul."

The frequency of the chopper's vibrating floor panel rose to a buzz. Then my seat pushed against my butt and I clutched my safety belt with my free hand and held my rifle with the other. I looked out through the windows but saw only blackness. I had no relativity. A moment later, the nose of the chopper tilted and my back was pressed into the seat. I prayed the aircraft was fast, because my disoriented inner ear and compressed stomach didn't want to be in these modes very long.

Sergeant Mason leaned forward, reached across me, and touched the soldier sitting next to me. "Hey, Kansas, is that you?"

"Yeah, Sarge."

"Give this kid your radio and all your M14 ammo." He nudged my side. "You need anything else, Kugi?"

I patted the pistol strapped to my leg for assurance. "Just off this thing." I clutched my stomach.

"First ride?"

I nodded.

272

"It takes a little getting used to," the Sergeant said. "Try to relax. This won't take long."

I busied myself by filling my pockets with a half dozen clips of ammo handed to me by the soldier. In the dim light from the instrument panel, Kansas looked too young to be in the service. I guessed him to be eighteen. The young man pulled me forward and put something in my backpack. Then, he pushed me back and attached the radio to my shoulder. He took my hand and placed my index finger on a button.

"That button turns the radio on. You can than activate anytime, it's in a hands free voice activation mode. If you want it off, push the button again."

"Thanks," I said. "How old are you?"

"Eighteen."

"How long you been in country?"

"Ten days."

"I can't remember my first ten days," the pilot said. "Let's pray you both get to that point. Now knock off the chatter. The head sets are for information pertinent to the operation only."

I leaned back, closed my eyes, and wondered how banged-up Carl was handling Montana in her violated condition. I couldn't imagine the strain her condition must put on their relationship.

The ship bounced several times as if we had hit a series of pot holes. The floor continued its noiseless hum under my feet, although I could sense the horrific noise lurking on the other side of my earphones. My stomach gurgled near eruption.

I cleared my mind. I needed to focus on what I was going to do when I got to Nanakpur; what Carl would do.

Chapter 78

The good news was the rain had stopped; the bad news was the dense cloud cover blackened the night. There was nothing to see, nothing to hear, nothing to do, but sit, strapped into the flying helicopter.

My mind floated in the nothingness suspended like the vibrating chopper in the dark. I don't know if my exhaustion, my fears, or my blank surroundings caused my mind to drift, but the escape from the tension relaxed me. I wanted to stay in this state of limbo. I leaned my head back and closed my eyes. My body eased into a numb mass, joining my mind adrift in a soft, peaceful void.

"Staff Sergeant."

I opened my eyes and jerked upright. Blackness engulfed me except for some multi-colored lights on a panel in front of me. I had no idea where I was. Then Sergeant Mason's resonant baritone along with the buzzing floor helped me piece together my surroundings.

"Yes, Lieutenant Zak."

"We're over Nanakpur. There aren't any signs of life, no infrared images, no lights, no fires, nothing. It's about seven-thirty and these small villages always have some signs of life at this time of night. The place is either deserted or we're expected. What do you want to do?"

I yawned and shook myself fully awake. Everything came roaring back, my blood-smeared trip, the painful sacrifices, my fears, all of the things that had brought me to this place and my purpose. Had I really thought this through? The pilot, who had a hell of a lot more experience than me, knew these villages. He had probably flown over hundreds of small hamlets like Nanakpur at night and landed in many. The man had to know what he was saying when he said, "This place is either deserted or we're expected." Going into a place I didn't know, by myself, in the dark, not knowing who may be there was crazy. My getting captured or killed would only make things worse for my father and grandmother.

I rubbed my beard. It was too late for hindsight. Nanakpur had been my destination since the beginning of the journey. Now I was here. I had to go into the village. So I'd be alone; my grandmother had probably been alone for a long time.

I could sense the Sergeant's eyes on me.

"Drop me off, Sergeant," I said, my rested voice flat and lifeless. "I'll let you know what I find."

"Take her down, Lieutenant," Sergeant Mason said.

The chopper nosed down and banked hard left.

Sergeant Mason grabbed my arm. "Turn that radio on and leave it on, you hear me?"

"Yes, Sergeant," I said. The man made me feel like a boot camp private as I activated my radio.

The helicopter slowed, leveled, and hovered.

"Hot zone stations," the pilot commanded.

My nerves didn't need to hear those words. I sucked in a large breath of air and exhaled slowly.

Doors slid, cool wind blew, and men took positions behind side-mounted machine guns.

The Sergeant tugged on my arm again. "And, Kugi, if your grandfather is down there stay away from him. Hide and call me. Don't let your blood lines corrupt your logic. Remember who you're dealing with."

How could I ever forget or forgive Masoud Omar? The images of Mannik racing to save those bomb-strapped children, the stack of dead Sikhs, and the hurt in Montana's eyes had been branded into my mind.

275

I patted his hand on my arm. "Thanks, Sergeant Mason. I won't forget all you've done for me and my family."

My seat dropped out from under me and my stomach. The floor hummed at a different frequency. And suddenly the world below me lit up. We were dropping onto a dirt road that, a few hundred yards away, bisected two rows of huts, Nanakpur. Then my body bottomed into the seat as the chopper met the ground.

The landing lights went out returning the exterior to pitch-black darkness.

I removed the headset and was blasted by the noise of the engine. I unstrapped and stood bent at the waist, my rifle in one hand, the other holding my floppy hat on my head. Grabbing the door frame, I climbed out of the chopper. Crouched under the rotating blades, I jogged stiff-legged away from the chopper into the ebony, into what my mouth and eyes told me was a cloud of dust. The engine revved and the rotor wash pelted me with ground debris. I was forced to close my eyes and shield my face with the brim of the hat. When the wind and dust subsided, I opened my eyes. I was alone, left with nothing but darkness and the whopping noise of safety growing fainter and fainter.

Chapter 79

I stood on a dirt road, just outside of the village of Nanakpur. My wounds ached, I was alone and exhausted, and it was too dark to see, but I was here. Finally I was at my grandmother's village, after all this time. How long had I been in country, a week, maybe ten days? It had to have been longer than that. I tried to recount, had it only been five days? The days seem to all smear over each other with no nights, and little if any sleep.

Regardless of how long it had taken, the journey was behind me. I hoped and prayed my past would be the ugliest memory in my life. I didn't want to think about my future. I was too tired to think, too tired to move, but I was here, in Nanakpur.

Standing here in the dark produced nothing but more anxiety, I had to move, I had to explore this little hamlet.

I blindly hand-checked both my rifle and pistol and made sure they each had rounds chambered.

Now if only I could see.

My eyes were adjusting to the blackness and I could discern nearby lumps of grey versus black, buildings or huts, something other than blackness. I took an agonizing step in the direction of the structures and then was stopped by a thought.

Nanakpur was a Sikh village named after Guru Nanak, the founder of Sikh religion. Also Nanakpur was the birthplace for my Pops and the home of his mother and his deceased father. For some reason, long ago, a group of Sikhs decided to settle here and call this place home.

I tossed the floppy hat on the ground and laid the rifle on top of it. Next, I took off the poncho and my backpack. My fingers fumbled in the pack until I found my turban, my Sikh turban. After retying my hair, I wrapped my turban on my head. A Sikh was coming home, to the place where his grandparents had started a family.

If there were Taliban hiding in this village, so be it. I was Sikh. If I died tonight, I'd die a Sikh.

Being alone, unable to see, and not knowing what or who was in this village made it difficult to swallow let alone think. But when a gust of wind made me check my turban, my fears remained but lost control. Although my mouth was dry, my back was straight and my hands study.

I stowed my hat and poncho in my pack and slid the backpack over my shoulders. Cradling the M14 in my hands at hip level, I limped toward the village, each step a focused, jaw-clinching effort. The weapon was no longer just a rifle; the M14 had become my protective shield, my means of surviving, my friend.

A small one story stone hut took form to my right as I stepped through the darkness. I ducked below the side window and edged my way to the front corner. I peered around the front of the hut and more listened than looked.

The longer I listened, the more things I heard, inhuman things. Crickets chirped, an owl hooted in the distance, cicadas sang their brief but repeated song, and frogs croaked. In the background, water flowed somewhere behind the huts, a river. Owls and cicadas meant there were trees nearby and frogs were either in a pond or the stream. My backyard at home had taught me as a kid that all these noises only exist if there isn't a person or people close. I was alone. The thought by itself was depressing, but the fact that I had come all this way not to find either my grandmother or father alive caused my knees to buckle. I slid down the rough hut until my butt found the ground. I had never been so tired.

This was all a mistake, me and Pops coming to this damned country. I had known, before I had left home, the probabilities of finding Biji alive hadn't justified the risks. And coming to this village alone was almost as foolish. Maanik's horrible death and the rest of all the killing I had done could have been avoided. I'd still be an innocent, naïve, college graduate hunting for a job instead of a combat-hardened man burdened with nightmare-spawning memories. But no, Pops and I had to come here.

I leaned my head back against the hut and closed my eyes. I'd let what was left of Mother Nature's animal world in this war torn country sing me to sleep. Besides it was too dark to do any scouting. Carl would understand. I'd check out the village at first light. Right now, I needed rest, sleep.

And then as if someone had thrown a switch, all the noise stopped except the flowing water.

Chapter 80

The birds, frogs, and insects had quieted. I wasn't alone in this dark village. My eyes flipped open and I pushed up on my undamaged and yet weak leg to a standing position. My wounds ached, but I didn't care. I eased my head around the corner of the hut and looked into the darkness, nothing.

But then I heard a faint 'putt-putt' noise. The noise grew louder and I saw a bouncing haloed light in the distance approaching from the other end of the village. I pressed the rifle's stock into my shoulder, braced my support arm against the rough stone joint of the hut, and tracked the light through the scope.

As the 'putt-putts' grew louder, I recognized the sound. It was just like one of those Italian made scooters I'd seen back in Cincinnati. Some students rode them to school in the warm months.

As the hazy light came closer its bouncing beam outlined the village huts. I counted twenty-two, twelve on my side and ten on the other. The other side had an area in the middle of the village void of huts with a few trees. Maybe later, God willing, I'd climb one of those trees, a place to hide and sleep.

Sleep, I couldn't keep thinking about it, sleep would rule. I needed to be alert, aware, and afraid, not numb. This person could be a Sikh killer. I took a deep breath, exhaled, and shook every muscle in my body. The growing haze that had surrounded the scooter's light vanished.

The scooter slowed and stopped in front of a hut four down from the one I hid behind. The motor and the light were turned off, leaving me blind. My finger slid inside the trigger guard. Where was the rider? What was this person doing in this seemingly unoccupied village? Was this a Taliban scout? Was my grandfather and his band of killers close behind?

What should I do? Should I try to sneak up on this person? What if this person wasn't alone and there were others inside the huts? I could walk into a trap set for Pops. My turban wrapped hair prickled with sweat.

I decided to wait and see what happened next. Keeping the rifle aimed in the general direction of where the light had been, I eased my good leg down and rested on my knee.

A small light came on and shown on some saddle bags on the scooter. A small person, silhouetted in the light, removed something from a saddlebag on the scooter. Then the person followed the light across the road. This short mystery person was cloaked head to toe, in a burka. This mystery person was a woman.

What if . . . could this be? I bolted to my feet, shunned the pain, and lowered the rifle. I stepped toward this outline of a woman. I had come so far, been through so much, and was so tired. I had to know. The word foolishly, dangerously, leapt from my lips, "Biji?"

The silhouette stopped and so did my feet, my heart, my breath, and my good sense.

The light swung around and searched the huts until it came to rest on me, a frozen fool standing in the open.

I squinted into the light and raised my hand to shield my eyes.

"Who are you?" a female voice asked in Pashto.

"Is that you, Biji?" I asked. "I'm Kugi, Kugi Singh, your grandson."

"Kugi!" The jiggling light came at me, fast. "Oh thanks be to God, you're alive. I've been waiting here for days."

The voice sounded familiar, but it wasn't the voice of an elderly woman.

The veiled woman ran into my arms and hugged me. "I didn't think you'd ever come. I . . . I was afraid they . . . I'm so glad you're here." Her arms tighten around me.

The voice, the hug, her body, I knew this woman. I eased her to arms' length and took the light from her hand and shone it on her niqab-covered face. She removed the veil and Rashi Sundri's smiling, tear-streaked face glistened in the light.

Chapter 81

"Rashi, what . . . what are you doing here?" I asked, looking into her tear-glinted brown eyes in the glow of the flashlight. Though slightly bruised, her face was no longer swollen or bandaged. Her features combined to form a pretty backdrop for the smile of someone who had just found a missing loved one.

Why would she look at me like that? I was tired and couldn't trust my eyes or interpretations. But what was she doing here?

She sat down her bag and held out her arms, palms up. "You saved my son and me—"she dropped her arms and looked down for a second and then into my eyes—"you left us. We . . . I never had a chance to repay you. My husband," she blinked away an image, "and I had saved a little money, and I left most of it with my son. I used the rest to come here. Abdul and his wife, Nasiba—"her eyes read my reaction—"the young Sikh couple you left us with in Gerdi, agreed to help me. After the American woman left, Abdul drove me to Kabul, where I bought food, and then he brought me here, two days ago. And I—"

"You came here looking for me?" I asked. "Your son, Jodh, what happened to him?"

"He stayed with Nasiba. Abdul was going to take Jodh and his wife to Rawalpindi upon his return from Nanakpur, to Maanik's father's house." She yanked on the end of my jumpsuit sleeve. "But you didn't let me finish . . . I found her."

"Who?" I shook my head.

She raised her arms. "Your grandmother, Biji."

283

"What?" I staggered backward and leaned against the wall of the hut. "My grandmother, you found my grandmother?" I lurched forward and grabbed her arms. "Was . . . was she alive?"

She chuckled and smiled. "Very much so. She was fine. Your dad was taking good care of her."

"My dad?" I shook her. "You found my dad and my grandmother?"

She laughed and tears ran down her face into the dimples of her smile. "Yes, and they are fine. I took them to Kabul and—"

I kissed her on her thin pink lips. It was a reactionary peck, a gesture of thanks. She smelled like jasmine and her mouth was soft and sweet. My lips lingered along with my thoughts.

Biji and Pops were safe. This horrible trip would become memories, buried memories. Hopefully, the old Kugi would return and the calloused, cold, killing Kugi could be buried with the rest of the bloody experience.

This moment, this kiss opened a door to sanity and normalcy. I wanted to enjoy the moment and make it last as if it were my first kiss.

But this moment wasn't just about me. Poor Rashi, I had her clamped between my hands and my mouth. My hands gripped her arms so hard her shoulders scrunched up close to her ears. She must think I'm crazy.

I pulled away and looked at her face. Her eyebrows arched over her enlarged eyes. I wasn't sure if she was shocked, or questioning my act, or what. It didn't matter. My happiness and relief over my father and grandmother being alive and safe were all that mattered. The rest, her sweet mouth, my needs, her brave unselfish act for me, my ability to conquer my fears, and my mental numbness from fatigue, all of these things had merged to raise my joy to an unparalleled summit and brought my mouth back to hers.

She responded by sliding into my arms and kissing me back.

What was I doing, kissing a married woman? Though she had told me her husband had been killed, she had been

284

married, and not very long ago. Now she was a widowed mother, a dependent refugee with nowhere to go. Had I opened a door that would be difficult to close?

Her tongue found mine, raising my heart rate.

Why should I care about the past? This was a woman who had risked her life to find me, the woman who had searched out and found both my father and grandmother and had taken them to safety. And she wasn't pushing me away, far from it.

I hadn't kissed a woman, passionately, in so long. My pounding heart demanded more air. I approached the panting stage.

Using my flashlight and rifle holding hands, I pressed her body against mine.

I was tired; I couldn't trust my reactions to her responses. But I wasn't too exhausted to have forgotten where all this passion would take me if I let it. I wasn't sure it was right to go there. I should stop.

Rashi was a single mother who needed security for her son. She had to be desperate. Her needs trumped mine. I didn't want to mislead her or hurt her.

Her hands and fingers rubbed my back, finding the knots and kinks and messaging them. Like her lips and tongue, her hands were wonderful, beyond relaxing. Why would I even think about stopping this?

But prolonging this 'thank you' kiss, which had evolved way beyond gratitude, was taking advantage of a needy woman. I barely knew her and the chances of developing a relationship were miniscule. As soon as she took me to my family, I'd take Pops, Biji, and Carl, and we'd get out of this horrible country. This body-rubbing kiss was self-serving. My intentions were no better than the two Taliban men who had tried to rape her. This wasn't like me, or at least who I used to be.

As if she had read my thoughts, she pulled away. But then she tapped her fingers on my chest. "What is that?" Her words were panted more than spoken.

I gulped some air and touched my chest. "Oh, ah, that's my flak vest. Sorry."

Touching the vest revived a memory, my one last link with the outside world. I reached up and clicked off the radio.

"I came back here to tell you your family was safe." She rubbed my arms. "And I am so glad I did. I love how you kissed me."

She snuggled back into my arms and pressed her mouth to mine.

Her aggressive lips and tongue attacked and consumed my reluctance like a kid eating an ice cream cone on a hot summer day.

How could I not love how she tasted, or not enjoy her hands and her body against mine? I needed this and obviously, she did too. These huts had beds. All we needed was an hour or so. My eyelids flipped open. Without breaking our embrace, I would maneuver her to the hut's door.

The surroundings refocused my brain. We were in Nanakpur, a Sikh village, we couldn't stay here. This place was dangerous. We should leave now and go to Kabul, to my father and my grandmother. That was why I came here, along with Carl and Maanik. That was my purpose for this blood-trailed trip. This nightmare needed a happy ending. And staying a minute too long in this place could be disastrous.

Her hands went under my vest and found the zipper to my jumpsuit.

I gasped when her warm hands slid over the skin of my neck and shoulders, then down to my chest, touching, tweaking, and roving downward.

A body quake closed my eyes and caused me to stutter step back against the hut wall.

She moved with me, her mouth and hands glued to me, controlling me, owning me.

She was a young, pretty woman, and I was a young man. We both had needs. No one was being taken advantage of; we were a man and a woman responding to our natural, God-given

286

instincts. We had both been through hell and we both needed a tension release. Making love wasn't making a commitment; it was consenting to mutual pleasure, a gateway back to sanity.

Carl and Montana had had their release, their night of self-satisfying saneness, why shouldn't Rashi and I?

Her invasive arms wedged my jumpsuit zipper further down. All my thoughts melted into one; happy endings could always use some icing.

The rifle slid through my hand until the stock found the ground. I let it fall away. I stuffed the flashlight into my pants' pocket. My free hands roamed over her back, from her shoulders down to her round, flexed buttocks, caressing and pressing.

Our noses, sucking air as fast as possible, collided, and slid past each other as our lips rotated to a new position.

The point of no return for both of us was close, just a movement, a touch, another zipper tug, or button or two away.

I slid my left hand around to her waist, just below her breast.

My hand froze.

At first it was just a distant rumble, like thunder miles away. But the deep pounding grew louder and louder, until it became the distinct sound made by rolling trucks, many trucks.

Chapter 82

Rashi, panting, pulled away before I could push her there. I retrieved the flashlight and shone it on her. Her eyebrows pushed for a new height record and her mouth quivered.

"Rashi, get the scooter," I said as I zipped up my jumpsuit. "We must get out of here." I pointed to the direction I had entered, but then I saw lights coming from that direction. I looked the other way and lights were on that end of the road into town as well. I pointed across the street into the woods and she turned just in time to see beams bouncing through the woods toward us.

I grabbed her arm, bent down, retrieved my rifle, and ran to the scooter.

"The food." She twisted.

"Forget about it, there's no time," I said. "Push the scooter behind the huts."

"We are trapped," she said, her words vibrating with fear as she rolled the scooter off its stand.

We both knew what would happen to her if we were caught.

She leaned the scooter against the backside of a hut.

I grabbed her arm and pulled her away from the village.

"The river is about fifty meters behind the huts and the mountains are on the other side," she said. "There . . . there is nowhere to go."

"Can you swim?" I asked. I limped-ran, almost dragging her into the darkness behind the huts.

"No."

The closer we got to the river, the louder the water flowed. This was more than a stream. Roaring water meant a fast current. I was a strong swimmer. I had taken life-saving in high school. I'd get her across somehow. We didn't have a choice.

"How wide is the river?"

"Too wide and too deep. Maybe a hundred meters. And it is cold, mountain snow-shed water. If you try to swim me across, you will cramp up, and we will both drown. Teenagers drown in this river every summer. We are trapped."

"I am a good swimmer. I can—"

"Please," she shook her head. "I cannot do it . . . not the river."

We stood at the edge of the black ribbon slipping by us at a fast pace. I wrapped an arm around her slumped shoulders.

"That's why he wasn't at the cave," I said to no one. "He knew I would come here. And he could've been trapped in the cave. Here he can trap me. He probably sat outside the village and watched the chopper drop me off."

Enough Monday morning quarter-backing, I needed to get Rashi out of here. I pulled her along the bank searching for a log I could use to float us down river, out of this trap.

She grabbed my hand with both of hers and yanked me to a halt. "Who?"

I looked around the bank. There weren't any trees along the bank. I wasn't going to find a log. What a screwed up country, the only thing scarcer than trees was hope.

"My grandfather, Masoud Omar." I tugged her further along the bank.

"Mullah Omar's brother is your grandfather? Your grandfather is a Taliban General who has a Sikh grandson?"

I glanced back at the village; the huts were silhouetted in lights. "Yes. Now come on we've got to move."

"Why?" She stopped. "Why are we running?" she asked, her tone infected with optimism. "He won't hurt his grandson and hopefully he won't hurt the woman with him."

"You should tell that to all the dead Sikhs back in," I shook my head, "whatever that damned town was called. How can you trust a cold-blooded killer? I'd rather take my chances with the river."

It wouldn't take them long to find the scooter and then find us, minutes at best. I couldn't let them do to her what they had done to Montana. I couldn't.

Then I remember the radio.

Chapter 83

The Taliban truck lights lit up three sides of Nanakpur in the overcast night. Rashi and I stood at the river's edge on the northwest end of the town. With the wide, cold torrent at our backs, we were surrounded, trapped.

Hand-held waving, bouncing flashlights emerged behind the huts. It wouldn't be long before we were discovered.

I only had a few options, none of them good. I could call Sergeant Mason and tell him my grandfather and his militia were in Nanakpur. But the Sergeant wouldn't get here soon enough to prevent our capture or maybe killings. Another choice was to try to swim the river holding Rashi. The remaining choices were to surrender or to fight. We wouldn't last long in a firefight, there was no cover, and we were outgunned at least a hundred to one. The gun battle would probably take about as long as the raging, frigid waters of the river to end our lives.

I put my arm around Rashi and pulled her close, placing my mouth on her ear so she could hear me over the roar of the water.

"We're going to have to surrender or swim. And if we surrender, I won't be able to—"her fingers pressed against my lips.

She nodded her head, tiptoed up, and spoke into my ear. "I know." She glanced over her shoulder at the river. "If you try to swim the river holding me, we will both drown. And I am so afraid of water. I . . . I would rather take my chances with those maniacs. But you might be able to swim the river by yourself. I would not—"my mouth covered hers.

The kiss lasted but a moment, a sweet moment.

I stepped back. Unsnapping my holster, I removed my pistol and placed it with my rifle on the ground. I prayed surrendering wasn't a mistake. Rashi was so vulnerable. I had to make sure my grandfather had no reason to think Rashi even knew my father. If he did, he would make her talk. I'm sure he'd rather torture a Sikh woman than his Sikh grandson.

"I don't know how, but we will get through this. And after we do, I want to get to know everything about you."

"That sounds wonderful." She searched in the darkness and found my hand and squeezed it.

"There is something you must promise me."

She leaned against me and tiptoed up. "That will cost you another kiss."

"We don't have much time."

She wiggled her body into mine. "Just a little one."

I pressed my mouth to her warm, soft lips and reintroduced my tongue to hers.

She dropped my hand and slid both her hands under my vest.

I knew if she touched my skin again, this would not be a short kiss. I pulled back.

"Promise me, if the Taliban asks you where my grandmother or my father is, no matter what, tell them you don't know them. You came here because . . . because of me. Okay? No matter what."

Her hand stroked my bandaged cheek. "Well at least some of it is true. I promise."

I eased her soft, caring fingers from my cheek and turned on my radio. "Sergeant Mason, are you there? Hello."

"Yeah, Kugi, what's going on?"

His baritone voice gave me both hope and fear. He sounded so close, a comforting but useless stimulus.

I clutched Rashi and pulled her to my side. "There's a woman with me, Rashi Sundri, can you remember her name?"

"Rashi Sundri, got it."

I cleared my throat. "My grandfather and his horde are here. They have us surrounded, and we're going to surrender."

"Don't do that." The image of his piercing glare was conveyed by his tone. "I can be there in twenty minutes. Find a way to hold them off. Run, hide, or take a stand, but don't surrender."

"I knew that's what you'd say. But we have no choice. I'll leave the mic on until they take it. Don't come here. Do you understand me?"

"I hear you."

"If you and you chopper mounted cavalry come whopping in here, they will kill us. I'm going to try to talk to the old man. After all, he is my grandfather."

"Sergeant Thompson is going to be so pissed at me," Sergeant Mason said. "I should've never taken you there without at least setting a trap for those bastards."

"Masoud outsmarted both of us."

"I'm sorry."

The bobbing lights were closer, much closer.

"Tell Carl, ur, Sergeant Thompson, he's the best and Pops and Biji are safe in Kabul." A light found us. "I've got to go. May God bless you, Sergeant."

I raised my hands and motioned for Rashi to do the same and limped toward the lights.

Chapter 84

The bobbing flashlights became fixed when they shown on Rashi and me, followed by a burst of gunfire.

Rashi and I both flinched. My sensors double-checked my entire body searching for wounds, nothing.

A man yelled in Pashto, "We have found them, my leader."

At a moment when I should have been scared of dying, I was overwhelmed with curiosity. I was finally going to meet the mystery man, the man my parents had been keeping in the closet all my life.

"Move! To the village." A voice and a gun barrel prodded me.

Rashi and I, hands over our heads, walked into the lit street of Nanakpur, lighted by the headlights of at least thirty trucks. Most of these trucks were double-axle vehicles used for carrying heavy loads. The drone attack at the pass must have forced my grandfather to commandeer some of his poppy transports for this operation.

Hands grabbed my arms from behind, pulled them down and back, and bound them.

Two men grabbed Rashi. She screamed as they pulled her away.

"No!" I yelled in Pashto. "I am Kugi Singh, the grandson of Masoud Omar. The woman stays with me."

The two men wrestling with the struggling Rashi stopped.

A voice came out of the darkness, from the line of trucks, "So you think your bloodline gives you privileges?" The tone was deep and craggy, but firm. "You are a Sikh. Sikhs have no rights in Afghanistan, except to die."

A roar of agreement rose from the surrounding Taliban.

I fixed my eyes on Rashi. "She is with me. Wherever you take her, I go there as well. Whatever you do to her, you must do to me also."

She stopped squirming and looked at me like no woman had ever looked at me, a look of respect mixed with love and lust.

"So you want to be treated like a girl?" The craggy voice broke into a chuckle and the crowd joined in adding jeers and debasing remarks.

"Speaking of girls, why does a Taliban General hide in the darkness?" I asked. The night became quiet with only the faint noise of the distant river flow.

Something hard slammed into my kidney. The stabbing pain buckled my knees and dropped me to the ground. My shoulder's impact with the hard-packed road knocked my turban off and loosened my tied hair.

"No!" Rashi cried out.

My below-shoulder length hair whipped around as I writhed on the ground searching for a position to stop the pain.

"You squirm like a girl, and you have hair like a girl, maybe we should treat you like one." The voice was closer.

A pair of worn, dust covered, US Army boots, topped by dirty, black cotton pants, appeared at my eye level. I bit my lip to counter the relentless core of nausea in my lower back and looked up.

A bowed-back, lean man with a blue turban, failing to contain long oily white hair, stood over me. He wore a black long-sleeve tunic shirt, the collar up and the tail hanging over his pants. I thought the style of that shirt and the production had vanished with the Beatles.

I studied his face, looking for features relating him to my mother and to focus on something other than the pain. His crazed copper skin sagged all around a pair of inquisitive brown

295

eyes, topped by white bushy eyebrows. His weathered skin stretched over high cheek bones and drooped at his jaw line, flanking his narrow chin. His thin, straight nose, dotted with blackheads, flared into wide nostrils, shadowing a small, crack-lipped mouth.

Any resemblance to my mother had to have been eroded by age and too much exposure to the elements.

He scanned every square inch of me like I was an alien.

"And you claim to be my grandson?" When he opened his mouth to speak, at least half of his teeth were missing with the remainder blackened from betelnut. White foamed spittle gathered at the corners of his mouth. "Pick him up," he ordered someone behind me.

Rough hands grabbed my bound arms and pulled me to my feet. I rolled my lips together hard to squash a moan.

Fighting the lingering pain, I straightened my core and stood a head taller than the old man.

"I liked it better when I was looking down at you," he said with a sneer.

"At last, I meet the man who murdered my father's father," I said with as much disdain as I could muster.

He glanced away, chewed on something and then spit. When his eyes returned to mine, I knew I had made a mistake. His squinted eyes looked at me like I was a roach in his food. It took all of my self-control to keep from shuddering.

"Your child-stealing father tell you that?" he asked, spraying light-glinting specks of spit into the night air.

I held his eyes with mine, slowly shook my head, and lied for affect. "No, your daughter did."

Masoud looked down and away. "So, Raman has her believing his lies." He wagged his head. "How sad."

I strained against the bindings. "You killed him. That's all you know, killing." I sighed the anger away. "You murdered my grandfather when you found out your daughter had been impregnated by a Sikh."

"Daler's death was an accident!" His booming voice caused me to reel back.

I couldn't let him think I feared him. I leaned down close to his face. "How can you call a man with half his head shot off 'an accident'?"

He turned his head to the side, averted his eyes, and chewed. He took a deep breath and focused on someone behind me.

"Hameed, tie her to him, gag them, hood their heads, and put them in the bed of my truck. We need to get out of here." His eyes swung to me. "I'm sure he has—" his gaze stopped at my shoulder, the radio.

Masoud reached out and yanked the microphone and the loop of material it was clipped to, off my jumpsuit. His fingers traced the wire into my backpack.

I glanced at Rashi. Her upper teeth clamped her lower lip. Our link to the outside world, our salvation, was about to be severed.

He held the microphone to his mouth and in broken English said, "If you come, Kugi and the woman die."

How had this old man learned English? He had to have learned many things to aid his survival through all his years of fighting. Hell, he probably knew a bunch of Russian as well. He had taken the time to learn about his enemies.

I always thought Mom had a broader perspective about things than Pops, more worldly in her thinking. Hopefully, this old man and my mother were more alike than just intelligence.

"Hameed, untie him and remove his pack. Then tie him to her and throw his pack into the river. We must go, now!"

Chapter 85

Some uncaring son-of-a-bitch drove the dump truck cross country at a breakneck speed. I bruised my bruises as I bounced again and again on my right shoulder and hip onto the steel bed. I was helpless with my arms bound behind me tied to Rashi's back-bound arms. My discomfort was worsened by trying not to hurt Rashi when I bounced. No matter what I did, when I became air born, there was nothing I could do, I was out of control. I banged into her head, her legs, and landed on top of her several times causing air to whoosh out of her nose. I know how that hurt because she landed on top of me as well. Having a wounded leg and gagged with a hood over my head, added to my ordeal.

The ride lasted a zillion bucking potholes too long. The truck finally stopped, thank God. Rashi and I were dragged off the bed and stood on the ground. My right side, from my head to my feet, felt like a kid had tap danced on me. Back-to-back, Rashi and I wobbled against each other. Someone removed my gag and the tether joining Rashi and me. Being able to breathe through my mouth was almost as good as getting off that truck. Exhaust fumes hung in the air. I figured the convoy must have driven into a large cave. My hands remained bound behind me, and the hood stayed in place.

I prayed that Sergeant Mason had a drone tracking us. But even if he did, what would he do, blockade the entrance to the cave? My grandfather hadn't survived decades of fighting without an escape plan. The cave probably had multiple access tunnels. And I was sure the crusty ol' Sergeant knew that as well. Masoud Omar had earned his title and reputation and his longevity. We weren't going to be rescued, not tonight anyway.

Hands slipped a rope noose over my head, and I was led, limping and stumbling, next to Rashi. Our bodies collided on more than one occasion. My aching bruises became secondary to the fire lit in my leg wounds.

At one point, when we were shoulder to shoulder, Rashi whispered, "Kugi, because of you, I am no longer afraid."

"I have nothing to do with that. God is with you."

"But the devil is with these people," she said in a hushed tone.

"Who else would support the slaughter of woman and children?"

My rope yanked, and I stumbled.

"Be quiet," a male voice ordered.

Too many pain-filled steps later, Rashi whispered again, "Kugi, no matter what happens tonight, the taste of your kiss on my lips will get me through it. I ummm-ummm."

"I said be quiet."

A sweat-soiled rag was stuffed into my mouth. The foul taste and nose-breathing added to my plight.

Hopefully I would be allowed to lie down soon. Adrenaline, and very little of that, fueled my exhausted, air-starved body. I would've collapsed long before if it hadn't been for replaying over and over Rashi's news about Biji and Pops, Rashi's passionate kisses, and the meeting with my grandfather.

I was too tired to care about what happened to me now. My grandmother and father were safe. Pops had found his mother, and I had no doubt he would get her out of this country.

My ego and fears had blocked my faith in my father's abilities. My presence here hadn't been necessary. It was I who had failed, not Pops. I had become the liability. But I couldn't dwell on that thought now. I was too tired, and the costly conclusion was too painful.

The reason for this trip to hell had been accomplished. Nothing else mattered, except Rashi. Her life hung by a thread, a thread attached to me. Her survival was now my sole purpose.

The further we walked, the cooler the air. We were either descending or going deeper into a mountain. My inner ear failed to sense a downward slope, however, my stiff-legged limp probably helped fool my equilibrium.

What seemed like miles later, I was jerked to a halt, and a hand pushed me to the ground.

A muffled scream and shuffling of feet caused me to try to get up. A skin-splitting blow to the side of my head stopped me.

Brilliant spots of light flashed in the darkness behind my squinted closed eyelids. Rashi was gone, and I was spinning, spiraling downward. Waves of nausea and brow-sweating heat got worse and worse. I must—

Chapter 86

Consciousness returned with my head competing with my leg, both throbbing for attention. A cool wet cloth gently touched the side of my head. The gentle touch had to be that of a—Rashi. Rashi had to be caring for my new wound.

I forced my eyes open. The hood had been removed, and I had to blink away the brightness that greeted me. I was on my back, outside, looking up at the sun.

I tried to sit up, but a turban-wearing head appeared attached to a restraining arm. My hands were still bound behind my back.

"I have heard American youth sleep a lot, but you amazed me," a familiar male voice said in Pashto.

The voice registered and cleared my mental fog. Masoud Omar, my grandfather, had spoken to me.

I pushed up on an elbow. "Where's Rashi? The woman I was with. Where is she?"

I squinted and then saw the old man standing over me. My flack vest drooped on his frail frame. His pronounced jaw muscles and many of the lines in his forehead eased away. Had he been concerned for my condition? A man like him couldn't have feelings. He probably just had indigestion from living off the food he stole from poor people.

There were mountains behind him topped by a blue cloudless sky. I had no idea where I was or what time it was.

"The woman?" I asked again. He obviously needed to be reminded.

He swatted a hand at the air. "She is fine."

I pushed up to a seated position. A young Talib reached for me, and the old man held a stop-sign hand out.

"Bring her here. I want to see her."

"Later," he said.

"Why, what have your out-of-control zealots done to her?" I licked my dry lips. "How can you let them rape women and murder children and support their actions by saying 'In sa Allah'? Do you really think that's God's will?"

He looked away. "The woman is fine."

"Then bring her here. Let my eyes and ears tell me she is fine."

He gazed at the mountains for a moment as if expecting them to give him a response for me. "You do not believe your mother's father when he tells you something? Did your mother not raise you to respect your elders?"

I laughed.

He stepped away, momentarily straightening his bowed back.

His face turned to me. His facial scowl overwhelmed by his squinted visual conveyance of anger. "I see . . . you are your father's son."

"Yes, I am my father's son . . . and my mother's son. What I cannot understand is how my loving mother can be the daughter of a killer of defenseless people, people like my grandfather."

He stepped closer as if distance were important to his message. "Who are you to judge me? You were raised in a land where material things, skin color, and religion are the measures of a man. A man's values, his heart, and his actions are not considered, only his race, beliefs, and wealth. It does not matter how many women other than his wife he has slept with. It does not matter how many lives he has ruined to obtain his wealth. Nor does it matter how many women and children he killed serving his country.

"You claim to be a land of the free, and you tout your black President, but you cannot hide your prejudice. Tell me you

302

have never been assaulted because of your turban, and I will call you a liar.

"America is a land controlled by white Christians who say they worship Christ while they really worship money. They preach freedom, and use it as a means to invade weaker countries. There are no morals or scruples in such a place.

"Americans are puppets parroting what they are told. You cannot exist without all your toys for communications and information, television, radio, computers, computerized cell phones, and whatever they come out with next week. You live, breathe, and eat communications. And your government uses them to brain-wash you." He shook a finger at me. "And you naively believe whatever you are told by your government-controlled media."

He leaned closer to my face. "And these infidels want to come to my land and try to force their ways on us. These immoral capitalists have the arrogance and stupidity to suggest we replace Islam with Christianity and your tainted democracy. Can't you Americans understand we do not want to be like you . . . ever? We would rather die. Or better yet, we would rather cleanse this world of sinful hypocrites. And the best way to do that is to kill Americans before they kill us.

"And you dare to judge me? You cannot. You have not lived my life, so you will never understand what I have done or why I did it."

His words made sense in a skewed way. If I were an Afghan who had never left this country, I'd probably think the same way he did. But he had totally missed my point. This wasn't about Americans versus Afghans or Christians versus Moslems.

"So you're telling me not to believe my eyes, my ears, or any of my senses. I watched the people you control take two little, crying, scared-to-death Sikh children with bombs strapped on them and make them walk toward a Marine unit. I will never be the same after witnessing that explosion, the murder of two little kids. And my cousin, a Sikh and a good man, was blown to bits trying to save them. My senses will never forget being

303

covered with the bloody, smelly fragments of him and those children." My voice cracked through the last few words and my lips twitched with emotion.

I shook my head trying and yet knowing I would never clear those images from my mind. I cleared my throat instead and swallowed my emotions. If I were ever to be in control of my emotions, it had to be now, in front of this man.

"And I was on a rooftop in . . . oh yeah, Sar Kand Ow Baba Ziarat and saw and smelled a pile of dozens of dead Sikhs, old men, women, and children, that your cult of killers slaughtered per your orders, in your presence. You posed near them for a photograph." I glanced away and took a deep breath. Then I fixed on his little beady eyes and held his stare. I needed to have him see the emotion in my eyes when I spoke. "You, and you alone, are responsible for all of this killing of defenseless people because of your personal hatred of one man, a Sikh, my father. And you tell me I cannot judge you. You're right. I cannot. Only God can judge you. All I can do is hate you."

Chapter 87

I had a hood over my head and a gag stuffed in my mouth sitting somewhere cool, out of the sun, probably a cave. There had been no further conversation with my grandfather. I had closed that door. He had stomped away and moments later, a putrid rag was jammed in my mouth, and my eyes were covered. I was dragged away by my bound arms, stood up, hands temporarily freed to pee, retied, and then pushed a bunch until plopped here, wherever that was.

Pops had often told me I needed to be wiser about when to speak my mind. I should've paid more attention to his advice.

My concern wasn't about me, it was about Rashi. Before we had surrendered, I had promised her we'd get through this. After blurting my angry thoughts to my grandfather, she and I would've probably been better off to chance the raging river.

I didn't know that grizzled old man I was related to, and I had no clue how he'd respond to my hateful words. I had been a fool. My long hair flapped against my face as I shook my head and bit into the foul tasting rag.

What had happened to my plan about proposing my grandfather and my mother meet in some neutral place? I hadn't negotiated with him for a peaceful settlement; an agreement to stop killing Sikhs. No, not me, I had let my emotions control my mouth. All I accomplished was to piss him off. Just what Rashi, my father, Biji, and every surviving Afghan Sikh didn't want or need.

I had to start thinking and acting more like Pops and less like Carl.

In the middle of praying for a second chance with my grandfather, something thudded on the ground next to me. The something squirmed. I leaned close and smelled jasmine. Rashi sat next to me. I eased me hood-covered face, my cheek against her soft cheek.

She nuzzled her cheek against mine.

I prayed they hadn't violated her. I didn't want her to be permanently changed, mentally scared, like Montana.

Hands rolled up my hood to nose level and removed my gag. "Rashi, are you okay?"

"Be quiet," a young male voice ordered. "Use your mouth to eat only."

A chunk of curry-spiced lamb was wedged between my lips. I hadn't eaten in a while and the taste of the meat made my dry mouth salivate. I chewed slowly and savored each chomp. After I had consumed several chunks of meat, a tin of goat's milk was held to my lips, and I gulped a mouthful.

The wonderful process continued, meat, drink, meat, drink, until the gag returned.

I wagged my head, dodged the gag, and shouted, "I need to see my grandfather. Now. I—"

The gag found my mouth.

"I am fine," Rashi said. Nothing—"

A brief tussle next to me ended with foot pats trailing away.

Rashi and I sat pressed together forcing as much body contact as two bound, sitting people could. The opportunity of touching another caring, passionate woman probably wouldn't last long and may never happen again.

Snuggled against Rashi, a thought slammed me. I not only had to think like Pops, I had to think like Masoud Omar. Food had to be a precious commodity to him and his militia. He wouldn't waste it on someone he was about to kill. Yeah, I had most likely upset him, but what I said or did wasn't his primary interest. I, and maybe Rashi, was a valued commodity, a marketable stock to be traded for my father.

Masoud had one problem. He didn't know where my father was. Masoud couldn't communicate his proposed trade until he found Pops. My grandfather would assume I knew where my father was. My grandfather wouldn't believe my denial of Pops' location. And he knew how concerned I was about Rashi's well-being.

Masoud's next move was obvious.

I had been a thoughtless fool.

Chapter 88

Huddled together, Rashi and I sat, bound and gagged with hoods over our heads, for over an hour, maybe two. I don't know what my grandfather was waiting for; thanks to me, he and his horde of killers were probably out searching for more Sikhs to kill.

I tried to focus on the positive things, Rashi's warm body pressed against mine, I wasn't standing on my gimpy leg, and Biji, Pops, Carl, and Montana were alive and safe.

Many pairs of feet approached. Hands pulled me to my feet and shoved me. I hopped on my good leg. Bodies surrounded me and pushed me, but also kept me from falling when I lost my one-legged balance. Dozens of hops later, I reverted to my stiff-legged gait to keep my unscathed leg from cramping. The cool air walk continued through what had to be a large underground complex.

I used the time to organize my thoughts and prepare for what I would say to my grandfather. I'd apologize for my previous outburst. Humbleness and respect would garnish the words of a grandson who wanted to get to know his grandfather and to try to understand him.

What if Pops' father's death had been an accident as Masoud had said? I'd ask him to recant his story of the night that changed all my family's lives. And I'd listen. Unfortunately there had been too many wrongs to be righted, the murders of so many Sikhs including Maanik. But, humble and respectful, I'd listen, and I'd find a reason to end Masoud's crazy vendetta. There had to be something, something that would justify a reunion between my grandfather and my mother. He had to still care about his daughter. Why else would he be killing Sikhs? The proposed family gathering would have to be planned such that he couldn't kidnap her, and he would have assurance of not being captured. It could be done, most anything could be done with the right attitude, and I would have it. And if the meeting between father and daughter went well, maybe, just maybe my grandfather and father could meet. My faith had taught me that everyone, no matter how wicked they appear, can change. God existed within everyone like fragrance inside a flower or a reflection in a mirror. Possibly the four of us could find a way to forgive and forget, to bury the past and start anew as a family.

My proposal overflowed with 'ifs', and forgetting would be impossible causing forgiving to be even harder. But it could be done. And the effort would be well worth a positive outcome. No more killing of Sikhs, and Biji, Pops, Carl, Montana, Rashi, and I all free in a sane world again. And possibly, my mother would have a father again, and I a grandfather.

Limping along, halfway through my second revision of my presentation, hands stopped me and pushed me down onto what my body recognized as a metal folding chair. Fingers removed the hood and musky gag I had almost become used to. Bodies shuffled behind me.

My blinking eyes adjusted to the kerosene lamplight illuminating a domed stone room. A few steps in front of me was a shiny red leather chair behind a desk with nothing but a glowing lamp on it. An army cot with straight-edge bedding bordered the cave wall to one side. A night stand supporting another burning lamp sat at the head of the bed. A row of folding chairs bracketed by wooden crates topped with lit lamps lined the other side.

I was alone.

309

Chapter 89

I shook my long unkempt hair out of my face. The chair-back pinched my bound arms so I scooted forward and sat on the edge of the seat. The combination of the cool air in the cave, mouth-breathing without the gag, and my solitude enhanced my mental readiness. I was prepared to negotiate with my grandfather, prepared to bend, to forgive-'ish' at least for the moment with fingers crossed, or whatever it took, and more than ready to end this family feud.

Though my faith was founded on forgiveness, could I forgive Masoud? The images of his horrible deeds would never leave me. If I couldn't forget, was I fooling myself to believe I could forgive him? Had Pops forgiven him for the death of his father? Knowing Pops, he had. But I wasn't sure I was that strong.

I'd have to deal with my forgiveness later. The obstacle at hand was Masoud's obsession with killing my father. Masoud had to realize that if he killed Pops, he'd never see his daughter again. Could he disregard his *haumain,* a Sikh's self-pride, and trade his obsession for a chance to meet with his daughter?

My words must find Masoud's heart. I worried that he had become so calloused the words of a young Sikh wouldn't be able to penetrate his time-thickened soldier's shield.

The repeated slap of a sandaled foot alternated with a light thud behind me redirected my focus. I cranked my head to one side and saw a short, stocky man with a beard walk into the room. My eyes were drawn to his foot, he only had one. Like the character Long John Silver in Robert Louis Stevenson's

"Treasure Island", the man had a pegged leg. In this modern era, why would a man wear a wooden peg for his prosthesis?

I looked at his face. Gray tinged both his long head hair and beard. His lined forehead and sunken, black eyes followed an eagle's beak nose. The tip of his pink tongue poked out of the side of his mouth, like biting his tongue made walking possible. With every other step, his features jiggled when the rigid peg thudded on the floor.

The Russians had invaded at the end of 1979. This man seemed old enough; maybe he lost his leg then. Today, the Taliban probably didn't know what a field hospital was. Back in the eighties, a wooden peg leg in Afghanistan could have been state-of-the-art.

The unarmed man stopped in front of me and leaned on the front of the desk. He wore a black unbuttoned vest over a brown long sleeve shirt with the sleeves rolled to his elbows. His thin arms, overlaid with thick black hair, braced on the desk. His shirt hung out, over black cotton pants, which were too short to hide his sockless scandal-wrapped foot and the scarred wooden peg. Fat toes tipped his bared foot. His toenails were blackened with dirt and chipped versus clipped.

A twinge of guilt made me lift my eyes from his foot to his face. The man glared at me like I had done something horrible. My looking at his peg couldn't have upset him that much. Anyone seeing him for the first time would be curious. Then a more concerning thought raised bumps on my arms. Maybe some of the men I had killed were friends or relatives of his. How could they not be? His scowl put my enthusiasm for talking with my grandfather on hold. I would have to deal with this angry man first.

Without taking his eyes from me, the man reached inside his pants pocket and removed a slender wooden handle. He pressed a button and a six-inch steel blade slashed out of the handle's end. He slowly spun the handle between his fingers. The lamp light flashed and darted along the blade as he turned the knife.

Despite the cool cave air, the man's silent stare and the spinning knife caused perspiration tingles on my scalp and forehead. I had to look away.

If I spoke, I'd probably just make him madder. So I slumped back into the chair and stared at the gray cave floor.

The silence grew heavier with each passing minute. My aspirations, my confidence, and my courage bowed and weaken under the load. I prayed my grandfather would arrive soon before fear of what this man may do with that knife consumed me. My grandfather . . . my grandfather was this man's boss. What was I worried about? I had nothing to fear.

I straightened my spine and looked into the man's hateful eyes. "When is my grandfather, Masoud Omar, getting here?"

"He is not coming." His Pashto words were as intense as his stare.

"What?" I edged forward.

"I am Hameed Ahmed, the General's aid. He sent me here to give you a message . . . no that is not what he called it. Ah, yes, I am here to give you an ult-tim-mate-tum."

Here we go. My grandfather didn't want a confrontation. Strange. Masoud couldn't be afraid of me. Why would he send his lackey to give me an ultimatum? Sending a representative would be a lot easier for him. Maybe the ol' man had a heart, or at least a soft spot, after all. After all his years of soldiering and the few things I witnessed that he had ordered made it hard to believe.

"I don't want to talk to you. I want to talk to him. I must talk to him, to my grandfather." My voice rose with each sentence in pitch and volume.

The man stopped spinning the blade and sat motionless. My insolence had the same affect on him as it did on the cave walls.

Minutes ticked by and Hameed remained motionless as if he wanted to feed my impatience.

I couldn't stand his imperviousness any longer.

"Did you hear what I said? Go. And get my grandfather."

The man pushed up off the desk.

I nodded my acceptance.

He took one step toward me. "You will tell me where your father is, or that woman, Rashi, will suffer. You have five minutes."

Chapter 90

Hameed Ahmed sat at the desk in front of me and cleaned his dirty fingernails with the tip of his stiletto. My mental clock boomed inside my head ticking away Ahmed's five-minute limit. I would have been more receptive to 'Big Ben' chiming inside the domed cave room versus my head clock. I was down to a few minutes and had no clue how I would respond to my grandfather's ultimatum. Masoud wanted to know where my father was so Masoud could use me as bait to capture and most likely torture Pops to death.

I had a simple problem. I didn't know where Pops was. But Rashi did. I didn't want to involve her. But the Taliban did. Either I told them where Pops was hiding, or they would torture her, or even—no they wouldn't kill Masoud Omar's grandson's girlfriend. I had to do whatever I could to preclude her any pain. She had already suffered enough discomfort because of me. Being a hooded, bound, and gagged Taliban captive alone was enough to scare up some permanent wrinkles and a bunch of gray hair.

I only had one chance to keep her safe. I had to have a chance to talk with my grandfather, a chance to sway him to reason, to sanity. Masoud couldn't pass up the opportunity to see his daughter again, not if he had a heart.

But in order to have an audience with my grandfather, I had to play a card I didn't have. I had to lie. My mom always told me I was the worst liar she had ever known. She called me her 'hundred-foot liar,' because she could tell I was lying from that far away. I fixed that problem; I didn't lie. But not today, or

314

tonight, or whatever time it was, I needed to become an instant and convincing prevaricator.

When Hameed bent down to inspect one of his fingernails under the lamp, I mentally practiced my lies. The bindings on my arms were tight. If I strained against them, they would cut into my flesh. So that is what I did to help make my silent practice more believable. The pain diverted my focus, and hopefully made me believable. I had no choice but to try.

Flexing my arms, I cleared my throat. Hameed looked up from his nails.

"I, ah, I know where my father is." My voice sounded as strained as my arms. I prayed I was convincing. If nothing else, I had Hameed's attention. I gritted against the pain and continued. "But some things must happen before I divulge his location."

"'Some things'? What things?" He stabbed the knife into the table top, burying an inch of the blade's tip.

Either this man was always pissed off, or he hated Sikhs, or Americans, or maybe he hated liars. He had to know I was lying, but I had no choice.

I relaxed my arms, and a trickle of warm fluid slid down my hands and dripped off my finger tips.

"Bring Rashi here so I know she is safe. Leave her here with me. Then, and only then, will I tell my grandfather, and him alone, where my father is hiding."

The man spread his arms out and smiled, a mouth opened, gaped black teeth grin.

He had to know I was lying. Why else would a hateful man smile? This man was either a great button pusher, or he was extremely dangerous; either way, he had me shaking. If he didn't do what I asked, I had no other means to save Rashi from harm.

"You Sikhs are so, ah what is the word, oh yes, so arrogant. You think you can sit there with your arms bound and dictate terms to me?" He laughed, but it was the kind of laugh that tickled all my bones except my 'funny bone.'

315

"I will have the woman brought here as you wished." His smile morphed into a sneer. "And then we can test your arrogance. You will tell me where your father is, or you can watch her suffer. And trust me;" he ratcheted the knife back and forth and then yanked it out of the table, "I know how to make a woman scream." His smile returned.

Chapter 91

"Amir!" Hameed hollered. Running steps slid to a stop behind me.

"Yes, Saab," a young male voice said.

"Bring the woman here. And Amir," his eyes darted to me and back to the man, "bring my toys as well."

"Yes, Saab." Slapping scandals drifted away.

I was back where I started. Hameed was in control, and Rashi was in trouble. Convincing my grandfather to stop pursuing my father was my only hope. I needed to remind this aide who he was messing with.

I bolted to my feet and greeted my leg pain with a scowl. "You don't seem to understand. Masoud Omar is my grandfather. And I demand—"

"Sit down and be quiet!"

I took a step toward him. "No."

Hameed, with knife in hand, jumped to his feet sending the chair crashing into the cave wall.

"I want to speak to my grandfather, now."

He stepped around the desk, waving the stiletto back and forth in front of him like it was a symphony conductor's baton.

Disregarding my instant fear and my good sense, I held my ground.

When he was a stab away, I said, "I will tell my grandfather you said he was stupid for wasting Taliban lives killing Sikhs when they could be killing Americans."

He cocked his free arm and a blurred fist slammed into my solar plexus.

Doubled over in pain and whooshing air, I staggered backward colliding with and falling into the chair.

He moved closer to me. The lamp light dancing on the blade centered my focus as his free hand slid into a pants pocket. When I raised my head and opened my mouth to suck in some air, he stuffed another soiled rag in my mouth.

"As I said before, all of you Sikhs are arrogant, just like the Americans." He shook his head. "Masoud knows I would never question his orders. I cannot believe you are related to him. You are nothing like my General. You act just like your Sikh grandfather . . . the one I killed."

Hameed, not Masoud, killed my grandfather? Sucking air through my nostrils like a vacuum cleaner became secondary. Somehow, I needed to hurt this man. I pushed up on my feet.

Hameed grabbed a handful of my hair and yanked me down on the chair.

'Get up again, and I will cut you."

My need to feed my anger and repay my pain disappeared as a hooded and bound Rashi was pulled into the room by two men. Her hooded body-covering burka had been removed. Her blue blouse had been torn open in front to the waistband of her rumpled black skirt. Her rapid breathing pulsed the tops of her mounded copper breasts in and out of the cups of her black bra.

What had these bastards done to her? Worse yet, what were they going to do because of me? I strained against my bindings.

One of the men placed a canvas duffel bag on the desk.

"Remove her hood and gag," ordered Hameed, reseated on his throne.

Freed of the gag and hood, Rashi licked her lips and blinked her eyes. She looked down and bowed her shoulders inward in an attempt to cover her chest. Her enlarged brown eyes looked at Hameed, then her head turned, and her eyes found me.

"Kugi, thank God, you are—"

"You will speak only to me," Hameed yelled. "And only when I ask you to." He lifted the duffel bag off the desk and

318

jiggled it, metal clinked. "And I must tell you, if you refuse to answer me or lie to me, you will be painfully sorry." The bag thudded and clunked like metal striking metal when he dropped it on the desk. "Has this man," Hameed pointed at me, "told you where his father is?"

My spine involuntarily straightened as my what-seemed-like-a-month-ago words to Rashi at the river bank screamed inside my head. "Promise me, if the Taliban asks you where my grandmother or my father is, no matter what, tell them you don't know them. You came here because . . . because of me. Okay? No matter what."

I screamed into the gag, nodding my head.

Rashi's eyes darted to me and then back to Hameed. "No."

Hameed fished a hand inside the canvas bag.

Chapter 92

Hameed withdrew a three-foot long bolt cutter from the duffel bag on the desk. He opened the jaws and snapped them closed. A smile spread his beard.

I had been taught not to hate, but hate cut the bindings into my flesh.

"Amir, bring her to me and hold her hand on the edge of the desk," he ordered.

I leaped to my feet and squealed into the gag.

Hameed pointed the tool at me. "Sit down! If you get up again, I will cut off her hand instead of her fingers."

I plopped down but grimaced and growled.

Rashi's fear-filled eyes looked at me as she struggled with the two men pulling her to the desk.

Eyebrows raised, I nodded at her over and over again.

One of the men pinned one of Rashi's hands on the table and struggled with getting her fisted hand open.

My muffled pleas reverberated in the domed room.

Hameed threw the tool down and snatched up the stiletto. He glared at me. "Be quiet!" Then he swiped the knife down Rashi's front.

Blood flew from Rashi's chest, and she screamed.

I closed my eyes winching with her pain and stopped my verbal protests.

I opened my eyes. I had to do something.

Rashi squirmed and twisted around. A thin red line, oozing blood, ran down the middle of her chest. The center section of her black bra, which joined the cups, flapped open.

Grinding my teeth, I strained against the ropes binding my arms until I thought my veins would rupture. Of all the killing I had done, I had never wanted to kill someone as badly as I did at this moment.

Her tear-streaming eyes met mine. A body shaking sob escaped her pinched lips.

My body slumped in defeat. I closed my eyes and nodded my head. I prayed for her to tell Hameed where my father was.

"Straighten out her fingers," Hameed ordered.

My eyes sprung open, and my burning arms pulled against my constraints.

He stuck the knife into the table top and picked up the bolt cutter.

Amir forced Rashi's little finger out of her fist and pulled it straight.

Hameed pinched her finger between the jaws of the tool.

"No!" Rashi screamed. "Kugi's father is in Kabul at my cousin's apartment house near the center of the city, Argi Jumhuri."

"Amir, take notes," Hameed said. "What is the address?"

"Argi Jumhuri, ah, apartment house M, apartment 27," Rashi said in a weak voice. She lowered her head and broke into sobs.

Hameed closed the jaws until blood spurted from her finger.

"No!" she yelped.

"I want the truth." Hameed studied her face. The man expressed a look of confidence like a man experienced in interrogating people he tortured.

"I am telling you the truth." Rashi's eyes darted between her blood-squirting finger and Hameed's face inches from hers.

"Are you?" he asked.

"Yes," Rashi blurted. "Yes, I swear on my son's life, Raman is there. My cousin's name is Kartar Singh. He has a phone, and his address and phone number are listed in the Kabul directory."

Amir scribbled on a piece of paper with a pen.

321

"Did you get all of that, Amir?" Hameed asked.

The young man nodded and repeated the information.

"Go," Hameed said. "Go and check it. All the phone directories are by the south entrance where the reception is good. Go."

Amir ran out of the room.

The remaining young Taliban stood behind Rashi holding her by the elbow.

Hameed removed the cutters and sat them on the desk.

Rashi sighed, cupped her bleeding hand with her other hand, and glanced my way. She grimaced as she focused on her bleeding pinky and flexed the digit open and closed. Fisting her wounded hand, she used her good hand to clamp her blouse together.

I wanted to tell her she did what she had to do. She had no choice. I prayed she understood that. This wasn't her fight anyway. This was between Masoud and my father.

My father was in danger, but Pops was the smartest person I knew. He'd think of some way to save me without sacrificing his life. Hopefully this feud would end with no further bloodshed.

If only I could talk to Masoud. I could end this madness. Maybe now that he knew where Pops was, I'd get the chance.

Amir ran into the room. "It is as she said."

Hameed glanced at me with an expression of a victor looking at the defeated. Then he yanked the knife out of the desktop and in one blurred movement slashed Rashi's throat.

Chapter 93

Rashi's blood splattered the cave wall behind the desk. Mouth a gap, she clutched her blood-spewing throat and collapsed into the arms of the two men.

I was on my feet, running, making strange animal noises into the gag, a mixture of screams, moans, and crying. A step from the desk, hands came over my shoulders and others grabbed my arms. Twisting and kicking, I was pulled back to the chair and held there.

The two blood-smeared Taliban soldiers dragged Rashi's gurgling limp body out of the room leaving a trail of wet glistening blood on the stone floor.

Hameed, a sneer on his red speckled face, followed them.

He stopped near me. With his eyes glued to mine, he wiped the bloody knife's blade on my pants.

I tried to kick him, and he laughed.

He retracted the blade into the handle and pocketed the switchblade. "Arrogance." His laughter filled the domed room as he wiped his blood-covered hand on the sleeve of my jumpsuit.

Growling into the gag, I struggled against the strong hands to my feet. I had to get to Hameed, to bash his laughing mouth with my head. Something hard smashed into the back of my knees dropping me into the chair.

Hameed left, his laughter trailing after him.

Hands held me down as a man knelt in front of me and tied my feet to the chair. The men left.

323

Alone, I wished they had put the hood back on my head. I didn't want to sit here and watch Rashi's blood dry. I didn't need the constant reminder she was dead. But I couldn't take my eyes off the bright liquid. My peaked emotions fizzled and slipped into a void. Nothing mattered now. I was just a skin-covered hollow shell. Unmoving, eyes wide open and yet not seeing, not hearing anything but Rashi's last gasp, I sat head down staring at the red, spreading trail from the desk past my chair. Sat and watched Rashi's life congeal into the nooks and crevices in the cave floor.

One single thought repeated over and over in my head, "Fuck forgiveness."

Chapter 94

"Negative energy is a waste," my father's words echoed in my head. There was no way I could let that monster, Hameed, get his hands on my father. If it cost me my life to kill Hameed and hopefully my grandfather as well before they got to Pops, I would be happy. I diverted my eyes from the Rashi's blood trail and shook off the depressing images dominating my mind. My eyes came to rest on the desktop. Hameed and his boys, in their haste to tell my grandfather they had found Pops, had forgotten his bag of toys. His quest to taunt me had caused the bastard to make a mistake.

Though my hands were bound behind me, they still could serve a purpose. I pushed down until my hands clutched the back of the chair's seat. Then I rocked forward onto my feet. Bent like a duck-walker with my feet tied to the chair, I wobbled the chair from side to side and took tiny steps toward the desk.

When I got to the desk, I was sucking air through my nose, and my legs burned. Using the corner of the desk, I wedged the rag out of my mouth. I gulped air through my mouth until my system normalized. I maneuvered to where the canvas duffel bag sat on the desk and used my mouth to pull the bottom of the bag closer. I bit into the canvas and stood up as tall as I could. The contents tumbled out on the desk. As I had hoped, there was a knife, a big sharp butcher's knife. Maybe the rumors I had heard around the Marine base were true. Maybe the Taliban did cut people's faces off while they were still alive, one of the many reasons why Carl had told me never to get caught, alive. I would never underestimate Hameed's cruelty.

Biting the hard wooden knife handle, I placed the knife on the edge of the desk, handle outward. Then I turned my back to the desktop and grabbed the knife's handle with my hands. I sat down on the chair and gave my screaming legs a rest. Turning the blade vertical, I sawed the sharp edge across the ropes on my arms.

A face soaked with sweat later, my arms and hands were freed. My forearms looked like I had used them defensively in a knife fight. And my hands and fingers were streaked with my caked blood. I cut the ropes binding my feet to the chair and stood. My wounded leg burned. I glanced down, and blood had seeped through my bandages soaking my pants at both my thigh and calf. But who cared? I didn't. There were more important things on my mind, like killing a few people.

Chapter 95

I stood alone in the domed cave room by the desk. It had to be after midnight. I didn't have a clue about the time, just a guess.

Besides the knife and bolt cutter, the contents of Hameed's duffel bag of 'toys' included a pair of pliers, a hack saw, a two-three pound metal mallet, an ice pick, and a barbed strap.

I pocketed the ice pick and kept the knife and the hammer in my hands.

Locking my wounded leg, I limped toward the single entrance to the room. Rapid approaching scandal slaps on the stone floor caused me to hop to one side of the entrance.

Amir came to a sliding stop as he cleared the entrance. His startled expression conveyed his surprise to find the room empty.

The throwing motion of my left arm brought his gaping eyes to mine and then to the arcing hammer. The last thing he would ever see.

The two-pound mini-sledge hammer slammed into the top of his frontal bone, just above his forehead, emitting a thud hyphenated by a cracking noise. He collapsed to the cave floor like he was made of rubber, smacking the ground before his turban landed, a silent scream frozen on his face.

"Did Hameed send you back for his toys, Amir? Don't worry. I will take them to him."

Amir had a 40 caliber Glock automatic pistol and a knife tucked into the waistband of his pants. I mentally thanked him for his contribution to my defense, and then corrected my thought changing it to my offense. I checked the gun. It had fifteen rounds in the clip. I chambered a round and made sure the safety was off.

I picked up Amir's turban, piled up my long hair, and wrapped the turban around my head. Then I slipped on his vest. The turban and the vest could give me a second or two of surprise before my jumpsuit was noticed.

I separated the knives, putting them in opposite thigh pockets in my jumpsuit, the knife in my left pants pocket kept the ice pick company.

Blood-smeared hammer in my right hand and gun in my left, I peered around the entrance to the room. A six by six-foot tunnel disappeared around a curve about twenty yards away. Artificial light reflected off the wall at the bend in the tunnel. Either the tunnel was lit or the cave opened into another room around the bend.

I did my stiff-legged hop to the bend and eased my head into the turn.

Thirty yards further, the tunnel opened into a large lighted chamber. I could see the rear end of a truck near the opening. I had to be close to one of the complex's entrances.

I limp-trotted to the truck and crouched next to it. Unmoving, I listened for what seemed like a minute but was probably only fifty or sixty heart thumps. Silence, a friend, greeted me. Hopefully, everyone was asleep.

I rose up and scanned the area. I was in a large tunnel, dimly lit by only a couple of scattered wall torches roughly forty or fifty yards from a black opening on my left and a torch lit ongoing tunnel to my right. Several tunnels opened into this cavern on both sides. There were at least a dozen dump trucks, facing outward, obviously a lesson learned. The parked convoy lined the wall between where I stood and the opening. I stepped up on the running board and glanced inside the truck's cab. Keys dangled from the ignition. I had a chance. Thank God Pops had taught me how to drive a vehicle with a standard transmission. Now all I needed to do was to maneuver unseen to the lead truck.

I hopped off the truck.

I learned all over again how difficult it was to crouch with a stiff leg and try to move quickly. I imagined I must look like Quasimodo hobbling bent over from one truck to the next. That thought stopped me by the second truck. Quasimodo had saved his woman. I hadn't.

Negotiations had been cast aside by my grandfather and his aide, a mistake. Now there was only one way to resolve this feud, my grandfather had to die. And I prayed I was the one responsible for his death.

If I could escape, I'd get my father, Biji, and Carl out of this country, but I would stay. I'd kill Masoud and Hameed or die trying.

Hunched over, I gimped my way to the front of the third truck and prepared to run the gap. A man's voice yelled something garbled by the cave's acoustics. I froze. I had no idea where the voice was located in this hole in stone.

Grabbing the wheel well fender, I lowered my body to the ground and scanned the viewable area for feet. Nothing.

Then a man's voice, clear and too close, said in Pashto, "This is my third day in a row to be a night guard. I cannot sleep in the daytime. I have told Chaudry these very same words on too many occasions and yet here I am. I am afraid I will fall asleep. Do you know what they did to Gohar when they caught him sleeping? Amir strapped the skin off his back. Where is Amir anyway? He was going to talk to Chaudry to see if he could get a replacement for me tonight."

Two pair of scandal covered feet scuffed up the dust as they trod by the truck I lay behind.

"You complain too much. And that is not healthy. At least you do not have the outside duty. I think it is raining tonight. Now be quiet before Amir catches us. We have been warned too many times about talking while on guard duty."

329

One pair of feet stopped followed by the second. "You are a mindless, weak follower. You go guard the entrance. Someone will join you in a few minutes, but it will not be me. I am going to talk to Amir. Do you know where he is?"

"Yes, but you are an idiot. Amir is becoming as mean as his father. And Hameed is heartless. I heard about the woman."

"Where is he?"

"Amir went to retrieve Hameed's bag from the room where the woman was killed. Do not be gone long. Oh, and I will bet you one hundred Afghanis you will be on guard duty with me tonight."

"Now who is the idiot? That is a bet. I do not understand Hameed. Did you see that woman? What a waste. She was beautiful. We could have had many hours of fun with her."

Could there be one human being with a heart and morals in all of the Taliban? Fuck forgiveness.

The feet separated.

I had but a few minutes before the guard found Amir and set off an alarm.

At least my bitterness had been sweetened by the knowledge I had killed Hameed's son. I would give him time to suffer with his loss before I returned to kill him. Right now I had to get out of here.

I pulled my knees under me and, clutching the truck, grimaced as I rose to my feet. I stayed a truck behind the man going to guard the entrance. He and some outside guards were all that stood between me and my father.

Chapter 96

Two trucks from the cave entrance, I had gotten ahead of the Talib walking to his guard post at the opening. I slid between two trucks, crouched and waited. When he walked by, I stepped out and bashed the back of his head with the hammer. Crushing the man's skull with the heavy hammer reminded me of smashing pumpkins when I was a kid, the soft thud followed by the fracture of the shell. Head? Pumpkins? I must be going insane. But I didn't have time to think about my mental degradation or his, he deserved to die.

It wasn't my place to judge who lived and died. I could not and would not be a judge. I'd just kill as many of them as I could.

I traded the hammer for the man's AK-47 and a few thirty-round banana clips of ammunition and ran to the last truck. I used the mirror supports to pull my bad leg up on the running board, opened the driver's door, and entered the cab. I started the engine. A distant scream froze my hand on the gear shift. The body had been found. I jammed the truck in what I hoped was first gear and let out the clutch. The truck lurched forward.

I left the lights off and rolled out of the cave into the dark driving rain. I couldn't see. I flipped levers and turned knobs until I found the windshield wipers, but they didn't help. A ravine, a cliff, or a stone outcropping could be in my path, the typical geography of this damned country. I had no choice; I had to turn on the headlights.

The mud in front of me came to life when I flicked on the high beams. I guided the trucks into wheel tracks leading into the blackness. Shots boomed from the cave and bullets plinked off the steel bed behind the cab.

The wheel tracks led me through a gap between massive boulders. Just as I entered the gap, two men with rifles butted against their shoulders and aimed at me, stepped out from behind the stones blocking my path.

I slid down in the seat and floored the accelerator. A man screamed followed by a thud and slight bump. More shots shattered glass all around me. I closed my eyes and pressed harder on the gas pedal.

When the shots clanked on metal, I pushed up, brushing chunks of glass off my clothing.

I prayed the rain wouldn't wash out the tracks. I didn't know where I was going, but I was going to get there as fast as this old dump truck could take me.

Chapter 97

I drove for about five minutes as fast as the dump truck and my bouncing ass would let me. Then I stopped, climbed out into the downpour, limped behind the truck, and bashed out the tail lights. I glanced behind me and saw nothing but darkness, but they were coming. My grandfather needed me.

Back in the truck, leg screaming, I rolled on. The tire tracks led to a hard surface and disappeared. I held the wheel straight and drove on as fast as the light beams and topography would allow.

Nanakpur was only thirty or forty kilometers northwest of Kabul. How long had Rashi and I bounced around on the truck bed? Maybe thirty minutes? That torrential river and the foothills of the Hindu Kush Mountains were just to the west of Nanakpur. And we hadn't traveled on a road. So after we were captured, we had either traveled east or north out of Nanakpur.

I smacked the steering wheel with my open hand. I couldn't tell which direction I was going. Who cared? I'd drive until the sun came up or I ran out of gas and go from there.

That wouldn't work. I stopped the truck and doused the lights. I needed to think.

I gripped the wheel and pulled my body erect. I was wrong. Masoud wouldn't be pursuing me. He didn't need me anymore. He knew where my father was. He'd be going after Pops. I had to get to Pops before Masoud did. And since I didn't know where I was, I had only one choice. I turned the truck around and back tracked as fast as the truck would go.

Five minutes later, I saw their lights, a glow on the horizon. I turned off my headlights and drove as fast as I could with just parking lights. I came over a crest and flicked off my lights. There a half mile in front of me was a convoy of three trucks. Masoud didn't need many men to sneak into Kabul and capture Pops. I maneuvered the truck through the darkness in behind them and followed several hundred yards to their rear.

I prayed Masoud or at least Hameed was in the convoy. If I were Masoud, I'd be there. I wouldn't trust nor want anyone else to end my decades of pain.

When you can't see, the jolting and the bouncing, from rolling into holes or over objects, seemed much worse. I gripped the steering wheel like it was my trapeze bar and I didn't have a net.

Too many bone jarring jolts later, the dim middle-of-the night lights of Kabul glowed on the jagged horizon. I slowed and increased the distant from me and the rear truck in the convoy.

When we entered the city, my dilemma was I didn't know where they were going so I'd have to follow then without being seen. That should be real easy playing sneaky man in a big-ass dump truck.

Chapter 98

At somewhere close to or after one a.m., Kabul was like a large ghost town. The street lights were one per block at best and had low wattage. It would be damned difficult to read a book standing directly under one. You'd probably have better luck with a jar of lightning bugs.

The Taliban convoy didn't take a direct route. Frequently they would turn off for a few blocks and then continue in the same direction as before. Then they would do the same thing again but turn in the other direction for twice as many blocks and then head back on the original course, a zig-zag pattern. Kabul was an American and Afghan government controlled city. There had to be either patrols or check points throughout the city twenty-four-seven. Unfortunately, the Taliban had to know where the check points and patrols were.

My Taliban guided tour of Kabul didn't show me much of anything. The dim street lights coupled with no headlights and an overcast rain-filled night left only parallel lines of shadowy building silhouettes, some taller than others, gliding by the truck. The wet gloom, the smell of sewage wafting through my shot-out windows, and the unknown awaiting me, set the scene for my nerves.

Eyes strained, I rolled the dump truck through the city streets staying at least two blocks behind the three truck Taliban caravan. My hands fidgeted checking each of my guns, the ammunition, the knives, the ice pick, and then back through the weapons' check again. My only solace was my bruised ass appreciated the smooth streets for a change. While my hands worked and my ass rested, my mind raced around like a kid at his first visit to an amusement park. I needed a plan for when the Taliban and I arrived where Pops was hiding.

Three dump trucks equated to six to nine men; there was only one plan. I had to attack them before they got into the building. Hopefully, the gunfire would draw Americans or Afghan government troops.

We'd been in the city for at least twenty minutes; we had to be getting close to Pops' hiding place. I removed the turban, snuggled the AK-47 next to me on the seat, and closed the space with the trailing Taliban truck.

Chapter 99

Squinting into the rainy dimness of the poorly lit Kabul avenue, I eased off the accelerator as I watched the first two dump trucks of the Taliban convoy turn left onto another street. I slammed on the brakes when the third vehicle pulled across the entrance of the road, blocking access. Two assault-rifle-armed men jumped out of the cab and took defensive positions on each end of the idling high-bed steel leviathan. They had a plan. I didn't.

The bastards were going to barricade both ends of the avenue while the men in the middle truck went into a building somewhere on that street and either kidnapped or killed Pops and maybe Biji.

I was about a block-and-a-half back from the street's entrance. Being seen now was the least of my concerns. Jamming the accelerator to the floor, I rolled up to the next roadway and turned left. Maybe I could beat the first truck to the end of the block. Barreling down the thoroughfare, I saw an alley on my right and saw the lead vehicle go past. Though I couldn't beat that truck to the end of the block, God was on my side. I had a chance.

Locking the brakes and sliding to a stop, I backed up and pulled into the narrow alley. The truck bed had but inches to spare on either side. Short of the end of the alley, I stopped in the shadow of a tall building and shut off the engine. Grabbing the AK-47, with the pistol in a pocket, I jammed the door open as far as the tight alley would allow, and squeezed out landing on my good leg. Oblivious of my wounds, I ran to the end of the alley and peered around the corner. Roughly thirty or forty feet to my left on the same side of the street, the third truck idled in front of the large three-story structure I hid behind, an apartment building. Under a street lamp in the drizzling rain, two young men helped an old white-haired man down from the high cab.

I had been right; Masoud Ahmed had come to personally kill his son-in-law.

This was my only chance. I raced toward the group of men. The two men, arms steadying Masoud as he climbed off the truck, both looked in the direction of my pounding feet splashing through the puddles.

One of them released his grasp on Masoud and pulled his rifle off his shoulder. I slid to a stop, aimed, and fired a three-round burst into the man's chest. Each slug jerked the man back slamming him into the other two men.

Rifle aimed, I took several more steps within ten or so feet of the remaining two men.

Running feet slapped the pavement from both ends of the street, the others were coming.

The man holding Masoud had lost his rifle in the collision with the man I had shot. Spreading his arms, he shielded his leader.

Masoud, his turban knocked from his head, pulled a pistol, shook his long white hair out of his eyes, and aimed it at me over the man's shoulder.

I fired two shots into the chest of the human shield. Both men recoiled with each shot and fell to the ground, the young one on top of Masoud.

Guns fired behind me in concert with flame-streaked bullets ricocheting off the steel truck bed just in front of me. I pivoted, dropped to a knee, aimed, and fired a short burst. One of the two running men flung his arms outward and flopped into a sliding, limbs flopping mass. The second man, carrying a grenade launcher, ducked behind a parked car.

338

I rolled to the sidewalk and ran into the recessed entry of the building. Bullets chipped the apartment's stone façade from the other direction. I dropped down and saw a pair of legs walking along the other side of the truck. When that man got to the end of the truck, I'd be an unprotected target. I aimed and sprayed the legs with a burst. The man fell and I shot him twice more.

Unsure of how many shots I had taken, I retrieved another clip from a pants pocket, reloaded the rifle, and chambered a round.

I was pinched. As soon as the man with the grenade launcher got into position and fired, I'd be dead.

Bullets careened off the walls on both sides of me. I pulled at the solid wooden double doors of the apartment. They were locked. Another burst of gunfire caused me to drop my gun, hunker, and cover my head with my hands. My ducking, jerking body crouched face forward into the corner formed by the wall and the front door's frame. I couldn't stop my trembling as stone chips ripped the air around me. I had maybe seconds left. I wondered if death would be painful.

My father's advice for shedding fear blared in my head overwhelming the cacophony around me. I took a deep breath. Now was not the time to panic. I should die like a man, not like a coward cowering in a corner.

At least I had accomplished one of my goals; I had killed my soul-less grandfather. And the only remorse I had was that my father wasn't there to witness it. I twisted around to see the old man's body, and my head jerked. He wasn't there. Only the three young Taliban men lay in the street on the other side of the truck.

Something stung the back of my hand as I picked up the rifle. I'd make a final charge. Maybe, just maybe, I get another shot at that old son-of-a-bitch. Head down, fragments zinging all around me, I got my feet under me. My fears vanished, replaced by peacefulness in the midst of chaos. This would be for Pops, for all Sikhs.

Chapter 100

Bullet, stone, and wood chips slashed the singed air around me, whizzing, screeching, thudding, and whining.

I gripped the stock of the AK-47 like it was Masoud Omar's neck. I whispered a two-second prayer and braced a foot against the recessed portal's wall.

I hunched up over my braced foot prepared to launch into the street, to where my grandfather waited for me. The apartment's entry door creaked inward. I twisted around with my rifle at ready as a hand grabbed my shoulder. Pops smiled.

He pulled me into the foyer and slammed the thick, heavy door closed, bolting it with a cross bar.

An explosion roared and the door shuddered violently inward causing my father to push me against a wall and shield me with his body. Acrid smoke steamed through the cracks in the door.

"Kugi." He coughed. "My son, are you okay? Are you wounded? What did they do to you?"

He smelled like my youth, my home, my security, Old Spice Aftershave and Lux Soap. I wanted to hide in his warmth from the surrounding madness. His hugs had protected me before, a long, long time ago, a trip through Afghanistan ago. I eased him to arm's length.

"I've been better, but I'm okay. Thank God you and Biji are alright."

He glanced at the cracked door. "That's not going to keep them out. We need to move. Come." He tugged on my arm. "Upstairs. We'll barricade the steps. We can slow them down a

340

flight at a time. Unfortunately, those guns of yours won't compete with their grenade launchers."

He pulled me up the concrete stairs. "Your grandmother will be so glad to see you. She's on the third floor. Hopefully she has called the police by now. But who knows what they will do?"

Limping up the stairs behind him, a burst of shots thudded into the double doors.

At the first landing, I motioned him to go on, and I crouched by the wall and aimed at the door.

Another explosion jammed my ears. I ducked as a pressure wave rocketed by me. I looked up to see a cloud of dust and debris. And then a fast moving hunched-over shadow spewing spurts of fire ran through a hole where the doors used to be. I sprayed the shadow with bullets, jerking it upright and then slamming it to the foyer floor.

Four, maybe five down, three or four to go.

"Kugi, are you okay?" Pops called from above.

"Better than he is." I motioned to the foyer.

"You need to move, now." His tone brimmed with conviction. "Trust me."

I ran up the gray mortar steps. As he pulled me onto the second floor, a blast shook the building under my feet and knocked Pops and I onto the concrete floor.

"Damned grenade launchers," Pops said through the haze of dust.

I peered down to the first floor landing. The mortar walls were riddled with smoking holes. I flexed my jaws to clear the ringing in my ears.

"Too bad the steps aren't made of wood," Pops said. "They wouldn't be able to get up here. Pray they run out of those grenades soon. We've only got this floor, another landing, and the third floor to hide and delay them. How many are there?"

"Four maybe five, and Masoud is with them. I thought I killed him, but his body disappeared. I'd guess he's alive. If he were dead, the others would have left by now."

We choked on the burnt cordite fumes. I couldn't tell if his scrunched up face was from the smoke, or my news about Masoud Omar, his father-in-law. The man who Pops thought had killed his father.

"It's time for you to move up to the next landing," I said.

"Raman!" a male voice yelled in English. "Are you up there, Raman?"

"Masoud," my father said. "Yes, I am here. You sound just like you did so long ago, maybe a little older and obviously a whole bunch dumber."

"Still the insolent one . . . but not for much longer."

"Masoud, this is Kugi. This is insane. The killing must stop. Don't you realize that if you kill us, you will never see Surinder, ur . . . I mean you will never see Fatana again. Don't you want to see your daughter?"

"My grandson, the one who moments ago tried to kill me, asks me to stop the killing. You are just like your father. Someday I must thank you Americans for the vests. They work so well. And regarding my daughter, my Muslim daughter is dead."

"You are such a fool," my father said. "Fatana is so worth seeing. She is as lovely and—"

A burst of gun shots reverberated in the stairwell.

"Don't speak to me of this person _you_ will never see again, Raman." Whispered words were followed by shuffling feet. "Soon you, Kugi, will witness the death of your woman-stealing Sikh father. How appropriate that you get to watch me kill your father, just as I had to imagine him killing my Muslim daughter over and over for the past twenty plus years."

I leaned close to Pops and whispered. "Is there another way up here?"

"No," he whispered. "The elevator is broken. Only," he snapped his fingers, "the fire escape. Do you have another gun?"

I handed him my pistol, and he bolted down the hall and into a room.

342

"This feud is stupid," I yelled into the stairwell. "At first I thought you killed my grandfather, but today I found out that you didn't. Hameed did. And your daughter is alive. So at this point, we have no reason for killing each other. Put down your guns and go away. My father and I will take Biji and leave this country. You will never see us again, unless . . ."

"Unless what?" Masoud asked.

"Unless . . . someday you would want to see your daughter, sometime in the future when all of this is behind us."

A muffled burst of automatic rifle fire mingled with pistol shots from down the hall. Then there was silence.

"You are so like your father," Masoud said.

I waited and listened a long beard-tugging moment. When concern consumed my patience, I yelled, "Pops!"

Another long silent moment passed. And then my stomach rolled and fear-stirred anger jolted me with each clump of the hard peg on the floor in the room down the hall.

Chapter 101

What a difference a few weeks makes in one's life. Before this trip started I never could have imagined killing anything let alone a human being. And tonight I wanted to kill Hameed Ahmed more than I had ever wanted anything, even saving Biji. I owed him big, for Rashi and my grandfather, and now, maybe, oh God I prayed not, my father. Hameed must die.

But if I didn't control my boiling emotions, I'd be the one dying. Hameed was an old soldier, an experienced, smart killer. He hadn't lived this long by making mistakes.

Hameed was clumping around on his pegged leg in the room Pops had entered minutes earlier.

Running quietly in Army combat boots down a hallway was almost as easy as finding my grandmother. I ran on my "tippy toes" as Mom called them, down the apartment's second floor hall. Despite my painful effort, I still made noise. Halfway down the hall the peg leg thumping ceased. I slid to a stop, ten feet from the opened door to the room where Pops was.

I wanted to jump into the door opening and spray the room with AK-47's rounds, but Pops was in there somewhere. I held my breath, noiseless, and rigid against the hall wall. I prayed Pops was still alive.

"For my son, Amir," Hameed shouted. A burst of gun fire ripped holes in the room wall as well as the wall across the hall. The holes started at the door frame at chest level to within inches of where I stood, and then returned to the door at ankle height.

Metallic clicks of a clip being removed and another being inserted came from the room.

"Kugi, are you just going to stand out there and listen to me slowly kill your father?" Hameed asked in Pashto.

I could imagine the sneer on his bearded face, accentuating his beady brown eyes.

I had to do something. Just hours ago I sat and watched the sick bastard kill Rashi. Was I going to stand here and listen to him kill Pops? I had to do something, but what? He wanted me to charge in there, an easy kill.

"Ahhhhhh!" My father cried out.

"I told you he was still alive." Hameed laughed.

I needed to get Hameed to come to me, someway.

"I know a lot about you, stumpy, ur, I mean Hameed," I said in a flat Pashto. "My mother use to read grandfather's letters to me when I was young. He wrote that she need not worry about him for he had a young aide named Hameed who shadowed him and protected him. He said you kept him out of harm's way by teaching him to never take risks, to ambush your enemy, to shoot them in the back, and to only confront your enemies face-to-face when they had their hands bound behind them. Although his words did not say anything bad about you, he inferred that you were a back-shooting coward."

"General Omar would never say such things about me . . . never." His tone bordered on anger. "You want me to cut your father, don't you?"

"That is what you do best is it not, hurt old men, women, and children? How long have you been a soldier, thirty years? Think of all the good soldiers you have known who are dead. They fought. You hid. They were fools, and you are the wise one. The dead ones did not understand what it takes to survive, but you do. You never openly fight, you run from fights. You kill your enemies when they are asleep or tied up, never in a face to face gun fight.

345

"And you break your enemy's will to fight by butchering their loved ones, parents, wives, and children. That is why you are still alive after all these years."

"What do you know of war?" Hameed shouted. "You know nothing. You are an American propaganda-fed Sikh. You are not a soldier. Which of your father's ears would you like to have to remember him by?"

"No, I am not a soldier, and if you call yourself a soldier, I never want to be one. Go ahead, cut on a helpless old man. That is what you do best, that and running away."

"It is your coward father who ran."

"No. It was Masoud's daughter who wanted to leave. She did not want the man she loved to be ambushed like his father."

"Shut up!" A couple of peg thumps came closer to the door.

"I wondered how my grandfather lasted this long as a soldier. Now I know. You taught him how to shoot people in the back, or stab them in their beds, and to run."

"Shut up!"

I took out one of my knives and slid it across the floor toward the entrance to the room.

A rifle burst chipped the concrete floor in a dozen places and tore holes in the hall wall across from the room.

I pressed my fingers on my ears hoping to dampen the pain. "A little edgy are we? Masoud must know how afraid you are. He has to know what a coward you are. He has lived with you all these years. And he probably hates you. People do not like others who are like them. And you are just like him, a coward."

"I am going to kill your father now!"

Back in the cave, I had taken two knives. At the time I didn't know why I needed two knives until now. I took the second knife out of my other pocket. I brought the rifle to my shoulder and fingered the trigger. I bent over in a runner's starting stance. I slid the knife on the floor toward the opened door. Then I took two small steps, leaped, and slid into the open doorway, arriving with the knife.

346

Hameed twisted around. His head rose from the knife to face me with a look of surprise as if he'd expected just another sliding knife and not me. I fired six shots into his torso bouncing his body, jarring him backwards, until he dropped his rifle and fell onto his back.

I walked into the room and kicked Hameed's assault rifle away. My father lay face up on the floor near a bed. Blood soaked his shirt front, but his chest rose and fell in a slow rhythm. I leaned down and touched him. His eyes opened.

Carl's lessons about checking the fallen enemy shouted in my head. I glanced at Hameed. Though he wore a flak vest, he was still, lifeless. If not dead, he was minimally stunned and unconscious. My focus returned to my father.

"It's okay," I said. "I'm here." He tired to sit up, and I held him down. "You've been shot."

"I'll live." He patted my arm. "Thanks for coming after me. I just need a little rest. Give me a moment." He closed his eyes.

I laid my rifle on the bed. Reaching in my pants pocket, I retrieved the ice pick, Hameed's ice pick. I leaned over the unconscious Hameed, pulled off his black vest and then yanked the smoking flak vest he had taken from me over his head. There was no blood. I slapped his face hard several times until his eyes flipped opened.

He saw me and bolted up. I slammed him down with a punch to his hawk nose. Bone crunched. Blood flew.

"Noooo!" He tried to roll away, and I stepped on his chest.

His hand dove into his pocket.

I stomped on his arm over and over; each stomp linked by his screams until his arm went limp, and his hand fell out of his pants holding a closed knife.

I stepped on his wrist and leaned down close to his face.

Waving the ice pick in his eyes, I said, "Remember this, one of your 'toys'?"

He swung his free fisted hand at my face.

I caught his fist. I slid my foot off his other wrist and stabbed the pick through his hand.

347

He screamed.

Never had someone else's pain been so pleasing to me. I wanted more. My mind hungered for more. I kicked his fisted hand to the floor and stabbed his wrist, and, as if embodied by an evil spirit, I plunged the pick through his forearm, and then his bicep.

He kicked, yelped, and cried like a spoiled child.

I reached down and picked up the switchblade.

"This looks familiar." I pressed the button and released the long blade inches from his face. "Look, it still has Rashi's blood on the blade. How long does it take someone to die after their throat is slit? You, of all people, should know exactly how long it takes."

His enlarged beady eyes stared at mine, and his head shook violently. He pissed himself.

I swiped the blade hard across Hameed's throat and stepped away.

I finally knew who I was.

God help me, I had become Carl.

Chapter 102

I pulled a spread off the bed and threw it over the blood gushing, thrashing remains of Hameed Ahmed.

Bending on a knee, I unbuttoned my father's shirt. His eyes opened.

"What are you doing?" he asked. "Where's that God-awful man?" He tried to get up.

I stopped him.

"We need to get out of here," he pleaded.

"I must find out how bad you're hurt before we go anywhere. And 'that God-awful man' is dead or close to it. Now relax while I take a look."

He had a bullet hole just below his right clavicle and a chunk of meat missing from his left triceps. I raised my moaning father into a seated position and pulled his shirt off his shoulder. The bullet had passed through his upper chest and exited his upper back, missing bones and organs. I searched my many jumpsuit pockets and found several of the miracle bandages Carl had given me. In seconds, I had the bleeding stopped, and my father bandaged with antiseptics attacking any infection.

I helped him to his feet.

Then I found my pistol, checked the clip, and handed it to my father. "Let's go see if Masoud summoned enough courage to climb the stairs."

I led the way and peered into the hallway. It was clear. I jogged to the steps and peeked into the stairwell. No one was visible.

I turned and went down the hall until I saw my father appear. "Pops, it's all clear," I said in a hushed voice. "Go upstairs and get Biji. I'll sneak down to the landing and see if I can tell what's going on."

Pops shuffled down the hall behind me.

"None of that will be necessary," said a familiar voice from the stairway above.

Gun raised, I sighted on the stairs coming down from the third floor. Masoud stood in the middle of the steps behind a little white-haired woman. One of his hands covered her mouth; the other held a pistol at her temple.

I steadied my AK-47's gun barrel's bead on the middle of Masoud's forehead. "Let her go, Masoud. She has done nothing to you."

"Have Raman come up here, and I will let the old woman go."

"There are no more negotiations, Masoud," I said as I braced my back on the hall wall, firming my shooting platform. The man was only fifteen to twenty feet away. "You are not a man to be trusted. You are a liar and a killer of innocent people. Let her go or I will kill you."

"Kugi, between your father and the Westerners, they have polluted your mind. Come with me, Grandson. I know some of my blood pumps inside you. I have seen your courage. You are a warrior. In just weeks you will see these Americans for who they really are, invaders driven by their leaders' lust for money and power. You are young. You have no idea about the world or what your place should be. You are capable of doing great things. Let Allah be your guide. He has a plan for you. I have no doubt that in six months you will become a Mujaheddin, in a year a Talib. Come with me, and you have my word your father and grandmother will leave this place unharmed."

"And you have my word, let my grandmother go now, and I won't kill you. You like ultimatums, here is one for you. You have five seconds to release her, or I will kill you."

"You will not shoot your mother's father." Masoud looked at my father. "Raman, are you just going to stand there? Must both your parents die because of what you did? Perhaps it is Allah's will that I destroy your family as you did mine."

The gun shot boomed in the stairwell and hung there only to be diminished by the screams of my grandmother.

Chapter 103

Cincinnati, Ohio

Late October, 2011

About half-past three in the afternoon, I walked into the same little bar in Bethany where Carl and I had met a different life ago. The place was still small and dark and reeked of cigarette smoke.

Though I couldn't see anything, having just entered this cave from the bright afternoon sun, the place had to be full. The loud mingled conversations almost drowned out the hillbilly song blaring on the juke box.

I hesitated at the door and let my eyes adjust to the gloom. All of the bar stools were occupied, and I wanted to make sure that none of them held Moose or his Neanderthal friends. The place was far from safe, but at least Moose and his pilot fish weren't there.

The same pudgy bartender with dirty blonde hair in a half-buttoned blouse served drinks, déjà-vu. I wondered if she had gotten her missing tooth replaced.

I spied Carl sitting in the rear with his back against the far wall. I weaved my way through the mostly men-filled chairs around clustered tables.

At least a few things were different this time. Moose wasn't here, at least not yet, and Carl had on a sweatshirt stenciled with "US Marines" versus a tee shirt.

I glanced at my wrist watch. "You must be working first shift," I said, as I reached his table. "I would've thought you'd picked someplace other than this bar to meet again. What a place. I feel about as safe here as I did in . . . let see if I can get this right . . . oh yeah, Sar Kand Ow Baba Ziarat."

"Hello to you too," Carl said. "And yes, I'm workin' firsts at the Ford plant in Sharonville. Sar Kand whatever, I can't believe you remembered. I've been tryin' to forget that damned town." He spread his big arms. "And what's wrong with this place? The beer's cold, and it has a 'down home' ambiance."

"Ambiance?" I shook my head. "Don't tell me you've started reading Webster. I'm not sure my heart could take it." I glanced over my shoulder. "Why did you pick this place? Aren't you worried about Moose and his bookends?" I stiff-armed the air. "No, don't say it. You and Moose kissed and made up."

"Hey, the turban man is back," said the little blonde as she sat a bottle of Budweiser on the table in front of where I stood and another in front of Carl.

I stuck a hand in my pants pocket.

She patted my arm. "Don't bother, honey. Carl has already paid for the first several rounds plus a very generous tip." She winked at Carl, turned, and waddled away in her too tight, cellulite bouncing, black jeans.

"Cute kid," Carl said watching the blonde walk away. His focus returned to me. "Kugi, sit down and relax. Have a beer."

"How can I relax in here? Part of your ear lobe is around here somewhere." I looked around on the floor as I pulled out the chair and sat.

"Moose and I didn't make up, but he won't bother us again. Word is one of his 'boys' got nailed for drug dealin' and traded Moose's killin' Garman for a walk." His brown eyes squinted. "And who's this Webster guy?"

"He wrote an English language dictionary. And by the way, I think you looked better with copper skin."

He rubbed his cheeks. "That shit took forever to go away. Oh well, it was worth it. Speakin' of which, how's your dad and your grandma? Is your dad over the shootin'?"

Memories morphed into reliving the scene in the Kabul apartment, the sights, sounds, smells, and most of all the

353

emotions. My mind drifted as my fingers peeled the label off the beer bottle.

I had no idea how long the silence lingered.

"Ah, maybe I shouldn't have brought it up." Carl brushed the label peelings off the table. "It's just that your dad was so quiet durin' that long trip home. He just wasn't himself. Based on everythin' you both told me, he had no choice, he had to—"

My hand shot out toward his face. "Enough . . . please." I eased my hand down. "My father and Biji are both fine. Biji misses the simple life and her friends. And she's driving my mom crazy. And I thought you'd like to know, Uncle Parmajit is good, and his oldest son, a doctor in Rawalpindi, has taken in Mannik's family and adopted Jodh, Rashi's son."

He nodded. "That's great. Give your parents and Biji a hug from me." He cocked his head and studied me for a moment. "You look different."

"I do? In what way?"

"Older, taller, I don't know, different." He finished his beer. "Where you been? I've tried to call you several times since gettin' back from Chicago and—"

"Chicago?" My brow pushed upward. "You were in Chicago?"

A smile wedged dimples into his cheeks. "Yeah. I went up to the Windy City to spend a week with Montana. She's been assigned to the paper's home office as a local reporter. She's got . . . what did she call it?" His hand rubbed his chin as his eyes searched the ceiling. "Oh yeah, she's got a syndicated column now. Big bucks."

I took a gulp of beer. "So do I need to rent a tuxedo in the near future?"

"For what, a weddin'? Hell no. We're just long-distance lovers for the time bein'. I doubt if we get that serious. We're from different worlds with her bein' educated and me bein' a union guy."

"I don't think love cares."

354

He swallowed half of his second beer. "So back to my question, where you been?"

"I've been in Virginia for the past several weeks."

"What's in Virginia?"

"Quantico."

Carl's body jerked to attention.

"I joined the Marines and went to their officers' candidate school there."

Head shaking, he flipped his hands palms out. "Why in the hell did you do that?"

I drained my beer. "I'm going back."

The End

Author's Note:

Thank you for reading my novel. If you liked "Kugi's Story" please tell your friends and write a twenty plus word review in Amazon's 'Comment' section and Goodreads. And please review the descriptions of my other ebooks. Hopefully you'll find another story of mine that peaks your interest.

Respectfully,

Dave McDonald

Dave McDonald's other ebooks:

"Sam's Folly"

"Death Insurance"

"Killing by Numbers"

"A Common Uprising"

"Dead Winners"

Amazon Author's Page link:
http://www.amazon.com/David-McDonald/e/B009XGXN9W/ref=cm_sw_r_fa_nu_WdqPqb2F8DA84

Facebook link:
https://www.facebook.com/RDaveMcDonald?fref=ts

Twitter link:
https://twitter.com/AuthorDaveMcDon

And soon to be published,

"Too Many"

"Nesting on Empty"

"The Death Chase"

"The Federation"

About the author:

     A romanticist at heart, with a deductive mind, I am a graduate engineer who traveled the world keeping commercial jet engines flying safely. I thought I loved my first career until I found my second, writing.

     For decades, I traveled abroad. At the time I was performing my job. In retrospect, I was collecting data; sights, smells, emotions, experiences, and stories for my second career.

     I've written ten novels, with several more in seed.

     I live with my wife, Linda, and dog, Bentley, on Hilton Head Island, South Carolina.

Made in the USA
Charleston, SC
11 September 2015